the things we know in part

a novel

ALSO BY PAMELA GOSSIAUX

Horses and Hearts Inspirational Romance Series

Finding Hope
Healing Faith
Saving Grace

Russo Romantic Mystery Series

Mrs. Chartwell and the Cat Burglar (Book 1)
Trusting the Cat Burglar (Book 2)
Romancing the Cat Burglar (Book 3)
A Cat Burglar Christmas (A Russo Romantic Mystery
Novella)

Standalone Novels

Good Enough

Ordinary Girl

Why Is There a Lemon in My Fruit Salad? How to Stay
Sweet When Life Turns Sour

A Kid at Heart: Becoming a Child of Our Heavenly
Father

the things we know in part

a novel

by

Pamela Gossiaux

Tri-Cat Publishing

Scripture quotations are taken from *The Holy Bible,* New International Version, copyright 1973, 1978, 1984 by International Bible Society.

Visit the author's website at: PamelaGossiaux.com

First Printing, September 2022

ISBN#: 978-1-7348968-5-5 (Paperback)
ISBN#: 978-1-7348968-6-2 (ebook)

Cover Design: Llewellen Designs
Formatter: Dallas Hodge, Everything But the Book
Editor: Rachel Song, Songbird Editing
Author Photo: Vera Davis Photography

Published in the United States by Tri-Cat Publishing.
Chelsea, MI

In loving memory of Vern and Joyce Nixon
and for Cindy Nixon,
for inviting me into their world of horses.

And to my incredible parents
Floyd and Judy Millard,
who built me a barn so I could keep a few.

To Fanci Free, the best horse a girl could ever want.
Thirty-three years wasn't long enough. I miss you.

*For now we see through a glass, darkly; but
then face to face: now I know in part; but
then shall I know even as also I am known.*

– 1 Corinthians 13:12 (St. Paul)

chapter
1

FRANCIE DALTON STOOD IN HER BOX SEAT and watched her horse, White December, load into the starting gate. Eighty-three thousand screaming fans watched with her to see if her horse could win the third and most difficult of horse-racing's Triple Crown. White December was favored. He was a Cinderella story. A rescued horse, trained by a female trainer. He had won the Kentucky Derby and placed third in the Preakness. One race left, and they'd make history.

Frank Weaver, the man who had stood by her side through the journey, smiled at her. "He'll do it," he said.

Her cell phone rang, and she jumped. No one would call her *now* unless it was an emergency.

She looked at Frank, then glanced at the number. *Coastal Ridge Hospital.* It was a call from Florida. From home. Her stomach lurched in fear.

It rang again. She had about thirty seconds before the race started. She squinted to get a better look at White December. He was quiet in the gate. Ready. She answered her phone.

"Francie Dalton," she said.

"Francie Dalton?" The voice on the other end was unfamiliar. It had a slight, Southern drawl.

"Yes? Who is this?"

Somewhere out there, ABC Sports was panning their cameras across the crowd to get the pre-race reactions of the owners and trainers. She saw her face on the large screen in the middle of the track, her blond hair pulled back in a ponytail.

"This is Dr. McMurtry at Coastal Ridge Hospital," said the voice on the phone. "There's been an... an incident... involving Jack Banner. Your number is on his phone as an emergency contact."

Just then the bell rang, and thirteen horses burst from the starting gate. Fans screamed and cheered their horses on, waving ticket stubs. Francie put her finger in her other ear, blocking the outside noise. She could see December settling in at third place near the rail, his green and gold silks blazing in the sun.

Good, Steve, she whispered to the jockey. *Bide your time.*

Later it would surprise her when she remembered how her mind took it all in at once. The call, the race, the color of her silks as Steve volleyed for a good spot. She supposed adrenaline did that.

"Jack?" she said finally to the voice on the phone. *Dear God... no...*

"It was bad... is bad... " The doctor didn't seem to know what to say. Wasn't this man supposed to be a professional?

Jack... not again... he can't take any more.

On the track, the board flashed 24 and 2/3 seconds for the first quarter of the race. Steve held December in third place, letting the front-runners set the pace.

"You need to come." The call was breaking up. "He's asking for you," the doctor said through the static. "He's... screaming... for you." Then his voice took on a more definitive tone as he recited what he knew how to deal with.

"He's stabilized now and won't hurt himself in restraints, but the man's going to give himself a heart attack, especially after all of the Semitrex he gave himself." More broken sound as the signal wavered in and out. "Attempted suicide—" Static. "He was fighting the staff, trying to pull his IVs out."

"Restraints?" Francie's own voice rose several octaves but was lost in the mayhem around her. She was no longer focused on the race.

"Francie?" Frank said. Their eyes met.

Dear God... "Take the restraints off of him. Now! That's why he's screaming!" Francie was used to giving orders and used to people obeying them. *Oh, dear God...* "Do you hear me? Hello?"

The horses were coming around the fourth turn with a half mile to go when interference cut off the call. Francie vaguely saw Steve making his move with December as she realized her caller ID hadn't given her the hospital's number. She grabbed Frank's arm.

"It's Jack." She turned to her sister Sam, who was standing beside her. "Take care of things. I've got to go." She pushed her way past the others in the box and ran down the steps. Frank was right beside her. He always was.

In the parking lot, he flagged down a taxi. "Let's not waste time waiting for our driver," he said.

Francie heard the cheer of the crowd and vaguely wondered if they had won the race, but there was phone signal out here, so she was back on her cell, making arrangements with her pilot to get her out of New York.

"Our jet will be ready when we get there," she said, climbing into the cab. She frantically pushed at the buttons on her phone. The signal dropped again. "I can't get through to the hospital!" She realized her voice was taking on a panicked tone.

"Francie..." Frank's hand rested on her shoulder, a warm, familiar gesture, to get her attention. He waited until she looked at him before he spoke. He was infinitely patient and for that she was grateful. "Tell me what happened."

She swallowed hard. "It's Jack..."

She told him what she knew. "He's screaming for me. They—" She took a deep breath. "They've tied him down to the bed."

Frank pulled out his phone. "Keep trying the hospital. I'll make our landing arrangements."

There was a cab waiting for them when their jet landed in Florida, and in just three hours from the time White December crossed the finish line at the Belmont Stakes, they were at the hospital.

Francie hit the hospital entrance running, practically knocking the flowers out of the hands of a young man as he wheeled his wife and newborn out the door. She got Jack's room number and took the three flights up to the psychiatric ward. There was no time to wait for the elevator.

Frank, fifty-two and ten years her senior, was keeping up.

Jack Banner's hoarse screams greeted her as she left the stairwell. She ran toward them, her heart pounding, and burst into the room, realizing too late that her abrupt entrance probably wasn't going to help the situation. Several nervous doctors and nurses stood around the bed, doing their best to calm the man who was begging them to let him get up.

"We brought him out of the OD earlier. To give him anything more than a mild sedative to settle him down could kill him," a doctor was explaining to a nurse. He raised a hand to stop Francie and Frank, but Frank explained who they were.

"Jack, I'm here," Francie said.

She pushed her way through the crowd of people and sat on the side of his bed. Taking his face in her hands, she turned him toward her so she could look in his eyes.

"I'm here."

He struggled for control. His voice was low, cracking with emotion as he spoke, and hoarse.

"Get these off of me."

She tried. They were on his wrists, up around the thick muscles of his arms, and around his ankles. She could see how the doctors were afraid he'd break loose and tear out his IVs.

The buckles were strained, and she couldn't loosen them. "Somebody get me some scissors," she said firmly, but not too loudly.

"Ms. Dalton, that's not a good idea," said one of the doctors, but he didn't try to stop her. Jack had stopped screaming.

Frank was quickly opening drawers, searching for scissors.

Francie looked at the doctors. "Get out. All of you. *Now.*"

They shuffled nervously. One doctor spoke up, "I don't think—"

"Get *out!*"

They left, hovering just outside the door.

"Somebody find me some scissors!" Frank said.

A nurse was already coming in with a pair. She handed them to Francie.

"Thank you," Francie said quietly. "Call Ruth Isadora. She's his doctor."

The nurse left, and Frank closed the door and dimmed the lights, knowing from past episodes what Jack needed. Minimize the environmental stimulants. The lights, the noise, the crowd.

Francie talked as she cut through the straps on his legs.

"Jack, you have to stay in that bed, or you'll pull these IVs out, okay?"

The bed shook from his trembling.

"Okay?" She really didn't expect an answer.

She freed his legs, wrists, and arms, then pulled him toward her. Normally he hated to be touched, but she could see he was broken now, beyond caring. As she held him, she felt the shaking turn into sobs.

"It's okay now," she whispered.

Frank slipped out of the room to talk to the doctors.

After a few minutes, the sobs quieted, but Jack was still trembling. When she thought he was calm enough, she pulled back a little so she could look him in the face. He wouldn't meet her eyes. Her heart was breaking for him—this man, whom she loved like a brother. He was so much to her, especially now, after all they had been through.

"What happened?" Her voice was soft, almost a whisper. She took hold of both of his hands, careful not to hit the IV, and sat facing him.

"I don't know," he said quietly.

"They said you OD'd on Semitrex."

He looked up, his gray eyes still full of fear. He attempted a little smile.

"If I was going to kill myself, I would have chosen a more permanent fix," he said. "I'd have to be crazy to try death by Semitrex."

It was an attempt at humor. She knew how much he hated that drug. She smiled a little.

Whatever he still had in his system was starting to take affect now that he wasn't fighting it. His eyelids looked heavy.

"Why don't you lay back down," she said.

"Francie." His hands were still trembling. "If they tie me up again... "

"They won't," she said firmly, "and I'm going to get you moved out of psych and into a room with a view."

She knew how he felt about enclosed places, and this small room had no windows.

He lay back and closed his eyes. His hand squeezed hers.

"Don't leave me," he whispered.

She returned the squeeze. "I won't let go. I'll be right here when you wake up. I promise."

Francie woke up slowly, sensing Jack stirring in the bed next to her. She had fallen asleep sometime after 4 a.m., when Frank had left to go get her a change of clothes and to check on the farm.

Opening one sleepy eye, she peered at Jack. Sunlight was streaming across his bed from the window.

"Hey, Princess," he said. His voice was still hoarse, but the fear was gone.

"Hey, yourself. Did you sleep well?"

"Like the dead."

She removed her hand from his so she could stretch. After a big yawn she looked around. He had been sleeping for nearly ten hours.

"Do you like your new room?" she asked, raising an eyebrow.

"Better than the Hilton. We're going to have to quit sleeping together like this, you know. People are going to talk."

"Oooohhh, scandal. That sounds exciting." She smiled, glad of the light banter.

A nurse came in to take some blood and check his vitals, then an orderly brought in a breakfast tray. Francie used that time to go to the bathroom and wash up. When she got back, Jack hadn't touched his breakfast. She took his glass of orange juice and a bagel off his tray.

"How do you know I'm not going to eat that?" he asked.

"You still have eggs left... I guess that's what those are. And that goopy stuff. Is that oatmeal?" She stirred it around with a spoon, wrinkling her nose.

She was trying him out, trying to see what kind of a mood he was in. They had been friends for ten years. To see what the past seven months had done to him since the trauma... it broke her heart. His life had been forever divided into Before Stanton and After Stanton.

"You're going to have to talk about it eventually," she said, breaking the bagel in half and offering him a piece. He refused.

"You think talk can fix this?"

"What happened?" She sat down in the chair beside him, facing the door so she could share his food tray. He talked more freely when he didn't have to meet her eyes.

He stiffened. "I don't know."

"You've got to know. You were there."

"Repressed memory, I guess." He sounded tired.

"Mmmmm."

"They shouldn't have revived me." His voice was flat, emotionless.

Francie was silent for a while. When she regained control of her voice, she said in a tone carefully void of emotion, "You *promised* me. You promised me you wouldn't try suicide."

"I'm not sure I did," he said. "Try suicide, that is."

Frank walked in the room then. Francie rose and let him wrap her in his warm embrace.

"I see the patient is awake," he said over her shoulder.

"For better or worse," said Jack.

Frank offered Francie the duffel bag and sat in the chair while she went to change. She left the door cracked so she could hear. She knew Frank must be shocked at how bad Jack looked. His best friend's eyes had dark circles around them, and his wrists were bruised and raw from where he had fought the restraints.

"Guess I'm not too pretty right now," Jack said.

"Not a face *I* would want to kiss," Frank returned. Then, "You're not alone in this, man."

Jack said nothing so Frank turned the topic to the Belmont.

"We won the race," he said. "Did she tell you?"

"Oh, no... yesterday was the Belmont," Jack said. "Oh my gosh. Did... did she miss it?"

"We got the call from the hospital just as the horses broke from the gate. She said she almost didn't answer it."

She could practically hear Jack doing the mental math.

"You must have left right after they gave you the trophy," he said.

"Nope," Frank said. Francie heard the grin in his voice. "Have you ever known Francie to stall when she's on a mission? She heard you needed her and was down those steps and flagging down a taxi before poor December's nose crossed the finish line."

There was silence as Jack let the implication of that sink in.

Racing was Francie's life. Her *life*. Nothing, come Hell nor high water, kept her from missing a race when one of her horses was running. She used to be the head horse trainer, spending weeks at the track. But when Andrew was born, she'd handed the horses over to her assistant for the most part. She hadn't wanted to repeat the mistakes with Andrew that she had with her other children. But December was *her* horse, a special case, and she was there for him.

"I made her miss the Belmont?"

"Your timing couldn't have been better," Francie said, walking back into the room, more comfortable now in jeans and a t-shirt.

"Steve called this morning," Frank said. "He wondered if it was a new trend, the owner not coming to the winner's circle to accept the trophy."

Francie laughed.

They talked about the race until a doctor came in to check on Jack.

"I'm just going to look you over really quick, if you want to have your guests wait in the hall," the man said. He looked to be in his fifties, and he was balding. His ID read *Dr. Winans.* Francie didn't remember him from the night before.

Jack looked at her.

"You're just going to check his blood pressure?" she asked.

"And get him up. See if he can walk around without feeling light-headed," said the doctor. He seemed like a pleasant man.

She looked at Jack.

"Okay?" she asked.

"Just keep your hands off me," Jack said gruffly to the doctor.

"I'll be right outside," Francie said.

She cringed when the doctor shut the door all the way. She and Frank were alone in the hall, with Gunny, Jack's bodyguard, standing near the door.

"I went into his house to feed the cat," Frank said. "I found these."

Francie opened the envelope. Divorce papers. Annie had signed them.

Jack was sitting in the chair when she walked in. She had the papers in her hand.

"Frank found these," she said gently.

Jack glanced at the papers, then raised his scarred arms up in a gesture of defeat.

"She's gone," he said. He looked exhausted.

Francie didn't know what to say, so she didn't reply.

"After she left… " he paused. "I just wanted the shaking to stop. I thought I could give myself an injection, but the first one didn't work. That's all I remember."

She saw his jaw clench and his hands grip the sides of his chair. He seemed to be trying to work something out. He looked up at her, anger in his eyes.

"I did what you said. 'Persevere, Jack. Stand strong in the faith, Jack. God loves you, Jack. He'll take care of you.' Well, I believed that, Francie. I *believed*."

He stood, his eyes suddenly flashing with anger.

"Where's your God now?" he said. "Is He laughing? Is He suddenly feeling more awesome since He's pulled a power trip on his servant? See, Jack, see what I can do? It doesn't matter how much you love me, I can still take everything away from you, just like I did my servant Job. I am *God!*"

Francie dropped her gaze.

"Answer me!" Jack took a step toward her. "Where's your God now?"

She met his eyes. "He's your God too," she said quietly.

"He's no longer my God," said Jack. He strode toward the window and leaned heavily on its ledge, supporting himself. His hand went to his head as if he were dizzy.

"Jack…?" Francie started to go to him, but he swung around, a new anger in his face.

"Are you going to ask if I'm okay?" he said, raising his voice. "No, Francie, I'm *not* okay. I'm not okay at all. My wife just left me. You want to know what she said? She said she couldn't live with me the way I am now. She couldn't live knowing what had been done to me. I'm this… used… person. I've been beaten nearly to death. I've been tortured. I've been…" His voice caught. "I've spent the better part of my life in prison for a crime I didn't commit. Then there was Stanton..." He turned back to the window, clenching the sill with both hands, hanging on.

She understood him. That's all she had ever wanted too—to feel safe. She had spent her whole life and a lot of heartache trying to find a way to make herself and those she loved, safe. But it wasn't possible.

"God doesn't guarantee we'll be safe in this world," Francie said. "But I do know that He can take the most terrible things and use them to bless you in ways you never imagined possible."

"You think He can take this mess and bring something good out of it?" Jack laughed. "If God loved me, He would never have let all of this happen in the first place. I trusted Him. I *trusted* Him, Francie."

"You still can."

"Trust?" he spun to face her. "What do you know about trust? *You* trusted people. *You* trusted God. Look what happened to you." He was trembling.

Francie stood by the closed door and wept silently. She brushed the tears away with the back of her hand.

"But look what came out of the tragedies," she said. "And God isn't finished with the story yet."

They were quiet for a few moments, looking at each other.

Finally, Jack spoke, his voice soft, the fight gone out of him.

"I am. I'm finished," he said.

He was shaking. It started in his hands, as always, and Francie watched as it consumed his entire body. He raised his hands to his head.

"I can't do this anymore," he said, his voice now barely a whisper. He sank to his knees. "I can't do this anymore."

Francie looked down at the broken man on the floor in front of her, his body shaking, his head in his scarred hands. She went and knelt beside him and took him in her arms, holding him tight.

"I can't do this anymore," he whispered, just before the weeping took him. She held him, and wept with him, and it was a long time before the shaking stopped in either of them.

chapter 2

1970, Michigan

FRANCIE OFTEN WONDERED HOW HER LIFE would have been different if she had accepted that ride on Johnny Charger's Harley that cold spring night so many years ago. He sat astride the leather seat, looking at her with passion and longing through eyes that could penetrate her soul. But not even Johnny could get past the wall she had built around her heart.

"I love you." He spoke the words softly. He didn't need volume—his eyes said it all. "Please Francie. Please don't leave me."

Her hand was still in Tom Cutter's, the young man whose ring she had accepted the night before. The rain was blowing sideways, and the umbrella Tom was holding wasn't offering her much protection.

"Johnny, go home," she said, not unkindly.

She could still do it. She could forget wedding invitations and guest lists, and she could climb on board that bike and never look back. She'd wrap her arms around him and smell his musky cologne mixed with leather.

"Francie..." he pleaded.

No. She had made her choice. Consciously, she gripped Tom's hand tighter.

"Goodbye, Johnny."

She climbed in the car, and Tom shut her door. As they drove off, she looked back at Johnny out the window, his pattern shifting in the rivulets made from the rain on the glass. It reminded her of one of those kaleidoscopes she had played with at her grandparent's home. She touched her hand to the glass.

It was the last time she had seen Johnny alive.

She'd first met him when she was fifteen. Or almost fifteen.

She had been walking home from school with her sister Krista, swinging her book bag. She loved Krista as much as she envied her. Krista was so good to her, so sweet, and she was going to miss her horribly when she graduated in a few weeks and left home.

"You have the prettiest eyes," Krista said. "That's a pretty dress. It really brings out the blue in your eyes."

Francie blushed. "What's with all the compliments?"

Krista shrugged. "I guess I'm just going to miss you. And I'm afraid for you, Francie, with Mom and all. Don't let her get to you, okay?"

Francie's throat tightened. She concentrated on counting the sidewalk cracks to keep from crying. *Step on a crack, break your mother's back. Step on a line, break your father's spine.* It was a sick rhyme, and she wondered what psycho had come up with it. When she had herself under control, she looked up at Krista. "I'll be okay," she said. "Mom isn't that bad."

"Yes, she is," Krista insisted. The soft spring breeze blew Krista's hair in front of her face, and she brushed it back. "She's rotten, and it makes me mad." The breeze kept playing with her hair. Krista pushed the blond strand back again.

"She treats you like dirt," Krista continued. "You know that. I know that. Your brothers know that, and we do all we can to run interference, but I have no idea what will happen when we're all gone." The anger rose in Krista's voice, and she brushed her hair back again, this time with a little more force. "Francie, I'm going to tell you something, and I want you to remember it. You are a very beautiful young lady, and you are going to turn into a gorgeous woman. You're intelligent and more determined than anyone I have ever met. I think you'll go the farthest in life out of all of us if you just don't let Mom get in your way. Promise me you won't." Krista stopped and turned Francie around to face her.

"Krista..." Francie was uncomfortable with this whole conversation. "She's our mom."

"I know that, and I love her. But she's also a self-centered, rotten old crow at times, and I don't want her taking her mood swings out on you, that's all."

"Krista!" Francie laughed, a little shocked at Krista's anger.

"I'm sorry," Krista apologized. They continued walking. "Just remember what I said."

There was a whistle from the other side of the street.

"Hey, Krista!" It was Johnny, sitting astride his bike and wearing his black leather jacket. Francie's heart skipped a beat.

"Isn't he cute?" Krista whispered.

"Mom says he's no good," Francie said. *But who cares?* The way he combed his dark hair back so that one lock hung over his left eye... so what if he was four years older than her? "Mom says he only has his mind on one thing, and he'll never settle down and marry. She told us to stay away from him."

"It won't hurt to say 'hi'," Krista said. She started across the street. "Come on."

Krista smiled at Johnny. Her hair blew back in the wind, this time out of her face. She filled out her soft purple sweater in a very attractive way. It was no wonder she was going off to be a model in New York. Francie imagined Krista on the face of magazines, Krista on TV, Krista's face selling cosmetics to women around the world. She pulled her sweater tighter around her own shoulders, trying to hide her flat chest.

"Ready to graduate?" Johnny asked Krista when they reached him.

"More than ready," Krista said.

She was always so confident in front of the guys. Francie, on the other hand, stood there, trying to think of something clever to say. She noticed that he was looking at her.

"Hello, I'm Francie, Krista's sister." That was stupid, she thought the moment she said it. *Of course, he knows I'm Krista's sister!*

"Nice to meet you," Johnny said. He smelled of musky cologne and leather. His bike seat creaked as he moved. He revved the gears and exhaust burst out the back. The bike was like a stallion, eager to set off.

Johnny and Krista talked about graduation, but his eyes kept going to Francie.

Finally, he spoke to her again.

"Aren't you that kid who won the playwright contest? It was the script the senior class used this year for their play, right?"

"Uh... yeah. That was me." Francie smiled again.

"Cool," he said.

After a few minutes, Krista turned to go, and Francie followed.

"Bye," she said. Then she felt stupid again. *Is that all you can say? "Hi, bye" like you have no brain?*

Johnny smiled at her as they left. *He's probably laughing,* she thought.

"I think he likes you," Krista said when they were out of earshot.

"Yeah, *right!*" Francie laughed, but her heart skipped another beat. She knew Krista wouldn't tease her. "Maybe I'll invite him to my birthday party on Saturday," Francie joked. "Wouldn't that blow Mom's mind!" She was going to be fifteen. He was... well, eighteen.

"Ahhh, yes. Your Derby Day birthday. May 7. It's not often it falls on Kentucky Derby Day, but how fitting for you! What *are* you doing for your birthday?" Krista asked.

"Probably nothing. Mom said she doesn't have the time,"

"We don't need to bother her. We can plan it."

"No, that's okay. She said she doesn't need the mess."

"Just a few friends," Krista insisted. "We could have a barbecue in the back yard."

"Don't worry about it, Krista," Francie said a little too harshly. "I already asked her. She said no."

Krista dropped the subject, and it was just as well. Their mother had other plans.

The first Saturday in May dawned with promise.

Francie opened her eyes. Sunlight was streaming across the foot of her bed. Birds were singing outside. She glanced at the clock.

Eight o'clock! It struck her, suddenly, what day it was.

"Derby Day!" she shouted, tossing the covers back and jumping out of bed. She pulled on a blue t-shirt that featured a picture of a horse surrounded by a horseshoe-shaped cascade of roses. *Kentucky Derby Dreams* was written across the bottom. She struggled into a pair of jeans and ran downstairs, bypassing the bathroom in her hurry to get outside.

"Francie, why do you dress like a bum?" said her mother as she tore out of the front door.

"Good morning to you too, Mother," Francie said. Ahhh. There it was. The *Detroit Free Press.*

She grabbed the paper from the sidewalk (the paper boy never managed to get the paper in the paper box or even on the front porch) and flipped to the sports section. She found what she was looking for. Statistics from America's most famous horse race on page seven. She was a bit annoyed that it wasn't front-page news. But what could you expect here in Michigan? She sat on the front porch step and read.

Power Step was favored to win, but she didn't think the big gangly bay colt had it in him. She was more interested in the little chestnut, Slapstick. His odds were 14 to 1.

"He's got the talent and the speed. I wonder why people just can't see it?" she mumbled to herself.

Inside, she heard the phone ring.

"Got it!" she shouted, springing up and running inside.

Her mom was making her way toward the kitchen.

"I said I got it," Francie said, sprinting past her.

She grabbed the phone.

"Sunshine and eighty degrees expected, fast track today!" she said into the phone without even saying hello.

"Who's going to get the roses?" replied her grandfather on the other end of the line.

"Slapstick all the way!" said Francie.

"He'll get the roses, all right, but his jockey won't take him to the lead until the half pole if he knows what's good for him," said Grandpa.

"That'll never work. He doesn't like dirt in his face," Francie said. "Remember the Blue Grass Stakes?"

"Maybe so, but there are two speed horses that'll take the lead. He doesn't have the staying power to run in front from wire to wire."

"We'll see about that," Francie said.

They both laughed. It was tradition. Every year, on the first Saturday in May, Papaw called her from his home in Florida to discuss Derby statistics first thing in the morning. They both watched all the prep races and picked their favorite horses to win throughout the spring, then honed in on a Derby favorite or two. Whoever picked the winning horse bought lunch for the other one when they got together. But this year they liked the same horse.

"So who's buying lunch?" Papaw asked.

"We'll have to go Dutch this year, looks like," Francie said.

Her mother's voice interrupted.

"Francie, hang up that phone now. You're costing your grandfather an arm and a leg in long distance, and I have a party to get ready for. You're in my way."

"Sounds like the old bird is squawking," said Papaw. Francie loved that he didn't always speak fondly of his daughter.

"Yep, gotta go," Francie said.

"Happy Birthday, Tinkerbell."

She said her goodbyes and hung up.

"Not one of your finer moments, Mother," Francie mumbled.

"What?" said her mom, turning on her. "Just because you have this little... 'thing'... with your grandfather, this *obsession*, don't expect the world to stop. Nobody gives a hoot about horses the way you two do. There are real things in this world to get excited over, like your sister's pre-graduation party. Which reminds me, I need you to pick up some things."

"Mom, send Jim. I can't drive yet."

"Jim's not worth the shirt he's wearing," said her mom. "He can drive you, but I'll need you to get the items on this list." She produced a long list from her pants pocket. "I need it all this morning, except for the ice. You can't pick up the ice until about 5 p.m., because the party is at 6 p.m."

"Mom, the Derby is at 5:00. I'll be watching it live coverage from 4:30 until six. You know that."

"Francie, today is not the day to cross me," said her mom.

Francie sighed and grabbed the list from her mother.

"Fine," she said. "I'll get your stuff." She also figured she'd get ice and just not mention it until later.

"Brush your teeth and get some make-up on before you go out. You look a mess," said her mom.

Francie went back upstairs, suddenly aware of her full bladder. She used the bathroom and then knocked on Jim's door.

She heard mumbling inside.

"Are you decent?" she asked.

There was no answer, so she opened the door a crack. "Jim? You awake?"

There was the distinct odor of stale cigarette smoke and something sweeter. Pot.

Francie sat on the side of his bed and pulled the covers back.

"Oh, man," he said, shielding his eyes. "Bright light."

"Not really," she said. "Your shades are still pulled. Jim, have you been getting high again? Where were you last night? Mom would kill you, only she's too busy worrying over Krista's party."

"I'm fine, little sis," he said, sitting up and rubbing his eyes. "No highness here. Feeling pretty low, actually. What's up?"

"Mom wants you to drive me to the grocery store."

"Now?"

"Yes."

"All right. Let me get decent."

Francie wandered into the bathroom to brush her teeth while she waited for Jim to get dressed. She was pulling her long blond hair back into a ponytail when her five-year-old sister came in.

Sandra was a change of life baby and a person her mother considered a nuisance.

"Can I come?" she asked.

"You're still in your jammies, Sam," said Francie, tousling her hair. "We won't be gone long. But stay out of Mom's way today. She's in a tizzy."

"The party," said Sam knowingly.

"She's invited more of *her* friends than Krista's," Francie said. "I don't know why she wants to have those ladies over anyway. They're all stuffy."

Jim interrupted them. "Okay, out of the bathroom, girls. A guy's gotta go."

Sam giggled as Francie escorted her out.

"Hey, everybody's gotta pee at some point," said Francie. "Even boys. Now, let's get you dressed while I wait for Jim."

She steered her into the bedroom at the back of the house, a tiny room just big enough for a bed and a bookcase. Sam's clothes were all in the small closet, and Francie chose some pink pants and a flowered shirt.

"Here, put these on," she said.

"Sis!" Jim shouted from down the hall.

"Coming!" She turned to Sam. "I'll be home in a little while, and then I'll fix you some breakfast. Remember to stay out of Mom's way." Protecting Sam had become second nature to Francie. She felt more like her surrogate mother than an older sister. As an afterthought, she turned at the door and added, "Why don't you just stay in here and play for a while?"

"Okay." Sam sat on her bed, looking a bit forlorn. She grabbed Rolly Bear, the worn teddy her grandparents had given her for Christmas when she was three, and hugged him.

Jim grabbed Francie's arm.

"Let's go before Mom gets a good look at me," he said.

Jim was out the door before Francie had her shoes on, so she grabbed them and ran outside barefoot, taking the front door to avoid her mom.

"Bye, Mom!" she shouted.

"Francie, wait!" her mom said. "Here's the money."

Francie ducked back in, grabbed the money, and left.

"Put your shoes on!" her mom yelled behind her. That woman didn't miss a trick.

She settled in beside Jim, who was wearing his sunglasses even though they were still in the garage. He backed out, nodded to their mom, and turned down the street as Francie was pulling her shoes on.

"What kind of party is Mom having?" Jim asked.

"The pre-graduation party. You know, with the ladies' club from church. She's all set to have tea and crumpets or something I guess, in preparation for Krista's upcoming graduation. I don't know. Something weird."

Jim snorted.

"I can't wait until I'm old enough to drive."

"I can't wait until I'm old enough to leave home," Jim said.

"I'm fifteen. In just a year... "

"I'll be eighteen then, and I'm signing up for the army. I am *so* outta here." He put on the radio—some hard rock station that hurt Francie's ears.

He turned left.

"Where are you going? The store is that way," Francie said.

"I need to make a stop first."

He made a few more turns and pulled into the driveway of an older ranch home. A big black dog was tied up in the front yard, barking. The shades were still drawn in all the front rooms.

"I don't think anybody is up," said Francie.

"Wait here."

Jim got out and went up to the front door. Somebody opened it, and he disappeared inside. Within a minute or two he came out, returned to the car, and resumed driving.

They were both silent. Finally, Francie spoke.

"You don't need to throw your life away, you know. Drugs aren't the answer."

"Save it, Francie."

"Jim, you're smart and cute. If you'd cut your hair and..."

"Francie," he turned to her. "I know you love me, sis, but don't lecture. I'm your elder."

"Yes, a whole seventeen years old..."

"And much wiser. As soon as I can move out of the house, I won't need drugs anymore. They just help me relax in that hell we call home and be more creative. You know."

Francie sighed. She always lost this argument, so she decided to give it up today. It was, after all, Derby day. *And* her birthday.

At the store, Francie went in alone and bought everything on the list, in precisely the amounts and brands her mother liked. She had a little money left over and bought a lollipop for Sam, which she hid in her jeans pocket.

Then they picked up ice at the gas station.

That's when it happened.

Jim was making a left onto State Street when a car sped through a red light.

Francie felt the next few milliseconds occur in slow motion. She saw Jim look left, look right, and then pull out. Francie saw the car speeding up to miss the yellow light and knew the driver wasn't going to make it through the intersection before the light turned red. The driver tried to beat the light just as Jim's light turned green, and he pulled out.

The impact was enormous. What felt like a sledgehammer hit the driver's side of the car and shattered glass all over

Jim's body. His arms flew helplessly into the air as his head swung toward Francie from the impact, and then back toward the shattered window, where it hit with a thud on what was left of the glass.

Francie felt herself jerked sideways, and then her shoulder slammed against the passenger side door, taking the impact and saving her from a head injury.

The car slid sideways down the street and across the yellow line, where a pick-up truck slammed on its brakes and tumbled into a pair of garbage cans on the curb to avoid hitting them.

Then there was silence.

Francie sat there for a moment, frozen in terror. There was blood all over Jim. She'd heard somewhere that head wounds bled a lot, and she was afraid he was going to bleed to death right in front of her.

He was conscious. That was a good sign.

"Jim?"

He put his hands to his face and drew them back, his eyes widening at the sight of the blood. Then he cursed.

"Are you okay?" Francie asked.

"I've gotta get rid of this," he said, pulling a bag of weed from his pocket.

"Were you smoking that?"

"No, I swear," he said. "But it'll look bad if I'm caught with it."

Francie's heart was pounding. She saw her dad's empty thermos bottle that had rolled from under the front seat.

"Here," she said. "Put it in this."

She unscrewed the cap and Jim stuffed it in and got it under the seat just as they heard sirens approaching.

An officer got out of one of the cars and ran toward them. Someone else was going toward the driver of the car that had hit them, which had backed up and pulled over.

"You kids okay?" asked the officer.

"Yes, I think so," Jim said.

"He's not. He's bleeding. We need to get him to the hospital," said Francie.

The officer looked at Jim's head, then went back to the car to call an ambulance. Someone knocked on Francie's window and asked if there was a parent or anyone he could call.

"Well..." said Francie, looking at Jim.

Jim shrugged, and Francie gave the policeman her dad's name and phone number, hoping with all hope that her mother wouldn't answer the phone.

The ambulance arrived and the paramedics made both of them climb in and ride to the hospital.

They were taken to separate rooms. Francie waited for what seemed like an eternity. A doctor eventually came to look at her, and she checked out okay. Just a few nicks and bruises.

"You're going to be sore tomorrow," he said. "Just take some aspirin every four to six hours."

"I'm her father," said a voice in the hall, and he burst through the doors. He was an average looking man, "unspectacular" their mom said, and his thick glasses made his eyes look bigger than they were.

"Francie," he said, hugging her. "Are you okay?"

"I'm fine, Dad," she said. "How's Jim?"

"He'll be okay. He got a nasty bump on the head though," her dad said, then clenched his teeth. "Serves him right."

"What do you mean?"

"He should have been paying attention."

Francie started to tremble. It was so cold in the room.

"He was, Dad. The guy sped up and ran a red light."

"Don't stick up for him, Francie," her dad said. "He's a loser. He screws up everything he touches. He's not the son I hoped he'd become."

"Then what *did* you hope for, Dad?" said a voice from the door.

They turned, and there was Jim standing in the doorway.

Francie saw the muscles in her dad's temple start to work.

"I hoped for a son who would make something of himself in school and maybe go on to college like your brother Mark. Not a longhaired hippie boy who plays guitar in a loser band and can't even drive around the block. You've disappointed me, Jim, as always. I hope you figure out a way to pay for the car."

Their dad pushed past him, nearly knocking him down.

"Let's get home. Your mother will be furious."

Francie met Jim's eyes as she hopped down off the table. She gave him what she hoped was a look of encouragement. He put his arm around her shoulders.

"You okay, sis?" he asked. "I'm so sorry."

"It's not your fault," she said. "And yes, I'm fine. What time is it?"

They found a clock in the hallway that said it was 2 p.m. They had been gone for hours.

"The food!" Francie said. "The ice..."

Her heart started pounding furiously again. "Mom will be so... "

"We'll pick some up on the way home," said her dad.

Francie walked into the store wearing Jim's sunglasses and her hair down to hide the cuts and scratches on her face and arms caused by the flying glass. Jim and her dad stayed in the car.

By the time they arrived home, it was 3 p.m. and her mom was hysterical. Francie carried the groceries into the kitchen and helped unload, trying her best to tune out her mother's long tirade about their day and how their emergency had caused her gray hair and nearly a heart attack.

It was hard to imagine she had worried about them at all because there were several plates of tiny sandwiches cut up into triangles, a plate of cheese-filled pastries, and several relish trays. What she was going to do with the food they just bought, Francie couldn't imagine.

Her mom stopped to catch her breath. Perhaps she had run out of complaints for the moment. It was quiet. *Too* quiet.

"Where's Sam?" Francie asked.

"I put the little nuisance away for a bit," said her mother. "She was bothering me and here I have all this work to do, and Krista is still at work."

Francie ran upstairs.

"Sam?" she said. "Sam?"

She heard a faint voice from Sam's room and went inside. But she didn't see the little girl anywhere.

"Sam?"

"In here," said a timid voice.

Francie ran to the closet door. It was locked. She jiggled the handle then reached up on the ledge above for the key.

She opened the door and looked inside. There sat her little sister on a pile of clothes, with a stack of books and crayons beside her. She was drawing.

"Sam!" Francie rushed in and held the little girl in her arms. "Oh, Sam."

"It's not so bad," said Sam. "She gave me a flashlight."

Francie pulled back and took Sam's face in her hands. She looked the little girl in the eyes and saw fear, but brave little Sandra gave Francie a smile.

"See?" Sam said, turning the flashlight on.

Despite the horrible circumstances, or maybe because of them, Francie started laughing.

"Oh, Sam, I guess this is the safest place for you in some bizarre way," she said. "If I had taken you with us, I don't know what would have happened when we got hit by that car. And you're certainly out of Mom's way in here."

Jim appeared at the open closet door.

"What's up?" he said.

"Come and join us," said Francie. He crawled in.

"Shut the door," said Francie.

"Rolly Bear," Sam said.

Francie went and got the tired-looking stuffed animal and handed it to her little sister. Sam hugged it.

Jim shut the door. Sam turned on her little flashlight. The three of them sat huddled on piles of clothes, cramped in a dusty closet, and feeling closer and somehow safer than they had all day.

"Together, we can make it," said Francie, putting an arm around each of them.

Jim smiled but said nothing. He looked like a person who had lost hope.

"The accident wasn't your fault," said Francie.

"Dad took away my driving privileges," said Jim.

"For how long?"

"Forever. He says I'm irresponsible." Jim laughed, a small, sarcastic bark. "Wait until he finds the pot in his thermos."

"What's pot?" asked Sam.

"Something you cook in," said Francie.

"Why are there pots in Daddy's thermos?"

"Never mind." Francie hugged her closer.

"Ow. Something's poking me in the a—rear," said Jim. He pulled out a hardcover book of *Peter Pan*.

"Let's read!" said Sam, enthusiastically snuggling into Francie's lap.

"You," said Jim, handing Francie the book. "My head is throbbing."

So she read to them, passing the time away in the closet,and keeping her voice strong and confident. She was determined to turn every bad thing her mom did into a good thing; she wouldn't let her parents destroy their family. For a while, they were lost in the world of Never Land.

Finally, Sam had to go to the bathroom, and they crawled out, noticing that it was nearly 5 p.m.

"The Kentucky Derby!" said Francie. "I almost forgot!" She ran downstairs and into the den. She found the right channel and plopped herself down in front of the screen. There were some good smells coming from the kitchen. Despite all her faults, her mother was a good cook, and Francie was hungry. She realized she hadn't eaten all day.

The last commercial ended, and she got lost in the world of horses until a sharp voice interrupted her program.

"Francie! Turn that off. My guests are arriving."

"What?" For a minute Francie was confused. She had been so caught up in her program that she'd forgotten where she was.

"It's almost over," she said. "The horses are entering the starting gate."

"Now!" her mom said and stepped in front of her, turning the TV off.

"Mom!"

Francie had never missed a Derby. Never.

"Mom!" She was desperate. There was no other television in the house. "It's... it's my birthday!"

"You can have some of Krista's cake," said her mom, stepping back into the kitchen.

Francie had a stubborn streak in her, but she knew better than to touch the television. She glanced desperately at the clock. Soon the race would be over.

Maybe she could make it down the street to her girlfriend's house. She jumped up.

"Francie! Get in here. I need your help with this platter!" Her mom's sharp voice sounded so far away, and all the little cakes and sandwiches on the table started spinning and growing smaller and smaller. Francie grabbed the doorframe of the kitchen and suddenly pitched forward toward the floor. Then everything went black.

That night she lay in bed, staring out the window at the stars. The church ladies had been understanding. They had blamed it on not eating all day. They had blamed it on shock from the car accident. Maybe her iron was low.

Papaw had called shortly after she regained consciousness, and she'd crept around the corner with the phone into the living room and cried. Papaw tried his best to comfort her. He filled her in on everything she had missed about the Derby.

She was excused from the party since she had fainted and had been in bed ever since.

A knock came at her door then, and Krista quietly stepped in.

"Hey, sis," said Krista. She gave Francie a little smile and held out a plate with a slice of cake on it and a candle. The flame wavered as she walked.

"Happy Birthday," Krista said, sitting down on the bed.

"What's so happy about it?"

"You'll be okay," Krista said. "You always come out on top."

She blew out the candle and set the plate on Francie's nightstand.

"It's really pretty good cake. You should at least try it," she said. "But here. I brought you something."

Krista reached into her pocket and pulled out a little porcelain angel. Francie took it in her palm and carefully traced her finger along the delicate wings, down the golden hair, and across the robe. The angel had her arms outstretched and a slight smile on her lips. Her face was older and more serious, not cutesy like some of the angels that Francie had seen in Krista's collection. There was something powerful about her.

"You're giving me one of your angels?" Francie asked. Krista had collected angels since she was a little girl.

"She's a guardian angel," said Krista. "She'll take good care of you. We all have angels watching over us."

"Mine should be fired," Francie said.

"Well, she certainly has to work overtime to keep up with you," Krista said.

Both girls laughed.

Then, quietly, Krista added, "I have to go to New York. I have to chase my dreams, Francie. You understand, don't you? I know that you of all people... with your horses. I know you understand about dreams. Now is my chance to make mine a reality. And with modeling, it's not like I can wait around until I'm older to give it a go."

"I understand," Francie said. She lowered her eyes and closed her hand around the angel. "I'll take good care of her."

"My prayer is that she—or whoever your guardian angel is—will take good care of you," Krista said.

Francie put on a brave smile. "I'll be okay. As you said, I always am. Now let me try some of this cake, and you can tell me about your party."

The girls talked for a while, and then Krista left. Francie set the angel on the shelf across from her bed where she could lay and look at her. Then she lay back in the cool sheets, pulling her blankets around her.

"I wish you were real," she whispered. "I could use someone on my side right now."

The little porcelain figurine stared back at her, unmoving.

Then she turned out her light and went to bed, hoping that tomorrow would be a better day.

chapter 3

FRANCIE SAT IN THE BACKSEAT OF THE CAR next to Sam. Krista was over by the other window, and Francie was all too aware that these were her last few moments with her older sister before she wouldn't see her for... how long? Krista was off to New York. The three weeks since Francie's birthday had sped by, and now the day was here. Krista was leaving her.

The car horn sounded, and the girls jumped.

"Idiot drivers!" her dad cursed and slammed on his horn again. He hated traffic. "These confounded people can't maneuver a car to save their lives! Why did you have to go and get such an early flight?" he yelled back at Krista. "It's rush hour!"

"Don't yell at her," their mom said. "She's not going to be with us much longer."

"Norma, for heaven's sake, the girl isn't dying, she's just going to New York." Her dad pounded on his horn again, and the driver in front of him made an obscene gesture.

"*Just* to New York?" their mom cried. "Do you know how far away that is?"

They started to argue. Francie felt Sam tense.

They saw a sign that said there was construction ahead. Her dad cursed again.

"We have plenty of time," Krista said quietly. "The plane doesn't leave for an hour."

Thirty minutes passed as they sat in traffic, crawling. Their parents had quit fighting and were giving each other the silent treatment.

"Mommy?" Sam said in a soft little voice that barely broke the quiet in the car.

"What." Their mom's voice was cold and flat.

"I hope it's not too much longer," Sam said. "I have to go to the bathroom."

"Well, if you wet your pants, I'll whip you," their mom said. "You should have thought about that back at the house and went then."

Sam was silent again. Then she squirmed. "I really, *really* gotta go." Her voice was quavering.

"Be quiet. Your father's trying to concentrate on driving. We'll be there soon enough."

"There's a gas station!" Krista pointed out the window. They were out of the construction zone and were headed for the airport at a faster pace now. "Let's stop there really quick."

"We'll miss the plane," their dad said.

"We have time," Krista said, but he ignored her.

About twenty minutes later, they arrived at the airport. Their dad screeched to a halt just outside the terminal. "Honey," he turned to Krista, "I have to go park the car. Your plane leaves in ten minutes. Give me a hug, and good luck."

Krista awkwardly leaned across the car seat and hugged him. "Goodbye, Daddy," she said.

"I'll miss you," he said. There was genuine affection in the man's voice. Francie wondered what he used to be like, before he'd married her mom. Sometimes, she thought she caught a glimpse of the "nice guy" her grandparents had told her he had been when they'd first met him. Like the rare hug he had given Francie at the hospital.

"Let's go!" Their mom jumped out and grabbed the suitcases from the trunk. She took Krista's hand.

"Francie, come and see your sister off," her mom demanded. "Sam, you stay here. You'll get lost."

"But I have to go to the bathroom," Sam mumbled.

"Francie, *come on!*" her mom said, and the three of them rushed into the airport.

At the gate, their mother doted over Krista, hugging her and crying. Krista caught Francie's eye and winked. Francie wondered if she couldn't wait to get on the plane and away from her parents' suffocating love.

Krista ran to Francie and hugged her hard. "Remember what I said, sis," she whispered.

Francie bit her lip and refused to cry. There was no way she was going to show any emotion in front of her mother. She watched Krista pile into the plane with the other passengers. Krista looked back and waved one last time, and then she disappeared from their sight.

"My baby, my baby," her mom said, wiping the tears from her cheeks.

They watched the plane as it eddied away from the loading dock. Men were scurrying around below it, dwarfed by the big silver bird. Some were waving flags, and others were loading luggage onto planes. Krista's flight taxied around on the runway, and Francie watched it as it soared off into the blue sky, taking her sister with it. She felt very alone.

The ambiance was shattered as a rough voice behind her spoke to her mom. "Look what your daughter did!" Her dad roughly turned Sam around so that her mom could see her wet bottom. "She peed her pants!" he shouted. People in the area looked over at them. Francie was embarrassed, not because of what Sam had done, but because her parents were creating yet another scene. She took over, as she often did, before things got worse.

"I'll go clean her up." She reached for Sam's hand.

"How could you do this?" their mom shouted at Sam. Sam started to cry. "You're supposed to be a big girl. You have really disappointed Daddy and I." She turned to Francie. "Get her out of here. I don't want to see her until she's presentable."

Francie took Sam to the restroom.

Sam was crying as Francie tried her best to towel her off with the cheap paper. She washed the pants off with a damp paper towel, then stuffed some toilet paper down Sam's pants between her skin and her underwear so her skin would stay dry until they got home.

Then she turned the little girl around and hugged her. She could feel Sam shaking. "I didn't mean it, I really didn't!" Sam cried.

"Are you okay?"

Francie looked up. The kind voice belonged to a pretty, auburn-haired woman in her twenties. "Do you have any dry clothes for her?"

"Um, no. But we're fine," Francie said.

"Come out here. My fiancé can help," said the woman. Francie followed her out of the bathroom, where a handsome man stood, holding their bags. "Frank, I need a twenty," the woman said. The man looked at Francie. He had the kindest brown eyes she had ever seen. Without asking why, he dug out his wallet and gave the woman a twenty.

"Come on," the woman smiled and took Francie's hand. She followed her into a clothing store, where they purchased Sam a pair of pants. The woman took Sam into a small dressing room, had her put them on, and came out with the wet pants in the shopping bag.

"All set," she said. The whole thing had taken less than five minutes. Francie didn't know what to say. Outside the store, Frank smiled at her.

"Are your parents around?" he asked.

"Yes. Back at the terminal," Francie said. She tore her eyes away from Frank's to look at the woman. "Thank you," she said. She looked at Frank's kind eyes again. "Thank you so much."

He smiled. "It'll be okay, sweetheart," he said, meeting Francie's eyes and tousling Sam's hair. The way he said the words almost made Francie believe it.

Then she found her parents, and they left for home.

chapter 4

HORSES.

They had always been her escape, and truly an escape in the summer when her parents sent her to live with her grandparents on their Thoroughbred racehorse farm. Her siblings rarely joined her. They were busy with their own schedules and friends.

And this year, too, she was here alone, It was the last week in June, and she was flying across her grandfather's pasture with the wind whipping in her face and hooves pounding beneath her.

Star, her black Thoroughbred mare, marked only by the small white star on her forehead, was tugging at the bit and begging to run faster. Why not? The day was beautiful, the morning wind cool, and Francie felt *free*.

She gave the horse her head and nudged her on. The large metal gate loomed up ahead, dividing the pastureland from the wilder, undeveloped land beyond. Only a dirt footpath led past that toward the Atlantic, and over a hundred acres of undeveloped coastline that would make Francie's grandparents wealthy if they ever decided to sell it to developers.

But for now, there was nothing but sea salt, wild grass, and surf beyond that gate.

Star tugged at the bit again, asking her rider for permission to jump it.

"I don't know, girl, it's awfully tall and we're going pretty fast," Francie said.

Star, as if understanding her rider's words, tugged at the bit again.

Francie laughed. She had done it before—why stop to unlatch the gate when your horse was capable of jumping it? She checked her horse—slowing her up just a bit—and then felt the lurch of muscles as Star cleanly cleared the gate and landed on the other side.

"Yippee!" Francie yelled, and they took off for the beach, about a half-mile down the path. Soon, the waves crashing against the beach made such a noise that it drowned out Star's hooves against the dirt. Francie raced her mare into the surf, laughing as the water splashed up against the horse's belly and got Francie's bare feet all wet. She was riding without a saddle that day, so she turned Star in toward the water, and soon they were both soaked, the horse half running, half swimming. Then they turned back onto the firmer sand for some more running.

When she was on a horse's back, everything else went away. Her life, her parents, her problems... and the best part was knowing that when she went "home" that night, it would be to her grandparents' home. For the entire summer, she was surrounded by love, acceptance, and horses. Life couldn't be better.

She pulled Star down to a walk to let the mare catch her breath.

"There's our tree up there," Francie said. "Let's go rest."

At the tree, she dismounted and took the bridle off of her horse. Star immediately started grazing on the sea grass that grew sparsely along the coast there.

An outcropping of rock formed something of a little cave, and deep inside, Francie had placed a blanket wrapped in plastic. She pulled out the blanket and took it and spread it down under the tree. She had a little sack full of snacks tied to her side. She pulled out an apple, some walnuts, and a warm Coke.

"Oh, dear, not again," Francie said, looking at the Coke. It was bubbly from the riding and would most likely explode on her if she opened it. She set it aside and bit into the apple.

Star's ears pricked up, and she came over and nuzzled her owner.

"Yes, I brought you one too," Francie said, rubbing the soft, velvety muzzle. She gave the horse the rest of her apple and pulled out another one for herself.

Star whickered, nuzzling her again.

"No, this one is for *me*," Francie said.

She wasn't there long before she saw her grandpa coming down the path on his bay gelding. He stopped near her and dismounted, leaving his own horse to graze. He joined her on the blanket in the shade. He gazed out over the water, the corners of his eyes crinkling as he squinted against the sun. He pulled the western hat he was wearing down further over his forehead.

"I thought you had to work today," Francie said, handing him some walnuts.

"Thanks." He took them, popping a few into his mouth. "It's so *nice* today, I thought I'd go in late. That's the beauty of owning my own business. Also... I saw some young girl galloping off bareback on her horse and jumping my gate. I could swear I told her not to do that. Do you know why she did that? Did you see her? I think she came this way."

Francie cringed.

"Well..." she said. "That young girl got carried away is all, I guess, and she respectfully apologizes and hopes that her Papaw will forgive her and welcome her back into his home tonight."

Papaw laughed. "Oh, Tink, you know why I have that rule. The gate is tall—"

"And not collapsible, and if we hit it, we're going head over heels and will most likely get killed. I'll try not to do it again."

"Try hard."

They ate in silence for a while, listening to the waves crashing on the beach and the call of the sand plovers as they rooted for food along the surf.

"So Jim decided not to come with you this summer," Papaw said. It was more a statement than a question.

"Yeah," Francie said. She wouldn't admit it to anybody, but she had been a little glad that he hadn't. This way, she got her grandparents all to herself. "He says he hates horses."

"How *my* offspring could hate horses, I'll never understand," Papaw said. "It's in our blood. My daddy owned horses. *His* daddy owned horses... but your mother, now she refused to set foot in a barn as soon as she was able to walk." He chuckled. "When she was a baby, she had no choice. I carried her with me every morning on my feeding rounds."

He was quiet for a moment, then said more seriously, "Maybe that's why she hates them so much. Maybe she never really felt we gave her a choice."

"That's not true," Francie said. "Grandma told me that Mom was given frilly dresses and a canopy bed and enough parties so that she should find relief in simple solitude."

"Your Grandma said that?" Papaw chuckled.

"Yep."

"I think we spoiled her. But it was never enough."

Francie twisted her Coke open and shook the foam off her hands before she took a drink. "Why is Mom so cranky? You're so nice—so different from her."

Papaw looked off in the distance. "Your grandma and I weren't always like we are now," he said. "I made a lot of money, and we let it get to us. We had lots of parties, got caught up in social circles. As I said, we spoiled your mother. When we saw what our lifestyle was doing to our family, we changed. She was sixteen then and didn't like that. Not a bit. She wanted more—thought she was entitled to more. She has hated us ever since. And horses."

He winked at Francie. "But you're the girl who loves the horses."

"And Star is my favorite horse of all," said Francie.

At the sound of her name, the black mare pricked her ears in Francie's direction.

"You did a great job with her," said Papaw. "She's come a long way. She's not the scared, abused little horse she was when I gave her to you." He watched the mare, admiring her rippling, shiny coat and relaxed manner. When he had first found her, standing in a dirty stall, thin to the ribs, bleeding from whip marks across her hips, she'd trembled just from the sound of his voice. Somehow, he'd known that this was the horse for his granddaughter. Francie loved her dearly.

"You have a magic touch with horses, Francie," he said. "That's something not a lot of people have. It's a gift. Don't you ever forget that."

Francie was silent. When Papaw called her by her name instead of Tinkerbell, it meant he was serious.

"You can do a lot with that gift. Even make a horse run faster," he continued. He looked at her, and she raised her eyebrows in question.

"It's true," he said. "I've seen racehorses perform for a certain trainer or jockey when they wouldn't run for anybody else. It's all about heart. They run for *that person*. They want to please that person, and they give them all they've got."

Papaw stood up and brushed his pants off. "Speaking of which, this old man had better get to work or he won't be able to afford to *feed* his horses, and then they ain't gonna run for anybody! Why don't you ride back with me?"

Francie threw her apple core in the grass and got up. "You're not old, Papaw."

"Well, I sure ain't no spring chicken," he said, putting his foot in the stirrups and pulling himself up onto his horse. Francie hopped effortlessly up on her mare's tall, bare back.

"I used to be able to do that," he grinned.

Francie laughed, but she lingered back a bit so she could watch Papaw ride ahead of her, his head bobbing under his Stetson. His head seemed so dear to her suddenly, and even more precious because of the gray hair and wrinkled face. She wanted to throw her arms around him and beg him never to leave her. But that was silly. It was a beautiful day, and they were happy. She shrugged away her scary thoughts and nudged Star into a trot to catch up with him.

They rode back to the house, where the smell of fresh muffins greeted them from the kitchen window.

"God bless your grandmother," Papaw said. "Fresh cranberry muffins. My favorite! I'll have to stuff a few of those into my sack before I head off to work."

Francie grabbed one and put some butter on it. "Sam loves these," she said, momentarily feeling guilty that she was here and Sam wasn't. There had been a short fight with her mom about it all. Sam was too young to come, her mom had argued. Francie was unsure why her mom even cared, but she wouldn't worry. Jim had promised to look after the little girl.

Hopefully, he wasn't too high.

She closed her eyes and bit into the muffin, enjoying the flavor, and pushing all thoughts of home far from her mind.

Summer ended much too soon, and she was forced, by her mother, to return home. Why Norma insisted on parenting them, she couldn't understand. Her mother certainly didn't want them. It was probably that she didn't want anybody else to have them either.

It was dark when her dad picked her up from the airport. He didn't say much, just some talk about the yard and his golfing. When they got home, her mom was sitting in the kitchen, sipping wine with her friend Louise and slurring her words as they talked. She, of course, ignored Francie's entrance.

"I'm going out for a bit," her dad said, sticking his head in the door. When his wife didn't answer, he left.

Francie was at the hallway when she heard Louise's voice carry from the kitchen.

"Norma, I should go. You haven't seen your daughter all summer. I don't want to take your time away from her."

No, no, no! Francie silently pleaded. *Stay!*

"Oh, she doesn't mind. I can talk to her tomorrow."

Francie climbed the stairs to her room, ignoring the faint rumbling of her stomach. It wasn't worth the time in the kitchen it would take to make a sandwich. She peeked in Sam's room. The little girl was asleep. Francie saw a light under Jim's door and knocked quietly.

When he didn't answer, she turned the knob and peeked in.

"Hi," she said.

He was strumming his guitar quietly and looked up. "Hey, sis!" His eyes were clear and bright. "I was just writing this new song. Listen."

She came through the door and sat on the floor across from him. Clothes were strewn everywhere, and sheets of crumpled up paper were falling out of the wastepaper basket. A half-eaten Twinkie sat on his dresser.

The soft strands of music reached her, and she tuned into what he was singing. He sang quietly, and his words were beautiful; about love starting as a seed and growing into a tree. The branches spread wide, leaves burst forth, and life sprang from love. It had sexual undertones, but mostly it was about love and how, if properly cared for, it could multiply. It was about families and strength and wisdom and age.

She watched her brother play. His fingers moved so effortlessly across the strings. He played the guitar as if it were a part of him, an extension. This was his gift, she thought.

She closed her eyes and let the music carry her away, wondering if it had been written for one of the many girls he'd dated.

"Francie Ann Dalton!" Her mother's shout broke her reverie.

"I gotta go," Francie jumped up, hoping to make it to her room before Norma got up the stairs. She could pretend to be asleep.

She got through the door and shot under the covers just as her mom burst through.

"You insolent child!" she shrieked. "You've made me look bad in front of company. Now Louise thinks I don't take care of you. She thinks I should say hello to you and feed you. Why did you make her think that? *Why?*"

She tore the covers off of Francie, and that's when the girl noticed her mother was waving a butcher knife in the air. She grabbed Francie by the hair and jerked her up out of bed.

"You won't make me look like the fool again," she said. Her breath stank of alcohol. "When I get through with you—"

Francie screamed and kicked out. Her mother had always been mean, but she had never attacked Francie physically before. She tried to reach her hand back to support her neck, but her mom jerked on her hair again, pulling her head back. She brought the knife toward Francie.

Francie was scared. Scared for her life.

"Jim!" She screamed her brother's name.

Francie was jerked back by her hair again, and she felt her head slam against the wall. She saw Norma raise the knife and about that time someone grabbed her mother's arm and twisted it backward.

It was Jim.

Norma turned on him. "I will kill you!" she screamed. "You pathetic, no-good—"

Jim wrestled her to the ground, pinning her on the floor, his hand securing her wrist and the knife.

"Mom," he said. "Mom, give me the knife."

Norma hissed through her teeth and struggled, but he was too strong for her.

Finally, she went limp.

"Let me up," she said.

"Give me the knife first."

"James, I am your *mother*. Let me up."

Reluctantly and slowly, he began to release his grip on her. With a sudden burst of energy, she surged up and at Francie again. Jim grabbed for her wrist, and Norma turned quickly and thrust the knife at him. He put a hand up to block her, and the knife slashed through the palm of his left hand. Blood squirted out.

"What in tarnation is going on in here!" shouted her dad.

As soon as she saw her husband, Norma dropped the knife.

"Jim attacked me, Derek," she said, tears springing to her eyes. "I was talking to Francie for making me look like a fool in front of my girlfriend, and Jim just outright attacked me."

Her dad looked at the knife on the floor. He looked at Jim.

"What happened to your hand?" he said.

"Mom." Jim answered. He opened his hand. Francie could see bone. She retched.

"Norma, you're drunk," her dad said. "Go to bed."

Derek followed Norma down the hall, where he grabbed a towel and returned. He tossed it at his son.

"Wrap this around your hand. I'm taking you to the hospital for stitches before you bleed all over my house."

Within a minute, it seemed, the room cleared out. Francie heard the door slam shut and the car pull out. She heard her mom snoring loudly down the hall, passed out on her bed. Her stomach was churning, and she tasted acid. She retched again and just made it to the bathroom before her stomach emptied itself of its contents, mostly bile. Soon, she was dry heaving, and once that stopped, she crawled back to her own room and collapsed on the floor. It was two hours before she had the strength to go and check on Sam. She found the little girl hiding in the closet. Francie grabbed a blanket and sat down next to her, closing the door.

"I like the song Jim played for you," Sam said.

"Me too."

"So did the man at the record company. He wants Jim to play it for him this Saturday for a contract. That's a good thing, right?"

Sam yawned.

"The record company?" Francie said. Sam laid her head against Francie's shoulder and closed her eyes.

A record deal. That's why Jim had looked so happy. And so sober. She thought about his hand and the bone she had seen and felt sick inside again.

She stroked Sam's hair. The little girl was asleep.

Francie spent a sleepless night, listening for her mom to wake or her brother to return. By the time the sun rose, she had heard neither.

chapter 5

TWO WEEKS INTO THE NEW SCHOOL YEAR, Francie walked out of the building to see Johnny sitting on his bike. He smiled when he saw her, as if he had been looking for her specifically.

"Want a ride?" he asked.

"Sure," she said. *Who wouldn't?*

"Would you like a soda?" he asked as she was climbing onto the back of his bike, glad she hadn't worn a skirt that morning. She was keenly aware of her classmates watching her. Two of her closest friends raised their eyes as they walked by and one gave her a thumbs-up.

Her mom wouldn't be home until after 6 p.m., so she saw no problem hanging out with Johnny for a bit.

"Sure," she said again. Was that all she could say?

"Wrap your arms around me and hang on," said Johnny.

Wrap your arms around me? She thought she would die. She was aware of the difference in their ages and had no idea what he thought of her, but she was going to enjoy the moment anyway. So she wrapped her arms around his waist and breathed in his smell and never wanted the moment to end. But all too soon they were at the soda shop.

It was a little diner just a few blocks from school that was noted for its remarkable milkshakes and greasy burgers.

They sat at a booth, and Johnny ordered a root beer float. Francie went for the chocolate shake.

He smiled across the table at her as they waited for their drinks.

"How have you been?" he asked, as if they were old friends.

"Great," she said. "I spent the summer with my grandparents." She told him a little bit about the farm and that her grandfather was an architect and developer.

"Have you heard from Krista?" he asked.

So was this about Krista. "She's really busy but is doing well," Francie replied. "She was hired to do some commercials for hair shampoo, and last weekend she did a runway show for some fancy clothes designer."

"Wow," said Johnny.

Their drinks came. Hers was served in a cold metal cup, half of which the waitress poured into her glass. She topped it off with whipped cream and set it in front of Francie.

"Think you can handle all of that?" Johnny asked.

"Oh, yeah," Francie said, taking a big slurp. Whatever he was doing having drinks with her, she was going to let him know that she was old enough to enjoy the moment. Old enough to handle it.

"So when is your birthday, Francie Dalton?" he asked.

"May 7. You missed it." She smiled and took another big gulp. Too much. It gave her a brain freeze. She tried not to let it show, and Johnny made no mention that he noticed the searing pain she was in.

"So you're fifteen now," he said, as if weighing the years. "Well."

She had no idea what that meant, if it was too young or just a question to keep the conversation rolling.

"And when is *your* birthday?" she asked.

"November 3rd."

"You'll be... nineteen?"

"The girl can write *and* do math!" he said.

"I think my mother would kill me if she knew I were here," Francie admitted.

"Well, we should get you home then," he said. "I've got to get to work soon anyway."

They finished up their drinks and headed home. Francie asked him to drop her off a block from her house.

"Ashamed of me?" he grinned.

"Ashamed of my mother," she replied. She gave him a quick smile, and then he was off, disappearing around the corner on his bike. She stared after him for a moment, wondering what that past hour had been about. Then she sighed dreamily and decided it didn't matter. She was happy.

She didn't see Johnny anymore that fall. After a few weeks, she quit looking for him to be there to give her a ride home. School wore on into Thanksgiving and then Christmas.

On Christmas Eve, she was sitting on her bed re-reading a letter from Krista, who wasn't coming home this year, when her mom opened her door.

"Time for church," her mom said. She was holding Sam by the hand. The little girl's eyes were red from crying.

Francie reluctantly got up and followed them down the hall. Norma opened up Jim's door, and the sweet scent of pot filtered out. "Too late for you. You're headed for Hell," their mom muttered and pulled the door shut.

Church was stuffy and overheated, and the strong stench of an old lady's perfume next to her was making Francie nauseous. She half-listened to the minister as he told her why she should feel guilty and why she needed God's grace to forgive her.

When it was time for communion, her mom passed on the wine. Francie wasn't sure what had transpired after that night her mom attacked her, but her mom had quit drinking. Norma wasn't nicer, but she hadn't gotten physical with them again.

Sam sat quietly between them, fiddling with the braids in her hair, which were obviously too tight. Francie stared up at the Christ on the cross, his head hanging in a defeated gesture, his clothes torn away, his body bleeding.

She wanted nothing to do with a God who condoned suffering. She closed her Bible and her mom scowled at her, so she made sure to sing the closing hymn loudly. She went home upset, her stomach churning with acid.

Back at home, Francie put Sam to bed, then quietly knocked on Jim's room and let herself in. He hadn't moved from his seat by the window, it seemed. He had his head leaned back against the sill, his eyes closed.

Francie sat down on the floor, next to the guitar he hadn't touched in days. His hand had healed, but it wasn't the same. The fingers weren't as nimble, and he had all but given up on music. She had tried to get him to play that one song for her that he had played that night, but he always had an excuse not to, always seemed in a fog. They never talked about that night. He never mentioned the record deal that he had missed out on, and shamefully, she never asked.

"I hate God," she whispered.

He didn't respond for a moment, then quietly said, "What God?" He was barely there, off in whatever world he went to when he got high.

Francie wanted to scream at Jim. *I need you! I need somebody! Please come back to me!* Instead, she bit her lip to hold back the angry tears.

"Goodnight," she said and got up.

"Sis?"

She turned. Jim was looking at her.

"What's up?" she asked.

She looked at his scarred hand, which was fumbling with his cigarette pack, pulling one out.

"Nothing," he sighed. "Nothing."

She walked back down to her room and crawled into bed without bothering to change out of her dress.

The year was long and cold. Spring came late. Francie stayed out late with friends a few times, but sometimes, when she came home, Sam was locked in a closet. So she started staying in.

Then, blissfully, June arrived.

"I can't leave Sam here by herself," Francie said to Jim a few weeks before she left for Florida. Her brother was sitting at his windowsill again, the window cracked, smoking. "Can you keep an eye on her?"

He inhaled deeply, and for a few moments, Francie didn't think he'd answer.

"I'll watch her," he finally said.

He inhaled again, this time blowing smoke rings as he exhaled.

"But you work," Francie said. *And get high,* she added in her mind. Then she had an idea. "Come with me."

He laughed. "What? I hate horses. Besides, I have a job."

"Pumping gas."

Jim had become quiet and withdrawn and didn't have any plans after graduation. He barely graduated at all because his grades were so low, and he seemed content to pump gas at the corner station forever. He had given up playing guitar at all.

When he didn't answer, she added, "You quit the band. Your girl left you. What do you have left? Come with me. We'll take Sam. Give yourself a break."

He shook his head. "No. I have things here."

"Drugs?"

He didn't answer.

In the end, he refused to come, but her mom allowed Sam to go. Norma was delighted to have a summer of her own but warned them when they returned in the fall— and they *would* return—that she didn't expect them to be spoiled.

Francie and Sam flew off to Florida for a few months of peace. Francie worried about Jim, though, always a thought in the back of her mind, but at least she didn't have to worry about Sam for once.

Her second worry was the raging Vietnam War. Late that August, she watched television with her grandparents one evening and saw Jim's number drawn. Her brother was going to war.

Coastal Ridge Hospital, 1999

Francie watched Jack sleep. He was tossing fitfully in the hospital bed, the sheets tangled around him. At 1 a.m., he had finally agreed to take something to help him sleep. She wished *she* had.

Francie rubbed her face, running her fingers through her hair. She wished Jim were here. She remembered a conversation she had had with him that first year Jack was with them.

"Why can't he sleep?" she had asked. They were sitting outside on the swing under the grape arbor, a cool breeze tickling the grass at their feet. It was the middle of the night; nearly 3 a.m. There was a small light on in Jack's house that they could see from where they sat.

"Same reason I can't," Jim said. He had given up cigarettes by then, and she remembered him putting his fingers to his lips out of habit.

She was quiet, watching her brother. Jim didn't talk much, and she thought he wasn't going to answer her question when he finally spoke, very quietly.

"He's been through a lot. Men do awful things to each other in war, and he's seen the worst of it. Look at his scars. His arms were bound for a reason. They did things to him that they had to tie him down for."

He tapped his fingers against his lips again. Francie reached over and took Jim's other hand. "I'm glad he's here," she said softly.

Jim took a deep breath, then gave Francie's hand a squeeze before he withdrew his. "Me too."

"He's safe."

"From most things. Not from his memories."

Jim got up, and she could feel the coolness of the breeze touch her side as his warmth left her.

"But he'll get better," she said, making sure there was certainty in her voice. Jim only nodded.

"Goodnight, sis." He walked back toward the house, toward his own bedroom where the light came on often at night.

"Goodnight," she said quietly, and sat alone on the swing for a long time until the cold forced her to go inside.

Francie shook her head to clear the memory, and the hospital bed came back into focus. She sat and watched the man who had taken her brother's place. *No greater love hath a man than to lay down his life...*

"It should have been me," Jim had said to her.

"No." She said the words out loud, but Jack didn't waken. She sighed and ran her hands through her hair again, then laid her head back against the hospital recliner that was supposed to pass for a bed, willing sleep.

She needed rest. Tomorrow would be hard. She had to talk the doctor into releasing Jack and then...

And then what? What was she going to do with a suicidal man? She opened her eyes and looked at him again. He wouldn't kill himself. His life had come at too high of a price to throw it away.

Did she have regrets? Jim had asked her that. Heck, *Jack* had asked her that. As she watched him sleep, she knew she didn't. She'd go through everything all over again to have him here, next to her, alive. Had she sinned? She didn't think so. And she had tried to be sure no one else would get hurt. She'd done what she had to do at the time.

She closed her eyes. She thought of Star, and pretended she was sixteen again, riding with the wind out toward the beach where her grandpa was waiting. She smiled, and finally sleep came, and she drifted off with the feeling of the muscles of her horse under her, the sun on her shoulders, and Papaw standing on the beach, hands in his pockets, a broad smile on his face, waving.

chapter 6

Fall 1971

THE VERY FIRST DAY OF HER JUNIOR YEAR, she saw Johnny. She was one block from her house, walking to school. He pulled up on his motorcycle with his tight-fitting jeans, leather jacket, and great smell, and smiled at her.

"Want a ride?" he asked.

"Sure," she said, pleasantly surprised, and climbed on his bike.

In just a few minutes—not nearly long enough for her to soak in his closeness—he pulled up in front of the high school to drop her off.

"I'd like to buy you a soda," he said. "How about after school?"

"Um... sure," she said. "I get out at 3:10."

"I'll be here." He revved his gears and drove off.

Her girlfriends joined her. "What was that about?" Martha asked.

"I'm not sure," Francie said. "But I like it." They giggled and went inside to start their day. During second hour, Tom Cutter spoke to her. He was the star of the basketball team and very handsome.

"Would you like to go the back-to-school dance with me?" he asked.

Francie was polite but refused. She couldn't get her mind off of Johnny.

"You're insane," Martha said at lunch. "Tom is the guy every girl wants to catch."

Francie smiled and tried not to think about after school. It's just a soda, she told herself. And yet, as she left the building, her heart raced in her chest. It jumped at the sight of Johnny sitting there at the curb, straddling his bike.

"Hey," he said.

She smiled. "Hey."

He drove her to the same soda shop they had gone to last time, and they got a booth in the back. He put a coin in the jukebox and started playing *One* by Three Dog Night.

Their drinks came. He had ordered a root beer float. She took a long sip of her chocolate milkshake, so thick that it was hard to get through the straw. He was watching her.

"What are we doing?" she asked, licking some whipped cream off her upper lip.

"Enjoying something sweet," he said and smiled innocently.

"Seriously. Where were you for an entire year?"

"I was working in Ohio. Got a good job laying brick."

"I just wondered." She didn't want him to know she cared. Quickly, she tried to change the subject.

"Krista's doing great in New York," she said.

"That's nice," he said. His face grew serious.

"We weren't really a couple," he said, as if reading her mind. "I just took you out that one time. I was too old for you then, don't you think? And you said you couldn't date until you were sixteen. I didn't want to cause trouble with your parents."

"Oh."

"I wanted to write, but I had no idea where you disappeared to all summer. All I know about your grandparents is that they live somewhere in Florida."

He dug a small box out of his jacket pocket. It was wrapped in white tissue.

"Happy belated birthday."

She just stared.

"Your birthday was in May. May 7, right?"

"Yes," she said. She had no idea he remembered that.

"Here. Happy Sweet Sixteen."

She opened the package. It was a tiny gold ring with her birthstone in it.

"It's not a real stone, but I thought it was pretty," Johnny said.

"Thank you," she said and smiled at him.

"So would you like to go out with me now?"

She laughed. Life suddenly seemed so light and fun.

"You're still four years older. My parents would kill me!" she said, still laughing.

"We can tell them it's not a date. Didn't you say I was an old friend of Krista's? I won't even kiss you. So how about Friday night?"

She was enjoying this. "Sure," she said. "Friday night sounds wonderful."

They laughed and talked for the rest of the hour, and then he drove her home, dropping her off a block from her house. She got off his bike and stood next to him, listening to the motor idling.

"What time?" she asked.

"7:00?"

"Sure."

"Should I pick you up at your house or here?" He smiled, a playful twinkle in his eye.

"Might as well be at the house," she said. "I am, after all, sixteen now."

He leaned toward her. Gosh he smelled good. She could feel his breath on her face. She leaned in and their lips touched. His kiss was long and soft, drawing her in. Her feet felt like they were leaving the ground. She closed her eyes and drank in his scent, his strength, and his passion. When he drew back, she wanted more.

"I thought you said you wouldn't kiss me," she whispered.

"I meant on Friday night," he said.

"Oh."

She gave him a little smile, and then turned before he could see the big grin that took over her entire face.

chapter 7

ON FRIDAY MORNING, FRANCIE GRABBED a piece of toast and headed out the door. Sam was just finishing up her cereal.

"Can you and I play together tonight, Francie?" she asked.

Francie stopped.

"Sure. But... " her mother was sitting at the table too, finishing breakfast. The three of them were alone in the house. "I have a date tonight."

"With whom?" her mom asked.

"He's... he's an old friend of Krista's," Francie said. "It's just a casual thing. We'll probably... just talk about Krista." She gave a little uncertain laugh. *What an idiot I am!* Francie thought.

Her mother narrowed her eyes.

"Do I know him?" she asked.

"His name is Johnny," Francie said. "He's a nice guy."

"I need to know more about him," said Norma. The tone in her voice had changed. "Johnny... "

"I'm going to be late for school," Francie said.

"Me too!" Sam jumped up, grabbed her school bag, and brushed past Francie and out the door.

"Bye!" Francie turned and ran, taking her toast with her.

When Johnny roared up on his bike at 7 p.m. that night, Norma had a fit.

"Young lady, you are *not* going out with *him!*" shouted her mother.

Francie didn't say anything. She was trying to figure out if she should warn Johnny before he came into the house, or if she should just run out and disappear on his bike. But she'd have to return home sooner or later, and Sam would be left home in the aftermath.

Jim sauntered down the stairs.

"Mom, you're hilarious!" he said. "That isn't her boyfriend—that's my band buddy."

He winked at Francie and walked out the door.

"Johnny, my friend! Funny you have the same name as the guy who was about to pick up my sister for a date! Where's your guitar, dude?"

Johnny caught a look at Francie, standing pale and quiet in the door. He let Jim put his arm around him and lead him back to his bike.

"Dang, left it at home. I don't know where my brain is."

"Probably fried it out with drugs," muttered Norma.

"Go home and get your guitar, and I'll meet you at your house later," said Jim.

Francie saw Johnny nod and climb back on his bike.

"You are not going to hang out with *him*," Norma said to Jim when he walked back into the house.

"What does it matter to you if I smoke my brains out with pot or waste my life with my no good guitar, or whatever it is you think I do, Mom? I'm going off to Nam. I'll probably be dead in six months anyway."

He pushed past Norma and went upstairs.

Francie went to sit on the couch. She wasn't sure what to do, so she decided to just sit there. At about 7:30, she quietly wandered upstairs.

Jim was sitting at his window, smoking.

"Don't be dead in six months," she said quietly.

He looked up at her and motioned for her to close the door.

"I'll drive you to the park. He says he'll meet you there. I told him 8 p.m."

"Jim, you are the world's *best* brother!" Francie said. "I'll tell Mom that I'm meeting a girlfriend and that you're dropping me off."

Johnny was waiting for her on a park bench and took her hand when she arrived. He led her down a path away from the road, where the trees opened up to reveal a river. They sat on its bank, quiet for a while. He squeezed her hand.

She turned to him, focusing on his lips. He smelled so good, and he leaned closer, running his fingers through a few strands of her hair.

She tried to think of something to say.

"So how long are you back for?" she asked. "You don't have to leave again, do you? For your job in Ohio?"

He sat back. "No," he said. "That was just temporary. I'm working at a gas station right now. Only until I get my book finished."

"Your book?"

"Yeah," he looked a little embarrassed. "I'm writing a book."

"Really?" Francie was amazed. "About what?"

"I'll tell you when I get to know you a little better," he grinned. "I have to figure out if I can trust you or not."

"Trust me?"

"Yes," he laughed. "This book writing is personal, you know. I have to make sure you won't laugh. Bad boy Johnny writing books, you know."

She laughed. "You're crazy."

"No, just a little different." He winked at her.

He asked her some questions about herself then, and she told him more about her grandparents' farm and horses.

"I understand. Horses are kind of an escape for you, and a way for you to feel like more than you are. Kind of like an extension. That's how poetry is for me."

"You write poetry too?"

"Yeah," he smiled.

"I thought you weren't going to tell me."

"I decided I can trust you."

She looked over at him. "That's *exactly* what horses are for me. You said it perfectly." He had the most marvelous dark eyes. "You have a beautiful soul," she said.

He smiled. "And I always thought it was my body the girls were after."

"It is," she said and leaned forward. Her lips almost brushed his, and then he pulled back.

"I promised not to kiss you," he said. "Remember?"

"You can break your promise."

"I'm a man of my word."

She laughed, pulling back. "This is the best non-date I've ever been on!"

It was getting dark. He drove her home and dropped her off a block from her house. She walked the rest of the way home, floating on air.

The following Friday, they met at a little burger shack just outside of town. It was one of his favorite places, and she agreed to go, figuring nobody from school would be there to report back to her mother. Jim dropped her off.

After they ate, they went for a walk. The evening was cool, but he suggested going back to their "thinking spot" at the park. She rode on the back of his bike, and they hiked the short walk into the woods. Johnny spread out a blanket, and they sat down.

Francie saw a small flower that had survived the frost, and she picked it and held it up to her nose.

"A flower is nature's cloak,
God's creation,
But never was there a rose more lovely than thou."

Johnny quoted to her.

"Who wrote that?" Francie asked. She was familiar with a lot of poets, but she didn't recognize this line.

"I did," he said sheepishly.

She looked at him in amazement.

"It's beautiful," she said softly. He leaned toward her until she could feel his breath on her neck.

"I didn't promise not to kiss you on this date," he whispered in her ear. "May I?"

She reached hungrily for his lips, and he held her against him. Her heart was pounding, and all she knew was that she wanted this to last forever.

With Jim running interference, she dated Johnny through the winter. She learned that he had a rough home life and that his father was an alcoholic. After Jim left for the army, Martha helped her out so she could continue to date Johnny on the sly.

"I'll never drink," Johnny said over and over again. "I don't want to wrap my bike around a tree. What a waste of a life."

She tried to be with him whenever she could, and she thought of him when they were apart. There was a pull from Johnny that she couldn't understand.

"It's love," Martha told her. "You're in love."

One chilly day in late February, she lay on her back at their thinking spot, listening to Johnny read her love poems from his poetry book. He finished a poem, and after a few minutes of silence he asked, "Are you ashamed of me?"

She turned toward him. "Ashamed? Why would you say that?"

"Your parents have never properly met me. I have to drop you off a block from home, so they don't even know we go out.

"I'm sorry," she said. "But like I told you before, my mom's a nightmare."

"Do you love me?"

"Yes," she said without any hesitation, and she meant it. She rolled toward him and put her arms around him. He put his head against her chest. "Don't ever leave me, Francie," he said in a whisper. "I couldn't live without you."

So she didn't have to answer him, she put her lips to his and kissed him. She wished she could stay in his arms forever.

That night, Francie lay in her bed thinking about Johnny when her mom suddenly stormed into her room, opening the door so hard it slammed against the wall.

"My friend from church saw you on the riverbank with that Johnny character," her mom hissed. "You sleazy girl. You think you can live a life of sex and drugs like the rest of this horrid generation and not go to Hell?" Norma threw a Bible at her, and it hit her in the face, then fell to the ground, its thin pages fluttering. Francie held her arm up defensively, and sat up in bed.

"Mom, we're not having sex," she said, but her mother cut her off.

"I wasn't born yesterday, Francie. He's much older than you. I know what he wants, and I'm pretty sure you put out." Her mom approached her bed, and for a moment, Francie thought she had a knife. But instead, she threw some paper down on the bed. "I want a thousand sentences of confession before you go to sleep."

There was a quiet voice by the door. "Mommy?" The noise had awakened Sam.

Their mother pivoted on her heels and bore down on Sam. The little girl shrank in the doorway.

"You're going to grow up to be just like her, you little snot," Norma said. "Get to your room, and I'll deal with you later."

Sam ran.

"Mom... " Francie said, her heart pounding. "We didn't—"

"Don't lie to me, child," Norma said. "Your father will be in later to spank you. If I ever see you with Johnny again, I'll have him arrested for statutory rape."

Her mom turned and slammed the door closed. Francie jumped up and ran to the door, looking down the hall. Norma didn't stop at Sam's room but went downstairs to the kitchen.

Francie went and gathered Sam in her arms. "It's okay," she said.

"I think you should date somebody else," Sam said, "to make Mom happy."

Francie buried her face in Sam's hair. "It's okay," she said again. "It's okay."

She broke up with Johnny the next day after school, in the parking lot.

"Mom hates you," she explained.

"Your mom doesn't even *know* me," he said.

"I have to keep my sister safe." *And you.*

"Bring her with you on our dates."

Francie smiled. "You're sweet. I just can't. I can't be seen with you anymore." She turned and left before the tears started. She wouldn't let him see her cry.

She wasn't planning on dating anymore. Ever.

But on Sunday, in church, she opened her eyes during prayer and caught Tom Cutter peeking at her. The handsome guy from the basketball team.

He was friendly enough to her in school, but he hadn't asked her out again since that first time. He smiled.

Gosh, he was handsome. She closed her eyes and resumed praying. The minister said "Amen," then released them. As she was walking toward the exit, Tom walked up to her.

"Will you go with me to the Valentine's Dance?" he asked. "You can't blame a guy for trying again."

Francie caught her mom's eye and saw that Norma was smiling. Sam squeezed her hand.

"Um... okay," she said. His eyes were very blue when she looked up into them, and she felt herself blushing.

In the car, Norma turned around to look at her. "Francie, Tom is a good boy. That's the first wise decision you've ever made. We'll go out tonight and buy you a dress."

Francie was stunned. "Um... okay," she said.

"His dad is a deacon in the church, you know, and also a lawyer. Tom is going to be an engineer. He comes from good blood and will make good money."

How did her mom know all of this?

But true to her word, Norma took her shopping that evening. She bought Francie a beautiful burgundy dress and some matching heels. "There, don't you look lovely," said her mom as Francie came out of the dressing room. For a brief moment, she thought this must be what Krista felt like with their mom. It felt strange—and good—to have her mom's approval.

She wrote to Jim that week. She never knew for sure if he got all her letters. He hardly wrote back.

Johnny met me at our usual spot today, a block away from home. He offered me a ride to school. When I said no, he pleaded with me. I'm not sure I'm doing the right thing. What do you think? I wish you were here.

The dance went well. Tom held her in his arms, and she was the envy of all the girls. She was happy, for once, with the burden of Norma lightened a little bit.

They started dating regularly. He was kind and made her laugh, but she still found herself looking for Johnny's bike after school.

"Have lunch with my family on Sunday after church," he said after they had been dating a few months.

"What?" She was unsure. "I don't know, Tom."

"They'll love you."

Tom's family was so different from her own. They laughed and shared stories around the table. She already knew his little sister from school and liked the girl. It was so... easy. Everything was.

That Monday she left school with Tom's arm around her shoulders, and saw Johnny in the parking lot, astride his bike.

"Want a ride?" Johnny asked as she walked past him.

She shook her head. She felt Tom's arm pull her in protectively.

"Francie." She stopped at the sound of Johnny's voice behind her. "Let me take you to your junior prom," he said.

She turned. "Johnny... "

"She's *my* girl," Tom said angrily. "What right do you have—"

"Stop," said Francie and shrugged out of Tom's arm. "Give us a minute." She walked over to Johnny.

"I love you," Johnny said. His eyes never left Francie's. "And I know you love me. Why are you doing this? I can protect you and your sister." He reached his hand out and took hers.

At his touch, her heart started pounding in her ears, and she felt her breath quicken. It was still there, whatever she'd had with Johnny. She liked Tom, but she never felt this way with him.

"He'll never understand you the way I do," said Johnny, his voice low, for her ears only. "His life has been too easy."

She swallowed and was about to speak when Tom came up to her. "Let's go, Francie," he said. Several of his friends had gathered around.

"Is there trouble here?" one of them asked.

"No, we're good," said Tom and put his arm around Francie. He turned her around and she let herself be led away

chapter 8

S HE WENT TO JUNIOR PROM WITH TOM. Her mom made a big fuss and spent a lot of money on a dress. Tom held her in his arms, and once again, she was the envy of all the girls.

It was late when they left the dance. She walked out ahead with some of her girlfriends, while Tom stayed behind to use the restroom.

When she walked out into the dark parking lot, she saw Johnny, sitting astride his bike. His black jacket blended in with the night, and she might not have seen him except for the lit cigarette dangling from his lips. He saw her and put it out.

"Francie," he said.

Her girlfriends giggled and urged her to go meet him. "We'll keep Tom busy," said Martha.

She walked up to him. He smelled like alcohol. "You've been drinking," she said.

"Why?" he said. "I knew you were going, but as I sat at home and thought about it, I wondered *why?* Why not let me take you? You *are* ashamed of me." His words were slurred.

"No," she said, her heart breaking. What had she done? "But I'm not so happy you've been drinking. Johnny, go home. We'll talk tomorrow."

She turned to leave.

"Francie, get back here," Johnny said. He grabbed her by the wrist. She saw Tom coming out of the hall and twisted to get away. Johnny made another grab for her, a clumsy one, and got her by the back of the dress. It ripped.

"Is there trouble here?" Tom said, walking up to them.

"You stay out of this!" Johnny shouted at him. He looked at Francie's torn dress, suddenly realizing what he had done.

"Let's go home," Tom said, taking her hand.

Francie looked at Johnny. The anger had left his eyes. "Okay," she said.

The look in Johnny's eyes turned to confusion, then hurt. She allowed Tom to lead her away. Johnny didn't shout for her to come back or try to apologize. She knew he wouldn't. She never looked back as she climbed into Tom's car, and he drove her home.

She felt numb the whole way and hoped that her mother wasn't up. If she saw the torn dress...

Tom talked constantly, saying they should call the police, or tell his dad, and he kept asking her if she was okay. Something Johnny had once said came to her then. "Tom doesn't understand what it's like to have problems. He comes from an uncomplicated life. If there's ever hardship, he won't be able to handle it. You don't need that in your life, Francie. You need someone who understands you and who can roll with the punches."

Tom dropped her off, and she leaned over and kissed him. "Thanks for a great evening," she said. "Let's not let the end ruin it."

She wanted to go in the back door to avoid her mom, so she didn't walk her up.

The lights were on, but she didn't see Norma. She ran upstairs and changed, hiding her torn dress. When Norma realized she was home and peeked in her room, Francie was buried under the covers, pretending to be asleep. Thankfully, her mom left.

She didn't hear from Johnny all the next week. She thought about calling him but was too stubborn. After all, it was he who should apologize. By Friday, she was beginning to think she would never see him again.

Tom and Francie dated the three remaining weeks of school.

"Don't go to Florida this year," Tom said.

"You know I have to," she said.

"I don't get what you see in those horses. I keep waiting for you to outgrow it."

Outgrow it? Francie frowned.

He drove her to the airport. She gave Tom her grandparents' address, and he promised to write often. She still hadn't heard from Johnny. It was with a bit of a heavy heart that she left for Florida.

"Time flies when you're having fun," her grandpa said. They were in the barn feeding the horses one August evening, and she was lamenting the fact that she had to go home soon. The summer had flown by.

"And you'll get to see your young man again," Papaw said. "That's something to look forward to."

"I guess," Francie said. "You're right." Tom had written her weekly and called once every other week. She was grateful. She had found a good man. "But I'll miss the horses."

She kept busy all summer, breaking a few young horses to saddle, and gratefully she hadn't had time to think about Johnny or worry much about Jim away at war. The few letters she got from Krista told her that her sister was loving New York, and her older brother Mark even called a few times. Things were good.

Francie broke open the last bale of hay and fed it to the stalled horses.

"Here, Tinkerbell, let me get down another bale of hay," Papaw said and started to climb the ladder. Suddenly he clutched at his chest and fell.

"Papaw!" Francie ran to him. "Papaw!" He couldn't speak and seemed to be in a lot of pain. His face was very white.

In a panic, she ran to the barn phone and called for an ambulance. The paramedics were there in minutes and took him off to the hospital. As she watched the flashing light disappear around a bend, she felt like her heart would burst.

"Francie, come inside," Sam said.

The little girl had come down to the barn. "Grandma went with Papaw in the ambulance, so she doesn't have a way to get home. If they keep him."

Francie nodded shakily and finished feeding the horses. They walked together back to the house and sat at the table, quietly eating peanut butter sandwiches and waiting for a phone call. It was long past dark when Grandma finally called.

"It was a heart attack," she said. "He'll be all right. Get Sam to bed, and I'll be able to tell you more in the morning, after I talk to the doctors."

Papaw came home a few days later, weakened from the experience and with doctor's orders not to overdo it. Francie had to fly home the next day.

"I'll never get your grandfather to sit still," her grandma said to her as they dropped Francie off at the airport.

Francie hugged them goodbye and promised to come back next summer, before she started college. Her heart was in her throat as she and Sam got on the plane. She looked out the window and could see her grandparents standing in the terminal, waving.

The school year went well. She clung to Tom like a life preserver. He kept her afloat and out of the angry grasps of her parents. If she was with him, her parents were happy. Norma treated her special and assumed Tom was 'keeping an eye on her'. Francie still looked for Johnny after school, but he never showed up. She couldn't quite forget him. Fall passed and then snow arrived. With the bitter cold, her brother came back from war.

She went with her dad to pick Jim up at the airport. They watched as a few other GIs exited the plane and ran into the arms of their waiting girlfriends and mothers.

Jim came last, leaning heavily on a cane. Francie almost didn't recognize him with his short hair.

Her dad snorted. "He didn't even last a year before he got shot," he said, shaking his head.

Francie ignored her dad and walked up to greet Jim.

"Hi," she said.

Jim stopped and looked down at her. He looked so sad that she felt tears well up in her own eyes.

"I missed you," she said and pulled him into a hug.

"I missed you too," he said quietly. His one arm was in a sling, but he awkwardly pulled her to him. The other leaned heavily on his cane.

"What happened?" she said.

He pointed to his shoulder. "Shot." Then to his leg. "Broken." He gave her a wry smile.

She took his arm. "Let's go home."

Their dad stood a little ways off, arms crossed, waiting.

"From one hell to another," Jim muttered.

She did well on her college entrance exams and earned a scholarship to Michigan State University to study veterinary medicine. Tom was going there to study engineering. He came over to her house as soon as he got his entrance letter.

"I got a full scholarship!" he said. He grabbed her and hugged her. "Let's go out."

After a celebratory dinner, he drove her home. It was late, and after he turned the car off, he leaned over to kiss her.

"I'd like more than kisses," he said.

"We're in my driveway," Francie giggled.

"I know. Maybe we can meet up later?" He continued to kiss her, on the lips, down her neck.

"Tom," she pulled back a little. "Not here. We can't have sex. Mom says we'll go to Hell."

"I know. So marry me."

"What?"

"Marry me. We can have all the sex we want to then. And we can live together during college! It'll be perfect! Francie, I love you so much."

Francie wasn't sure what to say and didn't get the chance because someone turned the porch light on.

"I've got to go," she said.

He didn't bring it up again, so she was surprised when at his parents' Christmas party, with her parents present, that he proposed to her in front of everybody.

"I know we're young," he said. "But I love you, Francie."

He did it the old-fashioned way, down on one knee. He had asked her dad in advance.

Everyone in the room held their breath. Too embarrassed to say "no," Francie accepted his proposal.

Norma was thrilled.

Then, one snowy day in January, Francie walked out of the school at the end of the day, hand in hand with Tom, and saw a familiar motorcycle sitting by the curb. Only one person would drive a motorcycle in such weather. He came up to her from out of the crowd.

"I have to talk to you," Johnny said.

"She has nothing to say to you," Tom replied. Johnny looked tired and had lost some weight since Francie had last seen him.

"Please." He put his hand on her shoulder.

"Tom, give us just a minute," Francie said. Tom reluctantly released Francie's hand, and she followed Johnny away from the crowd.

"Francie, I'm sorry," he began. "Those things I said to you that night, they were wrong. I'm sorry I showed up at prom. I'm sorry I was drunk, and I'm sorry I tore your dress. I'll never do anything like that to you again."

"You'll never get the chance," Francie said. Suddenly, all the anger and hurt she had felt over the past year came rushing to the surface. "I waited for you to call and apologize, and I waited and waited. Finally, Johnny, I gave up on you. If you think I'm going to come back to you now, you're crazy. I love Tom."

"Francie," Johnny took both of her gloved hands in his, his eyes pleading. "I *love* you. I stayed away from you for a few weeks after prom because I was ashamed. I acted like a jerk. I don't know what got into me. I was just hurt. Then, I tried all summer to reach you. I called your house several times to get your grandparents' address, but your mother always answered, and she would just hang up on me. Then at the end of August"—his voice broke a little—"my dad got drunk and pounded on Mom. Anyway, she wound up in the hospital, and I guess he felt awful for what he did because he shot himself."

Johnny was talking fast now, holding back tears. "We moved Mom to her family's house in Ohio, and I had to find a job. To support her, you know, until she recovered. Francie, I tried to call, and I wrote letters to your house, but the last time I called, your mother said she had been throwing the letters away and threatened to call the police on me if I didn't leave you alone. I had to get in touch with you, so I rode up here to see you."

"You rode all the way from Ohio in this weather on your bike?" For some reason, that seemed more incredible than anything else he had told her. She focused on that. She had to focus on something. The school, the parking lot, it was all spinning. She was starting to feel sick. He had tried to contact her. Her mother...

"I had to," Johnny said. "We lost the car. My brother's business went under."

"Johnny." Francie didn't know what to say. Her life had been coming together with Tom. He was the perfect guy. He was good looking, he had a good career in mind, he was solid and dependable. He promised he'd make big bucks in his job and move her to her very own horse farm after college. She didn't know if she wanted to give that up for all of Johnny's problems. "I don't know what to say."

She wondered if she could make it to the bathroom. She thought she was going to be sick.

"Francie, I want to marry you," he said. "You'll be graduating in a few months. Come down to Ohio. I have a job at a restaurant right now, and I'll finish the book soon. It'll work out."

"Johnny, no." She pulled her hands out of his and put them to her face. The cold felt good. Ohio. No. Her horse farm was in Florida. Only Florida. "I don't want to live in Ohio."

"We'll move," he said. "To Florida if that's where you need to be."

"Johnny, all of this is so sudden."

"Let's go somewhere and talk," he said. Francie was starting to shiver in the cold snow. "I don't have much time. I have to be back to work tomorrow morning."

Francie looked at him. Her heart was pounding. She wanted to throw her arms around him, to tell him how she felt. She wanted to talk all of this through with him, the wedding, her feelings, her future. He would understand. He always had.

Johnny put a hand on her shoulder. "You're cold," he said. His touch was like fire to her, warming her from the inside. She was about to take his hand.

"Francie?" She heard Tom's voice behind her. "Is everything okay?"

She looked back at Tom, who was quietly waiting for her with a worried look, and she smiled.

"Johnny, I can't. I can't see you anymore. Go back home to Ohio and find another girl. It's over between us."

"Francie, *no*," he said. "Please. Tom isn't right for you. You're a free spirit. He won't be able to keep up." But she turned and walked away.

"Just give me a chance!" he shouted, and people stopped and looked at him. A few snickered.

Francie followed Tom to his car and didn't look back as he started up the Mustang and drove her home. Francie was so angry that she forgot to be afraid of her mom and let her have it when she got home.

"You hid them from me?" she shouted. "You *lied* to me!"

"He's no good," her mom said. "I did you a favor by hiding those letters."

"Give them to me."

"No. They're full of 'I love yous'. He doesn't love you. He *wants* you. There's a difference."

"You *read* them?"

"Of course I did." Norma folded her arms across her chest. "Stay away from Johnny. He's the pathway to Hell. And you're on it. Did you sleep with him? God will punish you for your sins, child."

Francie stormed upstairs and slammed her door.

In May, her grandpa had another heart attack. While in the hospital, the doctors discovered he had lung cancer, and that he had only a few weeks to live.

He came home, and her grandmother looked after him with the help of hospice care. Francie and her mom flew down to see them. Her grandmother looked horrible. She was thin and pale from taking care of Papaw, and the grief had worn her down.

Francie was even more shocked at the sight of her grandpa.

"Hi, Tinkerbell," he said, reaching a frail hand out to her. She grasped his hand and started crying. "Oh, no," he said slowly. Each word was difficult for him, and he was very short of breath. "Don't cry." He raised her hand to his mouth and gave it a tender kiss. "You'll take good care of Sunnyhill, Tink. Remember, it's your safehaven."

He had a coughing fit after that, then that evening, he lapsed into a coma. Those were the last words he ever spoke to Francie. She flew back home to finish final exams, and he died less than a week later. Francie's grandmother, out feeding the horses in the rain, contracted pneumonia. Within a week, she too was dead.

Tom flew down with Francie for the double funeral. Her siblings all came in, and she got to see them briefly. Even Jim was there.

It was a quick affair, and she had to return home for graduation. She picked up the mail on her way into the house and found a letter from Johnny. She went up to her room to read it alone.

He was back in Michigan and wanted to see her. He gave her his new phone number and asked her to call him. Almost without thinking, she lifted up the phone by her bed and dialed his number. He answered.

"Johnny?" she said.

"Francie?" he seemed shocked to hear from her. "Oh, I'm so glad you called."

"Johnny, my grandparents died."

"Oh my gosh." Silence. "Are you okay?"

"Yes. No. We just got back from the funeral. Can I see you?"

"Yes, I'd love that. Where do you want to meet?"

"At the park," she said. "Where you like to think." She smiled at the memory.

She borrowed her parents' car and an hour later she met him there. He was sitting in his favorite spot and stood up when she arrived. She ran to him, and as his arms embraced her, she began to sob. It was the first time since their deaths that she had been able to cry. She cried for them, for her breakup with Johnny, for everything that hurt. She sobbed uncontrollably, shaking, burying her face against his neck and inhaling his musky smell. She wanted so badly to feel safe. He made her feel safe.

Finally, when her tears subsided, she looked into his face.

"Johnny, I didn't come here to get back together with you," she said. "I don't know why I came here, really. It's just that... " she didn't know what to say. What she meant was that Tom just didn't understand about things like her grandparents' death and what that meant for her, and about her parents, and Sam, and everything. He had led too sheltered of a life and had never experienced any big disappointments or losses. He was sweet and good to her, but Johnny had been right: Tom just didn't get it. She loved him though, in a way, and liked his solid dependable nature.

"Francie," Johnny said tenderly. "You're my whole life."

She looked at him, fresh tears filling her eyes. "Why did you pick *me*, anyway? You could have had just about any girl in school, probably even my sister Krista, but you choose *me*. Why?"

"Because you're special." He took her by the shoulders and looked into her eyes. "You have an unquenchable fire. You're the only person I've ever found who really understands me. I *need* you, Francie."

She brushed the tears away as they streamed down her cheeks. "It's too late. I've lost the farm and my dream. Tom asked me to marry him. I want to settle down, Johnny, with someone dependable. I want to know that when I come home in the evening, he'll be there to hold me in his arms at night. I want a family. You're not that kind of man. You wouldn't be happy and in a few years. We'd wind up hating each other. I don't want that to happen."

"Francie, you love me. I know you do. You can't marry Tom. He's not right for you."

"Johnny, please try to understand."

"Francie... " Johnny looked lost. "You can't do this. The farm was your dream. You can't just give up that easily."

"I'm not giving up, Johnny. I'm going to veterinary school, and Tom is going to be an engineer. We'll make good money, and I'll be around animals. Someday we'll be rich enough to buy a little land and some horses. I could never do that with you. Tom understands my dream, and he's willing to help make it a reality." She turned to go. "Please, don't ever call me again. Don't ever visit me again. I love you, Johnny, but not enough to make it work."

As she walked out of the park, Johnny stood there in his leather jacket and faded blue jeans with tears running down his cheeks. She hated herself.

"I'm not giving up on you, Francie Dalton," he said. "I'm not."

The very next day she saw Johnny again. She and Tom had stopped by the town hall to register for their marriage, and Johnny was there, on his bike. She had no idea what he was doing downtown and didn't have the chance to ask. Tom told him to move on, they were here for their marriage license. Johnny begged Francie not to leave him.

In the pouring rain, she turned him down and climbed back in Tom's car. Johnny stood there, alone, and she watched him through her window until she could no longer see him.

Norma fussed about, making wedding preparations. She was telling the seamstress all about it, and about Tom's dad.

"He's not that wealthy, but he has good standing in the community, and they are very involved in our church. He's a deacon, you know."

Francie turned so the woman could add more pins to her dress. The fitting was taking a long time.

"Show her your ring, Francie," Norma said.

Francie dutifully held out her hand. The seamstress oooohhhed and ahhhhhed politely.

"I'm so proud of Francie for choosing well," Norma continued. "She gave us a scare for a while, dating this biker. Straight from Hell, he was. Straight to Hell he'll go too, I'm sure."

The seamstress stepped back and turned Francie to face the mirror.

"What do you think, honey?"

Francie stared at herself in the mirror and let her eyes travel down the dress to the ring resting on the fourth finger of her right hand; a ring with her birthstone in it.

"I think it's beautiful," she said, and knew that she would call him.

chapter
9

FRANCIE COULDN'T REACH JOHNNY and was in bed reading when Jim walked into her room that evening. She looked up at him. He stood there, with a newspaper in his hand, shuffling uncomfortably.

"I'm sorry, sis," he said.

Fear caught in her throat. "What?"

"I read the obits now," he laughed nervously. "Stupid hobby, but I see guys I know in there, local guys who were in the war. Anyway, I saw this."

He handed her the paper and pointed to one of the obituaries. "Johnny was killed last night. He hit a tree with his bike. They think he was drunk."

Francie numbly read the short write-up. She nodded.

"You okay?" Jim asked.

She nodded again. Her brother gave her shoulder an awkward squeeze and left, closing her door.

I don't want to get drunk and wrap my bike around a tree, Johnny's words rang through her mind. *What a waste of a life.*

She ran her shaking hands through her hair. If she had only climbed on his bike that night, he would still be alive. A sob escaped her, and she swallowed hard, fighting the tears. She, the person he had trusted the most, had let him down. Johnny was *dead*. Dead because of her. She imagined the rest of her life without him, and suddenly, she felt like she couldn't breathe. She grabbed her head between her hands and cried.

Francie lived in a state of numb shock for the next few days. Tom seemed to understand, and he didn't protest when she told him she was going to go to the funeral and wanted to go alone. What she didn't tell him—or her parents—was where it was. It was on the south side of town, where Johnny had grown up. It was not a safe place to go alone. To avoid driving, she took a cab.

She didn't know anybody, and the few people that were there didn't speak to her. There was an older woman sitting in a chair up front, quietly weeping, and Francie found it strange that she sat alone. Probably his mother. A couple of other people were talking, their voices a low mumble. There were a few flowers.

Francie went just to see the body. She had to be sure he was dead. In her mind, she couldn't accept that fact, and she kept denying it to herself. Johnny was laid out in a plain casket with his hands folded across his chest. His hair had been combed wrong. She resisted the urge to run her fingers through it and fix it the way he'd always worn it. He looked at peace. Francie stood by his side one last time, looking down at him, and she wondered what had become of the book of poetry he had been writing. Then she turned her back and walked out.

The funeral was the next day. It was raining, and the weather was dreary and depressing. She wore a plain black skirt and blouse and went alone to the cemetery, driving in her mother's car. When she got there, there were more people than she expected. She recognized his mother from the funeral home, and she guessed the young man standing beside her was Johnny's brother. No one spoke to her, and she stood alone in the back, listening to the words of the minister and tightly clutching her umbrella.

I killed him, she thought. *This is my fault.*

A few tears escaped her eyes, but she didn't break down. Long after the funeral service was over, and even long after his mother had left, she sat there in the rain near his gravesite. She didn't really think about anything, but just sat there, wishing he was beside her. She wanted to take back all the things she had said to him the last time she had been with him. She hadn't been cruel, but she hadn't given him a chance. By the time it grew dark out, she was chilled to the bone. She got stiffly up and started to walk back to the car, a few blocks away.

"Well, what d'we have here?" said a voice behind her. She was in a fog, in a dazed frame of mind, so it took her a moment to realize the voice was directed at her. She turned to find three guys following her. They were wearing a baggy assortment of jeans and leather and had various tattoos. The tallest, a dark-haired youth about her age, pulled out a knife and grinned.

Quickly, the other two walked ahead of her. She realized a bit too late that she was surrounded.

"Nice and fresh and from the other side of the tracks, guys," said the knife-wielding fiend. His grin reminded her of a rabid dog.

"Can't wait to taste it," said a thug to her right. She turned to him. His blond hair was cut short and spiked up with some sort of gel. His t-shirt read an obscenity.

She turned and ran. Right into the third guy.

His laugh curled her blood as his fingers dug into her arms.

"Leave me alone!" she screamed and kicked him hard in the shin. Then she brought her knee up and hit home.

He howled in pain and his knees buckled. She took advantage of the moment to break free, but the other two were on her.

She felt the knife-wielder grab her from behind and hold her arms down to her sides. His hot breath was on the back of her neck.

"Kill her!" said the third guy, holding his groin.

"Not until we play," said the one with the knife. "Then we'll cut her into pieces so's she can't tell."

Francie tried to fight her way loose, but he was a lot stronger than her. Then, as if in a dream, she saw an old brown Cadillac pulling up alongside the curb. The driver got out and ambled slowly toward them.

Jim stepped out. "What's up, guys?".

"You'd best just walk away and pretend like you didn't see nothin'," the voice said into her neck.

"I was thinkin' on a trade," said Jim. He reached into the pocket of his oversized bomber jacket and pulled out a bag of cocaine.

"You interested in some pussy?" said the third guy, recovering enough to stand.

"Nope," said Jim. "She's my sister."

Francie felt her captor's grip tighten, and he placed the knife blade along her neck. Then he laughed.

"Why don't you just hand me the stuff, and nobody will get hurt," he snarled.

Jim pulled out a knife of his own and put it up next to the bag.

"Or I could cut this little bag open, and we could have a snowstorm," he said. "What do ya think? There's about three-grand worth here. You pretty boys could snort it or sell it. Either way, it's worth more than a quick lay, don't you think?"

The goons exchanged glances.

"Drop the bag," said the one with the knife.

"Let the girl go," said Jim, staring evenly into his eyes.

He loosened his grip on Francie, and she broke away.

"Get in the car," said Jim as he dropped the bag in front of him.

"Nice doin' business with you," he said. He quickly got in the car and drove off, watching in his rearview mirror as the guys picked up the bag.

Francie was shaking.

"You okay?" he asked kindly.

"Fine," she said, although she wasn't. "Jim, if you hadn't come along when you did... " She started to cry.

"Shhhh. I came along, and that's all that matters. You're safe now."

"Mom's car... "

"I'll come back in the morning to get it."

They drove in silence for a while. Finally, in a shaky voice, Francie asked, "What were you doing in this part of town? And why... why do you have cocaine and a knife?"

He was silent for a while, and she thought he wasn't going to answer her. When he finally spoke, his voice was quiet and his eyes far away.

"There are some things that happened in... " he paused. "Sometimes, it's either this or suicide. And my life came at too high of a price for me to go and kill myself."

He swallowed hard. She couldn't be sure, but she thought she saw tears in his eyes.

"Too high of a price?"

He didn't answer, and she wrapped her arms around herself, still trembling.

It would be many years before she finally realized the depth of his words and the burden he carried with him.

She sat on her bed all the next day, staring out at the rain. The heavy thud of rainwater on the glass seemed to drown out her heartache, if she concentrated really hard on the patterns it made as it traveled down the pane to the sill, where it was collecting in a little puddle just below the window. She had it cracked so she could get some air. The room seemed stuffy.

There was a knock on her door that evening. She kept staring at the window. If only they'd all leave her alone! Her mom had tried several times to offer her some food but hadn't gone so far as to try to unlock the door to see if her daughter's silence was something she should be worried about. The knock came again, and as her eyes came back into focus, Francie realized how bad her head was hurting. The throbbing in her temples was keeping in cadence with the beat of her heart.

"Francie?"

It was Krista's voice, worried. "I just flew in. Mom told me about Johnny. Can I come in?"

Krista. She had come home. Somewhere in the back of her mind, Francie knew there was a reason for that.

"Francie?"

There was some scratching above the door as Krista felt for the key on the ledge. Then a click. The door opened slowly.

"Hey," she said quietly, shutting it behind her. She sat down on the bed and ran her hand down her long blond hair. Francie didn't look at her.

"It's almost time, huh?" Krista said.

Time. If only they all had more time. Time was the problem, Francie thought. If she could only go back in time a few more days, to the day Johnny had asked her to climb on board his Harley...

"Are you okay?"

The wedding. That was it. That was why Krista had come home. Francie finally turned to her sister and leaned her head on her shoulder.

"Krista, I've lost everything," she said in a whisper. "Grandma and Papaw, the farm, and now Johnny. I just don't know what to do."

"Do you want to postpone the wedding until you have some time to grieve?" Krista asked, concern in her voice.

"No." Everyone had worked so hard, and Krista had had enough trouble getting time off from work as it was. Francie didn't want to complicate things. "The wedding invitations have been printed and sent out. Mom has two hundred people coming. We can't tell two hundred people to cancel their plans and make it next month."

Krista stroked Francie's hair. "We can do whatever you want, little sis."

"No, I'll go through with it."

"Tell me the truth," Krista said. "Do you really love him?"

"Of course, I love him, Krista!" Francie pulled away, angry at the question. "He's all I've got!"

"He's not all you've got, Francie," said Krista. "You've got me. You'll always have me."

"Can you promise me that, Krista? Can you promise me that you'll never die or that you'll never leave me for some Hollywood glamour job or for the right man?"

"I can promise you that I'll never leave you," said Krista. "Not of my own accord. If the good Lord wants to take me, there's nothing I can do about that, but as long as I'm on this earth, I will always be here for you."

"The *good Lord*," Francie said bitterly. "I don't know what's good about him."

Francie refused to come down to dinner that night. Tom came over and saw her briefly in her room. She didn't feel like talking and asked him politely to leave. Then she heard her oldest brother, Mark, arrive.

She was facing the window but turned when she heard him come into her room. There was a slight quiver to her lower lip. She felt a rush of warmth flow up toward her face, making her headache worse. He stood there and opened his arms, saying nothing, because he knew there was nothing to say, no words of comfort that he could give.

She walked toward him and felt his warm arms fold around her and hold her tightly to him. It was then that the tears finally came.

"That's good," he whispered. "You've got to let it out."

She cried like a baby, and when she finally wiped her eyes and blew her nose on the tissue Mark offered, she laughed.

"I'm sorry," she said, a little embarrassed. "I guess I'm just a bit upset."

"Now doesn't that feel better?" Mark asked. "To let it all out? I know you, Francie, trying to be tough and keeping everything inside. It's not good for you, you know. If there had been any more tears inside you, you would have drowned!"

They talked a little bit, and he told her about his latest FBI assignment, or what he could tell her anyway. It was, after all, top secret. Then he went downstairs and got her some dinner and some aspirin for her headache. It had been so long since she had last seen him.

"Thanks," she said, picking at the food on her plate. He was sitting at the end of her bed, twirling a pillow around. "Are you going to stay until the wedding?"

"That's what I came home for," he said. "I see Jim is in his usual state. Useless."

That made Francie angry, but she let it go. It hurt her head to be mad or to talk. Mark and Jim had never gotten along, mostly because her dad compared them all the time. And Jim, of course, always came up short. The failed war veteran versus the man moving up the ladder of the FBI.

She smiled a little for Mark's benefit, then pushed the rest of her plate away. "I'm tired," she said. "I'd like to sleep a bit."

He nodded and kissed her on the head. "I'll be downstairs if you need me."

He left, and she crawled under the covers and slept.

Jim was dreaming.

There they were, his platoon, surrounded in the jungle. In a ravine with the enemy above them and only trees between them and death.

"We're going to die," the guy next to him whispered and started to cry.

Jim had an idea. He looked to his left. There were three of the best men he'd ever met, friends until the end. Nobody he had ever trusted more. He couldn't let them die. Not here. Not like this.

"Cover me," he said and charged forward and up the embankment. Shots rang off all around him, but he kept going. If he could only get to the top.

A sharp pain seared through his arm. He kept going. One pinged off his helmet. Another one through his leg. As he fell, he launched the grenade forward into the trees at the top of the ravine, where the enemy was hiding.

There was an enormous explosion, and Jim's world tilted wildly as his left ear drum blew out. Someone grabbed him and dragged him roughly up the embankment. Then he passed out.

In the dream, he always regained consciousness when they came to rescue him. He was a prisoner, his leg shattered and dangling at an awkward angle. But there was Paul, his hand on Jim's shoulder.

"I've got you, buddy," he said, and then shook Jim to keep him conscious. "We're getting out of here."

He was airlifted through gunfire up to the chopper, just as the enemy jumped Paul and the two other men who had saved him. They were buried under bodies.

"No!" Jim screamed and tried to jump from the chopper, to go back, to help. "No!" He screamed and screamed as the chopper flew away, having no choice but to retreat or be shot down. "No!" he screamed, reaching for his friends, until he was jolted awake, sweating and fighting the covers. "No," he said, more quietly, catching his breath, reorienting himself to his surroundings at home.

"What on earth?" his dad opened the door and flicked on the light. Pain seared behind Jim's eyes.

"Jim?" Francie said, pushing past his dad, but then Jim saw Mark behind her and was ashamed to realize there were tears on his cheeks from the nightmare. He brushed them away with the back of his hand.

Mark laughed. "Looks like a war dream," he said and shook his head. "Geez, Jim. I've seen worse combat as an FBI agent. People are always shooting at me. Get a grip."

Their dad shook his head and left the room.

"Idiot. Waking your sister up before her wedding weekend," said Mark, and he left too. He pushed past Krista and the others in the hall and sent them all back to bed.

"Jim?" Francie was starting to shiver in her nightgown.

"Go back to bed," he said, sitting up and lighting a cigarette. "I'm fine."

She stood there, wanting to reach out to him. "Mark's an idiot," she said, trying to help somehow.

"Go!" he said more firmly. "Leave me alone."

She turned and went back to her room, but it was a long time before she went back to sleep.

The weekend arrived in a whirlwind. After the rehearsal, they had dinner at a fine restaurant. Francie toyed with her salad and tried her best to smile for Tom. She was quiet, but that was typical for her, and she seemed fine to the rest of her family.

The wedding was beautiful, and she looked dazzling in her dress. She saw the empty pew where her grandparents should have been, and tears came to her eyes. She was in a daze, smiling only for the wedding photographs. Years later, when she looked at them, she could see how pale and miserable she looked, even behind the rows of white teeth.

She and Tom came back to her parents' house on Sunday to open their wedding gifts before they left the next day for their honeymoon in Acapulco.

While Francie was unwrapping a rolling pin, the doorbell rang.

"A wedding gift from Papaw," Sam said quietly.

"What?" Francie looked at her quizzically.

"It's someone looking for Francie Dalton," one of their guests shouted from the entryway.

"Francie Cutter, now," Tom squeezed her hand.

They brought the man into the living room. He was dressed in a suit and tie and looked vaguely familiar to Francie.

"Miss Dalton?" he said, extending his hand to her.

"Mrs. Cutter now," Tom said and gave a nervous little laugh.

"I'm Mr. Johnson, your grandfather's attorney."

Of course. That's where she had seen him. At the farm.

"Hi, Mr. Johnson," Francie finally spoke.

"I'm sorry to interrupt, but I think you'll be glad I found you," he said. "And I wanted the whole family together for this. I'm the lawyer who's handling your grandparents' estate."

"Oh?" Her heart skipped a beat. Why would this man be looking for *her?*

"We just got things settled down there, and it seems like I've got good news for you."

Francie waited, holding her breath. Could she dare to hope they had left her anything? Her mare, Star?

"It seems that your grandparents have left their entire estate to you. Congratulations!"

Francie was silent. Their *entire estate?* The farm was *hers?* This couldn't be happening!

"To *me?*" was all she could get out.

Her mom turned white.

"Yes. However, he did leave your mother $10,000. And there's a letter here he left for you. I'd like to take a minute to read it to the family, if that's okay."

"Um... sure," Francie said.

"Wait a minute," her mom stood up.

"Mrs. Dalton, please just listen," Mr. Johnson said and pulled out the letter.

Dear children and grandchildren,

If you're reading this, it means your grandma and I have passed on. I leave $10,000 cash to my daughter, Norma. The rest of my estate goes to my granddaughter, Francie Ann Dalton. Francie, you understand what Sunnyhill Farm is about, and you have the business sense and horse know-how to run the place as I have taught you over the years. You were my protégé. My contingency is you will open your new home and your heart to your siblings and anyone else who needs a home. Use it to shelter and protect, and to be a safehaven to anyone or animal who needs a place to be. Take care of each other, especially little Sam. I am proud of you all. And Jim, I know there's more to you than you let us see. Krista, you are as beautiful on the inside as the outside. Mark, as the eldest, *take care of them. I love each and every one of you, and I will see you someday in Heaven.*

Norma, I hope you find what you need in life to be happy. Your mother and I love you, but honey, I can't let you turn Sunnyhill into a beach resort. It is so much more than that.

Love, Papaw/Dad

The room was silent. Mr. Johnson folded the letter and put it in the vest pocket of his jacket.

"The last year was hard on your grandfather. He accumulated some bills because of his ill health."

"Wow," Francie whispered. "It's all *mine*. Are you serious?"

"Very. When can you get down to sign the papers?"

"Uh... this weekend?" Francie said.

"There doesn't need to be a rush. Are you going on a honeymoon? Did you want to wait and sign the papers next week?"

"No!" Francie said quickly. "I want to do it now." It seemed that if she waited, the entire farm could slip through her fingers. She couldn't risk losing it.

"Okay. Give me a call later, and we can arrange a time to meet." He handed her his business card and smiled down at her. "If only your grandfather could see you now. You look so radiant. And I'm sure he would be proud of the young man who captured your heart." Mr. Johnson extended his hand to shake Tom's.

Francie got up and gave Mr. Johnson a hug. "Thank you!" she said.

Someone showed him to the door. Francie glanced around the room. Nobody was talking. Her mom had turned from white to red. Her dad was frowning and had his arms folded across his chest.

"Happy wedding present," Sam said with a little smile. "I told you you'd like it."

The full realization finally hit Francie. She threw her arms around Tom and gave him a hug. "We're rich," she whispered into his ear. "Now we can have everything we ever wanted."

Krista came over and gave Francie a hug. "I'm happy for you. I have enough money of my own now, but I know I'll always have a home with you if I need it."

"We've got to move there this week!" Francie said to Tom.

"But Francie," he was still confused. "What about our honeymoon?"

"Tom, honey, forget our honeymoon! We've got a mansion to live in. We've got to go down and sign the papers and start moving in!"

"Francie," Tom wasn't getting too excited about the farm. "You're jumping into this. We have our educations planned for *here* this fall. We're both enrolled in college in Michigan. We can't move to Florida!"

"Tom," Francie was getting exasperated that he wasn't understanding. "Don't you see? We don't *need* our education. We can run the farm. My grandparents made good money with it. You can be the manager, and I'll do the horse training."

"Francie, wait," Tom's voice had an edge to it. "We don't know *anything* about running a farm!"

Francie was losing her patience. Her dream had finally come true, and here was this... *man*... hindering her. She didn't want to be disappointed, and she didn't want to come down from her high, even for a minute. Not after all the pain.

"You can go to school down *there*," she said. "You have good grades, so they should let you in anywhere, right? And I can stay home and run the farm. We'll have to call the airport and see if we can get our tickets refunded, and then we'll have to start packing to go down. Actually, we've already got some clothes packed, so I say we just head down there tomorrow, after we rent a U-Haul of course. . ."

Francie rambled away, thinking about racehorses and the blazing green and gold silks of Sunnyhill. She thought of Star and how she'd soon wake up and walk out to the barn to see her every morning. She opened up the rest of her wedding gifts at Krista's suggestion, but her mind was on the farm. Sunnyhill was *hers*. Life suddenly seemed so perfect.

Tom sat beside her and watched his new bride open the rest of her gifts in a flurry of excitement. She gradually felt him relax.

"You're so... *excited*," he said, as if searching for the right word. "It's nice to have you back."

She looked at him and gave him a quick kiss.

"I... I'm not so sure about all of this," he laughed nervously. "It's exciting, but... I mean... do Sam and Jim come and live with us? I guess we can move there *after* college... " He swallowed.

But Francie wasn't to be discouraged. She had made up her mind.

That night, when they were in their little bedroom in his parents' basement where they had planned on staying until they could move into student housing in the fall, he told her he'd go.

"We can't take Sam, though," he said. "Jim will keep an eye on her. She needs to be in school, and we need to figure all of this out—how to run the place and stuff."

She hugged him. "You are the best," she said, and she meant it.

They canceled their honeymoon plans, and the next day, they rented a U-Haul and packed up all their belongings.

By nightfall, they were on their way to their new home in Florida.

Little did Tom know that it was the beginning of the end.

chapter 10

Coastal Ridge Hospital, 1999

"I DO KNOW WHAT IT'S LIKE TO LOSE SOMEONE," said Francie. "I've lost nearly everyone I've ever been close to. My grandparents, my sister, my brother, my husband. God took them all."

She was quiet while she watched that sink in with Jack. It was unfair to use her own past to try to show empathy. There was no way her past pain could equal his. But she had to get Jack out of his self-pity. Anger, she felt, was better than pity. That, at least, would sustain him.

"And then God blessed you tenfold," Jack said, "as He did Job. Is that what we are? A game between God and the devil?"

He was back in the chair, she on the windowsill, letting the sun warm her back. The doctor had just given him a mild sedative.

"Are you glad that it happened that way, Francie? Have you *grown* from it?"

She couldn't tell if he was being sarcastic or asking her a serious question. She thought for a moment before answering.

"No," she said.

But it all made sense to her, finally. All the pain, all the death, all the trials. Even her near suicide. Without it, she wouldn't be here. Jack wouldn't have chosen to trust her, to open up to her, and, quite possibly, wouldn't have pulled through his trauma the way he had. Amazing, doctors had said. Amazing that he had come so far so fast, after what had happened to him. A miracle, they called it.

A miracle. The hand of God?

"*No,*" she repeated. "I'm not glad it happened. I'm not glad any of it happened. I often wonder how far back I would have to go to change things, and somehow, it all goes back to Johnny. If I had gotten on the back of that bike with him. Or if I had never even broken up with him. How far back do I go?"

And would they all still be alive if she had? Krista... dear, sweet Krista. How she missed her.

Jack looked at her, his eyes softening.

"I know you've been hurt," he said. "I don't mean to discount that in any way."

"I know."

"It's just... I've come to a place where the pain doesn't stop. The nightmares, the physical pain. Now my heart... " He put his hands on his chest and smiled, but there was no humor behind it. "And it's not Annie's fault. I couldn't be what she needed."

"It *is* Annie's fault," Francie said. She wasn't ready to give that one up yet. "She kicked you while you were down. She knew what she was getting into when she agreed to marry you. She knew your past."

"Did she? Not all of it. Not even I knew my past," he said. "We could go on blaming everyone. We could go as far back as your parents—"

"Oh, I *do* blame them," said Francie, folding her arms across her chest.

"But I'm too tired for that. I need to sleep."

He moved over to the bed and lay down, closing his eyes.

"I'll leave," Francie said, getting down off the windowsill.

"No, stay," he said. "Just until I get to sleep."

She sat down in the chair and watched as he drifted into a world she couldn't enter. His hand was warm as she slipped it into hers, and he smiled a little bit before the pills took him down.

"Tomorrow's another day," he said.

And he dreamed.

When Jack dreamed, he was always called by his birth name, which was Paul. Even after all these years, his mind hadn't made the correlation that he was now "Jack", perhaps because his dreams nearly always involved the past.

In the dream, his chopper circled over the group of Viet Cong who had Jim by the arms, dragging him. Jim's leg was bent backward, broken, and he was bleeding from the shoulder, probably a gunshot wound. The man in the chopper with Paul opened fire, scattering the enemy, and Paul dropped right down in the middle of the chaos, knocking Jim's captors off of him.

"Paul," Jim said, breathing heavily. His eyes kept rolling up in his head.

"Stay conscious," Paul slapped him a few times on the face and buckled him into the cot they had lowered from the chopper. Two more men came down, shooting the enemy back, and suddenly gunfire erupted all around them. They heard shouts in Vietnamese, and Paul tugged on the rope, and the chopper lifted Jim up and inside.

Paul took cover, diving into some brush and firing wildly. Suddenly, he was grabbed from behind.

More shouting in Vietnamese.

"No!" he heard Jim scream from the chopper.

Paul felt someone grab his arms, nearly pulling them out of their sockets as he was jerked backwards. He glanced up in time to see the chopper disappear. The pilot had to leave, or they'd all be shot down. There was no other choice.

He and the two other men who had been with him had their hands tied.

"Walk," someone said in a heavy accent, hitting him in the kidney with the rifle butt. He had been captured.

Coastal Ridge Hospital, 1999

Ruth Isadora was a licensed psychiatrist who specialized in working with vets and others who had PTSD. At age 62, she had an impressive list of publications, awards, and workshops, but it was more her personality that earned her the trust and respect of her patients. Affectionately known as "Dr. Ruth," like the famous sex doctor of 1970's fame, Ruth Isadora wasn't beyond hugging her patients or letting Francie call her anytime she needed to talk; she had even given Francie her personal cell phone number. Over the past year, Ruth had become more like a mentor than a therapist.

Now she sat across the table from Frank and Francie, pondering the fate of Jack. The room was small, with no windows, and the one lamp was dim, but the space afforded them the privacy they needed in the hospital.

Ruth had gray hair and was slightly portly, adding to her motherly charm. She stirred her coffee while she thought.

"So you don't think it was attempted suicide?" she asked Francie after hearing the story.

"No."

Ruth looked at Frank, questioning.

Francie frowned, irritated, and spoke up before Frank could say anything.

"No," she said more firmly. "It was not attempted suicide. He was just trying to dull the pain, and he didn't mean to overdose. Been there, done that."

"Okay." Ruth knew when not to push. "I'm going to release him under your supervision. Can you handle it?"

"You know I can."

"If I knew, I wouldn't be asking," Ruth said gently. "Francie, the man has lost a lot. I just want to be sure you realize—"

"You want to be sure that I realize there may come a point where I can no longer fix things," Francie finished for her. She ran her hands through her hair, frustrated with how long this was taking. "We went over this the last time, Ruth."

Ruth refused to be rushed. She took a sip of her coffee, then blew on it and stirred some more. She waited until Francie exhaled, and then she continued.

"What if we've come to that point?" Ruth said.

Francie looked up at her sharply. "You've never lost hope before."

"I haven't lost hope now," Ruth said. "I'm just being practical. Looking at the whole picture."

Francie glanced at the clock.

"You're in a hurry?" Ruth asked.

"You know I am." Francie sat back in her chair and crossed her arms.

"You can't be at his side twenty-four seven," Ruth said. Then she looked at Frank. "But actually, you will need to be close and vigilant if I send him home with you."

Frank nodded.

She looked back at Francie. "There's more to your life than saving Jack."

"I know that."

"You also don't always know when to quit."

"I'm not a quitter."

Ruth sighed and looked at Frank again. He smiled. "It's okay," he said. He looked tired, but he put his hand on Francie's shoulder. "I've got an eye on her."

"You always do," Ruth said. She took another sip of her coffee, then pushed it away, deciding no amount of cream or sugar was going to quell the bitterness. She pulled out some papers, filled out a few things, and then signed them.

"Francie," she said, her palm pressing the papers down against the desk. "Promise me you'll call the moment you need me"

"I will," Francie said.

"Promise me."

Francie smiled and relaxed a little. "Ruth, I always have. I promise I will call you if I need you."

"When you need me."

"When I need you."

"Because you will," Ruth said. "I can adjust his medication. Give you ideas on how to handle certain things that will probably come up. Whatever."

"I promise to call you when I need you," Francie said obediently.

"We'll talk in a few days," Ruth said. "Call me tomorrow to set up an appointment." She glanced at Frank again then slid the papers across the desk to Francie. "He's all yours."

chapter 11

1974

THE HOUSE WAS HUGE. Tom hadn't paid much attention to it when they made the quick trip for the funeral, but now, as they drove through the stone pillars at the end of the long driveway, he took in the full view with awe. According to Francie, Sunnyhill Farm consisted of a little over five-thousand acres, running from the front of the house to the back, which faced the Atlantic Ocean. They had several miles of beach, none of which was visible from the house. Francie said you had to walk through the woods, and then quite a way back before you reached the ocean. You couldn't even hear the crashing waves from where they were. A road led off into the trees, and Tom guessed that that was the way to take to get to the water. He had never seen the Atlantic before.

Several barns stood on the north end of the property, and acres of stained, wooden fences ran across the pastures, stretching out into the distance.

He pulled into the circular driveway in front of the house, where Mr. Johnson, the lawyer, was waiting with the key. He let them in.

"I'm home!" Francie twirled around in the kitchen with a smile on her face. Tom wrapped his hands around her waist and gave her a kiss.

"I'm glad to see you this happy," he said, and he meant it. After the way she had been acting lately, it was refreshing to see a smile on her face and a twinkle in her eyes at last.

"Let me give you a tour through the house," Francie said to Tom.

"Honey, we should talk business with the lawyer first," Tom said. He didn't want to keep Mr. Johnson waiting forever.

"Nonsense!" Francie said, walking out of the kitchen and waving for them to follow her. "He can come too."

Tom looked at Mr. Johnson and shrugged. They followed Francie into what looked like the dining room.

"This is where we used to have all the big dinners," Francie explained. "When owners and breeders came to discuss business with Papaw, they would sit in here, and often Grandma would cook them a big dinner, or just serve them tea and cake if she didn't know them very well. But they knew just about everybody."

The walls were papered with a delicate flowered paper, which matched the rose-colored rug. Halfway down the wall, a light, cream-colored molding separated the paper from cream-colored paint. It looked like it used to be a very elegant place. Now, however, it was a little faded, and the walls looked like they could use a new coat of paint. Tom wondered about that. With all the money Francie's grandparents had had, it seemed like they should have been able to hire someone to redecorate the place.

Francie showed them the sitting room, which Tom considered a living room. It was big, larger than the dining room, and was separated from the dining room by an open arch. The sitting room was decorated in light greens.

They toured the two bedrooms and bathroom on the first floor, then Francie led them upstairs. The stairs were large, and led up the middle of the room, from the far end of the dining room. Upstairs, a hall divided four more bedrooms, two on each side of the house, and the bathroom in between. The banisters themselves were made out of dark cherry wood and were very fancy looking. Francie turned to see if they were following her up.

"We're coming," Tom said, laughing at her excitement.

At the top of the stairs, Francie turned to the left and went to the end of the hall.

The whole upper hall was open, with a cherry railing that allowed a view of the dining room. Tom could imagine Francie as a youngster, sitting upstairs and peering down at business meetings below, longing to be included. He smiled to himself.

"This is the bedroom I always stayed in," Francie said, leading them in. It was decorated in light blues, and two large windows looked out over the pastures, one on the east side of the room and the other on the south. "The sun shines in through here in the morning and always wakes me up," she said with a smile. The bedroom also had a private bath, with a nice shower stall and a walk-in closet. One of the other bedrooms was the master bedroom, and it had two walk-in closets and a full bath. It looked like a suite in a rich hotel. Several chairs and a couch were placed in front of one of the windows to form a little reading room. She continued to show them around the rest of the place.

Upstairs, in between the bedrooms, was an office. She went in and ran her hands across the large walnut desk, then walked around behind it and opened a drawer. She pulled out a little bottle of sand.

"This is special," she said, her eyes lighting up. "When my grandparents first stood on the beach, long before their dreams were a reality, my grandma collected a little bit of sand. It's a memory that they started this farm from nothing, together. They kept it so they could look at it later and see what they had accomplished as a couple." She smiled at Tom and put the bottle back in the drawer.

They continued their tour. The house was enormous and had been updated with central air.

"Wow," Tom said in spite of himself. He was a little leery of this whole deal and didn't even think he wanted to live in Florida, but he *was* impressed. Besides, it made Francie happy.

"Let's go down to the kitchen table where we can talk," Mr. Johnson said. "We need to sort out all the legal stuff."

They followed the lawyer back down the stairs, and Francie found some glasses and a pitcher and made a packet of lemonade she found in the pantry. All of her grandparents' furniture was still there, along with the contents of the house.

"Everything is as they left it before they died," she said. "It's almost like they'll walk in the door at any moment and join us for lemonade.

"So," Tom said when they had all been seated. "What is this all about exactly?"

"Well," Mr. Johnson opened his briefcase and shuffled a few papers around, looking very lawyer-like. "It seems Francie's grandparents rewrote their will a few years ago and willed everything to her. And I mean *everything*. The house, the land, and all of the belongings you see around you. They're all yours." Francie squirmed with excitement.

"Your grandparents seemed to think that your mother was going to sell the property and put up condos or something. They thought you were the only one in the family that would keep it as it is and continue to run Sunnyhill Stables as a full working farm. They want their name to live on in racing, and they thought you could do it. Your grandfather said that as for the other grandchildren, you were the kind of person who would share your wealth when you became established, so he felt in a way he was leaving something for all of them. You will, of course, live up to his wishes, I hope."

Mr. Johnson looked at Francie over his glasses. "I've known your grandparents for many years. I want to see their wishes treated with respect and their dreams made a reality." He looked at Tom. "Somehow I believe this fiery woman can do it."

"This sounds too good to be true," Tom said, still skeptical. His family had had to work hard for everything they had, and he didn't believe that anything this big could just be given to him.

"Well, there are some problems," Mr. Johnson said.

I knew it, Tom thought and looked at Francie, but she didn't look disturbed.

"In the last year, your grandparents' health deteriorated rapidly. They accumulated debt several years ago by purchasing horses they couldn't afford and were hoping the breedings would pay off, which they should. But in the meantime, their health bills used up the savings. You are nearly penniless."

Francie was silent. Tom could see that she was struggling to keep her composure. "I miss them," she said quietly.

"So what does that mean?" Tom was worried. He always looked at the logical side of things, and if they couldn't afford to keep the farm, then they would have to review their options, and possibly sell it while it was still salvageable.

"Well, I was appointed to manage the affairs of the estate until Francie took over. Their first debt is paid off. I sold half of the horses and liquidated most of their large assets. What remains for you two, is to keep the place running until you can cash in on the breedings next January and February. Once the mares are serviced, you'll have enough cash flow to keep the farm running."

He paused. "Your other option is to sell. You also have to be able to pay the bills and taxes on this property, and it's quite expensive. You have a little bit of money left in the bank to get you started, but it'll only last you about six months, which should get you to breeding season. Then you're on your own, and you need to have this farm running and able to support itself by then."

"Okay," Francie said, undaunted. "What do I have to sign?"

Mr. Johnson laughed at her eagerness, but Tom fidgeted with his shirt sleeve. "You sign these," the lawyer said, opening a folder with a stack of papers in it.

They signed all the necessary papers and finished up their lemonade. Then Mr. Johnson packed up to leave. "You'll have to come downtown with me tomorrow and change the bank account over into your names. Then everything should be set. I recommend you hire someone who's familiar with managing a farm. Good luck, and I'll see you tomorrow."

Tom stood on the porch, his arm around Francie, and they waved at the lawyer as he drove away.

"We're so young," Tom said, still feeling unsure. "I guess that's a good thing, right? If we fail, we'll still be young enough to go to college and start all over again."

Francie smiled up at him. "We won't fail," she said.

chapter 12

THE NEXT WEEK FLEW BY. Francie and Tom were caught up in a whirlwind of business affairs, and they had to learn quickly. They had no experience with so much money or capital and were at a loss as to what to do. They were convinced, however, that they would soon get things going, and laid in bed at night dreaming of the wealth that they would soon accumulate. Mr. Johnson was kind enough to walk them through things.

They both decided against college for a while, so they could put their full efforts into the farm. They bought paint and stain and refinished all the barns on the farm. A lot of it had fallen into disrepair.

"Whew," Francie said, wiping sweat from her forehead late one afternoon. "I think we've got it." The barns were finally immaculate, and Tom had repaired what needed to be done on the stalls. Tom, who wasn't used to working with his hands, was quite pleased with himself.

"It looks wonderful," Tom said, hugging Francie close to him. "And it's all ours."

Francie leaned against him and closed her eyes. She couldn't ever remember being so happy.

They lay in bed together, looking at the stars out their bedroom window. They had decided to sleep in the blue bedroom at the end of hall that Francie had always stayed in as a child. It was plenty big enough for the two of them and had a beautiful view of the pastures and barns. Every night they talked of their accomplishments and dreamed of their future.

"I guess we're all done, for now," Tom said. "Now we just need to hire some help."

Francie closed her eyes and hugged Tom tight. Everything was so perfect. She had all she wanted in life, and at such as young age. It seemed like it had all happened so easily.

The pregnancy wasn't planned. She hadn't been feeling well and went to the doctor, and that's when she found out.

She drove home with mixed emotions but thought it through and realized that she wanted the chance to give this baby the love she had never received from her own parents. By the time she got home, she was excited and ran to the barn to tell Tom.

Tom was shocked at first but took it in stride. He was dirty and sweaty, but she didn't care, and she let him swoop her up in a big hug.

"We're going to be a family," Tom whispered into her ear as he hugged her close. "A baby! A wonderful baby!" She knew he had always dreamed of settling down with a wife and kids. Of course, he'd thought he would have his engineering degree by then, but things had turned out a little differently.

He told her that night that they were quickly running out of money. But she was confident they'd be fine when breeding season rolled around.

November and December went well. Francie gave riding lessons to bring in additional income, but she was getting larger now that she was nearly five months along, so she had to quit training horses.

A few weeks before Christmas, they got a call from Tom's parents, inviting them up for the holidays. They offered to buy the young couple two plane tickets and wanted them to stay for a week or longer. Tom was excited when Francie hung up the phone and told him the news.

"But we can't, Tom," she said, annoyed that he hadn't thought of the problems himself. "Someone has to feed and take care of the horses. We haven't hired anyone yet. And I wouldn't feel right at this late of a date to hire just anybody to take care of them. They're worth too much money."

Tom looked dismayed. "But there has to be some way."

In the end, Francie and Tom stayed home. They ate chicken for Christmas, because that was all they could afford, and neither of them felt in a holiday mood with the sun shining and the weather a tropical 78 degrees. Tom was disappointed. He pouted all day and refused to talk unless asked questions. They opened what little presents they had with an air of gloom, then Francie disappeared to the barns to brush horses.

She was running a brush through Star's mane when he showed up about an hour later.

"I was just disappointed," he explained. "I guess I'm just a little homesick. You get all those letters from Jim and Krista, and even Sam, and that seems to be enough for you. You don't want to go back home. But I miss my parents and my sister."

"I know, honey," Francie said, stroking his hair back behind his ear. It was getting a little long, and she knew he hated it touching his ears. He said it tickled. "Soon we'll be able to hire someone, and then we'll go up and visit. I promise."

But he was wearing thin. One night, Francie came down late to find Tom sitting at the kitchen table, papers strewn all about, and his head in his hands.

"What's wrong, honey?" Francie asked. She startled him, and he quickly brushed his eyes. He had been crying.

"Tom?" She was concerned. Something was wrong. Was he dying? Was he leaving her? Stupid thoughts rushed through her head. Tom had never shown much emotion in front of her. Her heart started pounding.

"I'm okay," he smiled. "It's just"—he looked at the papers, discouraged—"it's just the books. I can't seem to get ahead. Almost all our money is gone. We've put it into repairs. We can't get outside jobs, because trying to keep this farm running takes twelve hours a day. I just don't know what to do."

"I'll start training," Francie said. "I'll try to get a job at the track."

"You can't do anything with that stomach." Tom was afraid the horses would bump against her or hurt her in some way. He absolutely refused to let her ride.

"Then we'll hire someone who can," Francie said.

"Honey, we're out of money already. We can't afford to hire anyone."

"But if we can find someone who will work for cheap, someone who knows how to manage a farm and bring in customers, we'll be ahead in the long run. Even if we have to take out a loan to pay him. Besides, we'll be getting breeding contracts for the next season. We'll be fine then."

"We could sell the farm," Tom said quietly. "With the money we would get from the farm, we could buy a house back in Michigan and live comfortably while I go to school and get my engineering degree."

"No!" Francie was dead set against the idea, and Tom knew there was no arguing with her. They had discussed it before. So, the next Sunday, an ad went in the employment section of the metro paper and in a few horse magazines around the country. On Monday, they received a call. Francie set up an interview with the man and looked forward to meeting him. Finally, maybe they could get someone to help them out.

chapter
13

FRANK WEAVER DROVE ALONG I-75 in his rusted-out lime green Ford pickup, jamming to "Give Me That Good Old Country Gospel" on the radio. It wasn't that he couldn't afford a better vehicle but that this one had character. He rested his left arm on the window, smiling at how much tanner it was than his right, and he sang along with the chorus—the only part he knew.

Beside him sat a black leather suitcase that used to belong to his father. He'd inherited that along with a few other things when his dad passed away a few years back. He reached for a lukewarm bottle of Pepsi and popped the top open, making a face when the warm froth hit his tongue. Not too pleasant, but at least he'd managed to open it without giving himself a suds bath.

The Florida weather was hot—hotter than he had expected it to be in February. Although it was hot out west where he had come from, it wasn't as sticky. His cotton shirt was damp, and even with the sleeves rolled up, he was sweltering.

He pulled a map out of the visor overhead and noted where he had to turn, which was just up ahead. Only a few more miles down the road and he'd be there.

He wasn't sure why he had just driven over 3000 miles for a job interview he didn't even think he wanted. But then again, he didn't have a plan or a place to stay. He had quit his managerial position at Brandenberry Farm when Tracy died. Even though it paid well and kept his mind occupied, he found that there were too many memories around of her.

Tracy. They would have been married by now. He absently fingered the gold ring he kept around his neck on a chain. His wedding ring. She had engraved it with "Forever yours, Tracy" on the inside.

He had been working the day she fainted, and a friend who was over for lunch had taken her to the hospital. Leukemia. He'd gotten to the hospital as quickly as he could and held her and they'd both cried at the shock of the news. The cancer was pretty far along, which was why she had been so tired all those months. They had just chalked it up to all the stress and excitement of planning the wedding.

It took her a year to die. Frank had wanted to marry her, but she refused. She said she wanted to wait until she could walk down the aisle, perfectly healed, and know that she would be an asset to him and not a burden. They both knew she wasn't a burden to him, not then, not ever. But he respected her wishes and postponed the wedding.

Exactly eleven months and thirteen days later, despite chemotherapy, she died in his arms quietly one morning and the pain was gone. Gone for *her*, anyway.

It always seemed odd to him that she died in the morning. He had thought of death as being a night stalker, taking someone away in the dark. But not in the morning. Not when the sun was streaming across her bed and the birds were singing and the day was so full of promise. It was then that she closed her eyes and left him.

He shook himself out of his thoughts and noticed that he had passed the street he needed. It wasn't good for him to think of her all the time. That was why, when he was called for this interview, that he gave his notice, packed up what few belongings he had, and left. If this job didn't work out, he'd find something else. He'd stay in Florida for a while. It was about the farthest place he could be from Nevada.

He backtracked until he came to the right street and turned down it. He shut off the radio so he could concentrate, and then he saw the address. It was engraved on one of two towering stone pillars standing at the end of a drive so long he could barely see the house. And the house... the house was a mansion.

Above the stone pillars was a black, wrought-iron bar with the name "Sunnyhill Stables" written in intricate metalwork. Ivy twined itself up the sides of the stone and crowded into large magnolia trees set off to the side.

Not too shabby.

He noted that someone needed to take care of the weeds, but other than that, he was impressed.

The gate was open, and he turned into the long driveway and drove up to the house, clocking the distance. A quarter mile. Wow.

The house wasn't quite what he had expected. Once he got closer, he could see that large chunks of white paint were peeling off of portions of the house, and the front door was sagging on its hinges. And the flower gardens... now *those* were a mess. He couldn't see the flowers for the weeds.

A young man came out of the house and walked up to the truck. Blond and thin, his hair a bit unkempt. The fellow looked like he'd be more comfortable in a two-piece suit than in the dirty blue jeans he was wearing.

"Hi," he said, extending his hand into the truck. "I'm Tom."

"Frank. Glad to meet you." He was a bit taken aback with how young Tom was. He couldn't be more than twenty, if that.

Frank stepped out of the truck and looked around at the farm. It was a sad sight. Even the trees seemed to be struggling to survive as they reached through tall overgrown bushes up toward the sky. They sagged under Spanish moss.

The young man led Frank in through the sagging front door, which groaned a tired complaint as he pulled it open. They went through a kitchen and a formal dining room with fading wallpaper and out onto a porch. A young woman, younger than Tom, he thought, was at the table, pouring glasses of lemonade for them. "This is my wife, Francie."

She tucked her long blond hair back behind her ears and looked up at him. For a brief instant, shocked registered on her face, but she recovered quickly. Maybe he had imagined it.

"Mr. Weaver," she said, handing him a glass of lemonade. As she stood, he saw that her belly was swollen, pretty far along in her pregnancy. She kept starting at him, as if she had seen a ghost.

"Thank you." He nodded and accepted the glass.

After a brief pause, she smiled and gathered herself. Then a bigger smile spread across her face. "Would you please have a seat?" she said.

He pulled out one of the wooden chairs and sat down, shaded by a big umbrella above. A few honeybees were humming along the vase of freshly cut roses in the middle of the table, and their sweet scent touched his nostrils.

"Nice," he said.

"My grandpa was a real rose grower," said the woman. "He loved them. That was his hobby. When he was finished with the horses in the evenings he would go tend to his roses, and you could hear him whistling as he prodded around in the dirt."

She had a distant look in her eyes.

"They both passed away a little while ago—my grandparents did. I really miss them."

She looked at him wistfully, but her husband, Tom, got right down to business.

"Have you ever managed a horse farm before, Mr. Weaver?"

Frank had. He had been the manager of a multi-million-dollar operation in Nevada and had made a substantial salary. The young couple looked at each other in discouragement. He handed them his resume and a list of references.

"Well," Tom said, only half looking at them. "I'm afraid we can't afford you."

Francie looked at the resume. Frank had listed that he was good at bookkeeping and had helped the previous farm increase in productivity by fifty percent over the first few years alone.

"How much are you asking?" Francie asked him.

Frank met her eyes, which seemed to penetrate straight to his soul. There was something familiar about this woman. He didn't know her story and didn't have any idea how she and her young husband had come to own this farm, but something in her stirred him.

"I'll work for whatever you can pay," Frank heard himself saying. He smiled as he saw the woman's eye widen a little bit, but she returned to business quickly and made her offer. If she was embarrassed at how low it was, she didn't let that show. Her husband, on the other hand, was squirming.

"I'll accept," said Frank. Francie couldn't hide her pleasure and smiled, her eyes lighting up. He liked her already.

"Great," she breathed and squeezed Tom's arm. "When can you start?"

Frank spread his arms wide. "Now is as good a time as any."

"But you don't even know what the job is," Tom said. "We haven't told you all your responsibilities."

"I take care of the horses and manage the finances," Frank said. "I've been doing that for ten years for the farm I just left. I liked it then, I think I'll like it here. It's a beautiful place."

"Why did you leave the other farm?" Tom asked.

"Personal reasons," Frank said, not wanting to explain. "You can call the owner and talk to him if you like. He's the first name of the list of references that I gave you."

Francie didn't wait for Tom to respond. She started in chatting about an apartment in the main barn that he could live in, rent free. That would be included in his meager salary.

Then she got quiet again and looked him straight in the eyes.

"You don't remember me, do you?" she asked.

He thought for a moment, but had to shake his head no.

"You were the man at the airport. My little sister wet her pants and my parents were so angry and your fiancée asked you for some money. You were both so kind to us. You told me it would be okay."

Realization dawned on him. Yes, the kid at the airport. Tracy had talked about them for days, wondering if they were okay.

Frank had run 3000 miles to escape his past, and now, here it was, staring him in the face.

"Ahhh, yes," he said. He held her eyes and something passed between them then. Tom cleared his throat.

"Francie? Maybe you should give him the keys."

"Okay," she said. After she handed him directions and gave him a key, she left him to move in on his own. "I have work to do," she explained. "Oh—and be careful not to hit the cats!" Francie warned. He drove his old Ford back toward the apartment and prepared to settle into his new home.

chapter 14

THE NEXT MORNING, FRANK WAS UNPACKING the few boxes he had brought with him when he heard a knock at his door. It was early, only 7 a.m.

"I've come to give you the tour," said a bright-eyed Francie. She was smiling and held out a pitcher of orange juice. "Here. Fresh squeezed. Good morning, by the way."

Frank smiled and took the juice.

"You're up bright and early," he said.

"Always. There's so much to do around here." She pushed her hair back behind her ears. "Well? Come on!" She waved him out into the hall.

"Give me a second to put the juice in the fridge!" He was laughing as he walked into the kitchen. He returned and pulled on a pair of leather boots. He followed out to the small landing.

"This is the main barn," she said, sweeping her hands around so they took in the wide expanse below his apartment. "Of course, you know that. You live here."

She walked—nearly *skipped*—down the stairs, Frank close behind her. At the foot of the stairs, she turned back and took him through the indoor arena, which a window in his apartment overlooked. Connected to it was another barn. Both barns were long, containing about forty stalls each, and well kept. A smooth concrete floor ran down the middle with solid oak stalls lining the walkway. Each barn had a tack room where the saddles could be kept, and an area for grain, and, he noted, cat food. There seemed to be cats everywhere.

"My grandparents couldn't turn strays away," said Francie as she shooshed a gray tabby out of their way. "It looks like a lot, but we only have four. They follow me around."

Above the stalls was storage for hay and straw. Right now, though, most of it was empty.

"I've ordered some hay to get us through until we can cut our own fields," she explained. "I'll need you to put up hay in a few days. I'm not supposed to lift." She rubbed her belly.

She took him to the far end of the barns where several pastures were outlined by wooden fences. Lining the back of most pastures were trees; wide expanses of them. Frank was impressed by the caliber of horses he saw. They all had fine breeding. He had done a little research on this farm, and they had some fast Thoroughbreds.

"Beyond all that, somewhere, is the ocean," Francie said, waving her hands out and away from her.

"Wow," Frank said, whistling. "You go that far back?"

"Yep. Could make a fortune if we sold it. Oceanfront property for condos or hotels, and probably a nice subdivision where these barns are. But my grandparents wanted it to remain Sunnyhill Stables, and it will."

She pushed a stray piece of hair behind her ears and grew serious for a moment. "You'll help me make sure it survives, right?"

So young, Frank thought as he looked into those intense blue eyes. *And so beautiful.* Her light blond hair was blowing in the little breeze they had. *And so married*, he reminded himself.

"I'll try," he replied. *And* he reminded himself, *a good ten years younger than him.*

Francie smiled again and led him through the barn up toward the house.

"It's quite a walk, but if we take your pickup, you'll miss some of the sights," she said.

"That's fine."

The road led them up to the gate he had entered the night before on his way back to the barns. From there he could see the house, sprawling across a lawn that was in much need of care. The house was a white two-story, with three stories in the back if you counted the walk-out basement. Its front faced toward the road and the side they were looking at had a pair of French doors that walked out into a little garden area, the porch he had sat on yesterday. Hydrangea, roses and lavender lined a stone path and a couple of little benches were positioned under some trees, which themselves dripped with Spanish moss. At the edge sat a grape arbor, with a swing facing west. A nice spot to watch the sunset, he thought.

To his right was a much smaller house. It sat facing the big house and was about three acres away from it. The driveway they stood on curved up to the main house but split off to the smaller house.

"That's where the old manager used to live, or the groundskeeper, depending on who Papaw had hired at the time," said Francie. "We would have put you in there, but it needs so much work. The apartment is newer and really a lot nicer."

From the dilapidated look of the roof, Frank was pretty sure it leaked and was just as happy to be in the apartment.

The yard was beautiful, and a huge fenced-off area sat behind the house, close to eighty acres, Frank guessed.

"Way out there," she said, following his eyes, "is a stream. It's great because you can turn the broodmares out and don't have to worry about watering them."

They were walking down the drive toward the entrance. She skipped ahead and spun around to face him, walking backwards.

"My grandparents bought this place when they were in their twenties and made a go of it," she said. "They were one of the top breeders and owners of racehorses. Ever hear of Plenty Tough?" She didn't wait for Frank to nod his head. "He won the 1949 Kentucky Derby. Took second in the Preakness and nearly won the Belmont—only lost by a nose."

She grew more excited as she talked, her eyes shining.

"That's what I want for this place, Frank. I want to revive Sunnyhill to its former glory."

She smiled and turned, settling into place beside him.

He couldn't help but smile at her intensity. She had youth and naiveté on her side, giving her hope beyond hope.

"Well, here we are," she said, turning around and looking up.

They were standing just outside the entrance to the farm, under the same Sunnyhill Stables sign Frank had driven through the day before. In black ironwork, towering a good fifteen feet over their heads and intricately placed, the farm name arched across the driveway. The overgrown vines and branches winding up it didn't give it a run-down appearance at all now. Instead, Frank thought, they added character, almost as if nature were coming to help support what should never fall.

Francie turned and smiled. Despite her carefree demeanor, she had carefully watched Frank's reactions to the place, and he could tell she was pleased with him. She was thinking that he was going to work out. He was going to be part of her dream.

She spread her arms up over her head and smiled at him. "Welcome home," she said.

That night, Tom sat with the two of them on the porch. Francie poured them all a glass of lemonade.

"It sure is beautiful out here," Frank said, reclining back in his chair, his long legs stretched out in front of him.

Fireflies darted around the foliage, and overhead, stars shone brightly down on them in the moonless night. There was just enough of a breeze to discourage mosquitoes.

"It's more like a lot of work," said Tom, digging a root out from between the bricks with his toe.

Francie frowned at him but chose to ignore the comment.

"It's perfect," she said determinedly. "A great place to raise our child." She put her hand over her belly and smiled. "Right, honey?"

"I suppose," Tom said. He was tired and stressed from his latest bout with bill paying.

If he were home right now, he thought, back in Michigan, he would probably have gone out on the boat this evening with his friend Ron. Francie would like Ron's wife, Mandy. And he would be drinking a beer and listening to the Tiger's pre-season show. None of this horse stuff. He rubbed his hands together, wincing at the blisters he'd gotten yesterday while attempting to tame some of the vines on the porch with a pair of parrot jaws. He should put something on them, but he was too tired. He sighed, and hoped he'd sleep well tonight. He needed to get rested before the baby came.

Frank went to church every Sunday morning, and that bothered Francie. She told herself it didn't matter, but in truth, it did.

One Sunday, she made it a point to be outside working in the flowerbed when he pulled past her in his truck on his way to church. She stood up and waved. He stopped and rolled down the window.

"Going to church?" she asked casually.

"Yeah. You want to join me?"

She laughed. "No way. I had my taste of God growing up. Religion isn't for me."

"Okay." He put the truck back in gear. His lack of concern for her soul made her mad for some reason. Aren't Christians supposed to care who burns in Hell?

"Wait," she said. He looked at her, his eyebrows raised. "I want to talk about this later."

"Is my going to church a problem?"

"Oh—not at all," she said. Why was she even bringing this up in the first place? Her grandparents had been firm believers in God, but her mother...

"Good. 'Cause I didn't see 'must be an atheist' on my work application." He winked at her.

She brushed a hand across her forehead, leaving a streak of black dirt on her face.

"It's just... "

"Come on. I'm early. Go get Tom and you can both hop in the truck with me. I've got about fifteen minutes before we're late."

"No." She was even *more* flustered that he wanted her to go with him. What was *wrong* with her? "I have work to do. And Tom... "

"I'll go," said Tom, walking up to them. "We need some prayer in this family. Give me a minute to get cleaned up."

This was not going at all how Francie had wanted. She had no idea why she'd even started this discussion in the first place. It was just that she liked Frank so much, and kind of even looked up to him, and he seemed so perfect except for this. She wanted him to be separate from this—from... from *religion*.

She remembered her mother throwing the Bible at her so many times. Or telling her she was going to Hell. She didn't want Frank involved in *that*. She couldn't imagine mixing the two. Frank and religion. She had such high regard for one, and mistrust for the other.

Frank had shut the truck off.

"You coming?" Frank asked.

"Um... " Caught off guard, she suddenly wasn't sure what to do. "I guess I could."

How could Tom do this to her? He *knew* how she felt about religion!

Exasperated, but trying not to show it, she turned and went into the house and washed up. She put on a light blue maternity dress, grabbed a pair of sandals, and was ready to walk out the door when Tom was.

"Why are we doing this?" she hissed as they locked the door and walked down the back steps.

"Why not?" he said. "Nothing else seems to be working."

Francie frowned. Tom had been really short with her lately.

He went on ahead, opening the truck so she could slide in the middle. He didn't say anything more all the way there. It was a hot ride and windy with the windows down. Frank hummed a tune, and Francie sat in between the men and wondered how she had managed to get herself into this situation so quickly.

The church was a medium-sized building in the middle of town, with "First Congregational" printed on the sign out front. Families were entering through the building and into the cool sanctuary. Frank guided them to a pew about halfway up on the right-hand side. Several people stopped them to say "hi," and Frank respectfully introduced them as his employers. "But today's my day off, so now they're just my friends," he said and winked.

Francie recognized a few men from the track, looking out of place in a tie, surrounded by their families.

"Hmmm."

"What?' Frank asked.

"Nothing."

Frank looked at her and smiled.

"What's so funny?" she whispered.

"You don't really want to be here, do you?" Frank asked.

"No. God and I don't see eye to eye. When I left home, I swore I'd never set foot in church again."

She surprised herself at her own vehemence.

"I'm sure God is glad to have you back," Frank said, and it was then that the singing started, and they had to be quiet since it was the beginning of the service.

The sermon was on hope. Francie tried not to listen, but the pastor's words edged their way into her mind. She glanced over at Frank, who looked so calm and happy, and she felt a little shift in her heart. She reached out and took Tom's hand in hers. She was stuck here until the sermon was over. She might as well make the best of it.

The pastor preached from Jeremiah 29:11: *"For I know the plans I have for you," declares the Lord, "plans to prosper you and not to harm you, plans to give you hope and a future."*

Hope. She gave Tom's hand a little squeeze, and he smiled at her.

The word stuck with her the rest of the day.

chapter

15

NORMA SHOWED UP THAT WEEK with a court order. She didn't say hi, or mention how her daughter's stomach had grown, or ask about her first grandbaby. Instead, lifting her head high, she presented Francie immediately with a stack of documents.

"I'm taking the horses," she said. "My lawyer found a loophole in the will that all property is yours, but since the horses are a living creature, apparently the will doesn't clarify that those are yours too." She smiled triumphantly. "So I'm here to get them."

Behind her were six horse trailers.

Francie stared at her, speechless. It took her a few seconds to wrap her mind around what was happening.

"Mom—you can't take the horses. Our breeding stock is what keeps the farm running, and breeding season is about to start. We'll go under."

Norma laughed, a cruel sound. "Then you'll know exactly how I felt when you and your grandpa took my inheritance away from *me*."

She motioned to the men who were with her, and they pulled the trailers into the yard.

"Wait," Francie grabbed the papers. Tom walked up to stand beside her, and they read them together.

"I'll go call my dad," he said and went inside.

Meanwhile, her mom got in her truck and they started driving to the barns. Francie ran after them, and when she arrived, they were loading up the first horse.

"Not Glory," she said. "Mom, he's our main breeding stallion."

"And probably worth a few million," Norma said.

"Mom, they mean more than money to me. I've watched them grow up. Glory here is one of my favorites."

They ignored her and finished loading the first trailer.

"Drive it up front," Norma said.

"You can't take my horses!" Francie stepped in front of the truck.

"Move," Norma said. The driver chewed on a cigarette and waited.

"I won't," Francie said, but another man grabbed her arm and pulled her out of the way. She kicked him in the shin, but he recovered quickly and pulled her against him so she couldn't fight.

Francie tried to elbow him in the gut, but she couldn't get any power. She was too close.

The truck pulled forward, and as the man held her, a third man opened another stall and started taking one of her broodmares out. The mare was frightened and bulked and the man yanked down on the chain under her chin. Her head shot up and the whites of her eyes showed.

"You *cannot* take my horses!" Francie screamed and finally yanked herself free from the man. But she was outnumbered.

Her stomach was starting to cramp. She had an idea and ran back to the house.

Tom was on the phone when he heard the first shot. He peeked out the window and saw everyone looking toward the front porch. All action had stopped.

"Hang on, Dad. I'll call you back." He hung up.

Francie was standing on the porch, pointing a loaded rifle at her mother.

"I'll shoot you if you make one more move," she shouted down to her mom. "Those are *my* horses, and you're only taking them over my dead body!"

She was screaming her words and realized that she probably sounded hysterical. Tom came up behind her.

"Francie, this is crazy. Where did you get that? Put that down. Now."

Frank came striding across the lawn. He walked up onto the porch.

"Hey," he said gently. He put his hand on her shoulder. "Give me the gun."

"No," she said. "Not until they unload my horses."

Two police cars pulled up. Somebody had probably called the police from the barn phone. They got out and saw the rifle.

"Ma'am, put the gun down."

"No. They're stealing my horses."

There was some talk below. They looked at the papers.

"Ma'am, the court order is legitimate. This woman has the right to take your horses."

"All of them," Norma said.

"Not Star," Francie said.

"*All* of them," Norma repeated.

"Francie, you're scaring me. You're going to get us killed," Tom said. "Let the horses go. We'll sort this out later."

"Tom, go get Star's registration papers. My name is on them. They can't take a horse I legally own. They're up in the file cabinet, probably under M for Midnight Star."

Tom quickly left.

The second trailer pulled up.

"No," Francie said. "Unload it!"

An officer drew his gun. "Ma'am. Put the gun away."

Frank put his hand on her shoulder. "This isn't the way to do this. If you shoot your mother, you go to jail, and then you'll lose the farm as well."

Francie felt a sharp pain in her belly. She moaned and grabbed at her stomach.

Frank took advantage of the contraction to gently take the rifle. He put it down beside him.

"They can't take my horses," she said. "They can't. I've known them my whole life... they're mine." She began to cry.

"Shhhhh." Frank put his arms around her. "We'll work this out."

She was crying so hard that she could no longer see. Tom came out with the papers and ran across the lawn, handing them to the officer.

"The black horse stays," somebody said.

Francie sank to her knees. Frank's arms were around her.

"Not my horses!" she kept saying. "Please, Frank, stop them!"

He held her as he watched the six trailers, one by one, pull up from the barn until they had loaded all the horses. Then they pulled out and slowly disappeared down the road. They heard a lone whinny from the barn.

Tom came and sat down on the steps. "You still have Star," he said. He put his head in his hands. After a moment, he said, "I'll go back inside and call Dad."

Frank was sitting with them in the living room late that night when Tom's dad called them back. Francie was on the couch, her legs curled up under her. Her stomach had stopped cramping, and the baby seemed to be okay.

"It's all legitimate," Tom said. "Dad got a hold of a copy of the papers. Your mom wins today, but my dad says we can appeal. It'll be long and costly."

Francie just stared at him. There was nothing left to say. Finally, she said to Frank, "I can't afford to pay you. I had all these breeding rights lined up. Now... "

Frank looked at her, with her large belly. Her husband had been pacing all evening, nervous, and wasn't much help in calming her down. She was so young.

"We'll work it out in the morning," Frank said. "You need to try to get some sleep."

Tom turned, as if suddenly thinking of something. "Where did you get that gun, anyway?"

"Papaw has a few stashed around the place. I know how to use them. I could take out a pop can on Mom's head from the porch."

The two men looked at each other.

Frank stood up. "Get some sleep," he said. "I'm heading back to the barn. I'll make sure Star has some water."

The next morning, Francie walked out to the empty barn. Star greeted her with a whinny before she even entered. As she walked down the aisle, she was flooded with childhood memories...

"Hey, Tinkerbell."

It was her grandfather's voice. She heard it as clearly as if he was standing there.

"Papaw... "

The lines in his soft, tan face crinkled into a smile, his eyes sparkling.

"What do you think of her?" He had always talked to Francie like that. One horseman to another. With respect.

Francie had been thirteen then, young and full of plans. She looked at the black mare. The horse had backed into the corner of her stall, far away from the people. She pawed the ground and snorted, her ears twitching nervously. The white star on her forehead was prominent in the darkness.

"She's beautiful," Francie replied.

"She is."

Papaw came and stood beside her, his arms resting on the stall's half door. He pointed to the horse's left front leg, which was bandaged.

"That cut was pretty bad. She'll never race again. And she was badly mistreated."

A small smile played across Francie's face.

"Is that why you bought her? She's a charity case?"

She knew what a soft spot Papaw had in his heart for such animals.

He laughed out loud, startling the horse.

"Yes! And your grandmother took one look at me and said, 'Oh, Joe, not *another* one!'"

Although he owned a sizeable stable of well-bred thoroughbreds, about one third of his horses were abused or neglected animals that he "rescued," sometimes for large sums of money. Papaw was well known for taking cast-offs from the racetrack and rehabilitating them. He could work magic with a horse, and when one of Joe Frasier's horses stepped on the track, all eyes were on it.

"So if she can't race, what are you going to use her for?" Francie asked him. "Breeding?"

"No, Tinkerbell," he said. "I'm not going to rehab her. This one's yours. I'm giving her to you."

It took a minute for it to sink in. She had always wanted a horse—*always*—but had never dreamed...

"*Mine?*" Her voice quivered.

"Yours."

Papaw quietly put his arm around her shoulders and pulled her to him, giving her a little sideways squeeze. "You can work magic with horses, Francie. And this mare is special. Once you gain her trust, I think you'll have her as a friend for life."

Francie watched the horse for a minute.

"Star," she said finally. "I'm going to call her Star."

"For the marking on her face?" asked Papaw.

"No, for the spirit in her. She glows so bright. It's a shame no one else could see it."

"It sure is," Papaw said, looking tenderly down at his granddaughter, whose eyes were fixed on the horse. "It sure is."

Star bumped Francie's arm, bringing her back to the present.

"Hi, girl," she said, stroking Star's soft nose. "At least I still have you."

chapter 16

WHEN THE BABY WAS BORN, Tom's parents flew down for a few days to help out. After they left, life got back to normal for Tom, but Francie stayed inside to take care of little Becky.

"Soon," she said. "Soon you'll be big enough, and we'll go to the barn. I'll buy you your own pony."

Jim called one day while she was heating a bottle. "I'm moving to California," he said. "Mom hired a nanny—with *your* money"—Francie heard the sarcasm in his voice—"and she's really nice. Sam will be fine."

With a new baby and the farm, Francie hardly had time to bathe, much less to take care of Sam, so she was glad to hear about the nanny. She didn't dare ask Tom if they could bring Sam to live with them. They couldn't afford her.

They appealed the court order. The horses were being held off-site during the proceedings, but all assets were frozen, including breedings. Things got worse financially as they paid lawyers to fight for them.

Tom took a job in town at a grocery store and worked long hours. He came home grumpy and tired. Frank and Francie were looking at some broodmares to buy and breed to a stallion nearby. They could sell the foals the following year for profit.

Tom was furious. "We can't afford to feed the horse we have!" he said.

But they were able to work it out in the budget and got the animals. Francie was excited. To share the news with Tom, and to soften it, she made a celebratory meal.

"What's this?" Tom asked in a gruff voice, angry instead of pleased by the wonderful spread on the table.

"It's dinner, honey," Francie said in her nicest voice.

"Did you buy those horses?" he asked.

"Yes, we did. Don't be angry, because Frank and I worked out the budget, so we think it'll work."

"You *think?*"

"And Frank says that I can always sell them and double my money later if we can't afford to feed them. We got a good deal."

Tom exploded. He picked up the steaming pot roast and threw it against the wall. The china plate, a wedding gift from Tom's mother, shattered and fell to the ground in pieces. The roast left a greasy smear on the wallpaper, and potatoes bounced and rolled across the carpeting. As if that wasn't enough, Tom picked up the salad and threw it too. Francie tried to grab it and stop him, but he hit her sharply across the face with the back of his hand. She fell back, clutching one of the dining room chairs to keep her balance, and unwillingly, tears came to her eyes from the sting. Tom shouted at her, but she didn't hear the angry words. She was in too much shock from the blow. Becky started crying.

"Shut up!" Tom shouted up the stairs, as if a three-month old baby could understand. Then he stormed up the stairs, still yelling, and for a moment of panic, Francie thought he might be heading for the nursery to take out his anger on the baby, but then she heard their bedroom door slam shut. She ran up the stairs and grabbed Becky, holding her close. She heard the sound of the shower running, muffled through the door, and with a gasp of grief, she ran down the stairs and out of the house and didn't stop until she reached the barn.

She sat down on a balc of hay in front of Star's stall and rocked her baby, crying silently. Eventually, Becky drifted off to sleep again.

She didn't know how long she sat there, but Frank startled her when he walked into the barn to check the horses' water buckets. She looked up and smiled at him, trying to pretend that nothing was wrong. He stopped in front of her with a horrified look on his face.

"Are you okay?" he asked.

"Yes... why?" she asked, but as she put her hand up to her face and touched her eye, she realized it was sore and swollen and probably turning black.

"What happened?" he asked.

"Becky started crying, and I was running upstairs to quiet her, and I tripped and fell," Francie lied. "I hit my head on the banister."

"Oh," Frank said. Francie could see that he didn't believe her, but he didn't press the issue. Instead, he picked up the hose and headed down the aisle to fill the water buckets.

After a few minutes Frank returned and rolled the hose up.

"Why don't I walk you back to the house?" he asked. "I have some paperwork on your desk I need."

"Okay," she said and stood up. Her legs felt shaky. They walked back together in silence. A few stars were coming out in the darkening sky.

Tom hadn't come downstairs yet, and the house was quiet. Francie cringed when she saw the food, still laying on the dining room floor. She had forgotten about it.

She looked at Frank, and he raised an eyebrow.

"I guess you wouldn't believe me if I told you I was carrying the roast while I was running up the stairs and when I tripped, it fell and splattered against the wall?"

"And you were balancing the salad on top of the roast," Frank said, nodding. "It sounds like a good story to me." They both laughed.

"I can just get that paperwork tomorrow," Frank said. "Let me help you clean this up before I leave."

Francie put Becky in her playpen, and they worked together in silence. They threw the food out and stacked the dishes in the sink.

"We should wash these," he said.

"I'll get them later. I need to feed Becky and get her to bed."

Frank paused. "Are you going to be all right tonight?"

"Of course. I think Tom's in bed. I... " She didn't know how to finish.

"Okay," he said easily. "See you tomorrow."

She was grateful that he didn't push, but she was sad to see him leave. She heated a bottle for Becky and carried her upstairs to feed her. Then she made up the bed in the guest room and slept there, with Becky beside her.

Becky slept until morning, and by the time she woke Francie up, Tom had left for work.

Frank spent that next evening with Tom in the kitchen, showing him that they could afford to keep the horses for a while. That only convinced Tom that Frank was meddling in their affairs too much, and after Frank left the house, Tom confronted Francie.

"He's just doing his job," Francie said.

"Well, we can't afford him anyway," Tom said. "I'll give him his two weeks' notice tomorrow, and we're going to sell those horses."

"Tom, this *is* a horse farm," Francie said. "We need horses."

They argued for a while, and Francie convinced Tom to give Frank more time.

"All right," he finally said grudgingly. "Look, I'm sorry." He nodded toward her eye. "It won't happen again."

But he slept on the couch that night.

After that, Tom spent more time at work, coming home tired and grouchy. He didn't speak much during dinner and often went to bed early. They lost the court appeal. Apparently, the will wasn't as tight as it could have been.

Frank did most of the farm work but sat in the shade and held Becky each afternoon so Francie could work some of the horses.

One afternoon, she put Star away and came and sat beside him. Becky had fallen asleep in his arms.

"Why did you come to Florida?" Francie asked. "You could have gone anywhere with your experience and made a lot more money. We're hardly paying you."

"I just wanted to get away, and Florida was the farthest state away from Nevada that I could think of unless I wanted to go north, and I didn't. I wanted to be warm this winter."

She smiled. "But why work for such little pay?"

"Money's not everything," he said. "Look at you. You're nearly bankrupt, your marriage is stressed, and you're killing yourself trying to run this place and raise a baby. All for this farm. Sometimes things, or ideas, mean more than money. And I'm comfortable here. I don't have to deal with a lot of business deals or people. It's quiet, and I'm not under much pressure. I'm doing the best I can for you, and it's keeping my mind off of other things."

"Like your girlfriend."

He had briefly mentioned Tracy to her but hadn't told her the details.

He looked down at Becky.

"Yeah."

"What happened?" she asked quietly.

He stroked Becky's cheek, and the baby stirred slightly then nestled into his arm again. "She was my fiancée, actually," he said. "She died. Leukemia."

"Oh." Francie hadn't been expecting that. She knew he had come south to get away from memories, but she expected a jilted lover or angry in-laws. Not death. Not in one so young.

"Was she the woman I met in the airport?"

"Yes."

"Oh." A sudden sadness came over her, that someone so beautiful and so caring could actually die. She sighed.

"How are things with you and Tom?"

She laughed. "You summed it up nicely when you said my marriage was stressed. I think it might actually be falling apart."

"I'm sorry."

"No. It's true. He hates this place."

"Will you sell?"

"No."

They sat there quietly for a while.

Suddenly they heard a loud whinny and a violent kick. They ran to the barn and saw that one of their mares had kicked down her stall door. A large bee buzzed around her head before finding its way out the window. The horse was holding her foot up gingerly.

Blood was dripping from it.

"I'll call the vet," Frank said.

The vet stitched the horse up and was pulling out of the driveway just as Tom pulled in. They rolled down windows and chatted briefly, then Tom came straight to the barn.

"I'm not paying for this," Tom said, waving the vet bill at Francie.

Frank was in the feed room, mixing up a hot mash for the mare. Becky was at the house with a sitter, a teen girl who came over a few times a week.

"I've had it with this place," Tom said. "It's a money hole. We'll sell these horses and the farm, and then we'll use that money to pay the vet with. We'll move north and buy a house. I want to go to college. We can find a place to board Star so you can keep her. We'll have a ton of money, so none of that should be a problem."

"Tom... "

"No," he said. "No, Francie. I've given this my best try. I'm exhausted. I'm dirty all the time. I hate this place. Start packing. I spoke to a lawyer yesterday, and if we divide the land up commercially, it will double its value. We'll be rich. We can live a good life."

Francie couldn't believe what she was hearing.

"You can't sell this place! This is our home!"

"No, it's *your* home. Not mine. And you're my wife, and Becky is my child, and we should stay together. So we're moving. All of us."

Frank kept quiet in the feed room, not wanting to interfere.

"I have it all arranged," Tom said. "We can stay with my parents until we find a place."

"Tom! We're supposed to discuss these things together!"

"Francie, we don't discuss *anything*, anymore. That's the whole problem. You're selfish, and all you think about is what you want."

"Well, you're a selfish jerk yourself and a poor excuse for a father. Becky hardly ever sees you!"

"Because I'm *working* to pay *your* bills!" Tom shouted.

"They're your bills too!" Francie shouted back.

That was too much for Tom to take. Before he could stop himself, he struck his wife across the face, hard.

The blow surprised Francie, but she stood her ground and took its force. Then she raised her own hand and slapped him back sharply. Surprise and anger gleamed in his eyes.

"Don't you ever do that again, woman!" he shouted and raised his hand, this time in a fist. Frank stepped out of the feed room and caught Tom's arm in a strong grip.

"That's enough," he said, glaring at Tom with steely eyes. "She's your wife, man. Don't beat her."

The fire in Tom's eyes slowly lowered to a simmer. Frank released his arm and stepped back.

Tom looked Francie in the eyes. They stared at each other for a moment in silence. Francie had her chin high, her eyes defiant. Finally, Tom spoke. His face was hard, his own eyes cold.

"Don't expect to see me again," he said, and his voice rolled down the aisle and out over the fields. It was strong, decisive, and didn't seem to belong to him. Then he turned and walked out of the barn.

Francie and Frank were left standing in the aisle together. No one spoke at first, and Francie didn't even move. She just stood there, staring at her husband's figure as if trying to make up her mind about something. She watched Tom move farther and farther away from her, and her jaw twitched, as if she was about to shout for him, but she didn't. After he disappeared, she turned to the tack room and took a few brushes out.

"While I have a babysitter here, I might as well spend some time with this mare," she said. "I'll tie her in the aisle and brush her. You fix the stall."

Frank seemed like he wanted to say something, maybe to tell her to go to her husband, or to put his arm around her and tell her it was going to be okay. Instead, he nodded quietly and went to get his tools.

chapter
17

THEY SOLD TWO HORSES TO PAY THE VET and buy feed for another month.

"You can cut the rest of my salary," Frank said. Then he handed her a check.

"What's this?" she said.

"To tide us over while you look for work as a trainer," he said. "It's my savings. I don't want you to lose the farm."

"I can't take this."

"Francie, where am I going to go?" He was sitting on the couch holding Becky. Francie was leaving to go work the evening as a waitress in the local pub. It paid the bills. She smiled at him.

The baby reached for her.

"Goodnight, Becky," she bent down and kissed her downy head. "Mommy will see you in the morning."

"Be careful," was Frank's usual warning.

"I will."

Mornings came early for her.

She finished the bacon and eggs Frank made while she slept in. If you could call it sleeping in. She had returned at 2 a.m., and now it was only six.

Most nights Frank went back to his apartment to sleep, but on the nights that she worked at the pub, he slept in the guest room down the hall, so he could hear Becky if she woke.

This morning he was casually skimming over some papers while Francie ate and was telling her about the budget. Becky was in her playpen.

She watched him across the table. The relaxed hands, the lack of tension in his face, the calm in his eyes. It mystified her. He must have been born with calm genes, she thought.

And she... well, *her* head was spinning. She had a death grip on her coffee mug, and there was a little pile of napkin in front of her that she had shredded during their conversation.

She sighed, a long drawn-out breath.

"Heavy sigh?" Frank asked.

"Heavy sigh." She was going to let it go with that, but she couldn't. She thought of all the times he had remained unruffled, while exhausted from the baby or working over their pathetic budget or whatever.

"How do you do it?" she asked. "How do you... remain so darn calm? Or maybe a better question is, where do you get your peace?"

He looked into her eyes for a moment. "I get frustrated," he said, leaning back in his chair. He folded his hands across his lap. "I get upset."

"But not really," she said, noticing that she herself was already getting frustrated and upset at this very conversation.

"Not really?" he arched an eyebrow.

"No," she sighed, spreading her hands flat on the table and looking down at them. "You have this... peace... for lack of a better term. No, that's it. It's peace."

After a moment's silence, she raised her eyes to see if he had heard her. He was looking at her and seemed to be weighing how to respond. Finally, he spoke.

"It's Jesus," he said. He was serious.

Francie slapped the palm of her hand down on the table.

"I don't want to hear any religious crap," she said, pushing back her chair and standing up. She hadn't returned to church with Frank since that first time. Surprised at her own sudden anger, she took a deep breath and looked at her friend.

"I'm sorry, Frank, but my mother preached Jesus to us night and day. You can't wear tight shirts, drink, go to parties, date guys—or girls—chew gum in church, stay up late. Oh, and if you've behaved badly and upset your mother, let's not forget the rod. Spare the rod, spoil the child. Does that include locking little girls in closets? Because that's what she did to Sam."

Frank sat there, listening quietly, intently, and not moving. Francie paced and spilled about a dozen more atrocities her mother had committed. Her heart was pounding, and her palms were sweaty when she finally had to sit back down, exhausted.

"All in the name of Jesus," she said.

"Your mother's Jesus is a God of guilt," said Frank. "The true Jesus is a man who ate dinner with thieves and sinners, who shared a drink of water with a prostitute, who went to a party and turned water into wine because there weren't enough drinks to go around."

Francie just sat there, listening, emotionally spent.

"That's the true Jesus, Francie. He's not a god of laws. He's a god of grace."

He looked at her for a moment with his kind eyes, weighing his words, and when he spoke, his voice was quiet.

"He loves you more than you can possibly imagine. He loves *you*, Francie, right now, as you are. He wants a relationship with you. That's all," he said kindly. "He doesn't want to judge you. He wants to free you."

She stared at him for a long moment.

"Frank," she said and sighed again. She wished her heart would stop pounding. It sounded so loud in the quiet of the house that she wondered if he could hear it. She realized then that she wanted what he had.

"Maybe if I had known your Jesus when I was growing up, things would be different now, but I had religion forced down my throat. And I don't want to change who I am. I'd have to change."

"You mean because you're such a derelict now?" Frank asked.

She smiled. "No, silly. But I'd have to stop working in bars."

"You could tell them about Jesus while you serve up a beer."

She laughed, then grew serious again.

"Jesus couldn't do anything for me," she said quietly. "I'm beyond hope." She gave him a half smile, then ran her hands through her hair. "Augggh!"

She started to get up, but what he said next stopped her.

"Why not give him a chance?" He spoke gently. He leaned forward across the table and took her hand in his.

"He loves you and was willing to die so you could be happy. He'll give you peace."

Francie looked into his intent brown eyes, so full of compassion and kindness. She tried to imagine a savior with that kind of compassion. Maybe if Jesus were like Frank...

Her heart pounded in her chest. She needed so badly for something to be right in her life. She needed a savior.

"Okay," she said, finally. "I'll give this God of yours a chance. Tell me how."

And Frank did.

chapter 18

S HE HAD HEARD ABOUT THE COLT. Word around the track was that he was a hellion. He seemed to hate everyone and threw every rider who tried to sit on him. Was a shame, too, folks said. He had great bloodlines and long, lean legs. Could tear up a track when he put his mind to it. Could tear up people, too.

Sometimes in the mornings, she heard the screams from the colt (and from the grooms) as they tried to handle him for his morning workout. Sometimes, a lucky rider made it around the track without being thrown.

Francie made it a habit to be around during his workout times. She didn't know why she was drawn to this particular colt—there were certainly other rambunctious horses around. But she felt a kinship with him the moment she saw him.

She had stopped by the track this evening with the specific intent of taking a peek at him in his stall. "There's hardly a horse that can't be tamed," her grandfather had told her. "You just had to earn his trust."

There was no one around his stall. It was the dinner hour, and she had chosen the time on purpose, knowing that most of the men would be away at restaurants or cooling off at the local bar.

His stall was quiet. She stood outside it for a few minutes. There was more silence. She had the feeling that the horse was listening to her, just as she was listening for him.

She carefully leaned up against the wall of his stall, not too near the door so he couldn't suddenly lunge out and bite her. Then, quietly and slowly, she blew out her breath between her lips, as if she were blowing out a candle.

Horses talked that way, her grandfather had taught her. They blew into each other's nostrils to say hello.

She listened. Nothing.

She blew again, toward the area on the top of the stall door, where he could stick his head out if he were there.

There was a soft blow inside the stall. Then more silence.

Francie blew again.

The horse returned her noise with another blow of his own. She reached into her pocket for the apple slices she had for him, and slowly, carefully laid them on the top ledge of the door.

It seemed she had to wait a long time, but eventually she heard the straw rustle as he moved in his stall. Then his nose came forward, and he gently plucked an apple slice off the door and drew back. He ate it. When Francie didn't move, he ventured back toward the door and finished the other apple slices.

When he was done, Francie blew again.

The horse got braver and poked his head out. He gave her a long, sideways glance.

"Hello, there," Francie said, her voice barely a whisper. She lifted her arm, palm down, and offered him her hand. He cautiously stretched his head out and sniffed at it.

She let him snuffle it a bit, then turned her hand over and rubbed his soft muzzle very gently. He accepted her touch and let her stroke his face.

Having made friends, she dug out the rest of the apple and hand fed him.

"That's all for now," she said as he finished and nuzzled her for more. "I don't see what all this fuss is. You're not mean at all. People just don't understand you, do they? People have never quite understood me either. At least, most of the people in my life. It does get frustrating."

She gave him a final pat. "I'll be back tomorrow night. Maybe I can be your one friend in this world."

She turned to go and saw an older man sitting in a chair on her left. She recognized the cane and the hat and tie. It was Mr. Richards, the horse's owner.

"Very nice, Ms. Dalton," he said smiling. "You have quite a gift."

"Oh... yes. Um, how long have you been sitting there?" she asked, a bit startled.

"Long enough," he said, getting up slowly. "Hip is bothering me a bit today." He rubbed it. "Say, how would you like a job?"

"A job?" she said. "How do you know my name?"

"I've been watching you for a while," he said. "I've noticed your interest in my horse's workouts. What impresses you about him?"

"Well, his bloodlines, of course," she said.

"But it's more than that," he replied, looking at her with keen eyes.

"Yes. He's... he's got something special about him. He just needs someone who can understand him. He needs a chance."

"I agree," Mr. Richards said. "Maybe you're the person who might be able to understand him."

"About that job... " Francie said after a pause. "I have my own training stable."

"Yes, I know," he said with a smile. "And I'm asking you if you will train *my* horse, Francie Dalton."

Francie jumped out of the truck and ran into the house. When she burst into the kitchen, Frank was just putting some meatloaf on the table, and Becky was in her playpen, hugging a stuffed duck.

"I've got a job!" Francie said.

"Don't you have ten jobs? Or maybe eleven? I lost count," Frank said, laughing.

"No, Frank, a serious big-time job. Mr. Richards asked me to train his horse. You know, that red colt I love. You know the one."

"Flaming Star?" he said, incredulous.

"Yes! Yes, yes, *yes!*" Francie danced around the kitchen, then picked Becky up and danced with her.

"Mommy has a real horse to train, Becky! Mommy is soooo excited!"

The baby laughed out loud as Francie danced around with her.

"When do you start?" Frank asked.

"Now! I'm hired now! Oh, I'm so excited!"

"Well, you need to eat," Frank said. "Go wash up."

At dinner, Frank was the more pragmatic one, as usual.

"How are you going to keep that horse from killing you?" he said.

"He's not vicious, just scared," Francie said. "We'll be fine."

Frank looked across the table at her.

"Yes, you will," he said. "Congratulations."

Francie was at the track early the next morning. Mr. Richards arrived a few minutes later and walked over to the stall, where Francie was standing alone, watching the red colt finish up the last of his hay.

"You're on your own with him," he said. "I'm giving you all his duties. You'll be groom, feeding person, stall cleaner, and, if you can ever get on him, his rider. I know those aren't the duties of a trainer, but I figured if you're ever going to win him over, you need to spend a lot of time with him."

"Okay," she said.

"Can you work that around your other horses?"

She swallowed. "Honestly, sir, I don't have any other horses at the moment. I lost them in a lawsuit."

"Against your mother," he said. "Terrible thing. Your grandfather probably turned over in his grave."

She looked at him.

"Yes, I knew your grandfather," he said, his kind eyes on hers. "He was a dear friend. I saw you tagging around with him for years, and he told me over and over what a great trainer you'd make some day. I know about your situation, Ms. Dalton, and I'm willing to take a chance on you. Flame's a very expensive horse, but he's no good to me in his current condition. If you can get him to run for you and not kill someone, I'd be mighty grateful."

"I think I can do that, sir," she said.

"I think you can too." They stood and watched Flame for a few minutes. The colt, finished with his morning meal, pawed the ground with impatience.

Francie laughed. "He's ready to go," she said.

The horse nodded his head up and down. Mr. Richards reached for the animal's halter, which was hanging on a hook outside his stall door. Flame bared his teeth and launched at the old man, who was expecting the attack. He pulled away in time.

"He hates men," he said. "I've tried to make peace with him but can't."

"What happened to him?" Francie asked. "Horses aren't born this way—somebody makes them this way."

"When he was a foal, he was treated roughly by his stable hands. I imagine they forced a halter on him and used a whip to teach him to lead. He was a bit ornery anyway and started shaking his head every time they came around to halter him. So they started beating him over the head with a crop. Real helpful, huh?"

Francie shook her head.

"When they broke him to ride, he balked, so they used spurs to get him to move forward. When he comes out of his stall, you'll see scars from the spurs and whips they've used on him."

"I've seen them," she said.

"I bought him a few months ago, partially out of pity and partially because he's got great breeding. If he doesn't make a runner, I can make a fortune with him as a stud. I know he'll produce some fine colts. But my boys haven't been able to handle him. Last month, I had his feet trimmed and used a woman farrier. Things went much more smoothly. I think, since he's always been abused by men, a woman will have an easier time working with him."

He turned to her.

"And your grandfather said you have a gift. You can heal wounds that nobody else can."

She thought of Star and smiled. "I don't know if it's a gift," she said. "I just love them. That's all any of us are looking for—a little bit of love and a safe place to sleep."

"Safe Haven Farm," he said and smiled. "That's what your grandfather often called Sunnyhill."

"Safe Haven Farm," she said.

"I'll move him over to your place, then," said Mr. Richards. "Just be careful. If you get yourself killed, your grandfather will come back and haunt me."

chapter
19

THAT EVENING, A BIG TRAILER PULLED INTO the driveway. Francie went out to meet them, carrying Becky on her hip. Frank, who was working in the barn, heard them pull up and came out to greet them.

"Hi," he said, shaking Mr. Richard's hand. He introduced himself. "So you're bringing us the champ, huh?"

Mr. Richards laughed. "Well, he's not a champ yet. I think he could be, but he's been spoiled by rough treatment, and I'm not sure he'll ever be good to run."

"She can fix anything," Frank said as Francie approached them. Becky was cooing and twisting her hair. Frank leaned in to whisper to Mr. Richards. "She'll pretend to be all professional, but she really feels like a kid getting her first pony on her birthday," he said with a wink.

"He's right," Francie said, smiling. "Let's put him in a stall toward the middle. I put fresh bedding in."

"This is my groom, Mike, and this is my attorney, Dale Samson," said Mr. Richards. "He has a bit of paperwork for you to fill out to make you my official trainer."

There was a lot of commotion as Mike tried to get the horse out of the trailer. Kicking, scuffling, then in a red explosion, Flame burst out of the trailer backwards, reared up, and ripped the lead rope out of Mike's hands. He ran a few paces away, then stopped and turned to face them, unsure of where to go.

Frank slowly closed the gate, locking him in the area near the barns.

"He can't get back to the road now," he said. "He's safe in here."

Francie handed Becky to Frank. The baby was quiet, watching the horse with big eyes.

"Mommy's going to go pet him," Francie said.

"Be careful," warned Mr. Richards. "Just be careful."

Francie pulled a small bag of apple slices out of her pocket.

"Look what I have," she said, holding one out in her palm. "You remember these."

She didn't attempt to approach the horse. She just stood there, holding out her hand.

He watched her, ears pricked forward, then glanced nervously at the men.

"You guys back off a little bit," she said. "Go into the barn."

They did as she said. Flame watched them, ears twitching, nostrils flaring. He snorted.

"Here ya go," she said. She took a step toward him. He snorted again and pawed the ground nervously with his front hoof. The lead rope dangled from his halter, and he looked at it sideways, his eyes big.

"It's okay. It's just a silly old rope," Francie said.

She took a few casual steps toward him. He started to tremble a little and pawed again.

She stopped and held out her hand. She was almost close enough to touch him.

He stretched his neck out as far as he could, just barely reaching her palm. His upper lip started smacking the air, trying to lift the apple off of her hand without making contact. Finally, he gave up, moved a bit closer, snatched the apple, and backed off, chewing.

Francie smiled. "See? I don't bite," she said.

She stood there quietly, watching him chew. When he swallowed, she offered him another.

He stretched his neck out, and this time, it was she who moved closer. He snatched the apple slice.

He watched Francie as he chewed.

She walked a step closer, offering another apple slice and, at the same time, taking the dangling lead rope in her other hand.

The horse didn't seem to notice and nudged her hand for another piece of apple.

She gave it to him, then ran her hand down his neck. It was soft, glistening in the sun. He was a beautiful color, as red as fire, with a big, white blaze down his face.

She gave a little pull on the lead rope, and he let her lead him into the barn, snorting as they walked past the men.

At the stall door, he stopped and began trembling again.

"He was abused in his stall, wasn't he?" she asked quietly.

"Yes," Mr. Richards said. "They kept him cornered so they could tack him up. He won't tie."

"You won't tie?" Francie asked the horse. "Well, we'll have to work on that."

"He's not going in his stall," she said to the men. "I want to put him in the pasture out back. There's a lean-to he can use for shelter."

"He's a $600,000 horse," the attorney said nervously. "I'd feel much safer if he was in a stall... "

"It's okay." Mr. Richards put a hand on Samson's shoulder. "Let her do it her way."

"He'll feel less confined out there," Francie said. "He needs to relax before I can do anything with him."

She led him without trouble out behind the barn and turned him loose in the pasture.

"You'll never catch him again," Mike said, leaning on the fence post.

"I don't plan to catch him," she said. "I plan to let him come to me when he's ready."

She knew from experience with her grandpa's horses that nobody, not even horses, liked to be alone for too long.

And it was true. Within three days, she had him running to the fence to greet her every time she went out. She fed him apples, sugar cubes, and handfuls of grain, spoiling him rotten.

Frank watched her from inside the barn as he worked or from the window of his apartment. She spent hours standing in the pasture with Flame, stroking his neck, his shoulders, his back, and rubbing her hands all over him. Down his legs, across his face.

At first, anytime she came near his head, he'd jerk it up, expecting to be hit. Habit was there, and protecting his face had been ingrained in him since he was only a few weeks old. But she didn't try to put his halter back on or lead him anywhere, and she never moved quickly. Soon, he was letting her rub his forehead, his muzzle, and even his ears. She worked slowly, talking quietly, and her touch became an expected comfort to him.

He usually had itchy spots on his withers, just at the base of his neck where his back ended and his mane began. She'd dig in there with her fingernails, giving him a good scratch, and he'd respond by stretching his neck out, curling his upper lip, and making all sorts of faces filled with horsey pleasure.

Frank watched and laughed. "That's amazing," he said, shaking his head.

She smiled. The first few days, Frank had been afraid for her, but the horse had never made a move to harm her. The change in the horse in such a short time *was* amazing.

Then one day, when Frank peeked his head out of the stall he was cleaning, she was on Flame's back.

There was no saddle or bridle on the horse. She was just simply laying on him, her arms wrapped around his neck. He was grazing, unconcerned.

Frank stepped out into the aisle and stood, watching her. She stroked Flame's neck, rubbing behind his ears, and working her hands up under his mane. When she got to his withers, she sat up and scratched. Flame raised his head, curling his lip out in ecstasy, thoroughly enjoying the attention.

She squeezed her legs into Flame's side a little bit. The horse's ears pricked back, listening, and he moved forward into a walk.

"Good boy," she said, scratching his favorite spot again in reward. She noticed Frank watching her and smiled. Then she slid off his back.

When she got into the barn, she said, "He's ready to ride. I'm going to start training him tomorrow."

"Good job," Frank said. "You've really worked a miracle. And you've only had him a week. I can't wait to see what you do with him in a month."

That night, after Becky had been put to bed and the dinner dishes washed up, they were sitting on the porch, watching the sunset. Mr. Richards had been called over that afternoon, and he watched Francie climb up on his horse, no saddle or bridle.

"You think he'll be ready to race soon?" Mr. Richards asked.

"If we can find a jockey," she said. "I'm a little over the weight limit."

At 120 pounds, she was a bit heavy for the job. Most jockeys weighed in around 100, and horses usually carried around 126, which had to include jockey and saddle.

"I'd like to get him in the Bluegrass Stakes in April, but let's try a smaller race first. Something where we won't attract much attention."

They had left it at that, with Francie and Mr. Richards both agreeing to look for a good female jockey.

"We have to find somebody to ride him," she said. They were sitting at the dining room table, listening to the rain pelt against the windows.

"I don't know any female jockeys," Frank said.

Just then the doorbell rang.

Francie jumped up, startled.

"Easy," said Frank. "Probably just a salesman. Or Mr. Richards."

"Or my mom," Francie said. Nobody ever took the time to come down the long, winding drive for sales pitches, and they just didn't get any visitors. She swallowed. "Or Tom. Or his lawyer dad." Tom hadn't made any attempt to see Becky, but it was always at the back of her mind.

Frank smiled. "Instead of guessing, let's go see. The suspense is killing me."

It was Sam.

They looked down at her tiny figure, too stunned to speak. She was dressed in jeans and a purple shirt, with an unzipped hooded windbreaker on, which blocked only some of the rain. In her hand was a small suitcase.

"Can I stay?" she said.

Francie looked warily around. "Where's Mom?"

"At home."

"How'd you get here?"

"By bus."

"You *ran away?*" Francie said.

Frank pushed the door open further. "Come in, sweetheart," he said.

He closed the door behind her and went to get some towels, which he handed to Francie. She started towel drying her sister's hair.

"Why?"

Sam rolled her eyes. "You know why," she said. "Please don't make me go back."

"Let's get you changed," Francie said. "I supposed there are clothes in that suitcase?"

"And Rolly Bear," said Sam. "I couldn't leave him."

"Of course not."

Francie took her upstairs to the bathroom and ran a warm bath.

"Francie, it's horrible there," Sam said as Francie pulled her shirt over her head. "Mom scares me. She fired the nanny. I don't have anybody to look out for me, and last week Mom locked me in the closet and forgot about me until bedtime, and I had to pound on the door, and I had to pee so bad... "

Francie hugged her. "I know. I mean... I didn't know—I should have been checking on you... "

"Please let me stay with you. *Please.*"

"How did you get bus fare?

Sam looked at the floor. "I took it from Dad."

"Took it?

"Yes. Every week when he gets his spending money out, I'd sneak a few dollars. He never seemed to notice it was missing. Once I found a twenty in his drawer. Once I found $5 in the car. Eventually I had enough for a bus ticket."

"Wow."

Francie put her in the warm tub to soak and went to find Frank. He was making up the bed in the guest room.

"We've got to keep her," Francie said.

"That's why I'm making up the bed," Frank said. "You have to call your mom though, or the police will be after us."

"Ohhhh," she ran her hands through her hair. "I *cannot* talk to that woman."

"Sure you can," Frank said, keeping his voice low so the baby wouldn't wake up.

Francie turned to look at him, hands on her hips. "I'm not giving her back," she said.

"I don't think you should," he said.

"We'd be raising two kids... "

"We would," he said, unfazed.

Francie smiled. "You are, by far, the best thing that has ever happened to me, Frank Weaver."

"I'm a kept man," he said. "You are, after all, supporting me with your new career as a horse trainer."

She laughed.

"That's true," she said. "I am your boss."

"Technically, yes," he said. "But I am your elder. So which gets more rank?"

"Depends on the day and the subject," she said and winked at him. Then she went back into the bathroom to finish up with Sam.

When the little girl came out, all warm and dry, they took her to her bedroom. Frank had turned down the covers, sitting Rolly Bear by the pillows. Sam was a full ten-years-old now, but she looked so small and helpless.

"Are you going to keep me?" she asked, her eyes lighting up at the sight of her room.

"Yes, we're going to keep you," Francie said.

"Then will you read me a story?"

Francie sent Frank downstairs to make Sam some toast, and she went to get some of Becky's books.

Then the three of them sat in her room, the two sisters on the bed, Frank in a nearby rocking chair, and read books together. Sam snuggled in close to Francie, and soon her eyelids were heavy.

"Tomorrow you'll have to tell me more about your adventure," Francie said.

"This is like vacation," said Sam as Francie tucked her in. "Do I have to go to school?"

Francie laughed. "Not tomorrow, but eventually. You can't be on vacation forever."

Sam was asleep almost immediately. Frank and Francie went downstairs, where Frank took a seat at the kitchen table.

"I'll be your moral support," he said. "Call your mom."

She sighed but picked up the phone and dialed. Her mom answered.

"Hi Mom," she said.

"Francie? Sam is gone. Are you involved in this?" Norma's voice was so loud that Francie had to hold the phone away from her ear. She looked at Frank, who made a face, which made her smile.

"No, Mom, but I have her. She bought a bus ticket." Francie explained what she knew.

"Send her home," her mom said when she was done.

"I'm not going to do that, Mom," Francie said. "I want custody of her. You don't want her anyway. Just let me have her."

"Francie, you can't raise a child... "

"I am raising a child, your grandchild—"

"Which is exactly my point," her mom finished.

Francie looked at Frank again, who scrawled "lawyer" on a napkin and passed it to her.

"Mom, I have a lawyer, and I'll fight you on this," she said, and as the words came out, anger fueled her. "You took my horses, but you're not taking my sister. You tried to destroy me, but it will never happen again. Ever. Do you get that? If you want to fight me on this, I'll throw everything I have into it, and by the time I'm finished, you'll be in jail for child abuse. Do you want to go that route?"

There was a long silence on the phone. Finally, her mom said, "Fine, keep her."

"I'll send you papers to sign," said Francie. "I want full custodial rights."

"We'll see," her mom said.

"No, you'll sign them, or we go to court," Francie said.

"Fine," said her mom.

"My lawyer will be in touch." Francie hung up the phone.

"Bravo," Frank said. "Well done."

Francie sat down. "That felt kind of good."

"I'll bet it did."

She ran her hands through her hair, then laughed. "We're becoming quite a family," she said.

chapter
20

SHE HAD BEEN RIDING FLAME on her own track, a half-mile dirt oval tucked in a field behind the barns. At 5 a.m. that morning, when she unloaded him from their trailer at the city track, it was the horse's first glimpse of that track in two months.

Flame stepped off the ramp, his head held high and his nostrils flaring, taking in all the smells. It was still dark, and bright, white lights lit up the track. There were a few other early risers—men leaning on rails with stopwatches in hand, riders getting a leg up onto a horse for a workout. Francie laid a hand on Flame's sleek hide. The muscles beneath quivered with excitement.

"He knows what's up," Frank said.

"He sure does," Francie replied. She saw Mr. Richards walking down the path across the track toward them, emerging from a thin mist that swirled around his ankles. Voices carried in the still morning air, and she heard him greet the men at the rail.

Frank handed her the saddle. While she tacked Flame up, the horse stood quietly, minding his manners like she had taught him. The only clues that he was excited were his quivering muscles and heavier than normal breathing. Frank put the riding helmet on her head and checked the chin strap.

"Buckling me in?" she asked.

"I guess if you were an actress, now's the time I'd say break a leg," Frank said. "But since you're not—don't."

She smiled. Their eyes met and held.

"Go get 'em," he said and gave her a leg up.

As soon as Flame felt her weight, he started to dance, his white feet tiptoeing and side-stepping across the dirt.

"Hey, trainer," Mr. Richards greeted her and motioned for her to come over to him.

He kept his voice low, and she leaned down to hear him.

"There's curiosity among the viewers," he said, inclining his head toward the men at the rail. Francie looked and noticed that five more men, all exercise riders, had joined them. "They're waiting for him to toss you. There's not a one of them who has been able to stay in his saddle."

He winked at her.

"Show us what this horse can do."

Francie gathered up her reins and turned Flame toward the starting gate. They jogged through the clearing mist at a slow, steady pace. She could feel his muscles bunch beneath her, ready to spring forward at her request.

"Easy boy," she said.

There was the promise of daylight in the weak, pink streak along the horizon. Cigarette smoke curled up from a trainer near the rail, hanging in the thick air.

"Hey, chickee," someone said. "Don't break a nail when he throws you." There was a ripple of laughter from the other men.

Francie looked back, and Frank and Mr. Richards both gave her a nod.

She smiled. "Let's knock their socks off, boy," she said.

She turned at the gate and stopped. Crouching low, she steadied her horse, and then signaled him forward with her legs. Flame took off like a cannon had fired him. Francie kept a steady hold on the reins, counting quietly in her head as Flame's legs ate up the track. One thousand, two thousand, three thousand...

His ears pricked back, asking for more rein.

"Not yet," she breathed, holding him back. He wanted to run. She kept him steady up to the quarter pole.

Twenty-five thousand...

He begged, and she gave him a little more. The cool morning air blew into her face, making her eyes water. She felt the heat of her horse under her and caught a glimpse of the quickly pinkening sky.

They were at the half pole now, and she realized they were moving along at a pretty fast clip. She checked him, but he tugged, wanting more.

"In a minute," she said and held him at that pace.

The half pole flew by at forty-eight seconds.

They were around on the far side and coming up to the third pole when she let him go. He leaped forward, his long strides swallowing up the track in huge gulps. She was surprised at how much he had left and lost count of her timing. She leaned into his neck and urged him on.

"Go, Flame, go," she whispered, her hands working the reins, encouraging him onward. But he didn't need encouragement. He was running for the pure love of it, opening up with all he had. The last quarter mile flashed by in an instant it seemed, and they flew past the finish line, a full mile completed. She tried to pull him up, to tell him it was over, but the horse shook his head and fought her, asking to run some more.

"No, Flame," she said firmly. "Whoa." She stood in her irons, pulling him back. Reluctantly, he slowed his pace, shaking his head a few times to show his frustration. Then he was jogging again, and she posted along, back in control. She turned and jogged him back to Frank and Mr. Richards.

By the time she got there, there was a small crowd of men. Some of the trainers and riders she recognized. They were all chattering excitedly.

Mr. Richards looked up at her and smiled.

"Did you count it out?" he asked.

"I know we were moving," she said. "I lost count in the last quarter."

He laughed. "I wonder why."

Mr. Richards held up his stopwatch.

"Francie Dalton, you just broke the track record in a workout," he said. "Not only did you do the mile in 1:02, but you did that last quarter in 22 seconds, and you still have a lot of horse under you."

"When are you going to race him?" one of the trainers asked.

"Not sure, Bill," Mr. Richards said. "He won't let anybody ride him but her. She doesn't have her jockey's license—and she's my trainer."

There was some mumbling, and the men started back up in excited conversation.

"Here, let me have him," Frank said, taking the reins as Francie dismounted. He started to walk the horse to cool him down. Francie walked alongside to keep Flame calm, pulling her gloves off and removing her helmet. She was sweaty and out of breath.

"Wow," she said.

"Yeah, wow." Frank was grinning from ear to ear. "You two sure made them swallow their words!"

"That's her manager," someone said.

"Frank! Come over here a minute, son!" Mr. Richards called.

He handed her the reins. "Let me go handle your affairs now that you're famous," he winked.

Francie laughed and took her horse. They walked quietly together around the track, steam gently rising from one and a big smile on the other.

Later that afternoon they got a phone call. Since Francie wasn't eligible to ride in an official race, and since Flame wouldn't let anybody else ride him, it had been discussed that an unofficial race be set up.

The phone call confirmed that.

"Mr. Donald Suthers, owner of Tried and True, has challenged you and Flame to a match race," said Frank, holding the receiver aside. "Mr. Richards wonders if you accept."

Francie's eyes widened. "Tried and True? The Horse of the Year? Oh my gosh. Um, yes, we accept! But... I'm just... "

"She's speechless," Frank said into the phone, "but before she went speechless, she managed to squeak out 'I accept'."

She heard Mr. Richards' deep baritone laugh on the other end of the line.

"Here, he wants to talk to you," Frank handed her the phone.

"You don't need me to tell you what a great job you did out there this morning," Mr. Richards told her. "Let's have some fun. I think Flaming Star can beat the socks off of Tried and True. I'm going to put some money up to see that happen. Be prepared for some attention, because you're sure going to get it."

With the names of Samuel Richards and Donald Suthers, two of the biggest names in racing, being slung around, the next few weeks were crazy. Every sports enthusiast and reporter in the country wanted to interview Francie. A growing crowd watched Flame's workouts on the three days a week she took him to the track. The rest of the time, she trained him at home, away from the crowds. More than once, she had to politely ask people to leave her property. She found a few strangers in her barn. No one seemed threatening, merely curious. People just wanted to see this wonder horse that she had. But after that, Mr. Richards paid for security at her front gate.

The weeks before the race were busy. Reporters filled Francie's quiet, humble life on the farm with phone calls and visits. Every time she left the house, it seemed, someone would stop her.

The girls were thriving. The sitter they found—one willing to start at 5 a.m.—was great with the kids. Sam began to fill out her thin little frame a bit, and while she still looked frail, she actually seemed happy. Frank was a Godsend. He managed the farm and their finances, cooked, and watched the kids. Wherever he was needed, he stepped in without complaining. It felt like a family.

A few days before the race, Jim called.

"Hey, Sis."

"Hey yourself."

"What's this I hear? You're a famous person now? I saw you on the news."

"Yeah... weird, huh?"

"Mom must be beside herself," he said.

They both laughed.

"Krista and I are coming down for the race," Jim said.

"What? Really?" She hadn't seen either of them for nearly a year. They hadn't even seen Becky.

"Yep. We'll get in Friday afternoon, watch you win the race on Saturday, then we have to head back on Sunday. Krista has to be back in New York on Monday morning."

"Oh my gosh, Jim, I miss you so much!" Francie said, cradling the phone with both hands.

"Me too, Sis," he said.

"How are you?" she asked.

"Do you mean, am I high?"

There was a beat of silence. "Why do you always think I'm wondering that?"

He sighed. "I don't know. I'm not. I'm good."

"Jim?" she hesitated. "I... I found God."

He laughed. "I never knew you lost Him. Didn't Mom always make sure we knew right where He was? Always watching us. Waiting for us to screw up?"

"God isn't like that. He's not like that at all. He loves us, Jim. It's more about a relationship. I've started reading my Bible, and Frank told me how much God loves me. And you! He loves you too! I go to church now. I sing in the choir. I—"

"Are you trying to convert me?" Jim said. "Because I don't convert. Music is my religion. Or was."

There was a silence on his end.

Francie took a deep breath. "Jim, Jesus died to save us. All you have to do is ask and He will come into your heart. It's a free gift. It's incredible."

"Ask? Where was Jesus when Dad was beating me in his name? Where was He when Mom locked Sam in closets? Where was Jesus when I was at war and people were killing each other. And Paul... damn it, Francie."

"Jim, I'm sorry. It's just... my life used to suck too... "

"And now, with Jesus, it's so much better?"

"Yes," she said quietly, almost embarrassed.

"I'm glad He's taking care of you," Jim said, his voice gentler. "I'm sorry. I'm happy for you. You know I love you. Just don't preach to me when I come visit you."

chapter 21

THAT NIGHT, AFTER THE GIRLS WERE IN BED, Frank and Francie sat out back on the porch and talked. She told him more about her family, about Jim and his dreams to be a musician, about Krista's career, about Mark in the FBI, who they hardly saw and weren't allowed to know where he was.

"Mark loves me, but he has a cruel streak," she said. "Dad has always compared him and Jim, and he rubs that in. He hates Jim. But Jim... he's awesome. So is Krista."

Frank listened quietly, sipping at his glass of iced tea. He noticed that her face was glowing.

"You miss them," he said.

"Very much," she said, meeting his eyes. "Jim saved my life, you know. Twice."

This was news to Frank. "How?"

She told him about the attempted rape.

He was quiet for a moment. "Did you contact the police?"

"No. We were just kids. We didn't tell anybody." She swallowed hard. "And the other time... " She stopped and laughed a little. "Oh, you don't want to hear those stories. I'm blathering on." She waved it away with her hand, smiling.

"I *do* want to know," Frank said. "Tell me."

She looked into his dark, serious eyes and then looked down, her smile fading. "And the other time... my mother tried to kill me." She had never spoken of this before to anyone, not even Krista. Jim was the only one who knew.

"How?" Frank asked quietly.

Francie slowly, quietly told him the whole story, ending with the destruction of Jim's hand and him going off to Vietnam.

"Oh, Francie."

Frank was quiet for a long while. He reached over and took her hand. They sat there for a while, holding hands across the gulf between their chairs, looking out into the darkness at the stars.

"You're safe now," he said, giving her hand a little squeeze.

"I know," she said. When she was with him, which seemed like always, she felt safe, secure, and loved. She felt like she belonged. He was so much to her. Her friend, her protector... and what else? She glanced at him, at his solid features, his brown eyes and thick, wavy hair that was neither blond nor brown but somewhere in between. What else?

His eyes met hers and her heart beat a little faster. She pushed her thoughts down. Everything was perfect now. Perfect just the way it was. She didn't want to lose him like she had lost Johnny and Tom. And what was she to him? A newly divorced mother of one with a little sister in the mix?

"Is Jim still using?" Frank's question startled her.

"I don't know," she said. "That night he rescued me he had certainly bought some. A lot. But it was coke, and I think he only smoked pot."

"Well, I can't wait to meet them both," Frank said. "There's certainly plenty of room here at the house."

"There's enough room for you, too," Francie said, as she had offered at least a hundred times.

He let go of her hand. "I'll stay in my apartment above the barn," he said. "It wouldn't be proper. And I should go now." He drained his glass and stood up. "We've got another early morning ahead of us."

After dinner on Friday, Frank drove Francie to the airport in his truck, since Tom had taken the car when he left. Sam was buckled in the middle, and Becky was on Francie's lap.

"Do we really get to ride in the cab on the way home," Sam asked excitedly.

"That's the plan," Frank said. He had thrown a mattress in the back for makeshift seating.

"Cool," Sam said.

The plane, from a layover in Tennessee where her siblings had met, was on time, and the four of them waited and watched people getting off. Finally, a woman with thick, long blond hair exited, walking with a man with shoulder length, sandy blond hair, glasses and a pack of cigarettes in his shirt pocket. The woman was exquisitely dressed—even in jeans and a white blouse, she looked neat and tidy and clean. The man with her was a stark contrast, looking somewhere between a rock star and like he didn't give a care.

"Over here!" Francie waved.

"You didn't tell me she was so... pretty," Frank said.

"I told you she was a model," Francie said. "You should have figured that out for yourself."

"And the man with her must be—"

"Jim," Francie finished.

The couple spotted them and hurried forward. Sam ran ahead and threw her arms around first Krista and then Jim.

"Wow! Look how you've grown!" Krista said, and she and Jim both started talking to Sam at once.

Then they spotted Francie.

"Oh my goodness!" Krista said. "This must be Becky! Oh, Francie, she's beautiful! Look at those blond curls!"

"Sis—she's spectacular," Jim said.

Everyone was talking at once. Becky got passed around, and Krista and Jim produced lollipops and a stuffed horse for Sam out of their carry-on bags.

That's when Krista said, "And this is Frank?"

Frank had been standing quietly aside, watching all the commotion.

"Yes!" said Francie. "This is the man who saved my farm and my life and oh just about everything," she gushed and stepped back, waving her arm toward him with a flourish.

"You sound like a superhero," said Krista, meeting his eyes.

"Hardly," Frank extended his hand. "It's good to meet you." He shook both their hands. "Let's go get your luggage."

On the ride home, Krista sat in the front in between Frank and Jim. Frank tried to keep his mind on the road.

Krista was taller than Francie, probably close to 5' 9", he guessed. She smelled as good as she looked. The skin on her arm, which kept brushing against his, was cool and soft. They talked a little, Krista telling Frank how she got into modeling and Jim talking about the music he was writing. Mostly, they asked questions about the farm and the upcoming race.

The cab window was open, and every now and then, Francie piped up with a remark, or Sam had something to say. The excitement continued as they pulled up in the driveway of the farm. Then, when they got out, there were exclamations and fond remembrances and more hugging. Frank helped carry the luggage in, and Francie got them settled in their rooms and put Becky to bed. It was past ten, and Sam was exhausted, so they put her to bed too, promising to spend lots of time catching up in the morning.

Then they settled on the screened-in back porch in the dark, with only a soft light burning in the corner. It showed off the waves in Krista's hair, and the shadows created soft lines. They were finally quieting down, relaxing.

"I should go," Frank said, coming downstairs last after getting Sam a final drink of water.

"No, no, stay!" Francie said.

"Yeah, man," Jim said in his quiet voice. "You've taken good care of my sister, so you're like family now."

"Better than family," Krista said. "At least *our* family."

"Please, stay," Francie said.

"Okay," Frank said. "Seeing as how I'm outnumbered and all." He took the glass of water Francie offered and sat down next to her, across from Krista and Jim.

The porch was quiet for a while as each of them sat with their own thoughts. Then Frank asked Krista a little more about her job.

"She's up for Glamour Girl," Francie said.

Krista, in the dim light, blushed. "Maybe," she said.

"Wow," Frank said. They talked about New York, and Krista told them how much she loved living there.

"I'll be working in New York someday too," Francie said. "At Elmont Park, Sarasota... "

"The race tracks!" Krista laughed.

Jim sat quietly in his corner, watching them.

"What about you, Jim?" Frank asked.

"I have a few gigs I play at on weekends," he said. "Mostly I work at the factory."

"How's Elise... Alissa..." Francie couldn't remember the name of his latest girlfriend.

"Elise," he said. "Don't know. She left me a few months ago."

"Oh," Francie said. "Well, sorry. But you never tell me about your love life when we talk, so how could I know?"

"That's because there's a lack of one," he said.

"He goes through girls like I go through lipsticks," said Krista. "A new color every season." The words were spoken gently, and she gave him a playful wink. He scowled back.

"I need a smoke," he said, shaking one out of his pack and walking outside. He walked off toward the pool, away from them.

"What *does* he do?" Frank asked. Both girls glanced at Jim. He seemed out of earshot.

"No one really knows," Francie said. "He won't talk about himself."

"He works in a factory making parts of some sort," said Krista. "He's been there— what?" She glanced at Francie. "Nine months? He's making okay money."

"We just don't know what he does with it," Francie said.

"Mom says he snorts it," Krista says. "But we don't think so."

Francie was quiet, remembering the bag of white powder he had traded for her.

"He holds down a job," Krista continued. "He gets guitar gigs. But now he lives in a dump in a bad part of town. He was living with Elise for a while."

"He was?" Francie said. "I didn't know that."

"Yes. I met her once. Pretty. Sweet. He seemed madly in love."

"I *was* in love with her," Jim said. His voice startled them as he pushed the screen door open and sat back down with a sigh. "I still am."

"What happened?" Francie asked.

"She got smart," Jim said, "and she got tired of not having any money."

"Where does your money go?" Krista asked.

"Do you think I snort it like Mom says?" His voice was bitter.

"No," Francie said. Their eyes met. His eyes were clear, searching hers. "I don't," she said. "But there is the mystery, then, of what you do with your money." He looked tired, so very tired. Her heart went out to him.

"I know you're clean, Jim," Krista said.

There was a beat of silence.

"Insurance," he said. "I use it to buy insurance. The expensive kind."

No one said anything. They weren't sure if he was joking or not, but Jim didn't smile. Then Frank said, "Look at the time! Francie has a big race tomorrow. She should get some sleep."

There was agreement from all. Francie made sure Krista and Jim were settled in their separate rooms, then came back down to the kitchen. Frank was washing up the dinner dishes they had left in their hurry to get to the airport.

Francie grabbed a towel and started drying.

"You guys are close," Frank said. "That's nice."

"We are. And I saw you looking at Krista."

"Well, I looked at Jim too."

"Not the same way. Much to Jim's relief, I'm sure."

A smile played at the corners of his mouth.

"All men find her attractive," Francie smiled. "She's a model."

"I didn't say I found her attractive."

"Yes, you did. Earlier you called her pretty."

"That's not attractive. It's pretty. Different words."

Francie laughed. "Whatever!"

Frank glanced at her. "Would it bother you if I did?"

Francie felt her cheeks grow hot. "No! Of course not. But she lives in New York."

"I could move to New York."

Francie coiled up her towel and snapped him on the leg. "Don't you dare leave me now!"

"Ouch! Hey—you get to bed. And sleep in. I mean it."

"Yes, sir." She laid the towel on the sink. "You don't stay up late either. I need you sharp tomorrow."

"Yes, boss."

She smiled at that and headed off to bed.

She got ready and curled between the cool sheets, a smile on her face. It felt good to have the people she loved the most all under the same roof. That was her last and only thought before she drifted into a dreamless sleep.

Francie woke to Becky crying. A glance at the clock said it was 2 a.m. She threw on her robe and went down the hall.

"Everything okay?" Krista asked sleepily, her head poking out of her bedroom.

"I've got it. Go back to sleep."

Francie went in and took the little girl in her arms.

"What is it, honey?"

Becky was already falling back to sleep, her cheeks still damp with tears. Francie laid her back down and kissed her tenderly on her forehead. It must have been a bad dream.

Krista was in bed, but Jim's door was open. She peeked in. His bed was empty.

Francie walked past her office and down the stairs. The house was dark. Then she saw a spark of light from his cigarette outside. He was sitting by the pool.

She went out through the patio door, making enough sound so she wouldn't startle him. He saw her coming and put his cigarette out. She sat down by him on the bench.

"Hey," she said.

"Hey."

The sky was full of stars.

"Papaw used to sit out here with me and tell me the constellations," Francie said. Jim didn't answer. She noticed he was breathing a little fast.

"You okay?" She put an arm around him and felt his whole body trembling, as if he was cold. "You're shaking."

"I'm okay."

"No, you're not. Tell me what's wrong."

Jim was silent for a moment. When he spoke, his voice was low, hoarse. "Bad dream," he said. "I get them a lot since the war."

"Oh."

"It was too much for Elise. She never got any sleep. I kept her awake. That and the money."

Francie pulled him toward her in a sideways hug.

"You know I love you," she said.

"I know." He leaned his head against hers. "You may be the only one."

"Krista... "

He laughed and leaned back against the bench. "Krista tolerates me because she's an angel."

"Do you want to talk about it... the dream?"

"No." He rubbed his arms, as if he had a chill. "Let's go to bed. You have a big day tomorrow. I'll be fine. Like I said, this happens all the time."

They walked back in together. She went back to her own room and lay there in the darkness for a while, thinking about Jim and wondering why life was so hard for him. Why couldn't he get a break? She wanted something to go right for him for once. Soon her eyes grew tired, and she fell back to sleep. She dreamed of Flame and didn't awaken again until morning.

Sunlight filtered in through the window, and Francie woke with a start. She glanced at the clock. Ten a.m.! Then she remembered that she was *supposed* to sleep in. She lay back down, enjoying laziness for once. She couldn't remember the last time she had slept in—had it been years?—and she wallowed in the luxury of it for a few minutes. Were it anybody else in the world in charge of the farm, she'd be worried and up taking control, but she knew she could trust Frank to take care of the horses, and Krista, well, thanks to Krista, she knew the girls would be taken care of until she awoke.

Today was the big race. Flame was ready, and she knew he could win, even carrying her weight.

She got up and slowly dressed, then wandered down to the kitchen. Frank was sitting at the table doing some paperwork. The kitchen was clean. There was a plate at her place at the table, covered with a pan lid. She peeked under. Pancakes.

"Mmmmmmm," she said.

Frank looked up. "Good morning. Sleep well?"

"Oh my gosh, it was so nice to sleep in!" she said. "Thank you! Where is everybody?"

"Krista and Jim are taking a tour with Sam as their guide," he said.

Francie found the syrup and a bowl of sliced peaches in the fridge. She sat down to eat.

"Becky woke me up once, and then I saw Jim. I guess he had a nightmare. From the war, he said. But other than that, I slept like a rock."

"Good. We need you sharp today."

There was a lot riding on this race. The track officials had put it as the final race of the day, hoping to draw a record crowd and take advantage of early betting. It was being broadcast on national television. Since Tried and True was such a champ, everyone was excited to see if this new challenger could beat him. Flame was nothing to snuff at; with his pedigree and Mr. Richards' many years of success as an owner, he stood a good chance. But the colt was untried, while Tried and True was a proven veteran on the track.

"Early betting has Tried and True as the favorite," Frank said.

Francie snorted. "Shows what they know."

"If he wins, you'll probably land a lot of training jobs. You've already pulled in a few because of him."

"That's what I'm counting on," Francie said. "We sure need the money."

Just as she finished eating, the others returned.

"The place looks great," Krista said to her. "You've kept it up well."

"The place looks *empty*," Jim said. "You have a total of three horses in the barn, and one of them is yours."

"Mom took the rest," Francie said.

Everyone fell silent. Then, to break the mood, Francie said, "The other two are horses I've been hired to train."

"Awesome," Jim said.

"And after today, you'll be hired to train more," Krista added.

They high-fived.

"Let's get started!" Francie said.

As expected, a record crowd filled the stands for the sixth and final race of the day. The weather was perfect, the track surface good and dry.

In the saddling stall next to them, Tried and True was surrounded by his groom, trainer, various handlers, and his jockey.

Flame simply had Francie saddling him while Frank held the horse steady. Mr. Richards stood nearby, watching with a twinkle in his eye.

"You don't look nervous," Francie said to him.

"My dear," said Mr. Richards. "You don't get to be my age by being nervous all the time. Whatever the outcome of the race, this is a good day for me. I'm having fun."

Francie smiled.

"Ready?" Frank said and gave her a leg up.

"You don't look nervous either," Mr. Richards told her.

"Because I have the best horse," she said and ran her hand down Flame's red neck. But she *was* nervous and excited and filled with all sorts of emotions. For so many years, she had watched from the other side of the rail, and here she was, *finally*, on a horse she had trained. She gathered the reins in the black gloves that covered her sweaty palms and started her horse out on to the track.

Flame was ready. His muscles bunched and rolled beneath her as he pranced and side-stepped his way onto the track. It was customary for the racehorse to have a lead pony accompanying him to the starting gate, but Flame didn't want anything to do with a lead pony. Like his rider, he liked to do it all by himself.

The crowd cheered loudly as they saw the two horses. Flame's nostrils flared, and he looked up into the stands.

"Our family's up there somewhere," Francie said. Flame danced and pulled softly on the bit but held himself together, sensing that something big was about to happen. Francie caressed his foamy neck with her gloved fingers.

"Not yet, fella," she whispered. The loudspeaker boomed with the announcer's voice, giving the horses' names and other information that Francie tuned out. When the voice was finished, the crowd cheered wildly again. Flame shied away from the noise, scooting sideways across the track, but Francie calmed him, and he settled down right way because he trusted her.

"It's just you and me, big guy," she said. She rode him into the starting gate, telling the handlers she didn't need help. Then she pulled her goggles over her eyes and crouched low over Flame's neck.

Tried and True's jockey laughed and glanced her way.

"Don't smudge your lipstick," he said.

Francie refused to let herself get mad. *We'll take it out by beating his butt,* she thought. Then the bell rang, and the doors flew open.

Flame surged forward with such power that she felt like she was on a rocket. Ahead of them lay a mile and a quarter of dirt track, and she felt Flame's huge strides eating up the ground. The clock in her head ticked away—nine, ten, eleven seconds.

Tried and True was on the rail, which would have been a bigger issue with more horses in the race. But since there wasn't a large field to swing them wide on the turn, Francie settled back to ride about a half a stride behind Tried and True. Close enough to breath down his neck but not close enough to push him to increase the time.

Flame pulled on the reins, asking to go, and she said no, not yet. He settled into stride and waited.

Twenty-two, twenty-three, twenty-four…

The quarter pole flashed by around twenty-four, a good steady time she knew Flame could keep up. His rhythm was even, and they passed the half mile pole around the fifty-second mark. Flame's ears swiveled, asking again.

Let's press him a little bit, Francie thought as they headed into the backstretch, and she let Flame out a notch. He responded, his ears pricking forward. Tried and True's jockey caught them out of the side of his eye, and he urged his horse forward. Flame wanted to pass him, and pulled again, asking for more.

Not yet, Francie told him.

Seventy-three at the three-quarter pole.

She let him out another notch, content to stay where she was. Tried and True sped up, but she saw his nostrils blowing hard.

The mile pole was coming up. Flame edged up until Tried and True was just a half a head in front of him. Both horses passed the mile pole in 1:02, track record time if Francie was counting correctly. Tried and True's jockey showed his horse the whip, and she knew then that they had him.

Flame asked again, and this time Francie said yes. She let him go, and he surged forward as if he hadn't just run a mile, passing the other horse like he was standing still. His ears were back, and he was increasing the distance between himself and Tried and True in strides. Francie peeked under her arms and saw that Tried and True was in their dust.

"Go, boy, go!" she said, and Flame sailed under the wire to a deafening crowd who was on their feet, screaming his name as she defeated Horse of the Year and Eclipse winner Tried and True by twenty-three strides and set a new track record and a new national record by two seconds.

Francie stood in her irons and held her hand high, waving to the crowd, then slowed her horse to a lope. She rubbed his sweaty neck and pulled her goggles up on her helmet.

"We did it," she said, a smile on her face and tears washing streaks down the dirt on her cheeks. "We did it!"

Her eyes scanned the stands, searching for Frank, but she couldn't see him in the crowd.

Back at the winner's circle, things were crazy. Everyone was congratulating Mr. Richards and patting him on the back. Cameras flashed. Flame stood tall and proud, as if posing for the photographers. Francie undid the throat latch to her helmet. She scanned the crowd, looking for

Frank, and then she saw him making his way toward her, a huge smile on his face.

He stopped a few feet away until the formalities were over.

"We did it," she mouthed, and he gave her a thumbs up. She talked to reporters and Mr. Richards but kept her eyes on Frank. Finally, it was time to dismount, and she turned to jump off, and there was Frank, waiting to catch her.

"Come here," he said, and she fell into his arms, laughing and crying, and he twirled her around and around. The crowd loved it and cheered some more, startling Flame.

"I never could have done any of this without you," Francie said, hugging Frank tight. "Thank you."

"Francie," Mr. Richards said. "Take your horse."

She looked and saw Flame pulling away from the crowd. He had had enough.

Krista, Jim, and the girls were a few feet away, having made their way down from the stands.

"You want my hot walker to try to cool him off?" asked Mr. Richards. Flame snorted and stomped his front foot.

Francie laughed. "I guess not," she said and left Frank to take the reins from Mr. Richards. She slowly walked Flame to the barns, where she could hose him down and walk him until he was cool.

Krista and Jim and the girls joined Frank and Mr. Richards, and they walked toward the barns.

"I'm treating everyone to dinner," Mr. Richards said to them.

About three hours later, around 9 p.m., they met for a late dinner. They had a sitter for Becky, and Flame was settled into his stall. Over enormous plates of food, they laughed and talked, reliving the saga of the race over and over.

"I wish we could do that again," Francie said.

"There's no one left to beat," said Mr. Richards. "He beat the horse that beat everybody else. And he beat him bad!" The old man high-fived everyone around the table, and they ate and laughed some more. Then he grew serious. "We'll have to retire him, Francie," he said. "Nobody can handle him except you, and you don't have your jockey's license. You're a trainer. He'd be retired by the end of the year anyway, and he'll make us a fortune at stud."

"Us?" Francie said.

"Well, yeah. I'll keep him at your place, if that's okay. And I have a few other horses I'd like you to train for me."

Francie's eyes filled with tears. "Thank you, Mr. Richards. Thank you so much."

"No, thank *you*, Ms. Dalton," he said. "You gave an old man a reason to live a little bit longer. I can't die when we're having this much fun!"

After dinner, as the others headed out, Mr. Richards held Frank back. When they were alone, he spoke.

"I'm giving her the horse," Mr. Richards said.

Frank raised his eyebrows in surprise. "What?"

"Flame. I'm leaving him to her in my will, along with a few good brood mares. When I'm gone, she should be set for life. That's the way her grandfather wanted it, and her mother stole it all from her."

"Well, you're not going anywhere... "

"Bah," Mr. Richards waved a hand. "I'm an old man, Frank. I can't stick around forever. Her grandfather and I were good friends, and I know this is what he wanted for her. And who else would I leave it to? I don't have any family. Just a few faithful staff that I plan to reward handsomely. Now come on. Let's go before the others wonder what we're up to."

Mr. Richards put his fedora on and walked toward the exit. Frank, overwhelmed and speechless, followed.

A little before midnight, the phone rang. It was her brother Mark.

"Congratulations, little sister!" he said. His voice was far away, staticky.

"You saw it?"

"I watched it via satellite. Looks like your dream came true. Papaw would be proud."

"Thanks, Mark," she said.

"I gotta go," he said, keeping the conversation short as usual. "The world needs to be saved."

They said goodnight, and she wandered into Krista's room and sat on her bed. "So you had a good day," Krista said. Her suitcase was packed because her plane was leaving early the next morning.

"Yes, I did," Francie said.

"And Frank is quite a catch."

It took Francie a moment to understand what Krista was implying.

"What? Oh, no, it isn't like that," Francie said, shocked. "Seriously, Krista, we're just friends."

"Just friends? The way he swung you around in his arms today, and you hugged him back? The way you two are always making eye contact, reading each other like books? You even finish each other's sentences!"

Francie thought about that. "He's my best friend," she said.

"And?"

"And nothing. It's platonic. It's perfect just the way it is."

"Ahhh," Krista said. "You don't want to ruin what you have."

Francie frowned. "I'm done with this discussion. I'm going to bed." She got up to leave.

"Francie?"

She stopped and turned.

"I'm sorry. I didn't mean to press. Come here."

Francie walked back to her sister and the two hugged. She buried her face into Krista's hair.

"I love you," Francie said.

Krista hugged her harder. "I love you too."

She held Francie back and looked her in the eyes. "I know life hasn't been easy for you, but I think today your luck changed," Krista said. "I think this is the beginning of your life."

Francie smiled.

chapter 22

THEY PARTED WAYS AT DIFFERENT GATES the next morning. Krista was on her way to New York and Jim to California.

Jim got off the plane in LA with his carry-on. He made a couple of calls at a pay phone and then hailed a taxi. He had the driver stop at the bank, where he cashed his paycheck. He drew some additional cash out of his account and divided it, putting some in one envelope and making out a cashier's check for the rest.

"For my ex," he said to the teller. The man rolled his eyes knowingly, but it wasn't unusual for him to see large withdrawals at this office.

Jim had paid the cab driver to wait for him and instructed him where to go next.

"Two-fifty-two Walker," he said. The house was nestled in a subdivision in LA, about a twenty-minute drive from where they were. The place was small but neat, and in a safe neighborhood. He was taking good care of her.

The cabbie pulled into the driveway.

"Want me to wait?"

"Yeah. This shouldn't take long."

Jim knocked on the blue front door, noticing the daisies and gladiolas carefully planted on either side of the porch steps.

Elise opened the door. The sight of her, as always, took his breath away. She was leanly built, small, with delicate, angular features, but the pregnancy had rounded her out. Her face had a fullness, a flowing roundness to it, and her breasts were larger. Below them protruded her belly, about seven months pregnant.

Her gray eyes met his, and her dark, curly hair fell around her face, escaping from an up-do of some sort. She was wearing a simple turquoise sundress.

"Come in," she said.

He followed her to the kitchen, a place that held a world of memories: having coffee and making pancakes on their better days together; smashing a glass, yelling, on their worst.

On the counter was a manila envelope. She slid it over to him.

He pulled out the divorce papers.

"You can read them if you want—" she began.

"No need," he said. He flipped to the last page and signed where required.

Then he looked at her one last time.

"It's a girl," she said.

He said nothing, just pulled out the envelope with the cashier's check and handed it to her.

"Jim... " Her hand reached toward him. He stepped back.

"I won't bother you again," he said. He went outside and got in the cab, fighting back the tears that were already blinding him.

"Go," he said to the cab driver.

"Where to?"

"Anywhere. Just go."

The cabbie backed out of the driveway and started heading back the way they had come. He glanced in his rearview mirror.

"The only thing I know that can get to a man like that is a dame," he said.

Jim smiled. "My ex. Or at least she's my ex now. I just signed the divorce papers."

"I'm sorry, man," he said.

"It's my own fault," Jim said. He sighed and rubbed his eyes. "I knocked her up and then cheated on her."

"Wow."

"Yeah."

They rode in silence for a bit. Finally, Jim said, "643 Maxim Street is where I need to go next."

"Okay."

Jim continued. "Only once though. I only cheated on her once, and I didn't mean to. We were at a party, and she wanted to go home, and I wanted to drink. Finally, she asked a girlfriend to drive her home. I stayed at the party and was drunk and woke up the next morning in bed with a blond. I don't remember a thing. If a guy's gonna cheat, you'd think he'd at least remember it."

"Maybe you didn't."

"I'm pretty sure I did. Anyway, she probably could have forgiven that. But I haven't slept well since Nam and drinking helped, only it made me mean. And I couldn't hold down a steady job for more than a year, it seemed. Well, I quit drinking, and I've finally turned my life around, and I'm trying to quit smoking. I found a good job in a factory. But Elise deserves better than me. So does our baby."

"Maybe Elise should get to decide that, if you don't mind my saying."

"She did. I just happen to agree."

They talked about other things then; the weather, sports, and then finally fell into silence.

They arrived at Jim's destination, a shady part of town. The cabbie pulled up at a bar and let him off.

"You don't look like the kind of man to hang out in a place like this," he said.

"Just meeting some friends. I'll be fine."

"Good luck with everything."

"Thanks, man." Jim paid the fare and added a large tip.

The inside of the bar was dark and smoky. He sat in a booth in the back corner and ordered a burger. It was 2 p.m., and he hadn't eaten all day except for the granola bar Francie insisted he take with him when he refused to let her fix him breakfast.

He finished eating and was sopping up ketchup with the last fry when a man sat down across from him.

"You got it?" Jim asked.

In answer, the man produced a thick manila envelope and slid it across the table. Jim opened the clasp and peeked inside. Satisfied, he pulled out the envelope he had full of cash and slid it across to the man. The man peeked inside, discreetly counted, then grunted.

"Nice doin' business with ya," he said. "You know where to reach me." He slipped out of the booth and disappeared into the darkness of the bar.

Jim stuck the manila envelope in his backpack and got up. He called a cab, and then left the bar.

This time, he instructed the cab driver to take him to the federal prison.

Jim walked through the heavy metal doors, which slid shut behind him with a clang of finality. The guard escorting him punched a code in and the next set of doors opened briefly to let him through, then shut and locked.

He was walking deeper into a steel cage, one layer at a time. His first few visits here had given him anxiety and an overwhelming feeling of claustrophobia, but he had grown used to it, and he, at least, could leave whenever he wanted.

When he came to the visiting area, the two escorting guards left him. The guard sitting at the check-in desk nodded. Jim was a frequent visitor, the only one besides the prisoner's mom, who came to see him.

Jim pulled out the manila envelope, the one the man in the booth had given him. He had carried it in with no problem, as usual, even past all the security. They were looking for metal: guns, knives, things like that. Not envelopes. Plus, it helped that he slipped the front guard a $100 each time. At the check-in desk, he slid the envelope to the guard casually, and then signed in. The guard took it, put in his top desk drawer, and motioned Jim through.

He sat in the visiting area, too brightly lit with fluorescent lights. The metal chair was uncomfortable, as was the stark metal table in front of him, on which he set a small box.

They brought the prisoner in, and he smiled when he saw Jim. He sat across from him.

"Hey, Paul," Jim said.

"Hey, yourself," he said. Paul looked at the box sitting on the table. "Cookies?"

"From my sister," Jim said. "Francie heard I was coming to visit you and made me bring them."

"Ahh... and here I thought you baked them yourself," he joked.

"Nope."

"That woman's a saint."

"She barely knows your name. It's me she loves." Jim pushed the box toward him. "So how are things?"

Paul leaned back in his chair, aware that the guards were listening to every word they said. "Things have gotten remarkably better, and I've finally made some friends."

"Glad to hear that."

Paul leaned forward, clasping his hands in front of him on the table. He lowered his voice so the guards wouldn't hear him. "I thought it was my charming personality," he said, "but I'm suspecting it's not, since most of those guys don't like someone who's in for treason against his own country." His gray eyes met Jim's and held his gaze, questioning.

"I wouldn't know anything about that," Jim said, lowering his own eyes.

"Yeah, I bet you don't," Paul said.

Neither man said anything for a minute.

"Your life came at high price, bro," Paul said. "Don't waste it. Enjoy it. Live it. You don't owe me anything, so quit throwing your money away."

"I'm not throwing it away. I'm investing it."

"There are no dividends." They were both silent for a moment. "I assume you heard they're giving me the electric chair?"

"You'll appeal."

"I have."

"I'll get you out. I won't stop until I get you out."

Paul laughed. "I'll fry," he said. "Not a thing you can do about it. But I do appreciate the comfort level being raised a few bars while I'm here. It's nice to have friends."

Jim smiled.

"Go home. Go back to Elise and make things right. I know you love her."

"It's too late."

"Man, if I was in your shoes, I wouldn't be sitting here. I'd be back at her place loving her with everything I've got and treating her like the queen she is."

"You're forgetting she threw me out."

"That's because your priorities are mixed up."

"Time's up!" the guard shouted.

Paul's eyes clouded. He peeked in the box. "Mmmm. Oatmeal raisin."

"They're from a box mix. She can't bake," Jim said.

"Good enough," he said. He closed the top and stood up just before the guard roughly grabbed his arm.

He turned back to Jim and held the box up.

"Jim? Thanks. For everything."

Jim nodded and watched as they led his best friend through the doors and back into the prison, the metal doors swallowing him up. Jim was left with a cold, empty feeling in the pit of his stomach and a numb bottom from the hard chair.

part two

chapter
23

KENTUCKY DERBY DAY WAS PERFECT. The weather was 75 degrees with no humidity. The track was fast. Twenty-three horses were entered in America's most exciting race, but there was only one of them everybody was talking about.

Starfire's Image.

The spitting image of his sire, Flaming Star, Starfire had been beating everything he ran against since his two-year-old year.

"Maybe we'll finally have a Triple Crown winner," were the whispers around the racing world. "If anyone can do it, that colt can."

But more exciting than the prospect of a colt capturing America's three jeweled races in seven weeks, was the team that raced him. They were all women.

His young trainer, Francie Dalton, was a very sought-after hire—the best owners were vying for her to saddle their horses. And riding Starfire's Image was her sixteen-year-old sister, Sam.

"We're finally here, Sam," Francie said. "Let's go get 'em."

Sam was wearing the gold and green silks of Sunnyhill Farm. Francie was dressed up in beige slacks, a cream top, and of course, a big Derby hat.

As always, Frank was by her side, looking handsome in his new suit.

"Rider's up!" came the call.

Francie gave Sam a let up onto the horse and then went into the stands to watch from her private box. She glanced at the chair where Mr. Richards had sat just two years ago, before he'd had a stroke and died suddenly one quiet Sunday morning while he was getting ready for church.

"You'll have your own horse here soon," he said. And sure enough, today she did. Although she had picked up enough work to provide for them quite well after the match race, his gift of Flame and some breeding stock had set her up financially for life. The first thing she had done with the money was build a fence around her property, with surveillance cameras. Then she had hired security and built a gatehouse at the entrance to the farm. There was only one way in and out of Sunnyhill, and Francie approved it all.

"Mom will never get in here again to take my horses," she said. "Now, anything or anyone inside of Sunnyhill is safe. Finally."

Frank had merely raised an eyebrow or two. She was happy, so he let her be. Outsiders simply thought she was protecting her breeding stock. Many farms had security because the horses were worth millions. But it was more than that she was protecting.

The band played "My Old Kentucky Home" and her eyes grew teary. She and Frank and Becky sang along, Becky's small voice piping up loudly. She was seven now, and cute, but quite a handful. She was an angel with Frank but liked to challenge her mom. She grasped Francie's hand now, and Francie smiled down at her and gave it a little squeeze. On the other side of Becky was Krista, gorgeous as ever, and wearing a very stylish hat. She had flown in for the Derby and got more press attention than even Francie.

Krista was a supermodel now, her face on the cover of magazines, billboards, and make-up packages everywhere. She was the face of Glamour Girl, and everyone knew her. She frequented talk shows and morning shows and was asked to be a special guest on various programs, including *Friday Night Live.* She had even had a few small cameos in television shows.

The other talk about town was another young jockey, Steven Cadrell. His mount for the race was a long shot, but his age had gotten him some attention. He, too, was only sixteen.

Down on the track, the horses were loaded in the gate. He glanced over at Sam. "You're the best-looking jockey I've seen," he said and winked. "Want to have dinner with me tonight?"

Sam smiled coyly. "You've gotta catch me first."

The bell rang and the gates burst open.

Image surged forward, and Sam moved him quickly toward the rail, smoothly transferring from the twelfth pole position to third on the rail. Steve, on Keep In Step, followed her, but his horse didn't break from the gate as fast, so he was behind her, in fifth, and two horses out from the rail. If he wasn't careful, he'd be trapped, but it was too early in the race to worry about that.

Image's ears were swiveling back and forth—forward, then back, awaiting a signal from Sam, asking to run. *Is it time? Is it time yet?*

"Not yet," she murmured, counting in her head. The pace was fast. If she hung in at third, he might tire.

The leader was a speed horse, known for setting a fast pace and then burning himself out. He might do well in the shorter Preakness in two weeks, but Sam doubted he could maintain this pace for the Derby's mile and a quarter.

She had two choices: stay the pace and hope for the best, or go around them, become the front runner, and set the pace herself. Pulling back wasn't an option, not with the half-mile pole coming up.

Up in the stands, Francie had an iron grip on her binoculars, and her other hand was digging into Frank's bicep.

"Oh, Sam, hang in there," she said.

Frank glanced at the clock on the board as they swept past the half mile pole.

"It's a fast pace," he said. "The front-runner should burn out."

"As long as the horses in the back don't have a lot of kick left, we might be okay," she said.

Francie saw the long shot, Keep in Step, was a half-length behind Image, living up to his name. He was keeping in step with her horse, shadowing him.

"Look at number 11," she said.

"Mmmmm," Frank agreed.

Down on the track, they rounded the three-quarter mark. The two front runners began to tire. As they dropped back, Sam moved Image around them to take the rail. She glanced under her elbow to make sure it was all clear, but there was Keep In Step, shadowing her.

"Darn him!" she thought. She was two off the rail, but she had the lead. Pushing from behind were three horses that had a little more left. They were soon breathing down her neck.

Image pinned his ears back as he sensed the challenge. He pulled on the bit.

Now?

"Not yet," Sam said. She gave him a notch to keep ahead of the others but didn't let him go. He fought her a little, wanting to run, asking to be let out. She realized she had a lot of horse left, and they had just rounded the final turn, coming into the homestretch.

"Now!" she said and let him go. He exploded under her, and the power of his haunches pushing him forward nearly threw her up on his neck. He left the three challengers in the dust, and his strides quickly ate up the track, putting space between himself and the rest of the field.

Except for Keep in Step.

"Dang!" Sam said, glancing to her left. The bay colt was only a half-stride behind them.

She nudged Image on, and he responded. Slowly, very slowly, he inched ahead of Keep In Step—half-stride, three-quarters of a stride—but the colt hung on, refusing to be shaken.

The crowd was all on their feet, cheering at the unexpected match between the favorite and the long shot. Either way, it would be an exciting finish. Both were young jockeys in their first year of riding. One was a long shot. The other was a girl.

The two colts sailed along the last strip of track, flaming red against dark copper. Neither jockey raised a whip. Both colts were running for all they had.

Sam's hands urged Image on, and he didn't let her down. He held his spot, ears pinned back, refusing to give Keep in Step any ground. When they sailed under the wire, they were only a half-length apart. Keep in Step's nose was even with Sam's boot.

The crowd, already pumped up, went wild. Around the nation, news reporters were already talking about how a female jockey had won the Kentucky Derby for the first time, on a horse trained by a female trainer. It was unprecedented.

"If only the horse had been a filly," many joked.

Up in the stands, Francie finally let go of her crushing grip on Frank's arm and threw her arms around him instead. "We did it!" she screamed. She was laughing and crying at the same time. Frank held her, laughing and shouting back over the crowd, thankful his sunglasses hid the tears in his own eyes.

Then Francie hugged Krista, Becky, Jim, and a few strangers before Frank said. "You'd better get down there and accept your trophy."

"Come on!" she said.

She ran down the steps, Frank close on her heels.

On the track, Sam finally had Image down to a jog and had turned him to head back to the winner's circle. The board said 2:02, a track record, and one second slower than his daddy in the famous match race against Tried and True.

Steve jogged up beside her on Keep in Step. Both horses were lathered, their nostrils still flaring from their recent effort. Image laid his ears back when the other horse approached.

Sam laughed. "It's okay, boy," she said, patting his neck. "The race is over. And you beat him."

"Does that mean you won't go out to dinner with me?" Steve asked.

Sam looked over at him. "You didn't catch me," she said.

"We gave it our best shot," he said, patting his own horse.

She nodded. "You sure did. Where did that speed come from?"

"We had incentive. I told him if he won me dinner with a pretty girl, there would be an extra scoop of oats in his bucket tonight."

"Well... it worked," Sam said.

"Really?"

Just then, a reporter on horseback caught up with them and started asking Sam questions on live television.

Sam looked over at Steve.

"Our victory party, tonight at the Stalwart Hotel. 8:00 p.m. You can be my date!"

The reporter held his mic over to Sam and asked her to describe her win. She saw Steve pump his fist into the air and mouth the words "yes!" just as he was overtaken by another reporter to discuss his second-place win.

There were a lot of smiles in the winner's circle. They hung a blanket of roses across Image's neck, and Sam closed her eyes, breathing in their scent. Frank picked one off and gave it to Francie.

"Roses for the ladies!" someone said, and flashbulbs went off all around them.

A reporter held a microphone up to Francie.

"What do you think, Ms. Dalton?"

"I think this is probably the happiest moment of my life," she said. She held back the tears of joy that threatened to spill out. All those years watching the Kentucky Derby on television, and now she was *here*. A winner.

They asked her some questions and went over a replay of the race, then handed her the trophy.

"I want to dedicate this," Francie said, holding it up, "to Mr. Richards, the breeder of Image's sire, and to my grandpa, the late Joe Frasier, who passed his dreams on to me. Without those men, and a few others, I probably wouldn't be here today." She met Frank's gaze, and he acknowledged her words with a slight nod. "Thank you."

There was more talk about women in the sport, then the reporter asked, "Are you going to the Preakness? Do you think Image can capture racing's second jewel?"

"We're sure going to give it a try!" Francie said, smiling at Sam. "Now I need to get my horse back to the barn and cool him off."

Steve showed up at precisely at 8 p.m., holding a mask in front of his eyes with a stick.

"Is it a costume party?" he whispered to Sam.

"No," she said, eyeing him suspiciously. He set the mask aside, nonchalantly. "Glad I didn't go with my first costume choice," he said. "I was going to come dressed as a jockey."

Sam laughed. Instead, he wore a three-piece suit, cut in a fine black linen. He looked quite handsome, she had to admit.

His brown eyes sparkled. "Would you like to dance?" he held out a hand to her.

"Not yet!" she giggled. "There's no dancing until after the dinner!"

"With you, beautiful, every footstep feels like we're dancing."

Sam rolled her eyes.

The party was an extravagant one. There was a lot of food on a buffet with hotel staff serving and walking around, offering wine and hors d'oeuvres. The hall was decorated in green and gold, Sunnyhill's colors, and there was a band playing quiet background music.

Frank looked dashing in his tux, but Jim looked quite uncomfortable in his dress clothes and couldn't seem to figure out what to do with his hands. He was very handsome, though, with his wavy blond hair and blue eyes. Several women were checking him out.

Francie had invited their entire staff—exercise riders, grooms, everyone connected with their farm. She had also invited several racing friends. There were at least a hundred people in the room.

Francie made her entrance then, walking through the double doors at the top of the stairs. Sam heard a gasp and murmur in the room as all eyes turned to her sister. Francie had her hair pulled up in a soft knot on top of her head, with tendrils hanging down. She wore a light blue gown in a shimmering pearl.

Sam had told her she looked more beautiful than even Krista, and, like always, she had a presence about her that turned all eyes in her direction.

"Good evening everyone, and thanks for coming!" Francie said, smiling. "Most of you here have had a part in making this possible! I value every one of you. Now let's win the Preakness in two weeks!"

There was a cheer in the room. Francie held up her hand to silence them. "But tonight, let's party!"

She laughed and everybody cheered and clapped and toasted.

Francie walked over to where Frank was standing with Krista, Jim, Sam and Steve.

"You look nice," Frank told her.

"Thanks."

"Nice?" Krista said. "She looks incredible!"

Francie looked over at Steve. "So you're Sam's date?"

He inclined his head. "Pleased to meet you and honored to be in the presence of Horse Racing's first female Derby winning trainer."

Francie smiled. "I like him," she said to Sam.

"The jury is still out," Sam said.

"What?" Steve feigned shock. "And here I thought I won your heart at hello."

"You actually never said hello," Sam said. "You arrived a masked man."

Frank finished his dinner and stood up. He held his hand out to Krista. "Would you care to dance?"

Krista quickly looked at Francie, as if caught. "Ummm... "

Francie waved her hand. "Go," she said.

Frank raised an eyebrow. "I didn't know I needed her permission," he said to Krista. "I'm off the clock."

Krista laughed. "No, it's just... I just thought... shouldn't you ask Francie to dance first? It's her night."

Frank and Francie looked at each other.

"That would be awkward," Frank said. "She's my employer."

Francie smiled at him. "And it's not *my* night. It's *our* night. Go. Dance with the supermodel."

Krista laughed. "That's all I am to you, Francie, a trophy sister. I knew it."

Krista took Frank's hand and he led her to the dance floor. The band was playing a waltz and Frank surprised them all by knowing how to dance. He expertly led Krista around the dance floor.

"They look good together," Jim said.

"They do," Francie said, watching them. "My best friend and my sister."

"She *is* beautiful," Jim said. "Men will line up tonight to ask her to dance. I've seen it before."

"So have I," Francie said. "Like at school dances."

"I prefer my women shorter," Steve said.

They all three looked at him.

"I'm just say'n."

"So Steve, what are you interested in besides my little sister?" Francie asked.

"Anything fast," Steve said. "Except women. No tall, fast women."

Sam said, "Steve likes to fix up sports cars when he's not riding horses. And he jumps dirt bikes."

"An adrenaline junkie," Francie said.

"Those long legs like Krista has?" Steve continued, "Makes them fast, but also tall... "

"Sam's an artist," Francie said, eyeing him steadily. She was usually good at judging character, but she wasn't sure what to make of him. "A nice, *quiet* artist."

"And a jockey," Steve pointed out. "So, consequently, short, and, I imagine, not so fast. Unless she's on your horse." He gave a nervous little laugh. Francie frowned.

"Francie... " Sam warned.

Steve was starting to sweat.

"Easy, Francie," Jim mumbled.

"Be good to her," Francie said. Sam rolled her eyes. Steve put his hand over his heart.

"I'll treat her like the queen she is," he said.

The music changed to a slow tune. Out on the dance floor, Krista put her arms around Frank's neck and stared into his kind, brown eyes.

"It has been a good day for you," she said.

"I can't complain."

His hands were around her waist, strong and firm and warm. She could feel them through her dress. Her heart fluttered a little, and she realized what she was feeling and wondered if it was wrong. Frank had become such a part of her life over the years through her sister. Francie always talked about him during their phone calls. When Krista came to stay at the house, there were late night monopoly games and lots of laughter and teasing. She was so relaxed around him, and she felt he had always looked at her as a friend, an equal. Most men were either so uncomfortable around her because of her supermodel status that they didn't know how to act, or they wanted her and couldn't see past her sexuality.

Frank was so kind. He had done so much for Francie. Her sister finally had some security in her life.

Krista looked into his eyes again. "You're a good man, Frank," she said. "You've taken such good care of my sister."

"Your sister's tough," Frank said. "She doesn't really need anybody to take care of her."

"But she needs someone on her team," Krista said. "Thank you for that."

Frank smiled and the music changed to a faster tune. Sam and Steve came onto the dance floor.

Jim and Francie were left alone at the table.

"That doesn't bother you?" Jim said.

"What?"

He nodded toward Krista and Frank on the dance floor.

Francie frowned. "Why does everyone think Frank and I have a thing?"

"Francie, I live with you, and I can see very clearly that you and Frank have a thing."

"It's not a thing," she said. "It's... friendship. He's the best friend I've ever had. Ever. That's it."

"Really?"

"Jim, he's ten years older than me. My first love got killed on his motorcycle, and my next love left me. I don't have a very good track record, so I prefer to keep things the way they are. They're perfect."

"Okay. So dance with me, your lonely bro."

"I don't dance."

Two women asked if they could join them and introduced themselves to Jim. Francie knew them as the daughters of another horse owner. They were attractive. Francie got up and left Jim to enjoy the flirting.

She felt restless and irritated with Jim. She glanced over at him, and he was already dancing with one of the young women. She smiled ruefully. Always the ladies' man. He was, no doubt, regaling her with stories of his days as a rock band guitarist.

Francie walked out onto the balcony, just off from their hall. It overlooked Louisville, and the city was alive with light. Traffic was still heavy, and she could see the restaurants were still full. She thought of Image and longed to be back at the barn, in the quiet. In a place she belonged.

"Hey."

Frank's voice startled her.

"Oh, hi," she said. "You're done dancing?"

"They picked up the pace. I needed a breather."

He came and stood beside her and looked out over the view. "The city's still celebrating your win," he said.

"Mmmm."

"Where were you just now when I walked up? I startled you."

"Back at the barn with Image."

Frank smiled. "You still prefer the company of horses to people."

"*Most* people," she agreed. They were silent for a few moments.

"I'm proud of you," he said gently.

Francie turned to look at him. "You helped. We're a team."

"We made it," he said. He put his arm around her shoulder and pulled her into a sideways hug. "Six years ago, we were dirt poor. Now we're millionaires with a Triple Crown contender. Or, rather, *you* are. I'm just along for the ride."

"Stop!" she said, laughing. "We're a team. I wouldn't be here if it wasn't for your support, your loan—"

"—which you paid back."

"But I will never forget it. Sunnyhill is your home."

"It would be better if you were there more," Frank said quietly.

"I know." She had been traveling a lot over the past several years, following her horses around to tracks all over the country.

She knew she wasn't the mother she should be, and she had wanted so much to be a better mother than her own. She wasn't cruel or mean, and she made sure Becky knew she loved her. She told her, she hugged her, and she cuddled her as often as she could. But she was hardly home. The racing circuit took her away a lot. She missed school field trips, plays, and dance recitals. She wasn't around when Becky lost her first tooth and got her first dollar from the tooth fairy. She had been in New York when Becky fell off a swing and fractured her wrist. It was Frank who took her to the ER. It was also Frank who had nursed Becky through a bout with the flu last fall and through other countless colds. Francie was always "there" on the other end of the phone line. She even read Becky stories over the phone.

But it wasn't the same as holding her in her arms, and they both knew it. Now she would go from Kentucky to Maryland for the Preakness, then hopefully up to New York for the Belmont. That was five more weeks away from home.

Sam joined them on the balcony, out of breath and laughing.

"That is the man I'm going to marry," she announced.

"Wow," Francie said. "Must have been quite a first date."

"He makes me laugh."

"Where is he?" Frank asked.

"Getting us something to drink. He invited himself to our Preakness party, assuming we have one, but I told him he'll have to earn it and catch me first."

"Don't give him too much incentive," Francie said. "He almost caught us this time."

They swept the Triple Crown.

Steve almost caught them in the shorter 1 1/16-mile Preakness aboard Keep in Step, but they beat him soundly in the 1 1/2 mile Belmont. Keep in Step finished fifth, a disappointing ending and 25 lengths behind Image, who raced home ten lengths ahead of the second-place finisher and set a new race record. Sam let Steve take her to the Belmont Party anyway.

The two "kids," as the press called them, were a pair now and hung out together in most of their spare time.

Francie finally returned home for a rest.

One night, while she sat in her office with Frank, they talked about how many horses they had.

"Rounding them up is a problem," Frank said. "We need a cow pony."

They had kept up the habit of meeting together every night in Francie's office after the kids were in bed—a thing they'd started when Becky was just an infant. They called it work, but really it was just catching up on their day.

Francie, who was sitting behind her desk, raised an eyebrow. "But we don't have any cows."

Frank, in his usual spot on the leather couch, to her left, propped his feet up on the chair across from her desk and ignored her comment.

"I found a Quarter Horse ranch close by. They have great reining horses for sale."

"Quarter Horses? An inferior breed."

"Not for herding cattle. Or horses."

"You can use your feet to herd our horses. Just walk out into the pasture and get them."

"It's not as much fun," Frank said. "And it's a lot of work. You have big pastures."

Francie looked at him for a minute. He stared back.

"*Seriously?* You want a cow pony?"

"Have I ever asked you for anything before?" Frank said, giving her puppy dog eyes.

Francie snorted.

Frank took a long sip of his iced tea to try to hide his smile.

"Okay. Tomorrow let's go see these cow ponies," Francie said.

Frank grinned. "Thanks, Boss."

Francie wadded up a piece of paper and threw it at him.

chapter 24

H ER NAME WAS JOEY, and she was a plucky little mare with beautiful confirmation that the gray-haired man led out for them to see. But she wasn't what caught Francie's eye first. It was the cowboy who walked over and leaned against the red pick-up parked by the barn.

"Howdy, ma'am." He tipped his ten-gallon hat. Beneath its rim, his blue eyes sparkled. He had a neatly trimmed moustache, which was either dark brown or black. His tall, muscular body was draped in a tan-colored duster, which fell down the length of his tight jeans to his dusty, black leather boots.

"H-hi," Francie stammered.

"This, here, is Ken, my son and top horse trainer," said Ron "Dusty" Moses, who had brought out the black mare for them.

"I'm... um... Francie Dalton."

Ken nodded, his eyes never leaving Francie's. There was a moment of silence.

Frank cleared his throat.

"Oh, this is Frank Weaver," Francie said, pointing to Frank. "He's just my farm manager. He works for me. We, uh, we work together."

Frank looked at Francie. She blushed.

"So Joey, here…" Dusty began to talk about the horse. Eventually, Frank got on and rode her. Francie kept glancing at the cowboy, who had not taken his eyes off of her, and then blushed and looked away. He seemed to be utterly relaxed and enjoying himself. She was so distracted that she missed most of what Dusty and Frank said, but she produced a checkbook when asked to and wrote out a check.

When the transaction was done, Ken straightened up and walked toward Francie. He had a bit of a swagger to his step, which made his duster sway.

He stopped in front of Francie.

"May I take you to dinner?" he asked.

"Yes," she said a bit too quickly.

"Tonight? 7 p.m.?"

"Yes."

Dusty got their address and promised to deliver Joey the next day.

Francie and Frank got in the truck and drove off.

"We bought a horse," Francie said.

"You sure about that?" Frank asked. "You seemed a bit distracted."

"I'm an idiot." She put her head in her hands.

"Just my *farm manager?* We *work* together?" he teased.

"I'm sorry."

"Francie, he's a *cowboy.*"

She sighed and looked dreamily out her window. "I know."

Frank chuckled, and they drove the rest of the short way home in silence.

Their first date went well. Ken turned out to be nearly perfect. He was smart, sweet, handsome, sexy, and he had the same love for horses that she did, even if (she teased), his Quarter Horses were an inferior breed of horse to her mighty Thoroughbreds. Ken also had a good head for business and ran his own farm well.

"You're smiling again," Jim said. He was sitting with her at the kitchen table, having lunch.

"He's perfect," Francie said. "Life is perfect."

"It's pretty close," he said, taking a bite of his soup.

She looked over at her brother who had changed so much in the past six years. He was covered in dirt now from the yardwork he had been doing all morning. He worked hard as her lawn and outdoor maintenance man and hadn't been high or drunk since that day he had shown up on her doorstep asking for help.

It had been a hot day—blistering hot. She had been in her office, working on some documents and avoiding the heat. "Your brother's here," her guard had said into the intercom.

"Mark?" Francie's heart skipped a beat. She was always a little unsure of him.

"No. Jim."

"Oh," Francie said, a bit of concern replacing her tension. "Let him in." The last she had known, he had been in California. It wasn't like Jim to just show up.

She put her computer screen to sleep and put the papers in a folder. Then she went downstairs to greet him.

He was standing on the porch, wearing a t-shirt that looked too big on him. She realized suddenly that it wasn't the shirt—it was *him*. He has lost a lot of weight.

"Hi," he said quietly. She wasn't able to see his eyes behind the dark sunglasses.

"Hi," she said. "I thought you were in California."

"I was." He had a duffle bag with him and a guitar was slung over his shoulder. His baggy jeans looked like they needed a wash. "I... uh... " He cleared his throat.

"Come in," she said. The sun was hot.

Jim just stood there. "I need a place to stay." He adjusted the pack's strap on his shoulder, pulling it up higher and lifting some of the weight off his back. His hand was trembling.

"You're high," she said.

"Francie, this is the last time. I promise." He took off the sunglasses, squinting at her in the light. His lids were low, his eyes bloodshot. "The factory had too many drugs available. I figured if I could be around family, around you... I need somebody to keep me accountable."

She searched his eyes. "Why?"

"Why?" He was struggling with the duffle bag. The sun was beating down on him, and he was sweating. "Because I have a new reason to live. I need to get better, and I can't do it alone."

She opened the door wider. "Come in," she said again. "Of course you can stay. Let's get your room set up."

He had been sober ever since.

Although he was still quiet and never seemed to have any money, he seemed happy. He flew to California about every other month to visit his best friend Paul, the soldier who had saved his life in Vietnam and was now in prison. Francie had never met the man, but often sent a box of cookies. She knew he meant a lot to Jim, and Jim meant a lot to her, so she helped where she could.

This last year had sped by in a blur. Francie's horses placed well, and Image won Horse of the Year at the prestigious Eclipse Awards. When Francie was home, she and Frank continued to meet in her office and go over their day, and they worked countless hours together. Frank was still filling all his roles in and around the house with the kids.

Francie floated through the year in love, buoyed by Frank's constant supportive presence and Ken's lavish attention. Ken bought her trinkets and flowers, but what she loved most was the way he'd tip his hat and wink at her when he was entering or leaving a room. He was flat out the sexiest man she had ever met, and he was kind to her. It helped that he had a wonderful Texas accent.

When Sam turned eighteen, she announced her engagement to Steve. They had both been at Churchill Downs, the track where they had first met, riding against each other in a small claiming race, when he proposed. Steve was in post position four, Sam in five. While in the starting gate waiting for the last horse to load, Steve looked over at Sam and popped the question.

"Will you marry me?"

Sam smiled from ear to ear, but said, "You've gotta catch me first," and the race was on. Steve not only caught her but beat her by two lengths. On his way back to the winner's circle, he trotted his horse up beside her and put the ring on her finger. A reporter caught it on camera, and it was soon national news.

"You're too young," Frank said when he heard the news. Francie was sitting at the kitchen table with him and Sam.

"Frank, we've been dating for two years!"

"Sam, you just graduated," Frank said. "Give it a year. If you're still together when you're 19, I'll walk you down the aisle myself."

Sam's face lit up. "You will? How'd you know I was going to ask you?"

"You were?" Frank's face folded into a smile. His warm eyes twinkled.

"Of course! Who else would I ask?" Sam turned to Francie. "I want you to be my maid of honor."

Francie smiled, then sighed.

"What's wrong?" Sam asked.

"Honey, he's not your faith," Francie said.

"He's not any faith," Sam said. "He's an atheist."

"That doesn't bother you?"

"No, Francie, it doesn't. Heck, not too long ago, *you* hated God. And church."

"I know."

"Francie, I'm not abandoning my faith. I love God. I have a special relationship with Jesus. He's in my heart. Nothing is going to change that. The Bible says that no one can take that away from me, and Steve would never even try."

"The Bible also says don't be unequally yoked," Frank said quietly.

Sam sighed. "I know. But he's so good to me."

They were all in agreement with that.

"Give it a year," said Frank. "One year."

Sam was quiet for a while. Finally, she said. "Okay. We haven't set a date yet, and that will give us time to plan."

"You have to book a photographer a year in advance anyway, I hear," said Francie.

When Sam told Steve later that evening, he said, "They hate me."

"No."

"They think I'm going to Hell."

"Well... maybe. But they love you so much that they want to save your soul."

He laughed. "And you?"

"I'd like to save your soul too, but maybe later. Right now I'm more interested in your body," and she leaned in for a kiss.

chapter 25

IT WAS A RAINY NOVEMBER DAY, and Francie was sitting in her office doing paperwork when she got a call from her security man out front.

"There's a man named Tom Cutter here to see you."

Francie froze.

"Ma'am?" came the voice over the phone.

Francie collected herself. "What does he want?"

There was a pause. Then, "To talk to you."

Becky was at a friend's house. Frank and Jim were working in the barn. Sam was upstairs painting.

"Send him in," she said, wishing Frank were there.

She went downstairs and stood at the kitchen window and watched him drive up to the long driveway. He parked his car—a nice, tan sedan—and climbed out. He looked around and ran his hand over his head, smoothing his hair down. It has grown thinner, she noticed. Then he walked through the rain toward the house. He hadn't changed much since she'd last seen him eight years ago when she signed the divorce papers.

Francie met him at the door.

"What do you want?" she said.

"Hi," he said. "May I come in?"

The rain was pelting off his coat, and his hair was now plastered against his scalp. Francie stepped back and let him enter.

He stood there, dripping, in her mud room.

"How are you?" he asked gently. "Well, I mean, I guess you're doing okay. I've seen you on television, on the news, and on the cover of *Sports Illustrated*." He smiled. "I'm happy for you."

"Thank you," she said. "What do you want?"

"I got married," he said. "She's wonderful. A nurse. We're happy."

Francie crossed her arms. Just then the door opened, bumping Tom, as Frank and Jim came in shaking water off their hats. When Frank saw Tom he stopped so fast that Jim ran into him.

Jim moaned. "Ouch. What the... oh."

Frank looked at Francie, then closed the door and sat down on a bench in the room to take his boots off. Jim did the same, then disappeared into the kitchen. Frank folded his arms across his chest and leaned back to listen.

"I'm happy that you're happy," Francie said coldly. "Now, for the third time, what do you want?"

Tom nervously glanced at Frank, then back to Francie. "Can we talk in private?"

"No," Francie and Frank said at the same time.

Tom frowned at Frank. "I don't know who you think you are... "

Frank interrupted him. "The last time I saw you, you took a swing at her," he said. "I'm not going anywhere unless she asks me to."

Tom looked hopefully at Francie.

"He stays," she said, arms still crossed.

"Fine," Tom said. "I want to see Becky."

"No," Francie said.

"She's my daughter."

"Who you haven't seen in eight years."

"I want to start. I want to be a father to her. I know I screwed up, but Jolie—my wife—has made me realize how important family is. You see, she can't have kids—"

"So she wants mine?"

"No, no. It's not like that," he stopped, realizing his mistake. "I want Becky in my life. I realize we'll have to start slow. I'll do supervised visits with her until she gets to know me, then maybe she can come and spend a week or two with me in Michigan."

"No," Francie said. "I'm not going to let you interfere now. We're happy. Just leave us alone."

"She's *our* daughter, Francie. Not just *yours*."

"Get out," Francie said.

"I'm not leaving until I get to see Becky," he said. "I came all the way from Michigan."

"You should have called first."

"Francie, please—"

"No." She looked at Frank. He stood up.

"Now isn't a good time to discuss this," Frank said. "Why don't you go?"

Tom turned. "Who do you think you are, taking over my family?"

"You *left* your family!" Francie shouted.

"Because you were *crazy!*" he shouted back.

"Get out!" Francie yelled.

"I didn't want this to be hard, Francie. But I'll fight you on this. I will. All I wanted was visitation, but now I'm going after full custody!"

"I can afford better lawyers!"

"All right," Frank said and put an arm around her shoulder. "Enough."

"Maybe," continued Tom, "but what judge is going to let you keep her? I have a stable home. You're living with a man you aren't even married to. Your brother's a drug addict and you are never home!"

Tom jabbed his finger at her, then stormed out to his car, slammed the door, and drove off.

Francie turned to Frank and buried her face in his chest. He pulled her close. "It's okay," he said.

"Is it?"

He held her. "I hope so."

Frank continued to hold her, saying nothing. Eventually, her breathing slowed down, and he felt her relax.

Very gently, he said, "You were a little harsh with him. He just wanted to talk."

"I know," she said, her voice muffled in his damp shirt. "It's just... I'm scared," she whispered.

"I know you are."

"Most of what he said is true. About me."

"We're not living together."

She pulled away from him and looked up into his eyes.

"Frank, he's going to come after me, just like Mom did."

She ran her hands through her hair and started pacing. "What are we going to do?"

"You have a strong team of lawyers," Frank said. "You're not going to lose her. But it might not hurt to let them meet."

"If he wants to try to be a father to her, you should give him a chance," Jim said. He was standing in the doorway of the kitchen. "Francie, I know you've been hurt by people who are supposed to love you, but everyone deserves a second chance, don't you think?"

She raised an eyebrow. "Really?"

He laughed. "Dad had his second chance with me. And his third." He grew serious. "I just know a little of what Tom may be feeling."

They were both staring at him now.

"It's not just Paul I visit when I go to California. I have a daughter. Her name is Lily. She's mine and Elise's."

He let that sink in for a minute. Francie's mind was working through several emotions. Finally, she said, "You mean I'm an aunt?"

He smiled. "Yes. She's six and a half years old." He came onto the back porch and sat down on one of the benches. Frank and Francie sat down on the other, across from him.

"You see, Francie, I loved Elise more than anyone I've ever met. She and I had a good thing, and I blew it. I even married her. Yes. I was married. But I couldn't quit using and when she was five months pregnant, I got drunk at a party and cheated on her. She kicked me out, rightfully so, and divorced me. But then I went back and asked to be a part of Lily's life. She was about 26 months old then, and although I had promised to stay out of Elise's life, I couldn't get Lily off my mind. Elise let me."

"That's why you quit drinking," Francie said.

"And smoking," Jim said. "And got a steady job, thanks to you. That's why I came to you for help. I cleaned up my act for Lily."

They sat there in silence for a while, absorbing everything that had just happened.

Francie looked at Frank. "What do you think?"

"About Tom? I think you should give him a chance to at least meet her," Frank said. "Becky has asked about him a lot. You know she's curious. He's not a bad guy, Francie. He just couldn't handle farm life. Things were hard then. You were both so young."

Francie reached over and patted Frank on the knee. Then she got up and gave Jim a hug. "I'm so proud of you," she whispered. "I'll go call up front and see if they got the license plate on the car he was driving. I don't know how else to get hold of Tom."

chapter
26

THE DAY OF THE WEDDING WAS SUNNY. Francie was maid-of-honor, and Krista and Becky were bridesmaids. Sam wore a simple white gown with a beautiful, lacey train. Frank walked her down the aisle and gave her away. Their parents weren't invited.

On Steve's side was his younger brother Kerry, who was Becky's age, and Jim. Steve's parents were wonderful, fun people, who beamed during the whole ceremony.

The reception, planned by Steve, was extravagant. The hall was filled with white vases of pink roses and the cake was four tiers tall. A live band provided music throughout the sit-down dinner, until the dancing started, at which time a DJ took over.

"You have to have the original albums," Steve said. "You can't dance to "Celebration" played by a *band*. Kool and the Gang has to be singing it."

It looked like a fairytale setting for a princess. It seemed extravagant for Sam, who was so tiny and shy, but Steve showered her with attention and claimed he wanted the world to know she was the woman he loved.

Around 11 p.m., feeling full and sleepy, Francie was dancing with her head on Ken's shoulder, her eyes closed. She felt so content, so *right*, wrapped in his arms, and a small smile touched her lips. Life was perfect.

After the song ended, Ken took her hand in his.

"Let's go outside," he whispered to her. She reluctantly lifted her head off his shoulder and let him lead her across the dance floor to the open balcony. They stepped outside.

The night air was cool and felt good on her warm skin. The balcony was deserted. Tiny white lights wrapped around the railing. The effect was magical.

Ken turned Francie to face him. She could see the table behind him, far inside the room. Frank and Krista were sitting close, talking and laughing. Frank reached out and touched Krista's face, gently caressing her cheek. Francie saw Sam glide by, looking like a fairy princess in her dress. The music carried outside to where they were, but the voices didn't, adding to the ambience. Francie turned her attention to Ken, who was looking at her intently. He was dressed in a dark navy suit and looked dashing. He took both her hands in his, then got down on one knee.

Francie suddenly realized what he was doing. *Oh, dear God.* How had she not seen this coming? Her heart started to pound.

"Francie," Ken said smoothly, a twinkle in his eye. "I love you, darlin', and I want to spend the rest of my life making you happy." Then came the lopsided grin that stole her heart every time. "Will you marry me?"

She looked into his blue eyes, full of love, and knew this man could make her happy. She glimpsed a future that just might be normal. Happy *and* normal. She stammered, then her eyes traveled up, behind him, and she saw Frank far across the room, reach over and take Krista's hand in his. Tears filled her eyes, and the room began to rock. She met Ken's eyes and locked on, trying to steady her world. But the room spun, and she collapsed. The last thing she saw before she lost consciousness was Ken reaching up to break her fall.

When she woke up, Ken, Frank, and Krista were all looking down at her.

"What happened?" Krista asked.

"I think she hyperventilated," Ken said. "Honey?" Ken was cradling her in his arms, his eyes full of concern.

Frank had his hand on her wrist and was checking her pulse. "Francie, can you sit up?"

"Easy," Ken said. Very gently, he helped her up into a sitting position.

"Are you dizzy?" Frank asked.

Francie shook her head no.

"Krista, get her some juice. Don't tell Sam. I don't want to worry her," Frank said.

"I think we should call an ambulance," Krista said.

"Me too," Ken said. "Or at least let me take her in somewhere."

"I'm fine," Francie said. "You guys are all talking about me like I'm not even here."

"Are you okay?" Frank asked.

Francie nodded as Ken helped her to her feet and over to a chair on the balcony.

"Your blood sugar?" Frank asked.

"Probably," she said.

"How do you know it's blood sugar?" Krista asked. "She fainted dead cold. I saw her drop from where we were sitting. If Ken hadn't caught her—"

"Krista, get me some juice," Francie interrupted.

Frank met Francie's eyes but spoke to Krista.

"This has happened before," he said. "Once at the track a few months ago. Once last year, washing dishes in the kitchen. I took her to the doctor. It's blood sugar. She needs to eat more frequently. She made me promise not to tell any of you so you wouldn't worry." He was still looking at her. The look in his eyes said, *I'm sorry for telling.*

Francie sighed and shrugged. *You're off the hook. This time.*

Krista scowled but hurried off for juice. Francie turned to Ken.

"I'm sorry," she said.

"Shhhh," he murmured. "We'll can talk later. Right now, I just want to be sure you're okay."

Ken sat beside her on the bench, his arm protectively around her shoulders. Krista brought her a glass of orange juice. She sipped it obediently.

No one said anything. After a few minutes, Steve and Sam came out. Sam was glowing with joy.

"We're off," she said, "on our honeymoon!" She squeezed Steve's arm. "Tonight, Florida. Tomorrow, Hawaii!"

Steve did a few quick hula dance steps, swinging his hips.

Sam put her arms around Frank. "Thank you for giving me away. Thank you for everything."

Frank held her, fighting back tears. "I was honored that you asked me."

They all hugged, then the DJ started playing their exit song.

"Aloha!" Steve said and swept Sam across the dance floor and out the door.

"Your eyes are a little damp, Frank," Francie said.

Frank sighed. "She just grew up a little too fast."

Francie looked back at the door, thinking the same thing.

They got home late, and Francie had already climbed into bed when Krista knocked on her door. "Francie?"

"Come in."

"You feeling better?" Krista asked, sitting on the edge of Francie's bed.

"Yeah, I just needed food."

"If you say so." Krista twirled her hair around her finger, quiet for a moment.

"Krista?"

"Yes?"

"Ken proposed to me tonight."

"When?"

"Right before I fainted."

For some reason this put both women into a fit of giggles. When they caught their breath, Krista asked, "And you said?"

"I didn't say anything. I didn't have time. I fainted."

They giggled again.

"Are you going to say yes?"

Francie sighed. "I love Ken."

"But... "

"Things are nice the way they are right now."

"Hmmmm."

"I'm afraid... "

"He's a good guy, Francie."

"I know. Maybe I'll say yes."

Krista played with her hair some more.

"Francie?"

"What?"

"Frank asked me to dinner tomorrow night."

"Oh. Where are you going? Maybe we can join you."

"It's a date."

Francie swallowed. "Oh. Well." She smiled. "Congratulations!"

Krista looked at her seriously. "Is that okay with you?"

Francie snorted. "As long as it's not on work time." She smiled more. "I don't think it'll interfere with our employee/employer relationship."

"That's not the relationship I was talking about."

Francie said, "Oh, Krista. And I'm dating Ken."

"And you just turned down his proposal," she said. "I just wanted to be sure that you and Frank—you know."

"I didn't turn down his proposal. I just didn't answer. And if Frank was interested in me, then he wouldn't be asking you. Frank and I are just fr—"

"Just friends, I know. I'm sorry I pushed." Krista got a dreamy look, still twirling her hair. "Are you sure, because... "

Francie swallowed again. The room felt a little bit like it was starting to sway again. Was she sure?

"Well... " she started.

"Because he is sooo amazing and the most perfect man I've ever met. You know, he likes me for who I *am*, not because I'm a supermodel. And we already have this great friendship as a starting point. I just think we could have something really special." Krista sighed.

"Krista... "

"Oh, honey. You must be exhausted. I'll leave and let you get some sleep."

Krista kissed her cheek and got up.

"Krista—"

Krista paused and looked back at her sister.

"It's just... just promise me you won't take him away from Sunnyhill," Francie said.

"I promise," Krista said.

Krista left, and Francie turned out the light and covered up her head.

It was decided that Sam and Steve would get the master bedroom, where their grandparents used to sleep. They moved in after their honeymoon, and Steve brought in a truckload of electronic stuff. Speakers, a top-of-the-line stereo system, and a television.

"Is all of that going to make noise?" Francie asked as he hauled the tenth box upstairs.

"Not to worry, sis," he said. "I have a plan."

Francie raised a skeptical brow. She was impressed later that week, however, when he hauled in special foam slabs that looked like drywall. Pulling all of the bedroom furniture into the middle of the room, he began to put up the wall panels.

"Sound-proofing," he said.

"Really? So I won't be able to hear the music?" Francie asked.

"Or anything else," Steve said and winked at her. Francie rolled her eyes. But she watched him for a while, then asked.

"Can you sound-proof my office?"

"Sure," said Steve. "That's easy, but as you can see, you'll lose about an inch and a half of space on each wall."

"That's okay," she said. "What about the door?"

"I bought a soundproof one. I can get you one too, with an electronic keypad if you want to lock people out and have keyless entry."

"Wow."

"Yeah. Pretty cool, huh?"

The months sped by, and the visitation between Tom and Becky were going surprisingly well. Eventually, Francie let Tom take Becky out for ice cream, just the two of them. Becky loved him, and he seemed like he genuinely loved her. Francie could see that Tom was trying. As much as she wanted to keep her daughter safe and under her care, she could see how much the girl loved her father. She started to ease up and to not watch his every move.

chapter 27

FRANCIE WAS AWAY IN NEW YORK AT A RACE, so Frank was in her office working on a stack of papers when Ken came in. He sat down across from the desk. Frank looked up.

Ken gave him a crooked grin and took his hat off, turning it in his hands.

Frank offered him an iced tea, which he refused, then went back to his work. He could tell something was on Ken's mind, but he knew he'd say it when he was ready. Ken was easy-going, never in a hurry. That was his style.

"Frank?" he finally said.

"Hmmmm?"

"Why won't Francie marry me?"

Frank put down his pen and looked up, giving Ken his full attention. He leaned back in his chair and took his time answering.

"My guess is because she's afraid," he said.

"Afraid of what?"

"Being hurt. Being left. Losing you."

"I would never hurt her."

"I believe she's so happy with you that she's afraid if she changes the situation, something will go wrong. It would hurt too much to lose you, so she's keeping you at arm's length."

Ken was quiet for a few minutes.

"I proposed to her again last weekend," he said quietly. "She said she wasn't ready. Then she told me not to give up on her."

"Are you ready to give up on her?"

"No. I want to marry her," Ken said.

"You're a patient man."

"I've waited six years. What's a few more?"

Frank looked at Ken. The two men had become good friends. Ken had even taught Frank to golf, and now he loved the sport.

"A man needs a sport other than horses," Ken had said. "Golf allows a man to get his balls out... "

Frank swallowed his smile at the memory and said, "Why are you asking *me* this, instead of her sisters? She's probably confided more in them."

Ken laughed. "Oh, I doubt that. She trusts you and loves you as much or maybe *more* than the rest of us. Even *me*." He met Frank's eyes.

Frank felt a familiar twinge in his chest, as if his heart was trying to get out. He had learned to ignore it long ago. "No. She doesn't love me the same way she loves you," Frank said. "You know that."

The two men looked at each other.

"Ken," Frank broke the silence. "You're good for her. Remember that and don't give up on her. She needs you."

Ken nodded and put his hat back on.

"Okay," he said. He got up. "I'll keep trying."

Francie and Frank were meeting as usual in her office one evening. She had been out to dinner with Ken and then taken a long stroll along the boardwalk. But promptly at 8

p.m., Ken had dropped her off, and she climbed the stairs to her office.

Now she was shuffling through papers, asking Frank questions about the farm and what had happened while she was away. Frank was twirling a pen between his fingers, his eyes lost in thought.

"Frank?"

"Hmmm?" He looked up.

"You didn't even hear my last question."

"I was thinking."

"About what?"

"Francie, do you love Ken?"

She looked surprised at the change of subject but said, "Of course I love Ken."

"Then why won't you marry him?"

There was a long silence. Frank waited. Francie opened her mouth to speak, then closed it again. Then finally she said, "I don't know."

"Tell me what you love about him."

"Well… he's a good man. He makes me laugh. He makes me feel special. He's kind, generous, patient—"

"Very patient."

"Very patient," Francie smiled.

"What if he's tired of being patient?" Frank said. "Maybe he's tired of waiting for you and wants to move on or settle down."

The color drained from her face. Frank let that sink in for a minute. Then he said, "Ken never said that. I said that. But I could tell from the look on your face that you don't want to lose him."

Francie was quiet.

"Francie, he's a good man. When you're with him, you're happy."

"I'm always happy."

"No, you're driven. You love what you do, but your life is goal oriented. Ken makes you have fun. He takes you out of your work and you play. He transforms you."

Francie swallowed.

"You play cards," Frank said. "You take walks. Actual walks. Before Ken came into your life, you were always running places. You cook together. You watch movies. You dance. The man has actually taught you to dance, and you love it!"

Francie laughed.

"He loves you," Frank said. "And I know you love him."

Francie looked into her friend's eyes.

"Yes," she said. "I do."

"Then I think the next time he asks you to marry him, you should say 'yes'."

chapter 28

SAM SAT ON THEIR BED, TWISTING THE COVERS between her fingers.

"I'm going to quit riding," she said to Steve. He was sitting on the bed with her, rubbing her feet.

"Why?"

"Because that's probably why I lost the baby."

A fresh tear escaped and trailed down her cheek. She had been at the hospital the night before—a miscarriage, the doctor had said. She hadn't even realized she was pregnant. She was only about eight weeks along.

"Not necessarily."

"I think it was. That's what happened last time too."

This was her second miscarriage. With the first one, she and Steve hadn't even told anybody she was pregnant because it had been so early. She was careful, and it had been during the winter, so by the time she found out she was pregnant, she was finished riding. But still, she wondered if riding during those first few weeks had been the cause.

This time, she hadn't even known she was pregnant because she was so busy with her schedule, and then she had taken a fall out on the track last week.

"Okay," Steve said. "But you love it."

"I know... " Sam said, her voice trailing off. She glanced at a painting she was working on, then out the window at the sunlight glistening off the leaves of the Cyprus tree. "But I love painting more. I just want to stay home and live an uneventful life, painting."

Steve was quiet.

"It hasn't been good for my health either," she said. "I had a brief encounter with an eating disorder a few years back."

Steve nodded. "But you're eating now?"

"Mostly."

He looked up at her.

"So maybe it's time to quit," she said. "We can concentrate on starting a family. I can concentrate on being healthy."

"Okay," he said. "I can take over your mounts for the rest of the year."

"You'll have to give up riding for others and focus mostly on Francie's horses," Sam said.

"That isn't so bad," Steve said. "They tend to win."

Sam smiled.

"Do you want me to tell Francie for you?" he asked.

"Yes," Sam said. "I'd like that. She might get mad at me."

Steve laughed. "She won't. But if she does get mad... well, she's *always* mad at me."

"That's because you harass her terribly."

Steve bent forward, kissing his wife on the tip of her nose. "Somebody has to." He took Sam's hands in his. "Hey," he said. She looked up at him. "We'll try again. We'll have a whole house full of kids."

Sam smiled.

Tom brought Becky home with a kitten. They had stopped at the Humane Society on their way to the farm. "I hope you don't mind," he said. "She's already named him Mittens."

He returned to Michigan and after that and made plans to bring her there for a visit.

Francie reluctantly agreed, but her heart tugged at her when she saw how excited Becky was about it all.

Francie was sitting at her desk, holding the framed photo of Starfire's Image in the winner's circle after his Kentucky Derby victory. Frank walked in with some papers for her to sign.

"What's up?" he said. "You look sad."

She set the photo down gently on her desk.

"Look how happy I am in that photo," she said.

Frank glanced at it and smiled. "I remember."

"But look how sad Becky is."

He looked at the photo again. "I know," he said quietly. "Why?"

He hesitated, then said. "That's when you said it was the happiest day of your life. That hurt her. That night when I put her to bed she cried, and said she wished the happiest day of your life was the day she was born."

Francie swallowed the lump in her throat.

"Why didn't you ever tell me?"

"I tried," he said quietly. "Many times."

She was quiet for a few minutes, staring at the photo.

"Find me an assistant trainer," she said softly. "I want to be home more." Rain beat against the window, but the rest of the room was deathly quiet.

Frank sat down in the chair across from her desk. She ran her hands through her hair, which was limp and wet. She had just come in from the barn.

"I want to be a better mother."

"Okay," he said. "But don't beat yourself up."

"Just find me a trainer," she said. "Please."

The past year had been hard on her, sharing Becky with Tom. She had thrown herself into her work and lost at least ten pounds. She knew Tom meant well, but she just couldn't let go.

"I'm tired," she said.

"I know."

That week, Frank hired Donovan Brach, a promising young guy who had a soft, gentle way with horses. He was good at his job.

Francie began to stay home a little more, trusting Donovan to handle the horses while she showed up a day or two before the races. When they were stabled at home, she still took the lead with their training, but she was glad not to be on the road so much.

Becky was great friends with a little blond girl at her school. Jessica, an orphan, had tagged around with them for years. With extra time on her hands, Francie bought Jessica a horse and started taking the girls riding once or twice a week.

"Mom?" Becky said one day. "Why do we have to send Jessica home in the evenings? Why can't she just stay here?"

"She has spent the night before."

"No. I mean... "

"Forever?" Francie said.

"Yeah."

Francie saw a spark in her daughter's eye that hadn't been there for a long time. And she herself loved Jessica as if she were her own daughter, anyway. Why not?

So she adopted her. Because Jessica was an orphan, the process was quick and easy.

She also handled the idea of Sam quitting quite well and simply pulled Steve on board to ride the other mounts that Sam had been up on. *I'm doing well*, Francie told herself. *I'm doing well.*

chapter
29

IT TOOK FOUR MORE YEARS for Ken to propose again.
In that time, Jessica had settled in as part of the family. Frank hired a sixteen-year-old boy named Mickey to help out around the farm. They found out his dad beat him, evidenced by the bruises on his body. He was a great kid, and Frank had grown to love him like a son. Francie called child services and offered to foster him. Eventually, she adopted him, but he lived with Frank up in the apartment above the barn. Their family was growing; the farm was full of youth and life.

"Are you trying to save the world?" Ken asked. "Kids, horses... you take in everyone who needs a home."

"That was my grandpa's plan for this place," she said.

Sam couldn't seem to get pregnant again. She regularly visited the orphanage where Jessica had lived and taught painting to the kids. She had grown to love a little seven-year-old red-headed freckle faced girl named Lexie. She and Steve started to bring her home for visits and even bought her a horse.

"We're going to foster her," Sam said.

"Might as well add her to the bunch," Francie said. The bedrooms were filling up fast at Sunnyhill.

It was a warm day in June when Ken showed up mid-morning with a large box tucked under his arm. He often dropped in during his workday to say "hi," but today he called Francie down into the kitchen.

"I don't want to walk on the carpet with my boots on," he yelled, so she could hear him from her office.

"I'll be right down!"

When Francie stepped into the kitchen, he set the box down on the floor. They were alone.

"What's this?" It was then that the box moved.

Francie jumped, then laughed. "What is it?"

"Open it and find out." Ken was grinning.

Francie knelt and united the ribbon. When she lifted the top off, a puppy peeked out. The dog was a bundle of gray fur with a pink tongue. It was the cutest thing she had ever seen.

"Awww!" She picked it up, and it licked her, it's tail wagging furiously. She noticed it had a note attached to its collar.

She looked suspiciously at Ken, then unrolled the note with the puppy squiggling and squirming on her lap. She read:

My name is Rascal, and I would love to live with you. Ken would love to live with you too and very humbly asks you to marry him. If you refuse (again) he will still love you, but can I live here anyway?"

Francie hugged Rascal, then looked up at Ken, her eyes shining with tears.

"Yes," she said.

Ken looked surprised. "What?"

"Yes. I said yes!"

"Really?"

Francie stood up, laughing. "Yes! I'll marry you, cowboy. Now hug me!"

He gathered her and the pup in his arms, and, laughing and crying, he hugged them both.

Francie kept Rascal hidden in her room until dinner was ready and everybody was seated. Then she walked down the stairs, carrying the pup.

"Where'd you get that thing?" Steve asked. Everyone looked up.

"What thing?" Francie said. "This?" She acknowledged the pup. "Or this?" She held up her left hand so everyone could see the glistening engagement ring.

Sam squealed at the ring, and the kids all erupted in "awww"s and "ohhhh"s over the puppy. Francie met Frank's eyes. He was grinning and acknowledged her with a nod.

"It's about time," he said.

It took a while to get dinner started because everyone was talking at once. Rascal ran around the table, licking everyone and chewing on toes. The kids were laughing, and Ken and Francie were hugging again. Steve took his fork and started tapping his glass. They kissed, and the room erupted in cheers.

"Thank God!" Steve said.

"There you go, talking to God again," Ken said. "It's almost as if you believe in him."

"I'm just sayin'," Steve said. "Maybe people around here will be less tense now. I mean, have you seen any action in the past eight or ten years? This house is full of sexually frustrated adults—"

Mickey sputtered and spit some water out.

"Steve!" Sam hissed. "There are kids here."

"Seriously. I've never seen him in her room. All that pent up energy—"

Sam kicked him under the table.

"Owww!"

Ken produced a rubber band from somewhere and shot it at Steve.

Steve picked it up. "Well, at least he has a rubber—"

Francie grabbed Steve by the ear and twisted. "Hush, small man, or I'll sic my dog on you."

"Is that what you call him now?" Steve squeaked, his face turning red from the pain. Francie started laughing and everybody laughed until their sides hurt. The girls were so enthralled with the puppy that fortunately they missed most of the conversation.

Jim slapped Mickey on the back. "And you wanted to live in this family?"

By the time they started eating, the chicken was quite cold, but nobody cared. They were warm enough on the inside, happy and full of talk.

Francie and Ken were married a month later. It was a quiet ceremony out on the beach by the ocean, with just the family. When they left for the honeymoon, Frank hugged her. "I'm so happy for you," he said into her hair. "I'll run the place until you get back. Just have fun and don't worry."

They drove off toward the Keys, to spend time alone, at long last.

When they returned, they moved Ken in and spent the day unpacking boxes. That evening, around 8 p.m. they remembered their past routine—only now Francie didn't send Ken home—and they laughed.

"Hey, I used to do a lot of work after that," she said. "I met with Frank. Actually, I need to go talk to him now for a few minutes and get tomorrow's plans figured out." She kissed Ken. He kissed her back, long and gently.

"I'm going to shower and then hit the sack," he said. "I've got a lot of work to do in the morning. But wake me when you come to bed." He winked.

Francie smiled coyly. "I'm glad I had Steve soundproof our bedroom," she said.

Ken went to their room, and Francie stopped in her office where Frank was finishing up some paperwork. She closed the door, sat down at her desk, and looked at the pile of papers.

"I'm glad to see you so happy," Frank said.

She smiled, then pointed to a contract. "What's that one?"

"That's from Marigold farm," Frank said. "They want to reserve three breedings from Image."

They talked for a few minutes about the farm, and Francie signed the contracts he had for her. Then she kicked back in her chair, ready to tell Frank about some of the sights they had seen on their honeymoon, and this great restaurant they'd eaten at, and all the tourist places they'd visited which she thought she'd hate but had ended up loving. She'd hardly had any one-on-one time with Frank since they'd been back, and she missed him.

But Frank was putting his files away and getting up out of his chair.

"Aren't you... going to stay awhile?" Francie asked.

Frank looked at his watch. "It's 9:30. You have a husband now. You need to go spend time with him." Frank smiled. "I'll see you in the morning. Early." Then he left.

She heard his footsteps descend the stairs and heard him softly close the door. Francie sat there for a while, her heart pounding.

Down the hall, her husband slept in their big brass bed, waiting for her.

Her office suddenly seemed empty, almost as if it would echo if she spoke. In the silence, she heard the blood pounding in her ears, and the sudden quiet scared her.

She jumped up and quietly ran down the stairs and outside.

Frank was about halfway across the yard, barely visible in the darkness of the moonless night.

She ran, barefoot, across the damp grass, as fast as she could toward him.

"Frank!" she called out when she was close enough to be heard without shouting.

He stopped and turned.

"Frank," she said again, when she reached him. She was breathless, even though she hadn't run very far. "Frank... I... "

How could she explain this sudden emptiness that had overtaken her? An emptiness that she was sure only *he* could fill? But uncharacteristically, her emotions took over and everything started coming out.

"Frank, you have to come back. I don't want to lose our evenings together. You're my best friend. There's nothing I love more than sitting with you and talking—just sitting"— she laughed a bit nervously—"and even doing nothing, as long as we're together. I'm just afraid that now things will be different. I don't want to lose you—or lose what we have, whatever it is. Frank, the fact is... the fact is... "

"Francie," he used that steady, calm voice of his. "Relax. I'm right here."

"No, you don't understand. I'm afraid... I'm afraid I married the wrong man. I love Ken, I do, I really do, but"—the next few words came out in a whisper—"but I think I'm in love with you."

She stopped, shocked at herself and at the words she'd just uttered. She swallowed hard and watched his face as best she could in the darkness.

"Francie, you are *not* in love with me," he said. "We've been friends forever, and that's all we are, *friends*. You chose who you wanted to be with, and I'm in love with Krista."

"No," said Francie. "We were wrong. It's more."

"Stop it," said Frank. His voice was angry. "That's enough of this foolishness."

"I can't... "

"Listen to me," he said. "Listen." His voice was cold, hard. "We are *not* in love with each other."

She started to protest but he suddenly grabbed her face between his hands and pulled her toward him, meeting her lips. He kissed her long and hard and then stepped back.

"There," he said, still angry. "I didn't feel anything. No sparks, nothing. Did you? *Did* you?"

"No... " she said. Her voice quavered. "Nothing," she whispered.

Frank looked at her. She suddenly felt so small and fragile. When had the tough, stubborn woman she knew herself to be left and replaced her with someone who needed him so much?

But then, she had always needed him.

He took a deep, cleansing breath and took hold of her hands. She was shaking.

"You need to go home," he said, not unkindly. "You're tired. I'm tired."

She took her hands from his and rubbed them together, suddenly cold.

"Okay," she said quietly. "You're right. I was being silly. I'm sorry."

Frank chuckled a little bit and turned to start back home.

"Goodnight," he said. "We'll just forget this ever happened and life will be back to normal in the morning."

"Right," said Francie. She turned and walked slowly back to the house. Frank walked toward his apartment.

She forced herself not to look back as she entered the house and went upstairs to bed.

When Frank reached the barn, he turned and watched her enter the house, her silhouette so far away as she moved through the kitchen, turning out lights. He sighed a heavy sigh and rubbed the back of his neck. Then, for a brief minute, he closed his eyes, as if savoring some scent in the air, and when he opened them again it was with a heavy heart that he walked up the stairs and into his apartment for the night.

The next morning, Francie met Frank at the track, early. Frank, as always, brought her coffee down to her; strong, no cream or sugar, just the way she liked it. He leaned against the rail in the cool morning air and watched her horse breeze around the track. Neither of them spoke for a while. They sipped their coffees and watched Vision clip off her time quickly. She was a pretty filly, a bay with four white socks and a blaze.

Francie clicked her stopwatch as Vision crossed the wire.

"What's her time?" Frank asked, the first words he had spoken that morning.

"1:04. Not bad, but she does better with Steve on her." Steve was in California riding in races. An exercise rider was up on Vision this morning, and he turned and headed the filly back to the barn to cool her off.

"Francie? About last night," Frank said.

"I thought we weren't going to talk about it," Francie said.

"I just needed to say this." He paused to make sure she was listening. "I promise I will never leave you." He turned to look at her and she looked up at him.

He knew what she needed to hear. Why wouldn't he? Who knew her better than him? So he told her the words she needed to hear, even though it broke his heart to say them.

"You don't love me, not in that way. What we have is different, but not necessarily less. Okay? I think you were afraid of losing what we had—have—and you need to know that you won't. Even if Krista and I get married someday, she told me that you made her promise not to take me away from Sunnyhill."

Francie ducked her head down and took a long sip of her coffee, hiding behind her drink.

"I don't *want* to leave," Frank said. "This is my home. I helped you build it, and this is where I belong. Beside you. Running this place."

She met his eyes again.

"You're free to love your husband, Francie. Love him, enjoy life, and try not to be afraid, because I'm not going anywhere."

A little smile played on her lips. "Thank you," she said simply, but Frank could see her eyes light up with relief and joy.

"I feel... free," she said, and he smiled.

Married life was awesome. Francie felt like she was living in one of those television series she had watched as a kid, where family members supported each other and had dinners together.

They began a regular family dinner hour at 6 p.m. every night. Everyone who could was expected to be there.

Ken encouraged Francie not to work as much after dinner, claiming that as family time. They attended Becky and Jessica's volleyball and basketball games, recitals, and other school activities. In the summer, they enrolled the girls in 4-H and went to horse shows and the 4-H fair.

Francie gave her assistant trainer Donovan even more of the work and stopped traveling so much to races.

They had family movies nights on Fridays when they were home, and Sunday evenings were family game time. Mostly they played board games, but sometimes Ken would start a football game outdoors which Steve and Mickey, and sometimes Frank joined in.

Saturday mornings were reserved for cartoons and pancakes. Ken could flip a flapjack straight into the air with the pan; sometimes he missed, catching it on the way down, and the girls always erupted in giggles.

When Krista came home, which was twice a month if she could, she always added sliced fruit to the pancakes.

Jim started playing his guitar more. Between Steve's sound system (which he piped through the house on strategically placed speakers) and Jim's strumming, the house was often filled with music. Sometimes one of the girls would accompany Jim on the piano, and they'd have a family sing-along.

They all went to church, except Steve, who stayed home on Sunday mornings to work on his cars. Sam taught Sunday school, and Francie and Ken sang in the choir. Mickey got involved with the church's youth group and went on mission trips, first to Miami and then to Haiti. He was applying for colleges, and Frank was facing an empty nest.

A year after Ken and Francie got married, Frank married Krista. They lived on the farm in the apartment, and she flew every other week to New York. She was at a point in her career where she could call some of the shots, and photographers began flying to *her* most of the time.

For a wedding gift, Francie gave them a piece of land on the ocean at the edge of her property, where her mom had wanted to build condos. Frank and Krista hired an architect and designed a beautiful house, which would involve floor to ceiling windows and a long porch stretching across the front to give the best ocean view.

Sometimes, on a cool evening or early morning, Frank and Ken would golf. Golf was Ken's other love, and he was thrilled to have a golfing partner. The two men were the best of friends.

Francie felt so relaxed and happy that she marveled that they got any work done at all. But the farm ran smoothly, her horses kept winning, her studs were in demand for breeding, and with Ken's farm's income, they were doing very well.

Life was good.

"Frank," Francie said one morning on their way back from the track. "Ever since I trusted God, life has been good. He has really been taking care of me. I feel protected."

"We are certainly blessed," agreed Frank.

Even Jim had finally invited Jesus into his life.

"Francie, you really need to redecorate this place," Krista said. "Seriously, have you done *anything* since Grandma died?"

"Hmmm?" Francie had been looking at blueprints for Frank and Krista's "dream house", which were spread out across the dining room table. In the kitchen, Chico was squawking. Becky had brought home a parrot from the Humane Society, and while Francie admired her for rescuing it, he was quite noisy. "What? Yes. I've changed things. A bit."

Krista put her hands on her hips. "Like what?"

"She sound-proofed the upstairs!" Steve shouted from above.

Francie harrumphed in triumph. "See?"

"I swear, he can hear like a horse," Krista muttered. "What else? These are Grandma's drapes and the same carpet."

"Keypad!" Steve yelled.

"What?"

"Keypad. She had keyless entry on her office door and the back door. Oh—and music piped throughout the house. She's also added video surveillance and a gate-keeper's house."

Krista frowned. "I'm talking about redecorating, not outfitting a fortress."

"That's not my thing," Francie said.

Krista brightened. "It's *my* thing. Can I do it? It'll take a while. I can practice on your house before I do my own."

"Okay. Just let me see the plans and samples first. I do have to live here."

From upstairs came the unseen voice. "Just don't mess up my wiring!"

chapter
30

FRANCIE WAS TROUNCING KEN AND STEVE in a game of cards at the kitchen table.

"Two kings!" Steve said triumphantly.

"Two aces!" Francie said. "Ha!" Ken just sighed and threw his hand down. Francie sang out, "I win again! I'm gonna do a little dance!" The parrot started squawking.

"Somebody, please, stop her!" Steve said and laid his hand down on the table.

Ken gathered up the cards. "Your deal," he said to Steve. "One more hand. I intend to beat the lady."

Jim had been standing in the doorway of the dining room, watching them for a few minutes. He walked up to Francie and interrupted her dance by touching her elbow.

"Francie?"

"Oh, thank you!" Steve said. "Thank God, and thank you, Jim."

"I thought you didn't believe in God," Ken teased.

"Figure of speech."

Francie looked at Jim and went quiet. His face was drawn and worried.

"What's wrong?"

The others looked up.

"Can we talk?" Jim said.

"Uh, yeah."

"In private?"

She followed him upstairs to her office. He closed and locked the door. Francie sat down at her desk, and he took the chair in front of it. He blew out a long breath.

"This room is soundproof?" he asked.

"Yes. And there are no bugs," Francie said. "The listening devices, not the creepy kind. Thanks to Steve."

Jim looked at her. "Do you have something to hide?"

"No. I just like the cool electronic gadgets Steve brings me."

"Well, that works for me." He got up and walked around nervously, then sat back down.

"I got a phone call this morning from Paul's mom," Jim said. "We lost the appeal."

"Oh, Jim. That was his last one, wasn't it?"

"They, um"—His voice broke—"they've scheduled his execution for next month."

Francie was silent. She reached across the desk and took his hand. He gently squeezed her fingers, looking down and fighting back tears. His pain made Francie's own eyes fill.

"Do you want me to go with you?" she said. She had been thinking about this moment, wondering if it would come. She knew she couldn't watch. She couldn't be there when it happened, but she could accompany Jim on the trip and be there for him when it was over.

He took her hand in both of his and looked across the desk at her, a tear coursing down his cheek. It was the first time she had ever seen him cry. His eyes were desperate, pleading, as he met her gaze.

"I want you to help me break him out."

Francie sat back, startled, and pulled her hand away. She gave a little laugh, but Jim kept looking at her intently. He was serious.

"Are you crazy?" she whispered.

"I thought this place was soundproof."

"It is!" she said. "It's just... What? How? You're asking me to *break a man out of a federal prison*. It's impossible. I wouldn't even know where to start."

"I've found some men who can do it."

"What? Oh, dear God, Jim! It's illegal!" She ran her hands through her hair.

Jim had regained control of his emotions, and his voice was strong.

"He saved my life. And by saving mine, he saved yours. I was alive to get you away from those men that night you were walking home from Johnny's funeral. If I hadn't come home from Vietnam... " He stopped.

She was quiet. His arms were on her desk, and she could see the white scar running across his left hand

"Francie, he's like a brother to me, and better than my real brother. And his mom has been like a mother to me."

"Jim... "

"Francie, please."

The look on his face was breaking her heart.

"He's innocent," he said, his voice wavering again, his eyes full of pain. "Do you know what it's like to die in the electric chair? It's... "

She interrupted him. "How much does something like this cost?"

"A lot." Jim sighed. "No one would know you were involved," he said. "All I need is cash." He wrote a number on a piece of paper and slid it over.

Her eyes widened. "I don't just keep this kind of cash lying around," she said. "I'd have to liquidate assets. We only have a month."

"So...does this mean you're considering it?"

"Maybe."

"If we get caught, we hang," he said. "Paul's in prison for treason. I need to do this, but I can't do it without your help."

Francie was quiet.

"Francie, he spent eighteen years in prison for a murder he didn't commit. He lost his girlfriend, and all his other friends have deserted him except his mom and me because they think he's a traitor to his country. Before that, he was tortured in a POW camp.

He looked at her. "You *rescue* things, Francie. That's what you *do*. You've taken in horses, kids, *me*. Didn't Papaw call this Safe Haven Farm? Paul needs a place to feel safe, to finally feel safe, and you have the means to do it."

"I can't just hide a fugitive here at the farm."

"They'll give him a new face and a new identity. It'll work. *Please.*"

She thought of her grandpa and wondered what he would do. His words rang in her head. *You'll know when somebody needs your help. Take them in.*

"I did offer to help you, but I meant a trip to California for the execution."

"Is that a yes?"

Francie looked into Jim's eyes. "Is he worth it?" she said. "Jim, is Paul really worth you risking your life? You'll go to jail. You won't see Lily grow up. Is Paul worth it?"

Jim looked her in the eyes. "Yes," he said. "I promised to get him out, and I intend to. He told me to leave, to get on with my life. But I can't do that, Francie. If you only knew what we have been through together."

Francie reached across the desk and took Jim's hands in hers. She couldn't believe what she was about to say. "Okay. I'll help you. Go, and let me figure out how I'm going to do this. Don't say a word about it outside of this room or to *anyone* besides me."

He stood. "I'll never be able to pay you back. I'll work for you for the rest of my life," he said. "You can cut my salary in half. I still need to support Lily, but I can work more hours."

"Jim," Francie said. "Go."

Francie started selling horses. She knew some breeders and racehorse owners who were dying to get their hands on some of her stock, so she carefully selected some, spreading them out in hope of not building one farm's breeding stock above another's, and leaving hers at the top. Most she sold privately; two she took to an auction.

"What are you doing?" Frank asked her.

"I have a plan that I'm financing," she said.

"Do you care to let me in on it because it's not in the business plan that *we* created."

"Not yet," she said. "But soon."

Francie was in town, looking at carpet samples that Krista had picked out. She decided on a cream color—not too white as to show dirt,but still light and airy. Satisfied with herself, she left the store and started walking down the sidewalk toward her car.

A black sedan pulled along beside her and slowed to a stop. The back window rolled down.

"I understand you want to do some business with us," a man said. He was older, with a large pock-marked nose and black hair.

"No," Francie said. "You must have me mistaken for someone else."

The door opened and the man got out.

"Francie Dalton," the man said firmly. "I'd like to offer you a ride. Get in the car."

Francie froze. Her keys were in her hands, and she considered running for her car. Instead, she faced the man.

"I thought Jim was handling the business end of things," she said.

"The boss prefers you."

Heart pounding, she got in. What had she gotten herself into? She looked the man in the eye as the car drove off and held her chin high. She wouldn't let him know how afraid she was.

"Where are you taking me?"

"To the boss."

"Then, will you bring me back to my car?"

The man gave her a long, hard look. "Well, if we kill you, it puts a damper on the business deal, so yeah, I guess so. As long as you don't tick off the boss. That's all you need to know."

They drove in silence for about ten minutes and came to a bar. The man got out and led Francie through the bar to a back room. He let her inside, then closed the door.

A middle-aged man with dark hair sat at a table with two other guys. They were eating sandwiches. One man was smoking.

"Welcome, Ms. Dalton!" the dark-haired man said. "I'm Vinnie. Would you like a sandwich? The turkey club is the best."

Francie shook her head. Vinnie got up and motioned for Francie to sit at the table across from him.

"Joe? Bring the lady something to drink. We're all gentlemen here. Let's treat Ms. Dalton with some hospitality." The smoking man stubbed out his cigarette and left.

Vinnie sat back down and carefully chewed and swallowed the last bite of his sandwich. Then he took a napkin and wiped his mouth off.

"So," he finally said. "You want to do business with me." It was a statement, not a question. His thug came back and set a glass of ice water in front of Francie.

"I thought it was my brother who you were going to do business with," Francie said. She hoped her voice didn't give her nerves away.

"You're the one supplying the money. You're the one with everything at stake. I prefer to do business directly with you."

Francie took a sip of her water to stall for time. There was condensation on the glass. The room seemed warm. "Okay," she said finally. "Then we have to do it my way. I don't want anyone to get hurt."

Vinnie sat back and laughed. "You're a good businesswoman," he said. "You have moxie. I like that." He grew serious. "You're paying me to deliver a product and that product will be unharmed. If he doesn't come willingly, we'll have to drug him, but that's all."

"You can tell him that Jim is helping him."

"There will be no time for explanations."

"I don't want any guards hurt either," Francie said.

"That will cost you a bit more," Vinnie said. "I'll have to pay people off."

"Just don't hurt anybody. I'll get you the money."

"I don't make it a habit of killing people, Francie Dalton. Only people who cross me."

His thug lit another cigarette.

"I need half the money up front in unmarked bills," Vinnie said. "The other half you can give me when you get your guy. We'll keep him about six weeks. He'll have cosmetic surgery to alter his face, and we'll give him a new identity. The six weeks will also give the feds a bit of time to lose interest in you. In the meantime, you're going to put an ad in the paper and racing magazines for an assistant farm manager. Interview a few people, but you will hire him. That will be his cover.

"Now listen carefully. Next Tuesday, shop on this street at 11 a.m.. Go into Maude's and buy a magazine. Carry a red tote bag in your right hand, a large one, and inside it, you'll have the cash. Go into the coffee shop and buy a coffee and sit down to read your magazine. Put the bag on the floor at your feet. A woman will approach you, say hello, and you will get up and hug her like you're meeting a friend. She'll stay five minutes and leave with the red bag.

"Three days later, you'll fly to New York to sign papers that you purchased a blue jeans company," he handed her an envelope. It contained two first-class tickets to Manhattan. "That's your cover for why you liquidated your assets. The place is a wreck, but we're pretending it's not, which is why you paid so much for it. Your job is to fix it up.

"About six weeks after we remove your man, we'll deliver him. Have Jim pick him up and bring the other half of the cash, this time in a backpack. He'll receive instructions later.

"After you get him, you're on your own."

He was quiet, waiting for her to speak next. She met his eyes. "Sounds like a plan," she said and smiled.

"Joe, take her back to her car."

Vinnie stood up and offered her his hand. Francie shook it and left, feeling a mixture of triumph and fear, and just a little bit dirty.

The cash drop was easy, but at home later that day, things were more difficult.

She was standing at Star's stall, stroking the mare on the neck and feeding her a sliced apple when Frank came and stood beside her.

"So what did you do with all that cash?" he asked.

"What cash?" She handed the horse another piece of apple.

"Francie, I keep your books."

"I'm buying a blue jean company."

"Really."

"Really." She turned to look at him. "I'm flying to Manhattan in three days to take a look at the place."

Frank frowned. "I don't get it. I don't understand."

"Come to my office at 4 p.m., and I'll explain everything to you." She knew it was time.

"Are you involved in something illegal?"

Francie opened her mouth, feigning shock. "Frank! You think—"

"Don't lie to me. I know you too well." His kind brown eyes looked deep into her blue ones. "After all these years... "

She turned back to her horse. She couldn't look at him anymore.

"I'll tell you everything later, I promise," she said. "4:00."

Frank nodded and turned to leave. He barely heard Francie when she spoke.

"Just remember, you promised never to leave me."

He looked back at her. Her eyes searched his, pleading.

He nodded and walked out of the barn.

At 3:00, she asked Ken to meet her in her office, figuring he should be the first to know. She locked the door, took her gadget, and scanned Ken for bugs.

He held his arms up.

"Want to strip search me, darlin'?" he asked.

She didn't smile.

Satisfied that they were completely alone, Francie sat down on the couch and offered Ken the chair, so they were looking at each other.

"I love you," she began.

"Uh-oh," he said.

"You're not going to like what I've done," Francie said. "I've done something illegal. I don't expect you to agree with or support it, but I'm hoping you'll love me and stick with me. I'm taking every precaution to be sure you're not going down with me if I get caught."

She paused. Ken swallowed.

She took a deep breath and continued. "You know of Jim's friend, Paul."

"Yes," Ken said. "He's due to be executed very soon, right?"

"No."

"No?"

"Well, yes, but I'm breaking him out of jail."

Ken laughed. Then he realized Francie wasn't joking. She saw understanding dawn in his eyes. "That's why you're selling off our horses. You need the money."

"Yes."

Ken stood up. "Francie, that's crazy. How would you even know how to begin?"

"Jim found some people."

"People?" Ken started to pace. "Darlin', you'll go to jail. You'll lose the farm. We'll all go to jail."

"I told you, I've taken precautions to keep the rest of you safe, and the farm too. If I get caught, only Jim and I go down."

"No," he said.

Francie raised an eyebrow.

"No. I won't let you do it," Ken said.

"It's too late," Francie said quietly. "It's already in motion." She explained to him what had happened so far.

Ken turned toward her, a mixture of hurt and anger in his eyes.

"Francie, we're supposed to be together. If I hadn't questioned why you were selling the horses, would you have even let me in on this?"

"I'm trying desperately to keep *you* out of this. This is my decision. My... my... "

"Crime?"

She looked away.

"Has it occurred to you this is illegal?"

"Ken, of course I know this is illegal."

Ken sat back down. "Tell me everything," he said.

Francie told him all that she knew. He listened quietly. He waited until she finished, then said, "You're putting us all at risk bringing him here. What if he really is a killer?"

"I believe he's innocent."

"Because Jim does? Have you ever met him?"

Francie sighed. "No. I just... I need to do this. I can't explain why."

"Why did you even tell me this? You could have hired him, as Frank's assistant, used the jean company as a cover. I didn't need to know."

"I needed you to know. Like you said, we're together."

"Why not tell me sooner?"

"I might have let you talk me out of it."

Ken laughed but his eyes were angry. Then he stood up. "I'm going to take a walk," he said, hurt and anger in his tone. "Alone. I'll be home for dinner."

Francie nodded. "I love you."

"I know." He put his hat back on, inclined his head to her, and left the room without kissing her.

Francie looked at the clock. Frank would be here in ten minutes. She took a long drink of water and sat on the window seat, looking out over her pastures, which were dotted with horses, although fourteen fewer now. She let her mind rest and was still sitting there when Frank walked in.

She asked him to lock the door, then take a seat.

"I'd rather stand."

"I really think you should sit."

They locked eyes, and after a moment, Frank sighed and sat down in the chair across from her desk. Francie hugged her knees, then moved from the window seat to her chair. She handed him the wand, and he scanned himself for bugs without asking why. Then she opened her desk drawer and pulled out the little bottle of sand.

"See this?"

"Yes. I know what that is."

"So you know the story. And you know how Papaw's dream was for this farm to be a safe haven for those who needed it."

Frank was quiet for a moment. Then, gently, he said, "Francie, tell me what you've done."

She swallowed. "I need you to still like me afterwards." She was upset to hear the tremor in her voice.

Frank's kind eyes gazed into hers, but his look was firm. "Tell me."

So Francie told him the entire story, and he sat quietly through it all, his face expressionless. She wondered how she had been blessed with two such sweet, gentle men in her life. When she finished, Frank took a long, deep breath.

"I'm not surprised you agreed to this," he said finally, his voice cold. "And I know why you did. Your brother is an asshole."

She was taken back by his anger toward Jim. She expected it to be directed at her.

"He knew you would never say no to him."

"Frank, he was hurting."

"He's going to be hurting a lot worse when they strap his butt into an electric chair next to Paul's. And yours. Francie, Paul is in prison for the murder of a general. That's treason against his country. *Treason.* They will find out who aided in his escape, and they will execute you."

"They won't find out."

"They will."

"I can't let him die."

"You can and you must," Frank said. "You've saved countless horses, Sam, Jim, Mickey, Jessica." Frank threw his hands into the air. "And who else? Too many to count. You have to let this one go."

"I need you to support me in this."

"I will not support you in this. This is crazy! I can't... "

Frank's voice broke with emotion. He rubbed his hand over his eyes. "I don't want to lose you."

Francie felt her own eyes tear up. "I don't want your support for what I'm doing," she said. "I just want you to support *me*. Don't give up on me. Just let me do this. Let him work with you. If this backfires, just still be my friend. If I wind up in jail, visit me. And yes, if they do execute me, at least come to say goodbye."

They were both crying now. Frank stood up and came around the desk and put his arms around her. She stood, and he pulled her against him.

"Don't do this," he whispered.

"It's too late. I've done it."

He held her for a few minutes, and when he stepped back, they both had their emotions under control.

"I promised to never leave you," he said. "And I'll stick to that promise. But go into this knowing that I don't agree with you. I know you've considered the legal implications, but what about the moral? Have you prayed about it?"

"And asked God to let me break the law?"

Frank waited for her to answer.

She sat back down in her chair and ran her hands through her hair. "Frank, he's innocent."

"And there are legal ways to pursue this."

"They've used up all their appeals. They lost."

"Apparently, the courts feel there's enough evidence to prove him guilty. This is the death penalty. They take it seriously. That's why he's been in there 18 years."

"I can't stop it, Frank. The plan has already been set in motion. These aren't the kind of guys you can go to and say, 'I changed my mind. Can I have my money back?'"

Frank went and sat back down in his chair. He laced his fingers together and put his hands behind his head, leaning back.

"Okay," he said. "Moral implications, then."

"Have I sinned?"

"Have you?"

"I honestly don't know."

"Well," Frank said. "Don't leave God out of this. You're going to need Him now more than ever. I'd start praying for us and for the farm."

She waited to see if he had more to say. He did.

"If they catch you, they'll confiscate the farm."

"I've thought of that," she said.

"And you have a plan," Frank said.

"I do." She pulled open her desk drawer and pulled out a manila envelope. She handed it to Frank and smiled a little. "Happy Birthday."

"My birthday isn't until next week."

"It's early. Open it."

Frank opened it and pulled out a birthday card. Inside it she had written:

This farm has always brought me joy. It wouldn't be here without you. Now it's your turn. Happy birthday,

Love Francie

He pulled a thick pile of papers out of the envelope. It was the deed to the farm. He read it for a minute, then looked up.

"You're selling me your farm for one dollar."

"Yes," she said, smiling. "It's not really the entire farm, just 60%. Controlling interest."

Frank was speechless.

"This way, if they catch me, the farm will be safe. I couldn't think of better hands to leave it in."

He swallowed. "You're giving up a lot for a man you don't even know."

"It's not for him," Francie said. "I'm doing it for Jim. You know that."

"And maybe a little bit for yourself," Frank said. "You've been rescuing things your whole life."

The two friends sat in silence for a while, each lost in their own thoughts.

"Okay," Frank said finally. "I'll work with him. It doesn't seem that I have another choice."

"It'll be okay." She smiled that sunny smile that made everyone believe she had the world in her hands.

"Francie," Frank said, his voice nearly a whisper. She looked up at him from across her desk. A strand of her blond hair fell across her face, and the evening sun caught it, turning it to gold. "I hope to God you're right."

Telling the others didn't go so well. When Krista came home later that evening, Francie gathered them all in her office, except for the kids. Then she told them.

"You're bringing a murderer into the house?" Steve said. "We have children here. Lexie is only eight."

"He's not a murderer," Jim said.

Krista turned on Frank, who was sitting on the corner of Francie's desk. "You support this?"

"No," he said.

"But you're... so *calm!*" Krista was angry, her voice harsh.

Ken leaned against the wall, arms crossed.

"Krista," Ken's voice was bitter. "It seems the deal is done. She's not asking for our permission." His eyes were still angry.

"We all live here," Steve said, his voice angry and loud. "I realize I'm not a blood relation, but you could have respected me enough to tell me before."

"No. That's exactly why she *didn't* tell us," Krista said. "She knew we'd say no. It's crazy, and you and Jim *both* are going to go to prison for this. James, what on earth were you thinking, bringing such a man into our lives? How do we know he won't rob us blind and leave? Or worse yet, kill us in our sleep?"

"He is *not* a murderer," Jim said between clenched teeth.

"Listen!" Francie said, standing up. "In the next week, this place will be crawling with feds. They're going to try to find him. If you don't want to send me to the electric chair, this can't be spoken of once we leave this room. Not ever. Not even to each other. As I told you, I've taken precautions to make sure you are all safe; you won't be implicated with me, and if I go down, the farm will stand."

"This is insane," Krista said. "Who exactly did you make a deal with, the mob?"

"It's dangerous," Steve said. The room got quiet.

Sam spoke for the first time. "It'll be okay," she said. "He's fine."

Steve looked at her. "How do you know?"

Frank stood up. "Sam knows things," he said.

They all looked at her.

"It will be okay," Francie said. "We're saving a man's life and giving him a new home. How can that be wrong?"

chapter

31

Her brother Mark showed up first.

"Paul has been sprung from jail," he said. "The man was on death row for murdering a general. It would take somebody with a lot of money or a lot of influence to do something like that."

"What are you implying?"

He arched an eyebrow.

Francie spread her hands. "He's not here. Look around."

"Oh, we'll look all right. And at Jim's and your bank accounts and everywhere you've been—they'll look at it all, Francie," he said kindly. "I've done my best to make sure they don't tear your place up while searching, but I can't protect you if they find anything."

"They won't find anything," she said, and gave a little laugh. "You think I'm that good that I could break a man out of a federal prison?"

"I learned long ago not to underestimate you," Mark said. He gave her a quick hug. "I love you, sis. Now I'm going to have a little chat with Jim."

For the next month, the feds searched every inch of the farm and everyone's transactions and kept them under constant surveillance. No one cracked, and after the first few weeks, the feds seemed more of a fly on the ceiling than Big Brother. They were there, parked outside the gates, watching, but not really in the way. After five weeks, they left to look elsewhere, and the story, which had been national news, began to take a back seat to other current world events.

He arrived six weeks after his escape, in a small yellow cab that stopped at the docks next to the marina. He was dressed in khaki pants and a blue t-shirt and carried a backpack.

Jim drove him home. At the gate, Jim rolled down his window. "The new hire is here," he said.

The guard waved him through.

If Paul—now Jack Banner—was impressed by his new home, he didn't say anything. He hadn't said a thing the whole drive home.

Jim unlocked the cottage door and motioned him through, then he closed the door.

"Your keys to your new house," he said and hung them up on a peg by the door. "We can talk freely," he said. "Francie went over this place with an instrument that picks up listening devices. It's clean."

Jack looked at his old friend. "Thanks doesn't seem like enough."

"Come here, man," Jim said, and the two men embraced in an awkward hug, with a few thumps on the back. "It's good to see you."

"How... " Jack began.

"Later," Jim said. "Francie told me to show you around the place and then let you get some rest. She wants to meet you in two hours at her office."

Jack looked around. The house was small, but uncluttered and clean. The front door that he was standing by opened up into a great room. An island separated the kitchen from a living room. To his left was a kitchen. To his right was the living room, with a sofa, two recliners, a television and a fireplace. The house was decorated in darker colors, with paneling on the walls, but there were enough windows to let in plenty of light.

Directly in front of him was a large oak kitchen table with four chairs. Beyond that were two doors: one led to a bathroom, and the other, Jim said, led to a master bedroom with its own bath. Also on the back wall was a door leading outside into a fenced-in back yard.

Jim showed Jack an envelope laying on the table. "There's $1000 cash in there. Francie told me you'll need clothes and assigned me the task of taking you shopping next week."

"Why?" Jack asked. "Why did you do this for me? There's no way I can ever repay you."

"Hey," Jim said. "You saved my life. I saved yours. We're even." He smiled. "Now, I'm leaving so you can get acclimated to your new life. I'll be back in two hours to pick you up and take you over to the house. If you need anything before then, the house number is there by the phone. You can reach me at that. Okay?"

Jack nodded.

After Jim left, he looked around. The little house was quiet and welcoming. He went into the kitchen and peeked around until he found a glass and ran himself a drink of water from the tap. There was a window above the sink with a tree outside it. Someone had hung and filled a birdfeeder, and there was a little black-capped bird feeding at it. Probably a chickadee, Jack thought, remembering the birds that used to visit his mom's feeder. His mom had loved wild birds. His eyes teared up at the thought of her, and he quickly turned away. He saw a little plaque hanging next to the window on the side of the cabinet. It read:

Faith is taking the first step, even when you don't see the whole staircase. - Martin Luther King, Jr.

He sat his glass down and went to use the bathroom. Even though there was no one in the house, he closed the door because he could. Privacy in the bathroom had been unknown in prison.

When he was finished, he washed his hands and dried them on the soft green towels in the bathroom.

Then he went into the bedroom. It was decorated in blues, with green for accents and a large plant on top of the dresser. The window was cracked open and outside, he could hear birds. The whole house had been decorated to give one the sense of being outside—of freedom. He appreciated that.

There was a shaft of sunlight across the bed. He sat down and slowly moved his hand across the comforter, feeling its warmth. Jack smiled. It had been a long time since he had seen sunlight anywhere on the inside.

The inside. He wondered how long it would take for him to stop thinking of the world in two hemispheres—the inside and the outside.

Carefully, he turned down a corner of the covers. The sheets underneath were a light blue, like the sky. He bent forward to smell them. They smelled cool and clean. There was a very faint trace of detergent, maybe citrus, but nothing like the strong and overpowering scent the prison sheets smelled like. She had layered the bed. Sheets, a soft cotton blanket, then the comforter. He sat there, enjoying it. It was so simple, and yet, it brought a wash of homesickness over him for what had been. For what he had missed. When was the last time he had laid in a real bed? One made up with care and love? Had it really been twenty years?

He lay back, stretching out. The pillow felt wonderful. He stared up at the ceiling for a while, wiping away the silent tears that spilled out. Eventually, he turned on his side with his back to the door for the first time in two decades and curled up into a ball. He pulled the comforter around himself and closed his eyes, drifting into a peaceful, dreamless sleep.

Finally, he felt safe.

chapter 32

FRANCIE SAT BEHIND HER GRANDFATHER'S WALNUT DESK, waiting to meet Jack Banner. It had been six weeks since he had been broken out of prison—long enough for his plastic surgery to heal. She had no idea where he had been all this time, or who he was with. She supposed it was better that way. A call had come in last night, telling Jim where to pick him up. He was to come alone today to get Jack.

"Take him to the guest house," Francie said. She had finished fixing up the little house yesterday, opening the windows to air the place out. She had promised Jim that she would let Jack get some rest and acclimate himself to the place before she intruded. Now she was waiting for him to arrive.

She figured her office would be the best place for them to meet first. With all her security measures—soundproof walls, no wireless devices, a hidden gun—she figured they were safest here to have an open discussion.

But she hated waiting. She realized, much to her dismay, that she had sharpened all her pencils while she sat there. She brushed the shavings into the trash and stashed them in her drawer. There was a light knock. The door was ajar; she had kept it open, so she'd appear ready to greet them.

Jim peeked his head in.

"Ready?" he said.

"Yep." She felt a twinge of butterflies in her stomach.

Jim stepped aside and motioned Jack into the room. The man was of average height, probably close to six feet and in great shape. He had steel gray eyes under a head of dark, wavy hair that was cut short. He wore a blue t-shirt and khaki pants and seemed as nervous as she felt.

Francie stood and motioned to a chair in front of her desk.

"Have a seat," she said.

Jack sat down, clasping his hands between his knees and letting them dangle down. He glanced at her and then looked around nervously.

"Welcome to Sunnyhill," she said.

"Thank you." He looked at her. "Thank you... for... what you did."

"Oh, well, you know. All in a day's work," she said. He didn't smile and looked down at his hands. He was a very handsome man, and she could see that his bone structure had been nice long before she paid for his face.

She looked up at Jim.

"I moved him into the house," Jim said. "Thanks for putting milk and cereal in the fridge. I didn't even think of giving the man food. Later, I'm going to pick up some more groceries for him. I figured we'd let him get used to the farm before he has to face the real world. A lot has changed in twenty years."

There was silence. Jack continued to look at his hands. Francie noticed they were trembling. She needed to take control of the situation. "Okay," she started to say, but when she spoke, he flinched. She sat back in her chair and took a deep breath.

"Jack," she said. "Is that what I should call you?"

"Yes," Jim said. "We can't use Paul anymore. Too risky."

Jack looked up again. "Should we even be having this conversation here?"

"We can speak freely here," Francie said. "You've probably noticed I'm a bit eccentric and have the place locked down better than Fort Knox."

No response. She dropped her attempt at light-hearted humor. Her tone turned more serious.

"That's because I love my horses and want to keep them, but it'll also come in handy protecting you," she said. "As for this room, it's protected as well, and nobody can trace or hear what is said in here. So I'm going to speak freely."

She softened her voice.

"I inherited this farm from my grandfather. It's called Sunnyhill, but he always said the 'SH' stood more for 'safe haven.' I don't know what you've been through, but I want you to know that you're safe now." She paused and saw him swallow. "The house Jim took you to is your home. You can come and go freely. You aren't a prisoner here, but I would appreciate you living here for a year or two so we can firmly establish your new identity and hopefully safeguard our secret."

He nodded.

She continued softly, as if talking to a frightened horse. "Can you look at me?"

Slowly, he raised his eyes to meet hers. They were clear and gray—intelligent eyes. Kind, she'd say, yet fearful. His hands were still trembling, and she noticed scars around both wrists.

"I didn't kill that man," he said.

"That's what Jim says," she said.

"It's important to me that you believe that," he said.

"I believe in Jim." She looked at her brother. "And he believes in you. That's good enough for me. Besides, you saved my brother's life. That means something."

There was another long silence. Jack rubbed his hands together, trying to quiet the trembling.

He was afraid. Of her? Of his past? Of being discovered and returned to prison? She'd be back in there with him, if that were the case. She almost asked, but it seemed too intimate of a question for their first meeting.

Jim saw her hesitate.

"He's been through a lot," said Jim. "He's disoriented. In the past six weeks he was dragged out of prison at 3 a.m., put through plastic surgery, given a new identity... "

"I know," she said quietly. "This has been a bit nervy for us all."

"You realize what you did is treason against your country," Jack said. "If you get caught —"

"If I get caught, we both go to jail," she said. "And I'll probably face execution. I know."

They looked at each other for a few heartbeats, searching. She sighed, frustrated by his fear. She hadn't expected that. Her heart went out to him, and she wanted to protect him, to help him realize that it was all going to be okay now. *Francie, stay out of it,* she told herself. *He's a man, not one of your horses, or the children you've brought in.*

She got back to business. "There aren't many rules," she said. "My biggest rule is no smoking anywhere near the barn." One of the first things she'd noticed was the pack of cigarettes bulging in his t-shirt pocket. "I'd also prefer you don't smoke in the house. You have a nice porch out back, so if you can smoke outside, I'd appreciate it. I just have a problem with fire. We had a barn almost burn down a few years ago." She smiled a little, to soften things.

"Yes, ma'am," he said, looking her in the eyes again. A lock of his hair fell across his forehead.

Gosh, he's handsome.

Francie blinked. "And please don't get drunk. You can drink, but I've never seen anything good come out of people who get drunk, and you and I have got quite the role-playing to do, so we have to stay sharp. Otherwise, we're both going to jail."

He smiled a little bit at that.

"I understand," he said.

"And don't call me ma'am. It makes me feel old. Call me Francie. From now on, if anybody asks, you're the assistant manager for my farm. That's what I hired you for, and I even have your resume. It was anonymously mailed to me a few weeks ago in response to the ad I placed in the paper."

The people she hired had done a remarkable job covering tracks and buying this man an entire life.

"You'll eventually work with my manager, Frank, and we'll find you some jobs here on the farm to do. Whatever you think you'd like to do or would be good at you can try. But for the next two weeks, just relax and re-acclimate yourself to life on the outside again."

"I was going to study architecture in school before I was drafted," Jack said. "I'm pretty good with numbers. And I'm strong. I'm not against getting dirty and doing some hard physical labor around the farm."

Francie smiled. "We could use you in both those areas," she said.

She stood. "If you have any questions, feel free to ask me any time. You and I are in this together, Jack. The adults who live here in this house know who you really are, but outside of that, mum's the word."

He stood and reached his hand across the desk to shake hers.

"Welcome home," she said and was surprised to see his eyes wet with unshed tears.

"Thank you," he said, and he and Jim left.

Not a minute had passed before Sam came in and shut the office door. She plunked herself down in the chair Jack had just been in.

"Oh my gosh, he's *gorgeous!*" she said. "How often do you think he works out? Like every day?"

"Sam, you're married!" Francie said.

"Yeah, but I'm not blind," she said. She giggled. "So... dish."

"He's a wreck," said Francie. "Seems like a nice guy, but he's a nervous wreck."

"Well, can you blame him?"

"No. He's been through a lot. Jim only knew part of his history, but I'm guessing abuse and mistrust play a pretty big role. I just wonder what they did to him in Vietnam."

"Jim said he doesn't remember most of it," Sam said.

"If that's true, he's blocked it out. And when it resurfaces, it won't be pretty."

"He'll be fine," Sam said.

Francie looked at her. "Is that a premonition?"

"Take it however you want," she said cryptically. "But you'll both be fine."

Ken walked in the office as Sam was leaving. "Did you enjoy your secret little meeting?" he asked Francie. He smiled and kissed her. He had gradually forgiven her and softened toward her these past few weeks.

"Yes, dear," Francie said, hugging him. "He's wonderful. Everything's wonderful."

"Mmmmmm," he said, hugging her closer.

"The office door is open!" Steve yelled from the hallway. "Can you two ever stop? Must be some pheromones in that hat you wear, Ken. Geesh."

Francie and Ken laughed, and Ken kicked the door closed with his foot.

"So you're not completely freaked out about having a criminal living in our home, among our children and near your horses?" he said.

"He's not technically *in* our home," Francie said. "And no. I'm not. I know in my heart I did the right thing. I think he's innocent."

"You *think*," said Ken. "That's comforting."

"You're having second thoughts?"

"I never had first thoughts," he said. "As you recall, you had your mind made up when you told me about your plan."

She drew back and looked at him.

"Are you still angry?"

"No, Francie. Honestly, I'd be surprised if you had decided not to do it. It's who you are. It's why I fell in love with you."

She laid her head on his shoulder.

"Thanks for letting me."

He snorted. "Letting isn't the word I'd use."

As Ken left, Frank walked in. The place was like Grand Central Station.

"Your turn," Ken said, tipped his hat, and pulled the door closed.

"Well?" Frank said. Steady brown eyes looked at hers. He raised an eyebrow.

"It's okay," she said.

"Is it?" he said.

"It is. Really."

Frank smiled and sat down in the chair.

"Oh, Frank," she sighed. "I've really gotten myself into it this time, haven't I?"

"You made it through the hard parts," he said. "You even fooled Mark, I think."

"I'm just not so sure I'm comfortable lying. I've always hated lying and swore I'd never do it, especially after what I went through with my parents. They always lied to us, we lied to them, everybody lied just to protect themselves. I said I'd never do that, and here I am. Lying."

"To protect someone," he finished.

"Yes."

"Maybe sometimes the end justifies the means."

"Does that make it okay?"

"I don't know." He gazed past her to look out the window. Some horses were grazing in the back near the stream. There should have been at least a dozen more horses out there this year, but they had been sold to liquidize her assets. "You didn't really do it to get anything out of it, so I guess you can't lose."

"What if he can't adjust to life on the outside? He's been in prison here for 18 years, and before that was a POW for two... "

"It's not like you to doubt," Frank said. "Just give him time and no pressure. The open fields, the sea—all of this freedom might be just the balm he needs. I'd like to meet him."

"I told Jim we'd all get together this afternoon. I'll call you."

"Okay." Frank stood to go. "Come here," he said and pulled her into a hug. "It always works out in the end."

The office was very quiet that afternoon as the others filed in. Jack was sitting on the couch. Francie noticed that no one sat next to him, so she closed the door and did so herself. She preferred standing, but she felt she needed to make a point.

"So," she said, motioning to the man at her right. "This is Jack Banner. Jack, this is Ken, Sam, Steve, Krista, and Frank. Frank is my farm manager, the man you've been hired to work with."

"Factiously hired," muttered Steve.

Francie ignored him. She briefly told Jack a little about each person.

"Hi," Sam said and held out her hand. "It's nice to meet you."

Jack leaned forward and shook her hand. Ken followed, which made Francie love him even more, and then Frank. No one else moved. Krista had her arms crossed. She looked casual, but Francie knew that meant she was mad.

"Do you like your house?" Sam asked.

"Um... yes. Very much," Jack said. His hands were trembling.

The room was too quiet. Francie looked at Ken for help.

Ken cleared his throat. "I think you'll like it here," he said in his slow, easy Texan manner. "Before long, you'll probably even have your own horse."

Jack nodded and attempted a smile. A bead of sweat ran down his temple. Francie realized he couldn't take much more.

Just as she was about to adjourn the meeting, Jack spoke.

"I... um... " He cleared his throat and clasped his hands together. He looked around the room at each of them. "I want to thank you all for what you've done for me," he said.

"*We* didn't do it," Steve said. "Francie did. With a little help from her bro." He jerked a thumb at Jim. "But I'm sure it'll be fun living with an escaped convict under the constant scrutiny of the feds. Now I can check that off my bucket list."

Steve laughed. No one else did.

"Seriously," Steve said. "Did you know we've got this here room so secure *God* can't even see us? Maybe that's a good thing." He smiled.

"Steve," Francie warned.

"What? I'm just trying to be friendly."

"You need a filter," she said. "Okay, meeting adjourned." She got up quickly, but Steve wasn't finished.

"Well, I'm just saying, Francie, how are you going to live with yourself? You've preached to me all these years about being a Christian, and now you've gone and broken all sorts of laws. And you want us to *lie* for you? Isn't God going to zap you down for this?"

Francie looked at him. The room was deathly quiet. Krista raised an eyebrow in question.

"We can talk about this later," Francie said.

"Later?" Steve said. "I think now is the perfect time." He turned to Jack. "This isn't your fault," he said. "I seriously doubt she asked you what *you* wanted. She's like that— does her own thing." He looked at Jim. "Apparently your so-called religion is only when it's convenient."

Frank stood up. "Steve," he said rather firmly. "Later."

Ken tipped his hat at Jack. "Nice to meet you," he said and helped Francie quickly usher everyone out.

Frank shook Jack's hand. "I look forward to working with you."

"Jack, can you stay a minute?" Francie asked. Jim lingered. "Just Jack," she said gently. "Please."

After they left, she closed the door and sat down in the chair across from Jack. She couldn't help letting out a long sigh.

"I'm sorry," she said. "I didn't exactly tell them I was breaking you out of prison until I had actually done it. It was a bit of a surprise to them. It's just going to take a while."

He swallowed and nodded, rubbing his hands.

"They're all good people," she said. "Steve... he's a bit obnoxious. But he's good. And they all support me. They're just scared. It has been an intense six weeks."

Jack looked at her. "You shouldn't have done this," he said. "If the feds find me—"

"They won't find you," she interrupted. "I want to show you something." She picked up a remote control and locked the door with it. Then she stood up and walked over to her bookcase, which covered the entire wall to the side of her desk. She moved aside a volume and reached her hand behind it. There was a click, and the bookcase slid aside to reveal an opening. A door.

"My grandfather built this house," Francie said. "He said if we ever went back to the days of slave trading or running the Jews out or Christian persecution or whoever, he wanted them to have a place to hide. It leads to Sam and Steve's closet, where you can exit from behind her dresses and escape out the window and down a trellis. Probably best to stay inside though."

She closed it and slid the book back in place.

"The only ones who know about it are Sam and me. And Frank. And now you."

"Not your husband?"

"I never really got around to telling him," Francie said. She sat back down and looked at his hands.

"You're safe here," she said.

"Maybe," he said.

She smiled. "Have faith. Now go home and get some rest. Jim is going to take you shopping tomorrow. Don't let him pick out your clothes though. He'll dress you like a rock star."

Jack smiled at that.

"Francie?" He seemed to struggle for words. "Thank you."

She smiled. "You're welcome." She unlocked the door, and he went home.

Krista jumped into redecorating with a flourish. Painters, carpenters, and carpet installers all turned the house into a dusty, noisy mess. They stripped wallpaper, removed moldings, sanded, laid carpet, and puttied. The chaos got to Francie, and she retreated to her office.

Even in the soundproof room, she felt the trembling of the house as it was violated. She couldn't take it anymore and decided to visit Jack. She had given him a week to get adjusted and wanted to see how he was doing. All she knew from Jim was that he was okay and that they had been bar-hopping several times and that Jack had brought home a new woman each night. She frowned when she saw a different car there for the third night in a row, but Ken smiled and said, "Give the man a break. He hasn't been with a woman in twenty years."

The night before, Jack had stayed home, so there were no visitors at his house. She knocked.

"Have you been to the barns yet?" she asked when he answered his door.

"No. Jim said that was your territory."

"Come on, I'll give you a tour."

They walked slowly toward the barns. Jack was wearing jeans and a t-shirt—both looked new.

"Did Jim pick those clothes out?" she asked.

"No. I took your advice and did my own shopping."

She laughed. "You did well!"

"You can't really go wrong with jeans and a t-shirt. I haven't shopped in twenty years, so was wondering if I was in style. I could look better."

Francie glanced over at him. *Anything would look good on that body.*

Out loud she said, "Hey, don't belittle your looks. I paid a lot of money for that face."

He smiled.

She showed him the stallion barn first and told him about Flame, then she took him into the barn that housed the mares and foals. Star poked her head over her stall door and nickered at Francie. Francie stopped and rubbed the mare on the nose.

"This is my horse," Francie said.

"Aren't they all your horses?"

She laughed. "Yes, I guess most of them are. But this one is special. My grandpa gave her to me when I was thirteen."

"Wow," Jack said. "How long do horses live?"

"Not long enough," Francie said and produced a carrot. She broke it in half and gave a piece to Jack.

"Usually early- to mid-twenties. Star is twenty-three." She fed her half carrot to Star and waited for Jack to do the same. He hesitated, but gingerly fed it to her, and the mare took it gently.

"These buildings are beautiful," Jack said, noting the stamped concrete in the aisle. "And so clean."

A cat came out from behind a bale of hay, followed by five kittens.

Jack smiled. "Who's this?"

"That's Pudgy," Francie said. "One of our grooms found her. She was a stray, and he brought her here. We named her Pudgy because we thought she was fat, but it turns out that she was pregnant."

She scooped up one of the kittens. He was a small gray with tiny white paws and a white throat.

"This little guy is my favorite," she said. "He's very affectionate." The kitten had already started purring.

"Here." Francie handed him to Jack, who held up his hand to stop her.

"Oh, no. I'm not really an animal person."

She laughed again. "Well, you'll have to get over that if you're going to live here," she said. "Besides, how do you know you're not an animal person? When's the last time you actually held a kitten?"

Their eyes met. After a moment, Jack awkwardly held out his hands. Francie set the tiny cat in them. It started to fidget.

"You have to hold him next to your body, so he feels secure," she said. "Like this." She gently reached forward to press his hands against his chest, but as soon as she touched him, he flinched. She let go, and the kitten, now against his chest, settled down and resumed purring.

"I don't like to be touched," he said quietly. Trying to put him at ease, she attempted humor. She tilted her head and put her hands on her hips.

"Except by the various ladies you've been bringing home every night."

It worked. He forgot his previous discomfort and was now embarrassed. He turned red.

"You noticed that, huh?"

"Can you pick *one?* Or maybe two? All these different women... I mean... eww."

Jack laughed. The kitten washed his ears and his paws and settled down to sleep, still purring.

"Now you have to stand here until his nap is over," Francie said.

Jack smiled, and they watched the tiny gray ball of fur. So peaceful. With his focus on the kitten, Jack relaxed.

"Do you want him?"

Jack looked up. "No, I'm not ready for a pet. I'm still getting used to the idea that I have to match my clothes."

She laughed, which woke the kitten. Jack gently set him down on the floor, where he ran back to join his littermates.

They started to walk back toward the house.

"If I may ask, how much did you pay for my face?"

She pushed her hands into the pockets of her jeans. "A girl doesn't ever tell a man what she paid for something," she said. "Especially when we don't get it on sale."

"That much, huh? And look what you got for it," he pointed to his chest. "Me. Pretty shabby deal."

"Actually, I got a blue jean company in New York too. It's not much now, but I envision big things. You can help me run it."

"Me? You're awfully confident."

"As I see it, we're stuck with each other for a couple of years. What else are we going to do?"

"Sounds like fun."

"Are you getting settled into your house? I wasn't really sure how to decorate it. I didn't know what your favorite colors were. I just tried to bring nature in and make it manly."

"It's perfect," he said. "I'm finally sleeping. I even take naps!"

She glanced at him. "Probably because you're too busy at *night* to sleep."

He smiled. "Despite the fact that I sometimes have company—"

"Sometimes?"

"—there is a great deal of actual sleeping."

They both laughed. She stopped at his door. "All right. Go take your nap. I'm going to go get some work done."

chapter

33

FRANCIE WALKED INTO THE HOUSE one day after doing barn chores. Becky was sitting at the table with Jack, eating an evening snack. Chico's cage was empty.

"Where's the bird?" Francie asked.

"I let him go," Becky said.

"You let him go?"

"Yeah. Nothing should have to live in a cage." Becky glanced at Jack, then realizing that was the wrong thing to do, quickly looked away. Francie followed her gaze to meet Jack's eyes.

"True enough," Francie said. "It's okay."

She started mixing up some tea, which was what she had come in for. "What did he do when you let him go?"

"There was a flock of Quaker parrots in the tree out front. He flew up to them. He found his friends."

"Oh," she said. "That's sweet."

Suddenly and unexpectedly, she felt tears forming. It was all too much. Chico's empty cage, the tension of the past weeks. The tears threatened to spill over. She bit her bottom lip and concentrated on stirring the tea, glad that they couldn't see her face. Despite her efforts, a tear escaped down her cheek at the same moment that Jim stepped into the kitchen, rattling his keys.

He didn't seem to notice.

"You ready?" he asked Jack.

"Yep." Jack got up from his chair.

"Bye, sis. We're going out. Don't wait up."

Francie just nodded, still stirring and looking down at her glass.

"I'm going to my room," Becky said and disappeared, leaving Francie alone with her tea.

The next morning, Frank brought her coffee to the track as usual.

"Thanks," she said and clicked her stopwatch. "This is a good colt."

"He looks like his daddy." He was the same brilliant red as Starfire's Image. Image was producing fast and sound offspring.

Francie took a sip of her coffee. "I don't think I fully realized the implications on the children when I did what I did," she said.

It took Frank a minute to realize what she was talking about.

"How do you mean?" he asked.

"Chico."

"The bird. I heard about that."

"The kids are rethinking what's right and what's wrong. Do you think I mixed that up for them?"

Frank glanced at her and raised his eyebrows.

Francie sighed. "I know. I broke the law."

"That's putting it mildly."

"But they don't know that. They don't know who he is."

They sipped their coffee some more.

"And Jack was alone in the kitchen with Becky yesterday when I walked in. Jim had gone upstairs to get his keys."

"Does that worry you?"

"I'm not sure. I never even thought about it until it happened. Should I be worried?"

"I think you should be cautious and vigilant, yes. You would with anybody you hired."

"True."

They watched the next colt exercise and didn't discuss it anymore.

Exactly two weeks after Jack arrived, Frank met with him in Francie's office with the door closed.

"Are you ready to start working?" Frank asked.

"It'll be good to have something to do," Jack said.

Frank put some ledgers on the desk. "I use these to run the farm. They tell us how many horses we have, how much hay we need, how many foals we have on the ground in the spring, etcetera. This one"—he picked up a red ledger—"tells us what staff we have and the jobs that need to be done along with corresponding hours. This includes contract work, like Jim's landscaping work, pavers, plumbers, and electricians. Whatever we need."

Jack interrupted him. "I suppose I could ask Jim this, but why didn't you give him this job and leave me to do the landscaping or something?"

"Jim wants time to think. He composes songs in his head while he's riding on the mower. He prefers to use his thinking energy for playing guitar in those gigs he has. In other words, he's happy where he is." Frank put his hand on the stack of ledgers. "I'd like you to spend some time going over these to familiarize yourself with our business, and what it takes to run it."

Jack nodded.

"The good part about teaching you all this is if I ever get sick or take a long vacation, you should be able to run the place."

"And the bad part?"

Frank didn't answer.

"She's trusting me with a lot," Jack concluded.

"She's already put her life at stake for you, so I guess she figured she might as well jump in with both feet. We've needed an assistant manager for some time, and you have as much at stake here as she does. That is, if you both want to stay alive."

Jack looked across the desk at Frank.

"And do you want me to stay alive, Frank?"

Frank sighed. "Yes, I do. Francie has done a lot to give you a second chance at life, and I intend to help her succeed. I don't support how you came to be here, but now that you're here, I promised her I would support you both. You need to know I'm on your side."

Jack swallowed, unable to answer for a moment. He kept expecting people to hate him, and instead, he kept getting mercy. "I won't let you down. I owe you my life and am indebted to you."

"You're not indebted," Frank said. "That's the beauty of it. She wants you to be free, so please don't do this because you feel like you owe us. We're just helping you get started."

"You can't just give me so much and expect nothing in return," Jack said.

"Sure we can," Frank said. "It's called grace." He smiled. "Now let's get started."

chapter
34

LIFE RETURNED TO NORMAL AFTER THAT, or as normal as things could be with various adopted children and America's Most Wanted hidden in the house.

Fall came, and the University of Michigan accepted Mickey on a scholarship to study computer science and engineering, leaving Frank and Krista with an empty bedroom. The girls went back to school. The redecorating was finished, and things quieted down.

The house looked incredible, and Krista took her creativity outdoors to the landscaping. Racing season ended, and Francie came home permanently until the start of spring.

The Sunday after Thanksgiving was cool and cloudy, and Krista decided to decorate for Christmas. They hauled boxes up from the basement.

"Oh, Francie, this won't do," she said, looking at the faded decorations and old boxes. "Let's change things around a bit."

So the two of them went shopping and picked a theme. Angels, of course.

Krista found throw pillows, figurines, bulbs, candle holders, and table runners.

When they got home, Ken had a big crock pot of beef stew cooking, and the house smelled wonderful. He and Frank had put the tree up, and the kids had the ornament boxes out, waiting.

"I invited Jack to join us," Ken said, wrapping his arm around Francie in a warm hello.

"You are so sweet," Francie said. She and Krista were arranging their new decorations when Jack arrived. Steve put on some Christmas music to set the mood. The kids dug in.

"Where did this ornament come from?" Jessica asked, holding up a little wooden doll from one of the old boxes.

"That was Grandma's. A friend went to Germany and brought it back to her," Francie said.

Steve unwrapped a bright, shiny pickle. "This, my father gave to me," he said.

"I don't want to know why," Francie said.

"Well, if you must know... "

"I said I don't want to."

"If you must know, the pickle is a Polish tradition. Or maybe German. I'm not sure I'm either. Hmmm."

Jack was standing quietly by the living room door.

"Here." Jim handed him a box of bulbs. "Get to work."

Everyone was hanging ornaments, and for several, there were stories of where they had come from or memories attached. It took over an hour to decorate. Rascal found an old candy cane and ate it before anyone could stop her.

Finally, the tree was done, and Steve took the star out of a box. "The newest member of the family gets to put it on," he said. "Last year that was Krista."

"I wasn't really new," she said. "Been coming here since I was born."

"But you were newly married and new to us," Steve said. "This year," he looked around. "This year it's—drum roll please—Jack!" He handed him the star.

Jack hesitated but only for a moment. With a steady hand, he took the star and reached up and put it on the tree.

"God bless us, every one!" Krista said.

"Let's eat!" Ken said.

That night, Francie lay in bed in the darkness next to Ken.

"You are amazing," she said.

"Me?"

"Yes. Just all the support you've given me with Jack. And you are making such an attempt to include him. It was sweet of you to invite him to help decorate the tree."

He rolled over and whispered. "It's all part of the plan. When they come to arrest you, I'll say, 'Hey, don't look at me. I was inviting the guy over to dinner, asking him to Christmas, I had no idea.'"

Francie giggled.

"Seriously, though," Ken said, "it's not like he has any family he can go home to, and I really do like the guy. We also owe him a debt for fighting for our country. He was a POW. I wasn't. People like him fight so the rest of us can be free, stay home, watch TV, and order pizza."

"Well, no matter your motives, thank you."

"You're welcome, darlin'. Do you want to show me exactly how much you appreciate me?"

"Not with that attitude."

"Would it help if I put the hat on?"

France erupted in giggles and rolled over on top of Ken, locking lips with him and pulling the covers over their heads.

"We should invite Mark to Christmas," Krista said. "It would be fun to have us all here."

Francie shook her head. "No. That's exactly the problem. We're *all* here. I'm not going to put Jim through that."

Krista sighed. "We're all adults now. Don't you think we can get past that? Or that Jim can just let it roll off?"

Francie frowned. "Krista, don't you remember how cruel Dad and Mark were to Jim? Jim finally has his life together. I'm not going to bring Mark in to ruin things."

"I'll talk to Mark. He'll listen to me."

"I don't trust him."

Krista crossed her arms. "Well, Papaw *did* say that this farm was supposed to be a safe haven for us all, and that we were *all* invited here, right?"

"His exact words: *safe haven.* If Mark is here, it isn't safe for Jim. And as you just pointed out, Papaw left that decision up to me, didn't he?"

Krista scowled at her and turned and left the room, shutting the door rather firmly for emphasis.

It was an unusually cold December. Francie walked slowly across the yard toward Jack's house, Rascal at her heels and Mittens trailing behind her. At his door, she pointed to the dog.

"Sit," she said. Rascal obediently plunked her furry little rump down. "Good girl. Now, stay." The dog whined but obeyed.

Francie knocked on Jack's door. There was no answer. She looked down at Rascal. "He has to be home," she said. "It's not like he has a car. I guess he could be at the barn."

Mittens rubbed against her legs. She loved how the animals followed her around. She knocked again.

Jack opened the door. He looked terrible. He was trembling all over and sweating.

Francie was too stunned to speak, and neither of them said anything for a moment. Finally, she asked, "Are you okay?"

"No. I mean... yes."

"Which is it?"

"I just need a cigarette." He turned, leaving her standing in the open front door, and he walked through the house, disappearing out the back door.

She glanced at Rascal. "Stay."

Francie followed Jack. Something made her speak before she opened the screen door, but he still jumped. His hands were shaking so badly that he couldn't light his cigarette.

"Here," she reached for the lighter and lit it for him.

"Thanks." He puffed at it a few times, then took a long drag. He sat down in a deck chair and expelled the smoke slowly. Then he leaned his head back against the wall and closed his eyes.

Francie watched him for a few minutes, not sure if she should talk or leave.

"Why are you here?" he asked.

She jumped at the broken silence. "I came to invite you to Christmas dinner."

"On Christmas Day?"

"That's generally when we have it."

"You don't need to be a smart ass."

She frowned. "And you don't need to be so rude."

"I'm just... I'm just having a bad day."

"Look, I'm sorry," Francie said. "This was supposed to be a nice thing, but obviously my timing is bad. We can talk about it later." She turned to go. As she left, she put her hand on his shoulder, meaning to give him a little squeeze like she did to Jim all the time. But as soon as she touched him, he jumped out of the chair and jerked away from her.

"I told you I don't like to be touched!"

He frightened her, but she took a deep breath to calm her heart, then looked him in the eye.

"Tell me what happened to you."

"It's none of your damn business."

"It *is* my business. I made your business my business four months ago in case you forgot, and it would help me greatly—help *us*—if you would talk to me. I don't know any more about you now than the day I broke you out of prison." They both looked around nervously, as if someone was listening, but Francie continued, "I can't help you if I don't know what you need."

"I didn't ask for your help," he said quietly.

She stared at him. "Did you want to die in there?"

"No," he said. He took another long drag of his cigarette.

"Why do your hands shake?"

"Look, Francie, I just had a flashback, okay? A bad memory from the war. That's all. I'm sure your brother has them too. I'll be fine in a couple of minutes. Probably sooner if you leave me alone."

His hands shook when he hadn't just had a flashback too, but she wasn't going to mention that.

"We could find someone... " she said.

"Someone for me to talk to?" he finished bitterly. "You mean like a shrink? And tell him what? The story of my life? Which one? The real one or the fictitious one? They gave me a shrink when I first came out of Nam and was in prison. He tried to help me calm down and de-stress. I guess they didn't want me to be a nervous wreck when they strapped me in the electric chair."

His eyes met hers, challenging. She returned his gaze quietly, refusing to let him anger her.

"Jack," she said gently. "I just came to invite you to Christmas dinner. It's at 6 p.m." She continued to look at him, waiting.

He stubbed out his cigarette and smiled.

"Okay, Princess. I'll be there."

"Don't call me that."

His voice softened. "I'm sorry. It's just when the adrenaline gets going, I get nasty."

"Well, don't let it happen around the kids. I'll see you later."

She turned and left.

Jack watched her go. "Yeah," he muttered. "I'll try not to let it happen around the kids." He shook his head. "She's clueless. They all are." But actually, with Francie, he didn't quite believe that.

chapter
35

THE NEXT DAY AFTER DINNER, Jack showed up in her kitchen. She was drinking coffee with Ken, and both girls had their homework on the table, but it wasn't the topic of discussion.

"I don't see why I can't go to the school's holiday dance with him," Becky was saying. She sharpened a crayon for Lexie, who was coloring next to her.

"Honey," Ken said. "I told you. It's because he looks like a rock star and that means trouble."

"I think he's hot," Jessica said. "You should let her go. No woman should have to give up the chance for a date with a rock star."

Frank was on the phone talking to someone about breeding rights. The conversation was getting heated. Krista and Sam were washing and drying dishes.

"Sit," Francie motioned Jack to a chair. "Enjoy the chaos."

Ken broke from his discussion with Becky long enough to nod. "Hi, Jack."

"Hi, Ken," Jack said, taking a seat. He inclined his head to Francie. "Hi, Princess." He smiled.

She scowled. "Don't call me that."

"Princess!" Steve's loud voice rang out as he came into the house, letting the screen door slam behind him. "That is the perfect nickname for you! You sit up there in your little tower all day giving out commands to your many knights. I'm ashamed I didn't think of it myself."

Francie started to reply, but the sight of him—and his companion—stopped her.

"What is that thing?" she asked.

"This," Steve said with a flourish toward the large dog at his side, "is Guardian."

"Oh Daddy, can we keep him?" Lexie jumped out of her chair and ran to the door, gave Steve a big hug and then began petting Guardian. The dog was a large, black lab, who looked like he had never had a bath in his life. He sat there obediently by Steve's side, his tongue hanging out, taking in the scene, unconcerned with all the people around him and the little girl hugging him to death.

"You probably want to know his story and how he came about his name," Steve said.

"Go ahead, enlighten me," said Francie evenly.

"He saved my life, just this very day," Steve said.

"How unfortunate," Francie said.

"Francie, he saved Steve's life," Sam said, putting her drying rag down to come over and pet the dog. "Tell us about it, honey."

"Well," Steve said, "you know what a rough place the track can be. The other day I may have accidently cut off Buddy Larson's horse on the rail, causing him to place behind me. I don't know. The stewards discounted the claim. Anyway, today Buddy and his very large friend Bruno (I'm not sure of his name, but that one fits) decided to teach me a lesson. They cornered me in our tack room." He glanced at Francie. "You really need more security down there. So they had me cornered in the tack room and were going to talk to me"—he made invisible quotes in the air with his fingers—"about proper riding etiquette. Suddenly, this large dog appears and pushes his way past them and stands in between me and them. He starts to growl, and the hair on his back raises up. They asked me, 'Whose dog is that?' and I said, 'He's mine, and he's gonna eat you alive if you don't leave.' It was then that Guardian here barked and showed some fierce teeth, and they turned tail and ran." Steve patted him on the head. "So I named him Guardian and brought him home."

"We're not keeping him," Francie said. "We already have a dog." Rascal was hiding under the table, unsure of this new, large creature.

Steve brought his hands to his heart in distress. "But Princess"—here Francie glared at Jack—"I thought we brought in strays and gave them a home." He gestured one at a time toward Lexie, Jessica, and Jack. Jack, despite himself, smiled. "And where's Mickey?"

"Dad!" Lexie scolded.

"Come on, Guardian. Safe Haven is now your home too." He started through the kitchen.

"Whoa, whoa, whoa!" Krista stepped in front of him. "You are not taking that dog across these new carpets!"

"But he needs a bath, and I was intending to do it in my very own shower."

"Out!" Krista says. "The hose first!" She pointed her finger toward the door. Guardian's ears drooped.

"I want to help!" Lexie said and ran to the basement to get a bucket and scrub brush.

"Alright," Steve said. "Come on, hero. Daddy will clean you up, so Mrs. Francie lets you sleep in the house tonight."

He smiled at Francie. She put her hands on her hips. "He can stay," she said. "But if he messes on the carpet, you're paying for a new one."

After he left, Becky took up her discussion with Ken about the boy. "I'll make you a deal. I'll bring him home next week for dinner, and you can meet him first and then decide. It's not fair to judge him by his looks."

Ken looked at Francie. She shrugged. "Fair enough," Ken said.

That settled, everyone quieted down. Francie took a sip of her coffee and offered Jack a cup.

He shook his head. "Can we talk?" he asked quietly.

"Sure. Let's go upstairs."

She led the way up to her office and closed the door behind him.

"We're still bug-proof," she said. "I scanned the room this morning."

Jack smiled and sat down in the chair across from her desk.

"Well," he said, rubbing his hands together, "I came to apologize."

Francie raised an eyebrow.

"For yesterday. I was a jerk and was rude and... and I'm sorry. Can we start over?"

Francie laughed. "We don't have much choice. I meant it when I said we we're stuck together forever. Like it or not."

"I guess I'd kind of rather you liked it. Liked me. I was just... " he sighed and leaned back in his chair, at a loss for words.

"It's hard, you know?" he said. "There's so much for me to deal with. I didn't even know how to use the microwave. It's all so new." He grew serious and quiet. "And yes, it would help if you knew more about me, but the truth is, I don't remember much of it. I'm not sure of everything that happened to me as a POW. I came home and was thrown into federal prison and never really got to process it. The guys in there weren't too friendly with someone who was accused of treason against their country, so I went from survival mode right back into survival mode. The shrink—the one I told you about—said that sometimes things are too bad for the mind to deal with so it blocks it out. Sometimes memories come in flashes. That's what happened yesterday."

Francie listened quietly.

"I meant what I said when I told you I want you to feel safe here," she said. "Whatever you need for that to happen, let me know."

"Thanks. I just wanted to be sure that we were okay. I'll try not to be such a jerk again."

"And I'll try to be more sensitive to the situation," she said. "Tonight's Friday night. Are you and my brother going out... fishing?"

Jack laughed. "Fishing. Yes, we are. Only your brother never brings any home."

"Why is that?"

"He's still hung up on Elise. He loves her."

"She's married now," Francie said.

"He knows that. He just can't seem to find anybody who lives up to her. Or his ideal of her. And the ladies like him; he catches plenty when we go out."

"The ladies have always liked him," Francie said. "And I don't think until Elise he ever had a steady girlfriend more than a month." She laughed. "Mom was so religious and so against premarital sex, and I think Jim broke that rule quite a few times!"

Jack smiled. "I'm pleading the fifth on that."

"Yeah, I don't really want to know about my brother's sex life!" She smiled. "At least he's happy. Finally."

"Yeah. And he's clean. He never drinks. He usually just plays his guitar on open mic nights. Or with his band."

Francie nodded. "And you?"

"Only one beer. We're kind of pathetic. But I get the girls too because I'm friends with the cool guy with the guitar."

Francie laughed.

"Well, I should go bait the hook. He wants to leave at 6 p.m."

"Bait the hook?" Francie asked.

Jack smiled. "I'm going home to wash up. Get your mind out of the gutter."

Francie laughed.

"See you later, Princess. Have a good night."

Rick DuVarren, the "rock star" teen Becky liked, came over for dinner the following Monday, just one week before Christmas Eve. The dance was that Friday, and the kids were off then for two weeks.

Francie had managed to make it a small family meal; no one else was home.

Rick had an infectious smile, and despite his "rock star" shoulder length hair, both Francie and Ken found themselves warming up to him. Ken was fantastic with everybody, and Francie watched him as he made Rick feel welcome and asked him questions about his music and his interests. They found out that he was on the honor roll and that he had won several awards in music. With each of these announcements, Becky gave a triumphant little smile.

Rick had brought his guitar, and with a little encouragement, he took it out and played them a few songs after dinner. He chose hymns, How Great Thou Art and John Denver's Sunshine on My Shoulders, which both Francie and Ken later discussed were for their benefit and probably not on the top of Rick's play list.

At any rate, he got an "A" for effort, and Becky was allowed to go to the dance with him.

When Becky walked down the staircase the following Friday night wearing a soft velvet dress, Francie and Ken took lots of photos. Jessica was just as pretty in her blue silk dress, and her date was riding with Rick. The girls were going together, which also made their parents feel better.

Rick showed up driving his dad's car, and they told the kids not to be home late.

"It feels so perfect," Francie said. "We're just like a real, live family!"

Ken pulled her into a hug. "Of course we are, darlin'. There's nowhere I'd rather be than by your side."

"I want so much for them to have a good childhood," Francie said.

"Well, I was going to save this, but I've been thinking up a plan, and I believe you and I should take the kids to Disney World."

"Disney World?" Francie said. "Really?"

"Yes," Ken said. "That's what families do."

"But there are rides and people and lines... "

"And fun and memories to be made. We'll go in February, before racing season gets underway."

Francie thought about it for a bit, and decided that she liked the idea. Her life was starting to fall into place. She was actually settling down, she thought with a smile. Imagine that!

"I'll plan it," Ken said. "We'll go for a week. I figure five days in the park, and a few just hanging out at the pool."

"Wow, you really have been planning this out in your head!" Francie said. "I don't think I've ever been on a real vacation. Not one that wasn't connected to a racetrack, anyway. Will there be horses?"

Ken laughed. "We can survive without horses for one week," he said.

"Will you at least wear your hat?"

He laughed again. "I only wear that when I'm riding, darlin'," he said.

"Or when you're flirting."

"It worked, too, didn't it? Look at the filly I caught!"

She turned into him and kissed him on the lips. "The girls won't be home for several hours," she said.

"Ohhh... and as I recall, our bedroom is soundproof!"
Francie grinned and took his hand and led him up the staircase.

chapter
36

CHRISTMAS EVE WAS COOL AND CLEAR. They had just finished a simple meal of chili and cornbread at the dining room table.

"Is everybody coming to church tonight?" Ken asked.

"We're going," Frank said and smiled at Krista.

"Lexie and I are going," Sam said. "Can we ride with you?"

"Steve, you're not going?" Ken asked.

"Nope. Staying home and playing Nintendo."

"Steve," Francie said casually. She saw Frank shoot her a warning look, but she ignored him. "What does Christmas mean to you?"

"Presents," Steve said with a smile and high-fived Lexie.

"Steve!" Sam said.

"Okay," he grew serious and looked at Lexie. "It's the celebration of Christ's birth. I respect that and firmly agree that you should all go to church. Lexie, it's your faith."

"Jack, are you going?" Francie asked.

"Careful," Steve warned. "She'll try to convert you."

"Maybe I'll stay here and play Nintendo with Steve," he said.

"Alright!" Steve high-fived Jack.

"Steve!" Sam elbowed him. "Lexie, if you're done, why don't you go outside and play. It's nice out."

"No, Mickey promised to show me a new game on his computer."

Mickey, who was home on break, put his napkin down. "I'm finished," he said. "Come on." He and the three girls went into his bedroom.

Sam hit Steve in the arm.

"Ouch!"

"You promised."

"Promised what?"

"Not to make fun of my faith. Ever."

"I was just joking," he said.

"It's not a joke," Sam said. "Lexie thinks you're going to Hell."

"Well, where'd she get that idea? Do you think I'm going to Hell?"

There was silence in the room.

"Jack," Frank said, "you're staying home?"

"I'm kind of afraid to say one way or the other," he said. There was laughter, which broke up the tension. "I've already been to Hell, so I guess I'll try church."

"I'm surprised Jim hasn't conned you into going before now," Frank said.

"I invited him once or twice," Jim said. He was always so quiet that people almost forgot he was there until he spoke. "Sometimes he prefers to sleep in."

"Mmmmm-hmmmm," Francie said.

"Francie, give the man a break about the women! He's been in prison for twenty years!" Steve said.

Jack turned red.

"One thing Christmas Eve is supposed to be about is peace on earth," Frank said, "and that's not what this feels like!"

They laughed, and Ken got up to get dessert.

Francie was leaning against the car, waiting for the others so they could leave for church. The sky was brilliant with stars.

Jack walked across the yard and stood next to her.

"Where is everybody?" he asked.

"Inside. The girls are primping."

Jack looked up at the sky. "It has been a long time since I've seen anything other than a cinderblock ceiling," he said. "I can't get enough of the nighttime sky and fresh air."

"Did you go to church as a kid?" Francie asked.

"Sometimes. Christmas, Easter. My parents believed in God, but they never pushed the issue."

"Do you believe in God?"

"I used to," Jack said. "But God would never let a human being go through what I went through and not intervene. So I guess I gave up on God."

"God hasn't given up on you," Francie said.

Just then the door opened, and the girls spilled out, talking all at once. Mickey followed with Sam and Jim. Ken grabbed his hat and locked up.

"Krista and Frank are going to meet us there," Francie said.

Mickey drove all the kids, and the five adults piled into Ken's car.

The church was beautifully decorated with pine and holly and was lit with candlelight. It filled up quickly, and Francie was glad that Frank and Krista had saved them seats. They slid down, and she and her group squeezed in, taking up the whole row.

They sang many of the traditional Christmas carols, and Ken put his arm around her waist, as always. She snuggled in and listening to his beautiful baritone. She glanced at Jack, and saw him singing along too, and wondered if he had learned the songs as a child. He sang well. Maybe she'd ask him and Jim to sing to them on Christmas, because she remembered Jim saying they sang together a lot in the war.

The pastor gave a great sermon on peace, and how Christ had come so that all could have salvation and peace.

At the end, they all held lit candles and sang Silent Night. It was moving, and Francie wished that Steve were with them.

Then they all piled back into the cars and went home. It was well after midnight when they returned, and they all headed back into the house. Jack stayed behind and lit a cigarette.

"I'll be in in a minute," Francie told Ken. She wandered back down the driveway toward Jack. He had opened the back to Frank's truck bed and was sitting on the edge, dangling his feet. She leaned against her car, a little distance away from the cigarette smoke.

"That was nice," Jack said, taking in a long draw. "The church was beautiful. Thanks for inviting me."

"When's the last time you were in church?" Francie said.

"Oh… it's probably been… I don't know. We had a chapel in prison, and a chaplain, but I only went a few times. That was when I first got there. Other than that, probably when I was about ten."

"Wow."

"How about you? Were you raised going to church? You seem very religious."

"Very religious," Francie mused. "Why do you say that?"

"You go every Sunday, and your kids are heavily involved in youth group on Wednesday nights. You have a Bible on your desk that looks well read. Sometimes you quote scripture to Steve."

She laughed. "Yeah, that last one is probably not a good thing. I need to leave Steve alone. My mother was a very devout church-goer," she said. "But her God was an angry God, a punishing God, and I was always in trouble for something, or sinning, or on my way to Hell. So I hated the church and God and pretty much anything tied to it. Then I met Frank. He introduced me to the real God. A loving God who is full of grace, forgiveness, and love. Like the Christmas story: God sent His son to this world in order to save us. We don't have to work our way to Heaven or anything—salvation is a free gift. God wants to give it to us, and all we have to do is ask. It's that simple. I was just amazed at that when Frank told me, and he backed it up with scripture. So I accepted Jesus as my savior and haven't looked back. It's just so much more than religion. It's a relationship. A relationship with the living God. It's just amazing."

Then she turned to him. "I'm sorry. I got on a roll and rambled quite a bit there, didn't I?"

"And your life has been great ever since?" Jack asked.

"Great is a strong word, but yes, pretty much. I am very blessed. I had a nightmare of a childhood, and now here I am. I have a great husband, great health, just... everything I ever wanted."

"Because of God?"

"No... I don't think becoming a Christian means your world is hunky dory. I just think it means that when things get bad, we have someone to run to. God is always there for us. I can't imagine He would ever let me down."

"What if the worst possible thing happened to you? What if you cried out to God to make it all stop and it didn't?" Jack asked. "For example, what if one of your kids died, or Ken left you, or you lost the farm? Heck, let's be more realistic—what if you end up going to jail? Could you still trust in God then?"

"I hope so," she said.

"I hope you never have to find out," he said. He stubbed his cigarette out. The moonless sky made the stars really stand out. He looked up, taking in their beauty, and breathed in the fresh air.

"Is that what happened to you?" she asked. "You cried out to Him, and he wasn't there?"

"Yes."

"Jack, God isn't going to make all the bad stuff go away, but if you accept Him as your Lord and Savior, if you just ask Him into your heart, you'll at least have a starting point. Somewhere to cling. A rock to stand on."

"I don't need anywhere to cling," he said. "I learned long ago to trust me, and that's it."

She looked at him. "Do you trust me?"

Their eyes met. "I think you mean well," he said. "I really do. I just wonder what would happen if the going got tough. Really tough. Your world seems so much in your control right now. I'm not sure how you would do if you lost control."

"Oh."

"I don't mean that as an insult. I know you're pretty tough, especially after what you did for me. Jim has told me how you took care of Sam and how you all looked out for each other as kids. I don't know. Let's just drop it. I'm not interested in becoming 'saved' or whatever you call it. As far as I'm concerned, I'm already saved. I was in Hell, and now I'm not." He smiled. "And thank you for that. Now let's get some sleep."

She smiled. "Okay. You're right. It's late."

"Goodnight, Princess," Jack said.

"I hate it when you call me that."

Christmas Day was full of flurry and excitement. The kids woke at dawn and dashed downstairs to tear open gifts. Even though they were all teenagers, except for Lexie, there was a lot of energy. Ken, who loved holidays and anything with his family, was snapping pictures, taking video, and trying out all their new toys and electronic gadgets with them. Steve was putting together something with a screwdriver for Lexie.

Frank and Krista came just as the excitement started, and Jack wandered in in the middle of it all with a steaming cup of coffee in his hand. Everyone was there. Afterwards, when the room was strewn with wrapping paper, Francie went into the kitchen and heated up some cinnamon buns, which she brought into the living room on a big platter. Everybody dug in.

"Okay, now that the kids are done, it's time for the adults," Ken said, and he started passing out presents by name. There were even boxes for Jack, and he had brought over some small presents as well.

Francie's highlight was a diamond pendant necklace from Ken. She also got clothes and a scarf and some new riding boots. The guys got sweaters and shirts and various gadgets or tools. Krista, who didn't really need any more clothes, got a big box from Frank that he insisted she open in front of everybody.

It was huge, and he had to carry it in from outside. He had kept it hidden in the barn and had put it in his truck bed last night.

"What is this?" Krista asked.

Frank winked. "It's a little something I made. Open it."

Krista tore away the wrapping paper, while everyone waited with bated breath. Then she worked on getting the cardboard open. When she lifted the top, she gasped, and tears immediately came to her eyes.

"You made this?" she asked Frank, looking from the depths of the box into his eyes.

"Yes, I did. I've been working on it at our house site when you were out of town."

"What is it?" Francie asked. "Don't keep us in suspense!"

Krista ripped the box, so the contents were revealed to everyone, then she took Frank's hand.

There sat a beautiful bassinet, handmade out of dark walnut.

"Ohhhhh... " Francie breathed, then met Krista's eyes.

"Frank and I have an announcement," Krista said, her tears finally spilling over. "I'm pregnant!"

Francie jumped up and grabbed Krista in a big hug, crying along with her. "I'm going to be an aunt!" she said. "Oh, Krista." Then she threw her arms around Frank and hugged him hard.

"I'm so happy for you," she whispered into his ear. "I'm so happy."

"Me too, sweetheart," he said, giving Francie a big hug back. "Me too."

Everyone was talking at once, wanting to know if they had names picked out.

Krista laughed. "I'm not due until August," she said. "I'm only eight weeks pregnant and probably shouldn't even tell you all until... you know... we're sure everything is okay, but we are just so excited that we couldn't wait!"

Krista hugged Frank. "I love it. It's so beautiful," she said. "Thank you so much, honey!"

It took a great deal of time for everyone to calm down. Finally, Jim said in his quiet voice, "We have one last gift."

Everybody got quiet. "It's to Jack, from all of us."

Jack looked up from his third cinnamon bun, a bit startled. "What? Me? I think you've all given me quite enough this past year."

Jim walked out of the room, and a minute later, he returned with a new guitar case. "I was going to wrap it, but Francie and I couldn't figure out how to disguise it," he said, "so here. Merry Christmas."

Jack set down his breakfast and wiped his hands. Carefully, he opened up the case. "This is like the guitar I once had. It's the same style—he carefully stroked the wood—"the same make, the same wood grain. It's practically the same guitar." He looked up at Jim. "How did you find one?"

"It wasn't easy," Jim said. "But we thought since you use to play, that you should start again."

"And we'd love for you and Jim to entertain us with some Christmas songs," Francie added.

Jack brushed his eyes with the back of his hand. "You people sure know how to make a grown man cry," he said, laughing. "I don't even know what to say."

"Thank you is usually the custom," Jim said.

"Thank you!" Jack said, laughing. "Thank you, thank you, thank you!" He smiled, then he strummed a few chords and tuned it. "Hopefully I can remember how to play," he said. But his muscle memory was there, and the guitar felt so familiar in his hands. Something stirred inside him that was reminiscent of joy. Suddenly, he was aching to give the instrument a try. "Go get your guitar, James, and let's make some music!"

chapter 37

STAR DIED PEACEFULLY IN HER STALL on a cool January morning at the age of 23, with a good long life behind her. Frank buried her in the pasture out back, near the gate she loved to jump.

About a week later, when no one else was home, Francie dug up a young sapling from the woods behind her barns and drove it to the spot where Star was buried. Her arms were tired from the work, and she was streaked with dirt that was turning to mud in the misty rain that had begun.

She stopped to catch her breath, and she saw a familiar figure walking across the pasture toward her with a shovel. It was Jim. Jim, who never came back to the barns.

He reached her and without speaking, in his typical, quiet manner, started to dig. The two of them worked side by side until the hole was wide enough for the tree. Jim set the sapling in place and helped shovel dirt around it. Finally, they both got on their knees together in the mud and packed the dirt down with their hands. It was raining harder now, and Jim's glasses were speckled with water, and his hair was plastered against his face.

When they had the ground the way they wanted it, Jim pulled a stone out of his pocket, about the size of his palm. It was round and smooth—a river stone.

"I found this in California," he said. "I used to pick them up when I walked."

He laid it near the tree as a marker.

"Thank you," Francie said.

He nodded and stood up, then turned and walked slowly back toward the barns, away from her, his shovel in his hand.

She stood there, alone in the rain, but feeling fulfilled and somehow not so sad.

chapter
38

KEN TOOK FRANCIE AND THE TWO GIRLS to Disney World in February, as he had promised. They did all the things normal families did.

"Mom, this is awesome," Becky said as they were reading by the pool on the last day, which was unusually warm for that time of year. "I think Ken is the best thing that has happened to us. Ever."

"Me too," Francie said, glancing at Ken, who had gone to get them all something cold to drink.

"He celebrates everything," said Jessica. "Like birthdays, holidays—he's so into having fun."

Francie smiled. "I know, girls. I love that about him."

"And he bought you those silly Goofy slippers," laughed Becky. "Are you going to wear them?"

"Of course I'll wear them. Our house gets cold in the winter."

"Good," said Becky. "They'll remind us to laugh more."

Ken came back with a tray of glasses.

"Lemonade for everyone," he said. "I got cute little straws with umbrellas on them. And for you, darlin', a rose." He handed her a single cut flower.

"Oh, Ken! Where did you get this?"

He leaned down and whispered, "I snapped it off the bush over there."

The four of them erupted in laughter.

"This is definitely the best vacation ever," said Jessica.

When they got back home, racing season was beginning. Donovan had been exercising the horses, and they were ready for Francie's fine-tuning. The days got busy, and Ken was gone late at his own farm, working his horses. At Francie's request, he brought home a small, brown mare one day.

Francie settled it into the barn, and later that week, she took Jack down to see it.

"I got you a horse to ride," she said.

He looked at the animal warily. "I don't really like animals."

"But you manage a horse farm, so it's important that you learn to ride."

"I can ride," he said.

"You can?"

"I used to ride when I was a kid. My friends owned a horse."

"Hmmmm."

"Really. I'm not great, but I might remember a thing or two if I ever need to."

"Well, you need to today," said Francie, giving the saddle girth one last pull. "Climb on."

"What?"

"Climb on. That's why I told you to wear those fancy boots I got you at Christmas."

Jack looked at the horse.

"Unless you're afraid," Francie said, crossing her arms.

He looked at her. "Afraid? I'll have you know I've been in a war. I'm a trained special unit soldier. Fear isn't in my vocabulary."

"Good. Then let's go." She nodded toward the horse. "Frenchie," she said to her groom. "Is King ready for me?"

"Yes, ma'am."

"We're going to ride out and see Frank's new house," she said.

Jack looked at the horse.

"I'm not going for a ride."

"Yes, you are."

"You're pretty used to people doing what you tell them to do, aren't you?"

"Yes. So don't buck the system. Get on the horse."

Jack shook his head, but he put his foot in the stirrup and swung aboard. "How do I know this animal won't kill me?"

"Because we picked her out special, just for you. Ken trained her. He's owned her since she was a baby, and she has been used for riding lessons. For beginners. She's kid-safe."

"Hmmmpf," Jack said.

Francie got up on King.

Jack looked at her chestnut gelding. "Isn't that the horse you brought in here a few months ago all messed up?"

"Yes, it is. This is Chessman's Victory, or King, as I've chosen to call him. I started riding him last month. You really ought to get down to the barn more."

"Wasn't he a rescue horse?"

"I took him off the track with a little help from the Humane Society," Francie said. "His previous owner isn't too happy with me."

"I see."

They walked out of the barn and turned their horses toward the back of the property. "Have you been down to the building site recently?"

"Not since they broke ground," Jack said.

They eventually moved their horses up to a trot, then to an easy canter. Jack was a pretty good rider. His hands were naturally soft on the horse's mouth, and he stayed in the saddle.

After a while, they rode over a the crest of a hill.

"There it is," Francie said. "Wow."

Sitting up on a hill overlooking the ocean was the beginning of Frank and Krista's house. Francie had seen the plans many times, but not until now did she appreciate the beauty of the setting. The porch, when finished, would look out over the ocean. A strong breeze blew in, carrying salt and sea with it, and the sound of the waves slapping against the beach was soothing.

"Wow," echoed Jack. "That's some wedding present you gave them. How come you don't live here?"

"It's too hard to manage the horses with all this wind, sand, and noise," Francie said. "Papaw wanted his house settled some place quiet. He also wanted a basement."

They dismounted and left the horses, then walked through the open structure.

"When will it be finished?" Jack asked.

"Not for a year. They plan to move in next spring."

"It'll seem like a mansion after that little apartment."

They looked around some more, and Francie pointed out which rooms were going to be where. Then they went back to their horses and mounted up again.

"You look good on a horse," she said.

"Thank you, ma'am," Jack said. "I do my best."

"And I just realized that you've been a couple of hours now without a cigarette," Francie said.

"I'm trying to quit," he said.

"Really?"

"Yes. It's not good for me, and you don't like it."

Francie smiled.

"See?" Jack said. "Used to getting your own way."

"I'll race you back," Francie said. "Only when we get to the gate, you need to stop. King and I plan to jump it."

"Frank hates when you jump that gate," he said.

"I know," and she put King into a canter and took off.

The racing year was going exceptionally well. Francie didn't win the Triple Crown with her horse, but she captured a lot of stakes races. She reveled in her victory, because she knew that the following year would be slim. She had sold her best babies to pay for Jack's escape, and that would have been the year they would be racing.

Krista started to round out, and looked even more beautiful, if that were possible.

"Francie," she said in June. "God has sent me an angel. I finally have an angel." She rubbed her belly.

"Krista, you've always had angels," Francie said. "You've been surrounded by them. Our guardian angels, remember?"

Steve walked in with his dog trailing behind him. "You need those angels, Francie," he said. "You've made a few enemies around the track. King's owner, especially, has harsh words for you."

Steve sat down at the kitchen table with the two women and patted his dog on the head. "I think you should start taking Guardian with you when you go to the track."

Francie sighed. "I think they're all talk," she said.

"I don't know," Steve said. "You've taken in several horses and turned them into winners. You've made some men—long time trainers—look like fools."

"That wasn't my intention," she said.

"Still... " Steve said.

"Well, I need to run over there now." She glanced at the dog.

"I'll go with you," Steve said.

"You and the dog look tired," Francie said. "I just need to talk to Donovan and run down our schedule. He's leaving with the horses in the morning."

"I'll be leaving with him," Steve said.

"All the more reason to get some rest. I'll take Jack with me."

"Jack?"

"Ken is at his farm, Frank is at the bank. That leaves Jack. I don't really think I need a bodyguard anyway."

"Jack wouldn't be my first choice," Steve said.

"I thought you liked him."

"I do. But I said you might need protection. He's"—Steve leaned forward—"he's an escaped prisoner."

Francie laughed. "Yes, but he's *our* escaped prisoner," she whispered back. "I'll just go alone. I always go alone."

"Take Jack," Steve said. "I just have a bad feeling."

Francie sighed. "Go take your shower and get packed."

"Promise me."

"I'll try," Francie said.

She couldn't find Jack. After a cursory look around the yard and a knock on his door, she decided to go alone. After all, she had been going to the track alone since she was sixteen.

She pulled her truck into the parking lot and went to their stable area to find Donovan. He was packing up a tack trunk.

"Hi," she said.

"Hey, Francie. Give me a hand here." He had her sit on the trunk while he snapped the lid shut.

"A little too full, I guess," he said, wiping sweat from his brow. He was in his mid-thirties with wavy blond hair that was already starting to go gray around the temples.

He kept his hair trimmed short, but when it got damp the little tendrils on the back of his neck curled.

"How do things look?" Francie asked, walking along the aisle and peeking into the stalls.

"We're looking good," he said. "You'll be up on the weekends?"

"Some. Not all. I brought you my calendar. I have Krista's baby shower, and Ken is whisking me off for a short weekend getaway for our anniversary."

Donovan grinned. "Great. You party while I work."

"That's what you get paid for," she said. He threw a rag at her, and she ducked. It hit one of the grooms.

"What the... ?"

"Sorry, Davie. My bad," said Donovan. "Don't worry about a thing, Francie. We're looking really good going into the season."

"How's Dream?"

"Vet looked at him this morning, and his tendon has healed up. He'll be ready to race by next week."

"I'll be sending you one of my rescue horses in about three weeks," Francie said. "He's clocking 25 a quarter as you saw in last week's workout."

"I'm looking forward to working with him. He's a nice colt." Donovan leaned in and spoke quietly. "Be careful. There's talk around the track. You've pissed people off."

"Steve told me," she said.

"I don't think anybody would hurt you, but you never know. Just watch your back," he said.

Francie nodded. "I'll help you out."

She grabbed a water hose and went down the aisle, filling buckets. After she was done, she said her goodbyes and left.

She looked at her watch. 6 p.m. It was her turn to cook dinner tonight. It looked like it was going to be late.

The parking lot was deserted, since racing was going on. Most of the patrons were inside, betting and watching races, and most of the stable help was at dinner.

"If it isn't the horse rescuer," a voice said behind her.

She knew immediately who it was. She turned to see Butch, King's previous owner, and two other men walking slowly toward her. Butch had his thumbs in his belt loops and walked with a swagger. He had an evil grin on his face.

"You took my horse," he said.

"You nearly killed him," Francie said. "If I hadn't said something, somebody else would have."

She started backing away. The other two men spread out, coming at her from the side. She realized too late what was happening and turned to run, but they were already on top of her.

She kicked one in the shin, and somebody grabbed her from behind and slammed her down against the hood of a pickup. The back of her head hit, and she saw stars.

"Get off of me," she said through gritted teeth, wishing she had listened to Steve and brought the dog with her. She flung her knee up and got Butch in the groin. He moaned and his grip loosened, but the two other men were there, and pinned her arms down on either side of her.

Butch stood back up, putting his hand around her throat. "I'm going to teach you a lesson about taking what belongs to others," he said.

She felt her wind cut off.

"Maybe each of us will teach you a little lesson in our own way," grinned the one to his right. Francie tried to free her arms but couldn't. She tried to swing her knees up again, but Butch's weight had her entire body pinned against the truck. He was heavy, and his hand was tightening around her throat. Things were starting to go black.

Suddenly, Butch was lifted off the ground from behind and thrown off of her. She coughed and gasped, gulping in air. The guy on her right took a swing at the attacker and loosened his grip on her arm. She broke free and swung to her left, hitting the other guy in the face. He grabbed her harder and was about to throw her down when a punch landed square in his face, breaking his nose with a crack.

It was Jack. Butch rallied from behind, and the other guy came at Jack at the same time. He neatly sidestepped, sending Butch into the truck, and then turned to punch the other guy in the stomach. When the man bent over, gasping, Jack turned back to Butch and spun him around, elbowing him in the chin, then swiping his knees, taking him down. He then kicked him in the gut.

The guy with the broken nose came at Jack, and the other man jumped on his back. Jack flipped the guy on his back over his head and used the body's weight to take out the guy coming at him.

It was over in seconds. Three men lay on the ground, gasping for breath. Jack was untouched.

"Are you okay?" he asked.

"Yes, I think so," she said.

"Let's go." Jack grabbed her arm and led her toward his car. Actually, it was Steve's car. He put her in the passenger side and closed the door.

"My truck… "

"We'll come back for it later," he said. He turned on the engine and got out of there.

Francie rubbed the back of her head and her neck. "Thanks," she said. "How did you know where I was?"

"Steve sent me. I was walking from the barn toward home when Steve came running outside in his boxers, all wet from his shower, and cursing. He asked where you were. I told him I didn't know, and he said, 'That fool woman didn't listen to me,' threw me his keys, and told me to come find you. Good thing I did."

"Yeah," she said. "Not sure what they were planning to do to me, but I was losing."

He glanced over at her. She saw his knuckles were bleeding.

"Where did you learn to fight like that?" she asked.

"I was a soldier. I had special training."

"I guess."

They rode the rest of the way home in silence.

All of the adults were in the kitchen.

Francie was sitting on Ken's lap, and he had his arms around her. Steve was standing up, hyperventilating.

"What were you thinking?" Steve said.

"The fool woman didn't listen," Francie said, repeating his words back to him. She gave him a little smile. She had a nice bruise around her neck.

Sam opened a tin of salve and wet a paper towel.

"Here," she said, sitting down next to Jack. "Let me take care of that."

"It's fine," he said. "It's just a scrape."

"Which will get infected if we don't treat it." She looked at him firmly. "Give me your hand."

"I'd rather not."

Sam frowned. She pushed the salve over to Jack. "Put it on, and I'm going to sit here and watch until you do."

"So here is what we're going to do," said Steve, his hands on his hips. "Something I should have done a long time ago. I'm going to teach you women self-defense."

"I don't think I'm up for that," said Krista, rubbing her stomach.

"You can watch. You especially—a beautiful woman wandering around New York. Geez."

He turned on Francie again.

"And you fraternize with all sorts: the mob, shady track characters, etcetera." He crossed his arms.

"You don't think I'm beautiful too?"

He ignored her. "We start tomorrow. Daily training in the basement. 7 p.m. each evening. Be there."

"Steve," Francie started to protest.

"Francie, I'll teach you how to kick my butt."

She smiled at that. "Sounds fun."

Frank had been leaning up against the sink, arms crossed, listening.

"What if they report you?" he asked.

They all looked at him.

"Jack beat them up. What if they report him? What if the cops look into it?"

Everybody was quiet for a moment.

Francie said, "I think we should have this conversation in my office."

"Francie, it has been a year. Nobody is listening to our every word," Frank said.

"Why are you using that tone with me? This is not my fault."

He looked at her. "You were almost killed. Or worse."

"What's worse than being killed?" Steve asked.

"Lots of things," Jack said quietly.

"Do you two have a plan if they come after Jack?" Frank said, looking at Francie and then Jack.

"Yes," she said. "Not one I wish to discuss out in the open, but we have a plan." She looked at Jack. "We'll be fine. Butch is scum. If he does report the incident, they'll send him to jail, not us."

"The problem is, you need to report it," Frank said. "But you can't. What's to stop him from coming after you again? You've got yourself in a fix."

Ken put his arms around her tighter.

"Steve will teach me self-defense, and I won't go to the track alone," she said. "It's simple. We have a great dog, and I have several large men to protect me."

"I don't like it," Frank said. "But then again, when has my opinion ever mattered?"

"Why are you so angry with me?"

"You could have died, Francie," Sam said. "He cares."

Francie met Frank's eyes. "I'm sorry," she said quietly. Then she got up and went over to him, spreading her arms out. "Hug?"

He gave her a little smile and folded her into his arms.

"I'm sorry," she said again.

"Me too," he said.

chapter
39

THEY WERE IN THE YARD HAVING A BARBEQUE. Ken, true to himself, had found another reason for a party when he realized it was Jack's one-year anniversary at the farm. He had a fun evening planned.

Francie joined him. "Mark's at the gate. I'm not sure what he wants. I told them to let him in," she said.

Ken was poking at the meat when Mark pulled up to the house in his black Sedan. Mark got out of his car and gave Francie a hug. She felt his gun against his side. Another man, his partner, remained in the car.

"Hey, sis," he said. "You having a party?"

"Yes. My assistant manager has been with us for a year. Are you on duty?" she nodded toward his gun.

"Always," he smiled and walked over toward the men. The day was overcast and quiet; the air was heavy.

"Hi, Mark," Frank raised his glass.

The men said their hellos, politely.

Francie stood a little behind them, pushing her hands deep into her jeans pockets. Something didn't feel quite right to her about Mark's sudden visit.

"Do you want to join us?" Ken asked with a smile. "There's cake."

"No thanks." Mark looked around. "Where's Jim?"

"He took the kids to a movie," Francie said. "They'll be back for dinner."

"How many new people have you hired in the past year, Francie?" Mark asked.

Francie glanced at Frank. "A few," she said. She kept her eyes off Jack.

"Is he one of them?" Mark nodded at Jack.

"Yes."

"Francie." Mark walked a circle around the men, looking at each of them. He reminded Francie of a predator stalking its prey. "I think Paul might be right here on your property." He stopped and looked directly at her. "How do you know Jim hasn't snuck him in? We can't find him anywhere else. You could be in danger."

Francie held Mark's gaze, willing herself not to look at Jack.

"That's ridiculous," she said. "The Feds, the police, heck, half the world has searched my property. Besides, Jim doesn't have the means to pull that off."

"No," Mark said quietly, walking up to her. "But you do."

The two of them stood face to face. Francie tried not to show any emotion. "You're my brother," she said, "and yet I feel like you're threatening me."

Mark stepped back and began walking around again. "Maybe I will stay for the party. I'd like to chat with some of your staff. Are they all invited?"

"Leave," Francie said.

He turned, feigning hurt. "Francie, we're family."

"You're not acting like family. You're wearing your gun on my property, and you have an armed man in the car. Leave."

"This shouldn't be your property," Mark said. "But I guess you were Papaw's favorite. Didn't the will say something like you were supposed to let us all live here if we wanted?"

Krista and Sam had come to say hello, but sensing the tension, they had stopped on the porch.

"Mark, that's enough," Krista said.

"Do you have a warrant?" Francie asked.

Mark put his hands in his pockets, which brushed his jacket back, showing his gun.

"I don't need one," he said. "This is just a friendly visit." He walked over to Frank. "You know everything that goes on here, right?"

"Mark, put your gun in the car and have a glass of tea or leave," Frank said.

Mark shook his head. "Can't do that, Frank."

Frank got in Mark's face. "I don't know what suddenly turned you from a nice guy into an evil brother, but Krista—your sister—is very pregnant, and I am going to ask you one more time to put that gun in the car and back off. This is supposed to be a happy day."

The two men stood eye to eye for a moment. Mark's partner got out of the car and leaned up against the car door.

Francie turned and walked quietly into the house.

"Where are you going, Francie?" Mark called after her.

"I'm finished talking," she shot over her shoulder. The screen door slammed behind her.

Mark stepped away from Frank and turned to Jack.

"You're the assistant manager, right? What's your name? Jack, I think. You're pretty new here, aren't you?" It was more of a statement than a question. He waited for Jack's reply. The air hung heavy between them. Jack's eyes flashed dangerously.

In the silence, they heard the click of a rifle. All eyes turned toward the porch. Francie stood there, aiming her grandpa's rifle at Mark's heart.

Mark's man pulled his gun.

"Stand down," Mark said to his man. "Put your gun away. I don't want any shots fired here today."

The man started to protest, "But—"

"I said put your gun away," Mark said firmly. The man holstered his weapon. "She won't shoot me. I'm her brother."

"Get off my property, or I'll blow your frickin' knee cap off," Francie said, her sights still on Mark. She lowered her aim to his knee.

"You wouldn't shoot at me. You might miss and hit somebody else."

Krista and Sam went back inside.

"You and Papaw taught me to shoot," Francie said. "You know whatever I aim at, I won't miss."

Mark swore. "I'm here for your own good, Francie! We need to find this man. He's a killer, and he might be living right here under your nose. I wouldn't put it past Jim to bring him here and endanger you all. Now Francie, put the gun down!"

"Leave," Francie said, her voice cold.

"You're insane, woman!" he shouted. "Because I care, I will be back. I'll be back tomorrow with our stupid warrants!" he turned toward Jack. "And maybe a subpoena or two, and I won't leave until I'm sure this place is safe and free of vermin!" he said. "Now give me that rifle, Francie, before you kill somebody!"

A gun clicked behind Mark's head. He froze.

"The lady told you to leave," said Ken, holding the pistol against Mark's temple. "I suggest you listen to her."

Mark, swearing violently, walked toward the car, where his man had pulled his gun again.

"I told you to put that thing away!" he shouted. The two men got in the car. "This is not over," he said and slammed the door. They left in a cloud of dust, their tires tearing up grass along the way.

No one spoke for a minute. The silence was broken by Steve's voice carrying across the yard. He had been in the barn and just caught the end of things.

"Dude! I had no idea you kept a gun in your glove box!" he said.

Ken's truck door was still open. He put the safety back on and put the gun away.

"You never know," Ken said. "Back in Texas, we used to run across rattlesnakes. Looks like we have snakes here too." His eyes met Francie's. "Are you okay, darlin'?"

She lowered her gun. "Yeah. Thanks. For a minute there, I thought I was going to have to shoot him." Her voice was light, but there was a tremor to it. Ken walked up and put an arm around her. Francie looked at Steve. "Where was that dog when I needed him?"

"Why don't we put that rifle away before the kids get home?" Ken asked.

Ken walked back down to his pig spit. He picked up his glass of tea and took a drink. "I'm hungry," he said, and at the same time, they saw Jim coming up the driveway with the kids in his car.

Frank nodded. "We can talk about this later. Jack, hand me the corn."

The kids were all excited and talkative about their movie, and the others tried to rally their own optimism, but Jim could tell that something wasn't right.

Frank put his arm around his shoulders. "I'll tell you about it later," he said as he led him in the house.

They decided to eat inside since suddenly the openness of the deck seemed threatening.

They listened to the kids' accounts of their afternoon out with their uncle, while the adults toyed around with their food. After a few moments, the room fell silent.

Steve sighed. "Come on, guys," he said. "It's not like this is our last meal. You're all acting like it's the night before our execution."

Everyone looked at him. There was a beat of silence, and then Jack laid his fork down.

"Excuse me," Jack said and left.

"Nice," said Jim.

It dawned on Steve what he had said. "I'm an idiot."

"Do you have to talk?" Francie said. "At all?" She looked at Jim. "Maybe you should go check on him."

"No. It's best to leave him alone. He's not a talker. He needs to walk it off."

The rest of the meal was eaten in near silence. Krista tried to talk about the baby's room and managed to pull the girls into a bit of decoration discussion, but then it too fizzled out.

"What's wrong?" Becky asked more than once. No one answered her.

They got up to clear the dishes. "Should we cut the cake?" Krista asked Francie as they stood in the kitchen and looked at it.

"I don't know," Francie said. "The kids probably want some."

The phone rang. It was from the barn line. Francie picked it up. It was her groom, Frenchie.

She listened as he breathlessly talked. "Get King for me," she told him. "I'll be right there." She hung up and ignored Krista's raised eyebrows.

She grabbed her truck keys and took off for the barn.

"Where's she going?" Frank asked Krista as he came into the kitchen with a stack of dishes.

"I don't know," Krista said. "She got a call from the barn. Sounded like an emergency."

"I'd better go check," he said, kissing Krista on the cheek. "Ken?"

The two men ran for Frank's truck.

Francie arrived at the barn and ran down the aisleway. Frenchie was coming toward her with a saddle.

"I don't need a saddle," she said, slipping the bridle on King's head, who Frenchie had waiting in the cross ties. She swung on the horse bareback.

"Jack went that way, ma'am," Frenchie said, pointing out the back toward the fields. "He had a gun. I think he was meaning to use it on himself."

"Thanks, Frenchie," Francie said, already kicking King into a run.

She heard Frank yelling behind her, "Francie Dalton, don't you jump that gate on that horse!"

She ran King hard. They crested a hill, and she could see Jack far up ahead. The gate had slowed him down, because he had to stop to open it. Jack went through and shut it behind him.

She pressed King forward. "Come on, boy, you can do it," she said, squeezing with her knees to hang on. The little horse's ears pinned back as he faced the gate. He lifted himself up and over it smoothly.

"Attaboy," she said, urging him on. She knew she had Jack now. She was on a faster horse, and she was a stronger rider.

"Jack!" she shouted. "Stop! Wait!"

He turned back, saw her, and kicked his little brown mare into a faster run. But his mare was a schooling horse, and King was a retired racehorse. Francie felt King's powerful strides eat up the ground under her, and soon, she was almost next to Jack.

"Stop!" she shouted. They were nearing the ocean, and the wind was picking up. "Drop the gun!"

"Get out of here!" he shouted. "Leave me alone!"

"Who are you planning on shooting?"

"Myself. Now leave me alone!" He tried to swerve the horse away from her, but she leaned over and grabbed the mare's reins. She turned the horse and brought her toward her. Jack tried to jerk the reins away from Francie. He outsized her and was a lot stronger than her, but she had him beat in ability. She was an expert rider, and as they reached the sandy beach, she slid effortlessly from her horse onto his, grabbing him around the waist and taking him off the other side with her. They landed with a hard thump on the ground, Francie on top of Jack.

She grabbed the gun out of his hand and threw it as far from them as she could. He gasped for a moment, stunned at having the wind knocked out of him. Finally, he coughed and found his voice.

"Why are you here?" he shouted. "Why can't you leave me alone?"

She straddled him, but on the ground, he had the advantage. He sat up, rolled over, and pinned her to the ground under him, his hands holding her arms down.

"What do you want? We both know you'd be better off if I wasn't here. And I am not going back to prison!" He was shouting at her, pushing down hard on her arms. They were both out of breath.

She fought hard to speak, gasping both from the exertion and from the pain.

"You're... you're hurting me," she said.

The anger in Jack's eye was quickly replaced by grief. "I'm so sorry," he breathed and rolled off of her. The two of them lay on their backs, side-by-side, still breathing hard.

"I'm so sorry," he repeated. "I'm so, so sorry."

"It's okay. I'm okay," she said. "How about you? I took you off that horse pretty hard."

He didn't respond.

The sand was cool underneath her, and she could hear the waves from the ocean crashing onto the beach. She turned her head and saw the horses grazing on some sea grass nearby.

"What were you doing?" she asked.

"I already told you that."

"You stole Ken's gun."

"He would have gotten it back. I only needed one bullet."

She turned her head to look at him. "Why? Why would you do that?"

He refused to meet her gaze, still looking up into the gray sky.

"Because I would rather die than go back to prison," he said. "You heard Mark. He's coming back tomorrow with a warrant. Francie, you're better off without me around. You have children, and soon a baby in the family. I'm not an asset to your family. I'm dangerous to have around."

"Why not just leave?"

"And go where?" he gazed into the gray sky. His breathing had steadied.

"I won't let you go to prison."

"You can't stop them."

"I did today. We promised to protect you, and we will."

They were silent for a while.

Finally, Jack asked. "Are you okay? Did I hurt you?"

"I'm fine. Look, Jack, we only have a few more minutes before my rescue squad finds us. You know Ken and Frank are probably on their way after us. I need you to promise me you won't try suicide ever again."

"I can't do that. Not today."

"I need you to."

"Why do you even care what happens to me? Why? Why do you care so much?"

She turned her head to look at him again. This time he turned his head and met her eyes.

"Because you're my friend," she said. "Aren't you?"

He didn't know how to answer that. He looked at the sky again, unable to meet her eyes. Then he reached down and took hold of her hand in the sand beside him. He gave it a gentle squeeze. "Yes," he said finally. "I am your friend."

The wind was blowing a salty mist in from the ocean, bending the saw grass and scattering the sand around them. They heard hoof beats approaching. He let go of her hand, and she sat up.

Ken and Frank jumped off their horses at the same time. Ken picked up his gun as Francie got to her feet. Frank held out his hand, and Jack accepted it, pulling himself to his feet.

"Are you two okay?" Frank asked.

"We're fine," Francie said.

"And this?" Ken asked, holding up the gun.

"We'll talk about it later," Francie said. A light mist was starting to fall. "Let's get back to the house." She turned and looked at Jack, who nodded slightly.

The two men went to get the horses.

"My promise?" she said, looking at Jack.

He looked at her. "I'm not ready for that," he said. "But I do promise I will never lie to you. Ever. When and if I make you that promise, you can count on it."

Ken arrived with both horses and handed each their reins. The four of them mounted and rode back to the barn, to Sunnyhill, also known as Safe Haven. A sharp wind cut across their backs, driving in from the sea, and brought a chill to their bones. Francie rubbed her arms for warmth. Nothing, it seemed, would ever be safe again.

Later that night, Francie was sitting at her desk when Jack stepped in her office doorway.

"Jim said you wanted to see me. I hope it's not too late at night."

She glanced at her watch and saw that it was already 10 p.m. She had gotten so lost in her work she hadn't realized the time.

"Come in," she said. "Close the door."

She stretched and yawned then put her paperwork away. Her desk lamp softened the shadows and gave the room a cozy glow. She laced her fingers together, staring at her hands, trying to think how to start.

"We told the girls everything," she finally said. "Mickey is away, and Lexie is too young, but Becky and Jessica know who you are now."

She looked across her desk at Jack.

"What do they think?" he asked.

Francie shrugged. "They're teenagers, and the world revolves around them. They took it well, thought it was kind of cool. That's about it."

Jack nodded. He had dark circles under his eyes, and his hands were trembling. He looked like crap.

"Look, about tomorrow," she said. "I figured you could work in my office all day, and when they get here, you can hide in there." She pointed toward the bookcase.

"Until they leave?" Jack asked.

"Yes."

"And then what? They'll come back again and again until they find me."

She shrugged. "I'll shoot them?"

"Francie, I'll tell you how it's going to go. I'm not going to hide. Jim said when you got me out, you paid extra to be sure nobody got hurt. Hurting people is not in your genes. It's not who you are, and if you keep me here, eventually somebody is going to get hurt. So when they come for me, I'm going to resist arrest, and they will shoot me, and you will let them. I can't go back to prison. I can't. Do you understand?"

She swallowed. "What if they don't kill you?"

They both looked at each other for a long time, each weighing the implications of that.

"I can't go back," he whispered.

"I know," she said.

"Can you accept that?"

She buried her head in her hands, then looked up. "You don't owe me anything," she said. "I said there were no strings attached. But I'll take that much of the promise. You don't kill yourself—you let them do it if it comes to that."

He nodded. Francie ran her hands through her hair. This was not the way she had imagined this conversation going.

"I told you when you came here a year ago that this place was a safe haven for you, a place where you could finally feel safe. I meant that. I'm willing to do what it takes to see that through."

"I don't want you to shoot anybody for me."

A smile tugged at the corners of her mouth. "I wouldn't have killed Mark. I might have given him something to think about though."

"That's not who you are. I don't want you to change who you are."

Francie sighed and nodded. "Frank has always said that in the end, it all works out."

"I guess we'll find out tomorrow."

The next day, everyone pretended to work, but nothing much got done. Ken stayed at the farm in case "all Hell broke loose" as he put it. Steve took Sam, Krista, and the girls away from the house for the day. He left his dog Guardian with Francie.

Jack refused to work in Francie's office where she wanted him to be. Instead, he stayed in his house, quietly doing paperwork at his kitchen table. Frank worked on his truck. Jim did yardwork. Francie paced. She went from the house to the barn, then to Jack's house, then back up to her office, making a triangular pattern.

She had just settled into her chair for what felt like the tenth time when Frank burst into the room.

"Call him."

"What?" she said, startled. She was jumpy.

"It's 4 p.m. Call Mark. He's your brother. Just call him, and see where he is. I can't take this anymore."

"Okay." She picked up the phone and dialed his work number. It was the only number she had for him, and surprisingly, he answered it this time.

"Mark," Francie said, putting him on speakerphone so Frank could hear. Ken walked into the room. She put her fingers to her lips, silencing him.

"You got lucky, sis," Mark said. "The judge says we don't have enough evidence to grant a warrant."

Francie went from relief to anger immediately. "You could have called. You put me though... a lot."

"I'm just concerned for you," Mark said.

"You think I'm guilty?"

"No. I think you're naive."

Francie shot a look at Ken and Frank, who both motioned for her to calm down and ignore the jab.

"Would you have shot me, Francie?"

"Maybe. If you show up again, you might get a chance to find out."

There was a silence on the other end. Finally, he said. "I love you, sis."

She sighed. "I love you too. Just leave my staff and our family alone."

"Okay. For now. Maybe Paul's dead, who knows."

"Bye, Mark."

Francie hung up. All of them exhaled.

"I'll go tell Jack," she said.

He was still sitting at the table doing paperwork. He saw her through the screen door and motioned her in. An untouched glass of water sat in front of him, condensation dripping onto the wood. She fought the urge to put a coaster under it.

"You're back again?" he said.

She smiled. "This time with good news." She pulled a chair out and sat down. "The judge won't grant a warrant. He says there isn't sufficient evidence. They think Paul might be dead."

He stared at her for a moment, then put his elbows on the table and buried his face in his trembling hands.

"Are you okay?" she asked gently. He nodded, his head still in his hands. "Because I'm not sure that I am," she said.

He looked across the table at her, and she held up her own hands. They were shaking.

"Great," Jack said wryly. "Now we're twins."

She got up. "So... carry on with whatever you were doing. Looks like you don't get to die today either." She smiled and turned to go. He watched her walk toward the door.

"Do you think this is it?" he asked.

"I do. At least for now. Mark, in his own way, loves me. He said he'll leave us alone for now, and I believe he will."

Jack nodded, and Francie walked back to her house.

chapter 40

SOMETHING CLOSED OFF IN JACK after that day. The little bit of thawing that had come over the past year had disappeared. He worked hard but mostly kept to himself in the evenings or went out with Jim. He stopped bringing home women. On the positive side, he had also managed to quit smoking.

On August 14, Krista and Frank became parents. Krista's water broke at 2 a.m., and Frank drove her to the hospital in their new navy SUV with a car seat strapped in the back. He called Francie on his way out the door, so she, Ken, Sam, Jim, and the girls were in the waiting room when Angela Christine Weaver came into the world. A perfect baby, healthy and eager to nurse.

Krista looked radiant when the gang was finally let in to see her.

"My angel," she said, smiling and holding the sleeping infant.

Frank couldn't quit smiling. Francie had never seen him so happy.

"I'm a daddy," he said, hugging her.

She laughed and hugged him back. "Can I hold my niece?"

Life got back into a rhythm then. School, work, parenting. Pancakes on Saturday mornings. Ken started to plan next year's vacation.

"Already?" Francie said.

"It's fun to have something to look forward to," he said. They looked at brochures for the Grand Canyon, Washington D.C., and Sea World. "Maybe Paris," Ken said. "Why not think big? The girls would love it." So Francie looked into getting them all passports.

In October, Francie and Ken flew up to New York to look at the blue jeans company. The 32-floor building was usable but needed work. They hired an inspector and followed up on what he said, updating the electrical and putting in some new windows. Then they hired painters and ordered new carpeting. They went home to wait while all the work was done.

"What are you going to do with that place?" Steve asked.

"I think I'm going to make and sell blue jeans," Francie said. "All the equipment is already there."

"I'll invest," Steve said.

"Really?"

"Yes. I'd like to be a stockholder if you're selling shares. Most of what you touch seems to turn to gold."

"I am very blessed," Francie said and reached over and squeezed Ken's hand.

Christmas was joyous, mostly because of little Angela. They took her to visit Santa and got the cutest photo of him holding her, her big blue eyes looking up into his. Then there were all the baby gifts. While she was too young to play with anything yet, they bought dolls, dollhouses, a wooden rocking horse, stuffed animals, wooden puzzles, and an assortment of books. Jack and Jim wrote her a song called "Littlest Angel," which they sang to her on Christmas eve as a gift to Krista and Frank. It was sweet, but also light-hearted and fun, a song she would love to sing when she got older.

"She's only four months old, and Frank's already talking about daddy/daughter dances," Krista said. "He saw a cute little dress the other day in the mall and said we should buy that now, so she'll have it when we go to a daddy/daughter dance."

"Really?"

"Yes, isn't that sweet?"

"Did you buy it?" Francie asked.

"No. I told him we ladies like to pick out our own dresses. I mean, what if fashion is totally different in eight years?"

Francie pulled out her blueprints of the New York office for them to look at.

They called it a day around 9 p.m. Jack left to go home, his arms full of leftovers for lunch the next day. Francie went up to her office to put her blueprints away.

"Hey," said Frank, coming in behind her.

She smiled. "Are you here for our nightly talk? We haven't done that in a while."

"I just thought I'd check in and see how you're doing," he said, taking a seat in his usual chair. "I've been sleep-deprived these past few months and thought I might have missed something."

"No, everything is great," Francie said. She sat down at her desk, fingering her cross pendant. "The reason for the season."

He smiled. "Amen." He took a sip of his coffee. She carefully rolled the blueprints up and put them back in a tube.

"So now you want to make blue jeans?" Frank said.

"Yeah. What do you think?"

"I think you'll make blue jeans," he said. "And do a fine job. You're business-savvy."

She smiled. "You taught me everything I know."

"Our house will be ready to move into in April," Frank said.

"Krista's excited. You guys have an awesome view."

"I'll get to show Angel the dolphins," Frank said. Then, grinning like a schoolboy, he added, "I just love being a daddy."

Jim stuck his head in the doorway. "Hey, I'm off to bed. My flight for LA leaves early in the morning. I just came to say goodbye."

Francie stood up. "Come here and give me a hug. She hugged him. "I love you, bro. Be careful, and give my niece a hug from me. Someday I want to meet her."

"Will do," he said. "I love you too. Stay out of trouble."

Frank stood up, and they gave each other a hug. "Thanks for the song," Frank said. "We'll have to make a recording of it when you get back."

"That's right," said Jim. "Maybe we'll make a whole album. That could be fun!"

He smiled and walked out the door. It was the last time they would see him alive.

chapter 41

THE CALL CAME ON JANUARY SECOND. Trembling, Ken walked into Francie's office, tears running down his face.

"It's Jim," he said.

The color drained from her face. "No."

She stood up, and Ken opened his arms. She entered them and let the warm expanse engulf her and swallow up her sobs.

The funeral was small. Jim only had a few friends, mostly band buddies. Elise flew in with Lily, and the family met her for the first time.

Francie had spent the past few days alternating between crying and anger. The police had found Jim's body in a rundown alley next to an apartment known as a hang-out for drug users. He was alone and had apparently died from an overdose of heroin. His glasses were cracked, which she found odd, and no one had thought to fix them before she saw the body. She had taken them in herself to get them repaired.

Francie insisted he wasn't using drugs and demanded an investigation. So far there were no leads.

Elise was beautiful, not in a supermodel way, but in a natural way. Her long, dark hair was tied back in a ribbon, and she wore her make-up light, with a soft pink lipstick. Her dark, sea-colored dress was simple and brought out the color of her eyes. She let go of her husband's hand and came to stand by Francie.

"I never stopped loving him," she said quietly.

"He never stopped loving you, either," Francie said.

"I tried. I gave him a year to quit using. After I gave up and married another man, he finally cleaned himself up." She turned to Francie. "He didn't die from a drug overdose. He wouldn't kill himself."

"I know. We'll find out what happened."

They were silent for a moment. Lily was standing far across the room, looking at the casket with big eyes.

"You need to let the police fail," Elise said. "Don't pursue the investigation."

Francie looked at her.

"I know who Jack is," she said quietly. "I recognize his eyes. Jim was hiding a lot of things, and I'm pretty sure he paid someone to keep Jack alive in prison. They might be connected. I think you need to let it go."

Francie looked across the room at Jack, who sat in the corner by himself.

"It was worth it," Elise said. "Jim wouldn't have it any other way."

They watched as Jack got up and walked over near the casket and said something to Lily. The little girl took his hand.

"I wish we could have met under different circumstances," Elise said. "Jim said he wanted to keep Lily away from his family, to protect her from his parents. He didn't care for

Mark either, but he sure loved his sisters. I don't know why we didn't get together sooner."

"Lily was kind of young to travel," Francie said. "And I know you didn't want Jim to travel with her alone. He accepted that. It's okay."

They both looked at the body again, each lost in her own regrets.

It was a cold, gray day, spitting a misty rain. After the funeral service, they went right to the cemetery.

It was quick, with their church pastor officiating. Not many people were there—not even their parents. Francie had posted a guard at the entrance, who was instructed to call him if he saw her parents or Mark arrive. They had hated Jim while he was still living, so she wasn't going to let them near him now.

Ken held the black umbrella over Francie, his arm around her waist. When it was over, he asked her if she was ready to go.

"You go ahead," she said. "Give me a minute."

Jack stood alone, staring at the grave as the others mingled and departed. Francie walked over to him and stood beside him.

"He loved you," she said.

Jack nodded. "He came to visit me in prison every few months after he moved to Florida, and every Sunday when he lived there, in California. For 18 years he did that." He glanced at her. "How are you?"

"Terrible."

"Me too."

She hesitated, then reached over and took his hand. He didn't pull away and gave her hand a little squeeze.

Ken came up and put his hand on Francie's shoulder. "We should go."

She nodded, and the two of them turned to follow Ken back to the car.

chapter
42

TRAGEDY STRUCK AGAIN at the end of February.

Frank was sitting at Francie's big walnut desk, papers scattered in a semi-circle around him. He liked to get the taxes done early each year, "just in case."

"Just in case what?" Francie always asked, to which Frank would only shrug and say, "You never know."

Francie walked in and looked around at the papers piled across her desk and behind him, lined across the window seat.

"How's it going?' she asked.

"I've got a long way to go," he said and leaned back in the chair. He looked tired, but he smiled up at her. "What's up?"

"We're running out of groceries, and Krista says you guys are low on diapers, so we're all going to the store," she said.

"What time is it?"

"7 p.m."

Frank stretched his arms up over his head and yawned. "Tell Krista I need some razors."

"I'm here," Krista said, carrying Angela into the room. "We came to say bye." She leaned over to kiss Frank on the cheek, but he pulled her and the baby into his lap.

Angie, now six months old, smiled and laughed out loud. Frank wrapped his arms around Krista and kissed her, then bent to kiss the baby on the top of her soft head. "My two angels," he said.

Francie smiled at the sweet scene.

"Okay, let's go." Krista stood up. "I don't want to be out too late."

"Buy something fun, like cookies," Frank said. "Maybe Oreos. Or Nutter Butter."

They laughed.

"Seriously," he said. "Cookies for the man who's working. I have writer's cramp."

"Okay, cookies it is," Krista said, then gave him another kiss and left. The baby stretched her hand out after Frank. He waved.

He had just gotten back to work when Ken stuck his head in the door. "I need your car keys," he said. "It's easier for me to drive your car than move the car seat."

"I don't have them."

"Krista says they're in your pocket."

Frank dug his hand into his pants pocket.

"So they are," he said, tossing them to Ken.

"Thanks," Ken tipped his hat. "Pardner."

"Always the cowboy," Frank chuckled as he left. "Drive careful!"

Ken hollered up the stairs. "You bet! Precious cargo on board!"

Frank heard the back door shut, then bent his head to the papers and got back to work.

A steady rain beat against the windshield, and it was dark as they pulled onto the highway. Ken took hold of Francie's hand and gave it a little squeeze.

"I love you, darlin'."

"I love you too," she smiled.

"Aww, you two are so sweet," Krista said from the back seat. The baby started to fuss.

A semi-truck merged on the freeway from a ramp up ahead of them. His tires sent a muddy spray onto their windshield, and Ken drew back a little to get farther behind him. He checked his left mirror. Traffic was too heavy in the left lane to go around the truck.

Angela started to cry, and Krista unzipped the diaper bag to dig out the bottle. A car speeded by and swung in front of Ken, forcing him to hit the brakes. The bottle flew out of Krista's hand and rolled under the seat.

Ken let go of Francie's hand to grip the wheel. "Everybody okay?"

"Yep," Krista called from back seat. "The bottle rolled under your seat, Francie. Can you see it up there on the floor?"

Francie looked between her feet. "Yes, here it is." She reached for it.

The person in the car ahead of them that had cut them off put his blinker on. Ken slowed to give him more room, and the car shot out around the semi.

"I can't reach it," Francie said. She unbuckled her seat belt and leaned forward. She accidently kicked the bottle further forward. She leaned down, reaching further and just about had it in her grasp.

Ken saw the car that was in front of him swerve in front of the semi, cutting the truck driver off. The truck driver hit his brakes and began to skid across the wet pavement. In what seemed like slow motion, the semi slid sideways, jack-knifing across both lanes. Ken hit the brakes, knowing he was too close to the truck to stop. He watched, helpless, as his vehicle careened at 70 mph toward the belly of the truck. They were going to go under it.

Francie's hand closed around the bottle. Then her entire body was thrust forward and slammed into the small space in the floor. She heard a sickening crunch of metal and felt a tremendous pressure on her back and ribcage. Her right hand crushed the bottle, and several bones in her hand and fingers snapped. Her head slammed into the ground, bending her body in on itself, and she saw Ken's knee sliding under the steering wheel just before everything went black.

She dreamed she was suffocating. Something was squeezing her ribcage so tightly she couldn't get a deep breath. She opened her eyes and saw a light overhead. Her mind was gauzy and wrapped with cloth, it seemed, which would explain why she couldn't think. She saw Frank's face.

"He's hugging me," she thought. "That's what the squeezing is." But his head was in his hands, and his arms weren't around her. "If Frank's here, it must all be okay," her mind told her, and she went back to sleep.

The next time she awoke, he was still there. Had it been moments? Days? This time, he saw her looking at him.

"Hey," he said, and his eyes lit up.

Her lips were thick, and her mind was full of gauze. She couldn't find her right hand. The pressure was still around her lungs but not as bad. Something was missing.

She struggled to think what it was but was tugged back into sleep before she could formulate a thought.

She opened her eyes again, and this time tried to turn her head to get a better look at Frank. The pain stopped her.

Frank reached a hand up and softly touched her cheek with his finger.

She remembered what she was looking for.

"Ken?" she said. No sound came from her throat, but she made her lips form the word again. "Ken."

"Shh," Frank said. "He's in another room. You need to rest."

She tried to say more, but once again, she was pulled back into darkness.

When she woke this time, she felt stronger. She could breathe better. Frank was still there, sitting next to her bed. His head was resting on his arms on the edge of her bed. Morning sun was coming in the window.

She experimented and found that she could turn her head from side to side very gently but only a little. She could feel her toes. Her right hand wasn't really missing, it was just heavily bandaged, and she was hooked up to monitors.

With her left hand, she reached out and touched Frank's hair. He lifted his head to look at her. She smiled at him a little and hoped her mouth was making the shape she told it to.

"Hi, sweetheart," he said gently.

"Ken?" Her lips said again.

"Not yet," he said. "You still need rest. You were in a very bad car accident."

"Krista," Francie said. This time her voice came out in a husky whisper. "You should be with Krista."

He took hold of Francie's left hand.

"She doesn't need me right now," he said.

Francie wanted to say more. She had so much to say, but she was so very tired. She closed her eyes and nodded off.

She dreamed a lot. She saw Sam swimming through one of her paintings and heard her voice calling to Francie to wake up and come to the surface. Francie swam up to meet Sam, but the gauze kept getting in the way, tangling her arms, pulling her back down. Somewhere, Becky was crying and holding her hand, but when she opened her eyes, she saw Frank and Mickey in the doorway. Jim visited her, or maybe it was Steve, and she wanted to ask him where her riding boots were.

She kept reaching out for Ken's hand.

"You're getting better, Francie," Frank said, and she heard him. But still she slept.

"She'll wake up more this time," a woman's voice said. "We've cut back on her pain medication."

The voice left, and Francie's eyes fluttered open.

Frank was in the same chair beside her bed.

"Hi, again," he said.

She looked around and raised her right hand. It wasn't as heavy as she remembered. Some of the bandages seemed to be gone, but it was still wrapped. The pressure in her chest wasn't so bad, and she could breathe a little better.

"How do you feel?" Frank asked.

She thought about this for a minute.

"Okay," she said. Her voice was working. "What happened?"

"You were in a car accident."

She licked her lips. She was thirsty. "I want to see Ken."

Frank's eyes clouded. "You can't right now."

She tried to raise up and the room swam. Frank put a gentle hand on her arm. "Lay still," he said.

"Ken... " she tried again.

"Francie... "

She pushed herself up, and again, the room swam.

"Please"—a tear escaped Frank's eye—"lay still. You need to heal. I can't lose you too."

She lay back against her pillow.

"Where is Ken?" Her eyes met Frank's, and then she knew.

"No." Her voice faltered.

"He died in the car accident," Frank said. "It was instant. I'm so sorry." He took her left hand in both of his and brought it to his lips.

A tear escaped the corner of her eye.

"Krista?"

Frank nodded and squeezed her hand harder. "And the baby. My Angela. You are the only survivor." He leaned his forehead against her hand and fought back the tears.

"How long... " Francie was crying now, prone in bed, tears spilling out silently onto her pillow.

"Two weeks ago."

She moaned. "Two weeks? My head hurts," she said. Frank nodded and pushed the button on her morphine drip.

"Go to sleep," he whispered. "Just please, come back to me."

They raised her bed by degrees, and by the end of the day, she was sitting up. She grew tired, though, and within an hour had to lie back down.

She couldn't speak. Her head swam with questions, but every time she tried to talk, a sob came out. Frank stayed with her, hushing her, trying to get her to rest. Sam visited briefly and held her hand and wept with her. The nurses discouraged visitors. Only Frank stayed constantly.

They dosed her up again that night so she'd sleep. She didn't care. She welcomed the oblivion.

"We'll try to cut her medication back more tomorrow," Sharon, one of the nurses, told Frank. "They don't help with the depression."

Sharon was Frank's favorite nurse, and he welcomed her quiet comfort on their floor. She was older, a little heavy, and wore her graying blond hair back in a long braid. She was kind and had let Frank break most of the rules, including sleeping in Francie's room while she was in ICU. Sharon put her hand on Frank's shoulder. "She'll be out most of the night. Why don't you go home?"

Frank looked up at her. "To what?"

Sharon squeezed his shoulder. "Francie's a lucky lady to have you. I'll bring you a fresh blanket for your chair." She smiled. "She's going to make it. Tomorrow we'll try to get her up for a little walk." Sharon left and returned with a blanket and a chocolate chip cookie.

Frank smiled. "Thanks, Sharon." Then he turned out the light and settled back into the recliner, which had become his bed.

Francie was sitting up, toying with the vanilla pudding on her lunch tray. She had taken a short walk that morning, followed by a long nap, and was now attempting to eat her first full meal in two and a half weeks.

Frank had finished his sandwich and was looking through a newspaper he bought at the cafeteria.

"I wouldn't feed this stuff to our dogs," Francie said. Frank smiled.

"Of course not," he said. "You spoil the dogs."

"How is my dog?"

"Rascal is fine. Steve tried to smuggle her up here once when you were still in the coma, but he got caught. He didn't make it past the lobby. Jack said it's because he's too small to smuggle anything, and the bulge under his coat was a dead giveaway. Especially since it barked."

Francie gave up on her pudding and pushed it aside.

"You need to eat," Frank said. He looked like he had aged ten years. Deep lines etched his face, and he had dark circles under his eyes.

"When's the funeral?" Francie asked.

Frank folded up his paper carefully and took his time answering. When he got it folded and set down, he said gently, "There's not going to be a funeral."

She swallowed. "Why?"

Frank spoke evenly, carefully. "The SUV slid underneath a semi-truck at sixty miles per hour. Maybe seventy. Ken didn't even have time to brake. The truck sat low. The van was high. Everything above the bottom of the van's steering wheel was... destroyed."

Francie was looking at her sheets, twisting a corner around her finger. "How did I survive?"

"Since you were unbuckled, you were thrown onto the floor. The top crushed in on you, but not down that far. It took them over two hours to cut you out."

They were both silent for a while. The monitors quietly blinked, keeping track of her blood pressure, her oxygen, and her heart rate. The IV attached to her right arm dripped saline and pain medication into her veins.

"Did you see... the bodies?" she asked, not meeting his eyes.

"No," Frank said. "They wouldn't let me."

Francie nodded and slid her left hand across the sheet. He took it, and she squeezed it. She squeezed her eyes shut, fighting back the tears that were threatening to come again.

"We'll be okay," Frank said. "We have each other. I need you to be okay."

Francie nodded and squeezed his hand again but still couldn't meet his eyes. After a while, she asked him to lower her bed, and she lay back and pretended to sleep.

chapter 43

EXACTLY THREE WEEKS AND ONE DAY after she was admitted, Francie got to go home. Frank drove his truck up to the hospital entrance to get her, while Sam and Steve wheeled her down with all her flowers and cards.

He helped her in the passenger side, then loaded all her gifts and shut the door. When he climbed in, she was staring at the dashboard, as white as a sheet. Her breathing was heavy. She closed her eyes tight, unaware that he was looking at her.

"Are you okay?" he asked.

"I think I'm having a panic attack," she said, giving a nervous little laugh. Then she opened the door. "I've gotta get out of here."

Sam and Steve were already gone. Frank walked around to the side of the truck where she was standing, holding onto the edge of the door with a death grip.

Frank put his hands on her shoulders and looked her in the eyes. "You can't walk home," he said kindly. "We can do this. Together."

She took a deep breath, steadying herself. "I know. How many times have I fallen off a horse and gotten back on? I can ride in a stupid vehicle again."

But it took her five minutes to steady her nerves enough to get back in. Then she sat stiffly all the way home, her heart racing. She was glad to climb back out again.

"We made it," she said with another nervous laugh.

The farm looked good. Not much had changed while she was away. Ken's truck sat in the driveway where he had left it, and she felt a stab of pain when she saw it.

Steve came out to get her flowers, and Francie allowed Frank to lead her up the steps and into the house. She felt another stab of pain when she saw Ken's duster and boots on the porch.

Francie was trembling, more from fatigue than fear, and she asked to go straight upstairs to her room. Halfway up, she stopped to rest, and despite her protests, Frank scooped her up and carried her the rest of the way. He laid her down gently on the bed. Sam was there with a glass of water.

"Call me if you need me." Frank squeezed her arm and then reluctantly left.

"Pill time," Sam said.

Francie immediately took the medicine and a sip of water, then asked Sam to leave. "I need to be alone."

"I don't think that's a good idea," Sam said. "I brought a book. I'll sit and read."

"I don't need to be hovered over!" Francie snapped. Sam jumped. "I'm sorry... I just... "

The room was full of him. His watch was on the dresser. A discarded flannel shirt hung on the clothes tree. Francie wondered if it still smelled like him.

"Sam?" She hesitated. "Where's Ken's hat?"

Sam's face was a mix of emotions as she searched for an answer. Against her will, her eyes filled with tears.

"He... um... he was wearing it when the accident happened." She didn't offer any more details.

"Oh," Francie said quietly. She sank down into the covers and turned on her side, away from the door. "Please leave now. I'll call you if I need you. I promise."

"Okay." She heard Sam softly close the door behind her.

Francie buried her face in his pillow, breathing in deeply, trying to find his scent. The pillow was cold. She started crying and didn't stop for a very long time.

The girls brought her breakfast the next morning.

"Becky and I made eggs," Jessica said, setting a glass of orange juice on her nightstand. Francie managed a smile.

"Thanks, girls."

They stood there awkwardly, not sure what to do next. Jessica made a few comments about the weather. Becky started to tell her about the new baby birds in the barn, then stopped.

"Mom?" Becky said. "Are you going to be okay?"

"Of course," Francie said, sticking her fork in her scrambled eggs. "These look good." Both girls watched nervously as she took a bite and chewed. She swallowed. "I don't need babysitting," she said. "Do you want to talk?"

"No," they both said at the same time.

"Where's Frank?" Francie asked.

"Downstairs in the kitchen," Becky said. "He spent the night here last night. He slept in Jim's room. I don't think he's ready to go home yet."

"Has he been home at all?

"Only to get a few changes of clothes," Jessica said. "Do you want to see him?"

"No," Francie said. "I'd like to be alone for a little while, actually." She smiled apologetically. "After breakfast I might try to take a shower."

The girls, it seemed, were relieved to be excused. Francie was mentally exhausted from her pretense with them.

Sam poked her head in.

"Do you need anything?"

"I need to be alone," Francie said.

"I'd like to help you into the shower. In case you slip."

"I'll call you when I'm ready."

After she left, Francie pushed her breakfast aside and slowly stood up. She locked her bedroom door and walked toward the shower but stopped at the closet. There hung his clothes. His jeans, his shoes, his work shirts. She walked up to his shirts and wrapped the arm of one around her shoulder, then she traced her fingers along his ties. A small animal sound, like a whimper, came from her. She quickly went to the shower, turned it on, and undressed.

She stood under the water for a long time, and when she dried off, her skin was red from the heat. She was sore all over—muscles, joints, skin. She stared at herself in the mirror. Large purple bruises covered the upper half of her torso, and both of her eyes were ringed in black.

She put on some soft jeans, a t-shirt, and a pair of cotton socks and ran the comb through her hair. All the effort left her exhausted and her head throbbing.

She walked back toward the bed and stopped at the dresser to pick up Ken's watch. She put it around her wrist. She opened his sock drawer and peeked in and unfolded and refolded a handkerchief. Then she saw the flannel shirt hanging on the clothes rack and picked it up. It smelled like him.

She took it to bed with her and curled up on her side in a fetal position, hugging it. She closed her eyes and tried to pretend he was there next to her. She could smell him, but the throbbing of her head got in the way of her imagination. Annoyed, she looked at the clock and realized she was late taking her pain pills. She should have taken them at breakfast. She shook two out and swallowed them with the orange juice. But the pounding in her head was getting worse, so she shook out a few more into her hand and swallowed them. She just wanted the pain to stop. Then she curled around Ken's shirt and waited.

Frank rattled Francie's doorknob.

"Open up, Francie," he shouted again, knowing at this point that she wasn't going to answer him.

The girls stood in the hall, their arms folded, their backs against the wall. Jessica was chewing her nails.

"Let's kick the door in," Becky suggested.

"How can there not be a key?" Frank said to Sam again. She shrugged.

Steve ran out of his room, having fetched the screwdrivers he'd been sent for. He handed one to Frank, and the two men went to work on the door. In less than a minute they had it down.

Frank ran to the bed where Francie lay, pale and still. He saw the spilled, nearly empty pill bottle.

"Francie!" he shouted, patting her face.

"Oh, dear God," he heard Sam behind him.

"Francie!" He slapped her face harder. She moaned but didn't wake up. "Steve! Get your car ready!"

Steve ran down the stairs, and Frank scooped Francie up in his arms. By the time he was outside, Steve had the Vette's engine running and waiting.

"Call the ER and tell them we're on our way in and that she overdosed on these." Frank threw the pill bottle at Sam. He crawled into the passenger seat, pulling Francie on his lap.

"Francie, wake up!" He kept jostling her.

Steve peeled out, burning rubber.

"Let's not die before we make it to the hospital," Frank said to Steve.

"That's the plan," he said and gunned it faster.

"I meant... Oh, Francie, please wake up!" he said, bracing himself for a quick turn that plastered him against the door.

Before he knew it, they were at the hospital. Frank carried Francie in, and the ER staff put her on a gurney.

"I need to go with her!" he shouted, running after them.

"Sir, stay here. Let us do our job."

"I can't be away from her! I can't lose... her... " They disappeared behind a pair of double doors, leaving him standing alone in the hallway. Then Steve was at his side, putting a hand on his shoulder.

"Let them take care of her," he said.

They waited for what seemed like forever.

Frank paced the entire time, and Steve sat glued in a hard plastic chair, his eyes on Frank.

"Usually, I'm the one who has trouble sitting still," he said. Frank didn't answer. "I'll call Sam and tell her what we know. Which is nothing," Steve said and went to find a phone. He came back shortly, and Frank was still pacing.

He stopped in front of Steve.

"I can't lose her," Frank said. "She's all I have left."

Steve wasn't good at comforting people, and he searched for the right words.

"She's not all you have left," he said. "You have me. And the girls. You're like a father to them."

"Their father's dead."

"And Mickey."

"He's grown up."

A doctor came out and both men went to him.

"She's going to be okay," he said.

"Thank God." Frank rubbed his face with his hands. "Thank God."

"We got to her in time. You can go in and see her in a few minutes, and then we'll move her to a room. We want to keep her overnight for observation."

After the doctor left, Steve put in a quick call to Sam, then came back to where Frank was waiting next to the vending machine.

"Frank," he said. "I can stay with her tonight. After you see her, why you don't go home and get some rest. You look like hell, man."

"Go home to what?" Frank said. "The empty nursery? All my wife's clothes? What, Steve, do I have to go home to?" Frank punched the vending machine.

"You can see her now," a nurse said.

Francie was lying in a bed looking very pale and small in the white sheets. Frank took a deep breath and steeled himself.

"Hey," Francie said and reached her good hand out to Frank. He took it. "Why did you have to bring trouble along?" She nodded at Steve, then gave him a feeble wink.

"Francie... " Frank's voice faltered.

"Frank, I didn't want to die. I just wanted the pain to stop." Tears fell down her cheeks.

"I know, sweetheart, I know. Me too." He sat on the edge of her bed.

"Steve," she said, her voice low, her eyes drowsy. He came closer, and she reached for his hand. "I love you, bro."

"That must be the drugs talking," he said, but his eyes were stinging with tears. "You sure scared us."

"I'm sorry."

Two orderlies came and moved her to a room. Frank and Steve settled in with her. The doctor who had attended her in the hospital after her accident came down to see her and ordered another bed brought in for Frank. Soon, he and Francie were both sleeping, too exhausted to stay awake any more.

Steve decided to stay and spent an uncomfortable night in the chair, dozing off, then waking up with a start to make sure everybody was breathing.

The next day at noon Francie was released her to come home under "suicide watch" with the promise she'd return for counseling. This meant that someone had to stay with her at all times.

Frank got Francie settled in, then left her with Sam. Sam made her a late lunch, which Francie ate at the kitchen table. The house was quiet. The kids were at school, and Steve was napping.

"I'm tired," Francie told Sam. "I'm going to take a nap."

She went up to her room and sat on the bed. She noticed her meds were gone. She went into her bathroom. The Tylenol, Benadryl—anything that might be poison— were gone. She sighed. She decided that her room was too depressing, so she went down the hall to her office. She ran her hands over the big walnut desk, and considered, for a moment, trying to get a little work done. But the prospect seemed overwhelming, and her head hurt, so she curled up on the window seat behind her desk.

Sam came in and sat down on the couch with a book.

"You've got to be kidding," Francie said. "You're going to watch me sleep?"

"Doctor's orders," Sam said.

"I see you took all my medication," Francie said. "Did you get Ken's gun too?"

"Yep."

"I'll bet you forgot my rifle."

Sam froze.

Francie smiled. "It's strategically hidden."

"Francie... "

"Sam, I'm not going to kill myself."

"What were you trying to do then?"

Francie closed her eyes and pretended to sleep.

Sam sniffed and started reading her book.

About an hour later, Jack walked in. France kept her eyes closed.

"Let me sit with her awhile," he whispered. Sam nodded and left, shutting the door quietly behind her.

Jack sat on the couch and started sorting through a folder he'd brought with him.

Without opening her eyes, Francie mumbled, "So they're trusting the fugitive to sit with the suicidal woman. Sounds like the movie of the week."

Jack kept sorting his papers. "That's not nice."

"But it's true." She opened her eyes and looked at him as he shuffled through his papers and made a few notes in pen. He was wearing a soft gray t-shirt and jeans. His dark hair was cut short but was still wavy. She wondered what color it was naturally. She knew he dyed it as part of his cover. He was a very handsome man, and she knew, even without his cosmetic surgery, he must have been easy on the eyes. She wondered how many hearts he had broken or left behind when he went to war.

"It's a movie that has a bad ending," she said.

"For whom?"

"For both of us, probably. I'll probably die in the electric chair right next to you some day. So I should have just died in the car accident. It would have saved the taxpayers some money."

He finally looked at her. "You're angry."

"Yes."

"I can understand that."

She sighed and rolled over onto her back, looking up at the ceiling. "I guess if anyone understands pain, it would be you."

"Maybe. I never had half my family die all at once though."

They were silent for a while. Jack continued to work. Francie feigned sleep. Finally, she sighed and slowly sat up. She found that if she moved very slowly, her body didn't complain so much. Still, she felt lightheaded for a few moments.

Jack put his papers away. "I came to make a pact with you."

"A suicide pact?"

"I was thinking just the opposite."

She raised an eyebrow.

"I'm going to give you that promise you wanted," he said, his eyes meeting hers. His voice was serious. "I promise not to kill myself. And in return, I want you to promise me that you won't kill yourself either."

She regarded him for a moment. "What if they come to drag you back off to prison?" she challenged. "Back to confinement? Back to the electric chair? Are you going to keep your promise then?"

"Your anger gives you strength now," Jack said calmly, "but don't let it become the driving force in your life. It'll destroy you."

She looked down. "I'm sorry. I'm not angry at you."

"I know." He took a deep breath and let it out slowly. "Yes, the promise still holds, no matter what. I'll just have to trust you to get me out of prison again. Only next time, don't wait until the night before my execution. You cut it kind of close."

"The night before?"

"Yeah. I was scheduled for execution at 6 a.m. They pulled me out at 3 a.m."

"I'm sorry."

They were quiet for a moment.

She looked back up at him. "I don't really think I tried to kill myself. I just wanted the pain to stop."

"Good," he said. He got up and walked over to her. He held his pinky out.

"What are you doing?" she said.

He smiled. "Pinky promise. I've seen the girls do it. Lock pinkies with me, and let's promise not to kill ourselves."

A small smile crossed her lips. She held out her pinkie. "Okay," she said. "I promise not to kill myself."

"Me too," Jack said.

"Not good enough," Francie said. "You have to say the words."

Jack looked her straight in the eyes. "I promise not to kill myself," he said, then gave a small laugh. "I guess that means I'm in this for the long haul."

They locked pinkies. His steady hand felt warm and strong.

He then went back and sat down on the couch. "Are you done napping?"

"I wasn't really napping."

"I know."

She ran her hands through her hair, snagging some on the cast. She sighed and leaned back against a pillow that was propped up against the window.

"So you've been running the farm," she said.

"Trying my best," he said. "I'm doing things on the financial end, and Steve and Donovan are holding up the horsey end. We're in good shape."

"Thanks."

She looked at his hands again, steady as he shuffled his papers and put them back in the manila folder.

"So how long does it take to get over PTSD?"

"PTSD?"

"Post-traumatic stress disorder."

"I know what it is," Jack said. "Why?"

"I'm afraid to ride in automobiles."

Jack shrugged. "I'll let you know when I get over it."

"Where's Frank?"

"You're full of questions today. Were you this talkative with Sam?"

"No. I was napping."

He laughed.

"Sam's a pain in the butt. She took away all my meds and Ken's gun."

"Sam lost a sister too, you know. This isn't all about you."

"You're starting to be a pain in the butt too."

Jack regarded her for a few moments.

"Tell me who you're so angry at," he said quietly.

"So now you're a therapist?" She laughed, a humorless sound, and tried to run her hands through her hair again, then stopped, frustrated when the cast snagged. "Who am I angry at? The list is so long," she said. "The stupid driver who cut the truck off. The truck driver. The rain. The road. Our SUV. The stupid bottle that rolled under the seat because if I hadn't been unbuckled and reaching for it, I wouldn't have this." She held up her casted hand.

"And you'd be dead," he said quietly.

"Yes, I'd be dead. And glad."

"Where would that leave Frank?"

That stopped her for a moment. She opened her mouth to speak but no words came out.

"Francie, he hasn't left your side since the accident. He needs you. He was like a rock—held it all together all these weeks just for you. It was killing him, you not knowing and him realizing he'd have to be the one to tell you when you woke up. And he was so protective of you. He wouldn't let anybody make a move with you, even the doctors and nurses, unless he knew exactly what they were doing. He was terrified he was going to lose you."

While Jack was speaking, her eyes filled with tears. They spilled over and ran down her cheeks.

"I can't be that strong," she said. "Not like him."

"You already are that strong," Jack said. "And he needs you to survive. He needs you to be here with him. Alive."

Francie sniffed and reached for a tissue. She wiped her eyes.

"Where is he now?" she asked.

"He drove out to his new house. He told me he needed some time alone."

She wiped her eyes again and stood up.

"Will you take me there?"

"Sure," said Jack. "Come on."

He helped her down the stairs and out to the porch, where he left her while he went to get her keys. Fortunately, no one else was around. Sam must be in her room painting, Francie thought.

Jack helped her into the car. When he got in, he turned the ignition, then let the car idle. He looked over at her.

"Are you okay? You're pale."

"Yes. This might be good practice, tooling around the farm. Just no freeways."

"No freeways today," he said and slowly drove down their little road toward the ocean.

"Can we stop at the barn first?" Francie asked. "I want to see King."

Jack smiled and pulled up to the barn door. They got out, and he took her arm, walking with her. "I don't really need help," she said, but she felt wobbly, so she didn't push his arm away. "I thought you hated touch."

"I like it on my own terms," he said.

Francie breathed in the scent of horses, pine shavings, and hay. The smell was a healing balm to her senses, and for a moment, everything was okay. She pretended it was a normal day, and she was coming to the barn for a ride.

King saw her and whinnied.

"I forgot to bring him a treat," she said. He hung his head over the stall door, and when she reached him, he nuzzled her.

"Hi, boy."

Jack stepped back, and Francie rested her arms on the stall door. King nuzzled her hair, softly blowing on her cheek. She closed her eyes as the velvety muzzle caressed her face. With her good hand, she reached up and ran her fingers through his mane, then down his sleek neck. She rubbed behind his ears.

Jack watched them caress each other in this ritual of greeting. This girl and her horse. He shook his head in wonder.

"Okay," Francie said after a few minutes. "I'm ready to go."

By the time they got back to the car, she was trembling and out of breath.

"I'm a mess," she laughed as he opened the door for her.

"You're just weak. You were in bed for three weeks."

They drove on down the road and out past the gate, which Jack got out to open, then down to the home Frank and Krista had been building near the beach. The sun was setting, and there was a warm wind blowing in from the ocean. Frank's truck was parked near the unfinished garage.

They got out. "I think I need to be alone with him," she told Jack.

He hesitated. "I don't think I should leave you."

"I'll be okay. I don't break my promises."

He reached into his pocket and pulled out his cell phone. "Here. If you need anything, anything at all, call me on my house phone. I'll be here in an instant."

She smiled and took the phone in her good hand.

"Thanks, Jack."

He nodded and watched her walk toward the house. Just as she reached the door, he said, "Francie?"

She turned.

"Be good to yourself. Frank isn't the only one who needs you."

He looked very alone, standing there with the wind rippling his shirt and ruffling his hair. If she had had more energy, she would have probably hugged him. But now it was someone else who needed her more.

"I promise," she said, holding up her pinkie. She turned to go into the house. The front door was unlocked, and she went in, closing the wind and noise outside.

"Frank?"

The house was quiet. The countertops were finished in the kitchen, and the carpet had been laid. It was a creamy Berber, something that would stand up to toddler footprints tracking in sand, Krista had said.

She went through the kitchen into the living room.

"Frank?"

She heard a noise from the master bedroom and went toward it. That's where she found him.

There was no furniture in the room, just a few blankets folded in a corner, some clean paintbrushes, and a bucket. Frank was sitting on the floor, leaning back against the wall with his legs splayed out in front of him. A nearly empty bottle of whisky was on the floor next to him.

"This is where we were going to put the bed," he said. His speech was slurred.

Francie picked up the bottle. "Did you drink all of this?" She had never seen him touch alcohol before.

"And over there"—he pointed across the room—"is where we were going to put the dresser. But the bed had to go against this wall because she wanted a view."

Francie looked out the window across from them. Nearly the whole wall was a huge bay window with a window seat. It overlooked the vast ocean beyond.

"But I guess that won't happen now, will it?" He met her eyes. His were filled with pain.

"The baby's pictures came today," he said. They had gotten Angela's six-month photos taken just before the accident. "I couldn't open them. But I'm starting to forget what she looked like."

His voice broke.

"Francie... they wouldn't let me see the bodies. I never got to say goodbye." Tears were streaming down his cheeks now.

"Oh, Frank... "

"I was so afraid you were going to die too."

"I'm here," she said.

"I miss them so much." He began to sob.

"Me too," she said. She knelt beside him and wrapped her arms around him. He smelled of alcohol, but also of the warmth and safety she remembered. He leaned against her, and she held him, her tears flowing freely. He was broken now, sobbing, unable to stop. She could only hold him and wish that she could turn back time.

Eventually, he cried himself out and laid down, right there on the floor. She got the blankets and rolled one up into a pillow and slipped it under his head. Then she lay beside him, her knees up against him, and put her arm around him.

"Don't leave tonight," he said, his speech thick and heavy.

"I won't," she said. "I promise." And the two of them fell asleep.

chapter 44

THE FIRST THING SHE REALIZED when she woke up was that her head didn't hurt. She lay very still, enjoying the absence of pain. Frank lay beside her, facing away, and her arm was still around him. Light filtered across the floor from the window. It was morning.

She carefully removed her arm from around Frank and sat up. She touched her head. Still no pain. Her right hand didn't even hurt.

She smiled. It had never occurred to her before how marvelous the absence of pain could feel. It was like a gift.

Frank turned over, squinting at her.

"You're smiling," he mumbled.

"I don't have a headache," she said. It was all such a simple thing and yet so incredible to her, that some part of her pain, mental, spiritual or physical, could be eased.

"I do," Frank said, closing his eyes. "Ouch. What happened?"

"You drank most of a fifth of whisky."

"Oh."

"You don't remember?"

"Not... much. No." He opened his eyes again, squinting. "What are you doing here? Did you... sleep... here?"

She raised an eyebrow. "What if I did?" She got up. "I need to use the bathroom. Does the plumbing work?"

"Yes."

She walked into the master bathroom and closed the door. She saw some Listerine on the counter and swished it around in her mouth, still marveling at the absence of pain.

Frank watched her go, then sat up slowly, regretting his drinking with every move he made. He used the bathroom down the hall then came back into the room and slid back down against the wall, sitting again and squinting out the window at the ocean. Eventually his eyes adjusted. He felt heavy. Heavy with grief. Heavy with despair. He vaguely remembered last night, and crying, and Francie's arms. He had tried to be strong for her, but he was worn out and with all that alcohol in him... well, it didn't help.

"I found some aspirin in there," she said, holding out two in her hand and a small paper cup of water.

"Thanks." Frank swallowed the aspirin and continued to gaze out the window. He felt so tired.

Francie knelt, facing him. "Are you okay?"

He reached a hand out and gently brushed a wisp of hair away from her eyes, tucking it behind her ear. They had always been very comfortable around each other, all in a platonic way. It had never occurred to him until now to wonder what Krista thought of it. It was just so natural after so many years together.

"Frank?"

"No," he said. "I'm not okay. I can't go home. I don't want to go home."

"You can live with me," Francie said simply. "I've already been home. But I don't really want to go back there now. It's Saturday. The kids will be there. People will stare at me but pretend like they aren't and look away when I look at them."

"We could stay here forever," Frank said.

"Yes. I like that. We'll live off the fish from the ocean."

"When was the last time you ate?"

Francie shrugged. "I don't remember. Whenever it was, they pumped it out of me."

"Don't make light of that," Frank said. Oh, what a horrible two days it had been. "You scared me. Actually, what are you doing here? You're supposed to be under suicide watch. Who left you?"

"I made a pact with Jack. We agreed not to kill ourselves."

Frank frowned. "Somehow that doesn't soothe me."

"We did a pinky promise." She held up her pinky.

Frank stared at her for a minute. Then he laughed. "Ow, my head!" he said but started to laugh harder. Francie joined him, and soon both of them were laughing until tears ran down their cheeks.

"I don't know why that's so funny," Frank said.

"Maybe we've hit hysteria," Francie said. "We've finally cracked under the strain." She wiped her eyes.

"Wouldn't surprise me."

"More likely it's blood sugar," Francie said and pulled a cell phone out of her jeans' pocket.

"You got a cell phone? " Frank asked.

"It's Jack's. I'm going to call his house and invite us to breakfast."

By the time they got to Jack's, he had fried up a whole plateful of eggs and bacon, toasted some toast, and pulled out some donuts. He was glad they had called him.

They ate hungrily. Jack knew it helped that there were no memories here or reminders of things past. The little house was simply decorated and filled with his things; his coat hanging on a peg by the door, his guitar leaning on its stand in the living room. He kept the house clean and tidy.

Jack sat at the table with them and sipped at his coffee. He had already eaten. They both looked dreadful—thin, haggard, and tired—but he noticed a new light in Francie's eyes. She claimed her headache was finally gone, so he supposed that gave her some room to cope with the other kinds of pain in her life.

"Thanks," she said, buttering her third piece of toast. "I honestly don't think I've eaten in weeks."

Frank was finally feeling better with aspirin and coffee and some food in him.

Jack wondered how their night had gone, or if Frank had even been conscious when Francie got there. They seemed okay now, relying on the emotional support that had buoyed them through most of their lives. He wondered for the hundredth time why they had never gotten together. Maybe they already had all they needed in each other.

After toying for a long time with the last bite of eggs on her plate, Francie finally finished and reluctantly put her fork down. She sighed. Frank raised an eyebrow in question.

"Now what?" she asked.

He shrugged.

"We could hide," Francie suggested.

"You certainly have places," Jack said.

"Shhhhhh." Francie put her finger to her lips. "Big Brother."

Jack smiled, enjoying her mood.

"You could stay here. I'll make you lunch in a few hours," he said.

"Mmmmm. Tempting."

"The people at the big house know you're with me, though. I had to give Sam a report both last night and this morning."

Francie's mood sobered. "If I'm going to... survive... this... " She closed her eyes and tried again. "I'm going to have to work. I could hide in my office. I need to stay busy." She looked at Jack. "You've buried your trauma. I'm planning to do the same."

"It'll visit you in your sleep," he said.

"She needs therapy," Frank said.

Francie snorted. "What's a therapist going to tell me?"

"I was thinking of grief counseling," Frank replied.

"Then you need it too."

"I didn't try to kill myself."

"Neither did I."

Jack cleared his throat loudly. They both looked at him. "Let's start with essentials," he said. "The first fuel of survival is to make sure basic needs are met. You ate, now Francie should rest."

Francie realized it was true. She did feel exhausted. Her body was using what little energy she had to digest her food, and her limbs felt heavy and leaden.

"The bed's made," Jack said. "Go lay down on top and pull that quilt over you." He looked at Frank. "There's only one bed, so you can have the couch, or if you want to share the bed with her, I won't think anything of it."

The two of them looked at each other.

"The couch is fine," Frank said.

"I'll call Sam and let her know where you are," Jack said. "After you both get some more rest, we can figure out what the next step is."

Francie watched as he started to clear the table. He glanced at her, and she gave him a little smile.

"Thank you, Jack," she said and left him to clean up. She curled up on the big queen-sized bed she had bought for him. Frank lay down on the couch. Jack brought him a blanket and lowered the shades to block out the morning light.

Francie was immediately sound asleep.

chapter 45

Two and a half weeks later, Francie, Jack, and Frank stood in front of a towering brick building in upper Manhattan, gazing skyward. Large lettering across the front read "Dalton."

"We figured we'd use my maiden name," Francie said. "Ken"—her voice broke, but she recovered—"Ken said it sounded flashy, modern. Strong." She laughed but it was carried off in the wind.

It was early April, with only a few buds on the trees and crocuses blooming in New York, but there was a biting wind blowing off from the Atlantic down the city's streets. It was cold, and Francie pulled her coat tighter around her. The sky was gray. With the sun, there would have been a little more hope of some warmth.

"Let's go inside," she said and pulled the keys out of her pocket. Twenty-two steps led up from the sidewalk to the all-glass front entrance. She punched some numbers into the security keypad and opened the doors. The smell of new paint and carpeting greeted them. They stood in a large lobby with an information desk and a lot of light, let in from the glass windows and doors across the front of the building. Several elevators stood across the lobby.

Francie locked the doors behind them. Jack whistled in appreciation.

"Wow," he said. "Nice."

"Come on," she said, pushing the button for an elevator. "I'll show you my office."

Jack hesitated. "I don't really like enclosed spaces."

Francie looked at him. "But you lived in a nine- by twelve-foot cell for 18 years. Without a window."

"Exactly."

Their eyes met, both steely. The elevator doors started to slide shut. She stuck out an arm to stop them.

"I was trapped in a three-foot by two-foot space underneath the dash of an SUV for two and a half hours. I don't like confined spaces either. Get in."

Jack glanced at Frank, who shrugged. Both men followed Francie into the elevator. She pushed the button numbered "20" and up they went. She closed her eyes.

She heard Jack's breathing speed up, as did her own.

"This isn't supposed to be easy," Francie said. "This whole thing isn't easy. Ken was here with me last time. We were building this company together."

"Yeah, well, you're not the only one with issues," Jack snapped.

"Let's give Jack a break. This is his first time out," Frank said, meaning beyond the small community they lived in. There had been no problems at airport security, where his fake ID was truly tested for the first time.

The doors slid open.

"Ladies first," Jack said, and Francie didn't hesitate.

They stepped into a large foyer. Across from them was a big room taking up most of the floor, encased in glass windows. On either side of them, a single door led into separate offices.

"That"—Francie pointed to the glass room—"is the executive conference room. We'll hold our meetings there.

Over here"—she pointed to the right—"is my office. And over there"—she pointed left—"is Jack's office." She smiled. "Surprise!"

There was a beat of silence.

"My office," Jack said.

"Yes!" Francie said. "Come on!" In her enthusiasm, she instinctively grabbed his hand to pull him along, and he jerked away like he had been bitten. She ignored her mistake and happily went into his office, knowing he'd follow.

She turned and opened her arms in a big, sweeping motion. "Ta-da!"

The room was beautiful. Large windows on either side looked out over the city, offering a panoramic view of Manhattan. At the back of the room there was another door.

"This is your own private bathroom," Francie said. She opened the door. It was roomy and spacious. "Here"—she knocked on the wall between the office and the bathroom—"was going to be a hidden room, but Ken never got to finish it. It wasn't exactly something we could put in the plans for the architects."

Jack was staring in silence.

"Congratulations," Frank said.

"Why do I need an office?" Jack asked.

"Because I'd like you to be my vice president."

Still no response.

"Of the entire company," Francie said. "Actually, we'll probably be really big and have many VPs in other areas, so your title can be Executive Vice President of Dalton Jeans. Or Dalton Enterprises when we really get going."

Jack turned to Frank. "Did you know about this?"

"Yes. You didn't, apparently." Frank shot a look at Francie.

"I've been distracted," she said. "Also, I thought it would be a fun surprise. The Lord knows, we need some fun around here." She smiled. "Come and see my office." She led them across the foyer to a similar room.

"Did you even ask Jack if this is what he wants?" Frank mumbled in her ear.

"Not exactly."

The windowsills were large, and Frank looked tired. He sat down on one.

"I really like the farm," Jack said. "I don't want to move to New York."

"Move?" Francie said. "Oh, honey, you're not moving. You can stay at the farm. I figured we'd come up a few days a month is all. You can work from home. Telecommute."

"Francie... " Jack started.

She looked at him, feeling deflated. Then she glanced at Frank, who was leaning forward with his elbows on his knees, his face in his hands. She just wanted to keep moving forward, to stay busy and to not think.

"Why are you doing all of this for me?" Jack said. He sounded angry. "I didn't ask for any of this. What's the catch?"

"The catch?"

"Yes. Nobody gives people stuff like this. What do you want from me? Or is it pity?" His eyes flashed anger. "I'm not one of your little ponies—"

"They're not ponies."

"—that you can rescue and patch up and put out on a track to win for you."

"Is that what you think this is?"

"Well, what is it?"

"Did it ever occur to your hard head that I've been very impressed with your work? You kept the farm running all these past months. Before that, you were a hard worker, you don't complain, and you're smart. Or at least, I thought that until now."

"You'd trust me with your company?" Jack asked.

"I trusted you with my farm."

"How do you know I didn't murder that man?"

"Did you?"

There was a beat of silence. The anger in his eyes dissolved.

"No," he said.

"Well then."

Jack shoved his hands into his pockets. "I'll be in my office," he said and stormed across the foyer.

There was no furniture, so Francie leaned against the wall and slid down onto her bottom. "It's really cold in here," she said, glancing at Frank.

Frank looked up. "Did it ever occur to you that he still doesn't trust you?" he said quietly.

"Why wouldn't he trust me?"

"Francie, who has he been able to trust in the past twenty years? Jim? He's gone. His mom? She's out of the picture too. Everyone else has betrayed him, even his country. Why trust us? You should understand that better than anybody."

"What is that supposed to mean?"

"Just that you have to be in control of everything. You have your own issues with trust."

Francie frowned but didn't say anything. She pulled her jacket tighter around her, letting his words run through her mind.

"Let's leave," Frank said. "I'm getting cold too."

"Let me talk to him first," Francie said.

Slowly, Francie got up. She still got tired easily and had learned to move carefully. She walked across to Jack's office where he was standing and looking out the window.

"It's beautiful," he said softly.

Francie came and stood beside him. They gazed out at the streets below, where people and cars looked so tiny. On the crowded sidewalk, a father was tying a red balloon to his son's wrist and was apparently having trouble because of the mittens the boy was wearing. The boy's face was too far away for them to read his expression, but by the way he was bouncing up and down, he looked very excited. The man hugged his little boy and gave him a pat on the head.

"I'm sorry," Jack said.

"Me too," Francie said. Below them, the man took the boy's hand and led him into an ice cream shop. "Look, you aren't a prisoner. I asked you to stay at the farm for a year or two until we were sure you were safe. You made it through airport security, so I think you're good. You can leave anytime you want. But... " She swallowed. "I'd really like for you to stay." She absently rubbed her right hand. It was aching.

Jack kept looking out the window, past the streets now, out to the horizon. The sky was gray and looked very cold.

"I'd like to stay too," he said eventually. Then he looked at her and gave her his charming grin. "And I'd be honored to be your executive vice president. I will do my best."

"I know you will." She held his eyes. "And I don't pity you."

"That was a cheap shot. I was mad."

"Or scared?"

He turned back toward the gray scene outside. The little boy and his father came out of the shop, the red balloon a bright spot in the scene. "Just... uncertain," he said.

She started to lay a hand on his shoulder and then stopped herself in time.

"Let's go," she said. "It's cold in here."

They ate dinner at a little Italian restaurant, just the three of them at a table in the back. They were quiet, each lost in his or her own thoughts, each still grieving. Francie ate her spaghetti in silence, twirling it around her fork and playing with it. Her mind wasn't really on the food. She longed to go to the restaurant she and Ken had eaten at last time, to sit at the table they had sat at together, to try to relive that happy evening.

She was dreading tomorrow. Their trip to New York was two-fold. They were here to look at the business, but also to go through Krista's apartment and see what they wanted to keep or sell before they let the lease expire.

Francie's anger and depression had ebbed into a type of emotionless gloom. She had two gears now: work hard and fast with energy, and tired gloom. Those seemed to be the only things she felt. She had tried to go back to training horses last week, but it wore her out physically. She could train from the rail but decided instead to let Donovan handle it all for now.

"Are you going to eat that?" Frank's voice was gentle.

She glanced up. Both men had emptied their plates.

"Sorry," she said and put a forkful into her mouth.

"What were you thinking about?" Frank asked.

"The usual." She took another bite.

Jack signaled to the waiter and asked for another glass of water. He squeezed lemon into it and stirred it around.

"About earlier," he said. "I do realize I'm a very lucky man. I'm sorry I got all cranky." He watched the ice swirl around in his glass.

"You're not lucky, you're blessed," Francie said. "God has a plan for you."

Jack looked up from his glass. "You mean to tell me that after all you've been through, you still believe in God?"

"Well... yes," Francie said. "Why wouldn't I?"

Frank watched them and played with a pack of sugar.

"To start with," Jack said, "He took nearly everyone you love."

"Not everyone."

"Nearly. Then you were in a horrible accident. You had a dreadful childhood. Your first marriage ended in divorce..."

Francie swallowed her food. It tasted like cardboard. "Are you trying to depress me?"

"What about you?" Jack looked at Frank.

Frank cleared his throat and took his time answering.

"I look at it this way: what if I was going through this and didn't have my faith?"

Jack looked back at Francie. "So what is God's plan?"

"I don't know," she said. "We can't see the whole picture, but God can. I trust Him. The Bible says we only see part now, but someday, we'll see all."

"For now, we see through a glass, darkly; but then face-to-face: now I know in part; but then shall I know even as also I am known," Frank quoted quietly.

"So Ken and Krista, the baby, Jim—their deaths are all part of His plan?" Jack asked. He spoke softly, kindly, trying to understand and not wanting to push too far into the pain.

"Maybe," Frank said. "I don't believe He made it happen. Or wanted it to happen. All I know is God can use what did happen for His glory. He can use it to bring other people to know Christ, or to strengthen someone's faith. I don't know. All I know is I trust Him, like Francie said."

"That doesn't mean I'm not angry at Him," Francie said. "It's unfair, and I'm hurting, and I don't understand. I've yelled at God a few times since the accident."

"You yelled at God?" Jack said, raising an eyebrow.

"God's big enough to handle my anger," Francie said. "And compassionate enough to understand my pain."

"Won't you like, go to Hell, if you yell at God?"

"Grace," Frank said.

"There's that word again," said Jack.

Francie smiled. "The Lord is my strength and my shield; my heart trusts in him, and he helps me. My heart leaps for joy, and with my song I praise him," she quoted from

Psalms 27:8. Suddenly, she felt better and finished her plate of food.

After a quiet night in a local hotel where Francie had reserved them each a room, they began the difficult task of sorting through Krista's apartment. The guys wanted to grab some coffee and donuts, but Francie insisted they have a sit-down breakfast in the hotel restaurant before they began.

"We need protein," she said, "for strength."

"Says the woman whose only breakfast is usually coffee," Frank mumbled.

The first few minutes in the apartment were the most difficult. Krista had tossed a sweater casually over the living room chair, and they almost expected her to walk up and grab it on her way out the door. There was a tube of her lipstick lying out on the bathroom counter. On her nightstand, a book she had been reading held a bookmark on page 168. She was more than halfway through, Francie saw. She never got to finish it.

But it was the forgotten toy that broke Frank. Next to the living room sofa, on the floor, a small stuffed dog had fallen and lay there. It had been one of Angela's favorites, and she must have dropped it the last time they were here.

Frank picked it up and choked back a sob. Francie, already teary-eyed from her walk through the apartment, started crying more. She walked to the window, her back to them, and took the box of tissue with her. Frank put his head in his hands and wept.

Jack, very uncomfortable with the situation, went out into the hall and leaned his back up against the wall, touching his lips with his fingers. Francie suspected that he desperately wished he hadn't given up smoking.

Over the past few weeks, Sam had helped both Francie and Frank sort through some items at home. She had asked Jack to carry several large bags and boxes out to Frank's truck. Then Frank had handed him the keys and asked him to drop them off at the Salvation Army.

There had been some debate as to what to do with Krista's dresses. They could have auctioned them off for quite a large profit, but it didn't feel right. Sam found a local charity called Fairy Tale Dresses, which took donations of used evening gowns for girls who couldn't afford their own dresses for prom. They anonymously donated them there. Again, Jack delivered them.

There had been no funeral or memorial service. Fans clamored for one for Krista, and news reporters spent several weeks at the entrance to the farm, seeking an interview with Frank or anyone willing to talk. Finally, they gave up and left. Francie's mom, up in Michigan, was more than willing to talk at length about her favorite daughter, so newspapers and magazines were filled with her quotes. Even she had respected Frank's space though and not insisted on a service. Since there were no bodies to view, and since Francie had been unconscious, no one seemed to know what to do. So two weeks ago, three bodies were buried quietly in the small cemetery just outside of town where Jim was buried. The only ones in attendance had been those living at the farm and Ken's dad. No one told Norma or Derek until afterward.

Francie peeked around the door. "It's safe to come back in now," she said to Jack.

Jack came in. Frank was going through the dishes.

"I've decided to take the personal items, like Krista's Bible, our family photos, and this quilt her grandma made," Frank announced. "And I'm going to hire someone to come in and do an estate sale for the rest. I did this at home. I can't do it again."

They both looked at him. Finally, Francie rubbed her hands together. "Okay," she said. "Let's get it and go. Then we'll do something fun." She turned to Jack. "We'll go pick out our office furniture."

That afternoon they walked into Miller Office Furniture, a big store on East Grand. Frank was quiet and withdrawn. He followed them around, clicked a few lamps on and off, then lost interest. Francie was uneasy. She was used to his constant, warm support and felt like she was missing something vital.

They spent some time looking at desks. Francie couldn't find one she liked.

"I'm going to have one custom made," she said. "I might as well, now that I have all this stupid money." She was referring to Ken's life insurance policy.

"Again... the anger," Jack said, pulling out a drawer.

"You haven't seen anything yet," she mumbled.

"You both look tired," he said. "Maybe today's not a good day for this."

"Jack," Francie said. "There are no more good days."

He looked at her for a moment, standing there with her hands on her hips, determined.

"Okay, Princess," he said. "Let's go find you a throne." He pointed back toward a sign hanging on the ceiling marked "Office Chairs."

She frowned at the nickname but followed him back.

They both found chairs they liked, then went back for desks again. By dinnertime, they had outfitted the entire office and scheduled delivery for their next trip to New York.

"Let's go eat," Frank said. "Our plane leaves at 8 p.m."

Francie wrote a check from her Dalton Jeans business account. She still got a thrill seeing it. After she paid for the furniture, they found a little restaurant close to the airport. At dinner, they toasted with iced teas and soda.

"To Dalton Jeans," she said.

"And a new beginning," said Jack.

It was late when they dropped Jack off at his house after the trip. He went inside, switching on the light, and walked over to the kitchen sink to get a drink of water. He saw the plaque with the Martin Luther King quote that Francie hung there, staring at him: *Faith is taking the first step even when you don't see the whole staircase.* He had read it so many times he had it memorized, but really, the words hadn't meant a lot to him.

Faith.

It made him think of what he had witnessed in New York as he watched both Frank and Francie struggle through grief. He knew all about pushing through the pain. And yet, there was something there that he couldn't put his finger on. Something that buoyed them above their grief.

He went outside and sat on his back patio to get some fresh air and look at the stars. *Faith.* Even though Francie had had nearly everything taken from her, she still loved God. Frank too. It amazed him.

He gazed up at the stars, his eyes catching the familiar constellations of Orion and the Big Dipper that his mother had taught him when he was little. There were so many stars up there, stars he would never know the names to, but he never tired of looking at them after 18 years of not seeing the nighttime sky.

He thought of God. He had cried out to Him so many times while he was a prisoner of war, begging for God either to save him or to kill him. Death had been preferable to what he was going through at the time. But God had never heard him.

Or maybe He had. Jack thought about it, about how much he had been blessed. Maybe God *had* heard him and saved him, but God's timing was different than his. After all, now he had a nice home, an amazing job, and friends who cared about him.

I wonder if you really are listening, Jack said to the nighttime sky. He thought of Francie, and of grace, a word she used frequently. "A free and unmerited gift from God," Francie said. *Free.* Something he didn't have to earn.

Jack noticed that his hands were trembling, and his heart was pounding. He suddenly desired to have what Francie and Frank had, and Sam too. He got off the chair and found himself on his knees.

He looked up at the stars, into the vastness of the universe, and felt so small and inconsequential. Was it possible that a creator was out there and wanted a relationship with *him?* Why would God take time for individual people? A God that vast, and yet that personal. His heart continued to pound in his chest as his eyes searched the heavens.

"I'm sorry," he whispered, not knowing why he was asking for forgiveness, or to whom. Then his lips formed the words, "Jesus," and he realized that tears were running down his cheeks.

He thought of Frank offering him grace. "You don't owe us anything," Frank had said. "We just want you to be free."

Jack realized that he wanted that grace that Jesus brought, and he wanted it with a hunger he hadn't realized he had. There was an emptiness in him that nothing had been able to fill.

"Please," he said. "I want you in my life. I'm not good at trusting, but I want to trust you. I turn my life over to you." *He'll take you as you are,* Francie had told him. "Be

Lord of my life too. Give me the grace and mercy you've given the others."

Jack felt a peace come over him, a completeness, a wholeness that he had never felt before. A weight lifted from him. He thought it must be his imagination, but it felt as if a warm blanket was laid across his shoulders, enveloping him in compassion and comfort. He had been touched, and it was good.

Jack knelt there for a long time on the cold patio, warmed by a spirit glowing within his heart. He felt alive.

Francie was upset. The trip, while a good one, had opened up a lot of memories of Ken and Krista, and she still couldn't get the image of the stuffed toy out of her mind and of Frank breaking down.

She hadn't slept well all night after they'd come home, but instead of giving up and going into her office to work, she had laid in bed and tossed and turned and tried to hide under the covers.

This morning, she found herself upset and angry. She was short with Frank at the track and had hardly spoken to Donovan while he worked the horses. She couldn't even remember what time her new colt had clocked. Instead of going to the barn afterwards, she came home and took a long, hot shower, then fixed herself another strong cup of coffee.

Now she was sitting at her desk, waiting for Jack to come for his 11 a.m. meeting in an hour. She opened up Solitaire on her computer because she wasn't in the mood to work. She was putting an ace up top when she saw her Bible sitting on her desk.

The truth was, she was mad at God. She had turned to Him for comfort but could feel any. Not now, not after her trip to New York and the memories it had stirred. Last night she'd read the scriptures she used to love, the Psalms and the promises of Jesus, and yet she couldn't understand why God had let everyone die. Why? She understood that life was often a series of random acts and that the hand of God wasn't causing these horrible things to happen. She also understood intellectually that God still loved her, but she didn't *feel* it. He could have stopped that accident they were in.

Despite her encouraging words to Jack at the restaurant, she had been struggling with her faith lately. What she had told Jack was true—she still believed in God, but she was angry at Him. He had let her down.

She ignored the Bible and put a two of hearts up on her ace, then she got a king and had a spot for it on the playing board. A queen. The game was going well.

She glanced at the Bible again, sighed and pulled it over to her. Frank had given it to her when she had first been saved, and he had written a scripture on the inside of it:

Trust the Lord with all your heart and lean not on your own understanding. In all your ways submit to him and he will direct your paths. - Proverbs 3:5–6

Trust. She snorted and slammed the cover closed. She went back to her Solitaire game, but she couldn't concentrate.

Trust? Francie thought. *I've trusted You and look what that brought me,* she said to God. *What good can possibly come out of this tragedy You've allowed into my life?*

She thought of all she had lost and then thought of all Jack had lost too. What kind of God would allow such things to happen?

She picked up her Bible again, this time turning to a passage on peace, Philippians 4:6–7:

Do not be anxious about anything, but in every situation, by prayer and petition, with thanksgiving, present your requests to God. And the peace of God, which transcends all understanding, will guard your hearts and your minds in Christ Jesus.

"I don't have any peace!" she said angrily. She stood up, smacking her palms down on her desk in anger, glad for the soundproof room. "I don't have any peace!" she shouted at God. "You call this peace? How can you possibly work the death of my family members into Your plan to bless me? Or am I being punished?"

Maybe that was it. She was being punished for breaking the law.

Francie picked up the Bible and shook it at the ceiling, feeling her anger turn into something like hate toward God.

"I can't trust You anymore!" she shouted and then heard her voice break in a sob. She brought her arm back and flung her Bible at the wall. It hit with a thud, the thin pages fluttering as it slid to the ground. She sat back down in her chair and wiped a tear from her cheek. She felt utterly defeated. "What good can come of this?"

Just then, someone knocked on her door. She wiped her other cheek and glanced at the Bible on the ground. At the same time, the door opened, and Jack came in. He shut the door behind him.

"You're early," she said, looking at her clock.

"Yeah," he said with a smile on his face. He didn't seem to notice the Bible on the floor. "I just wanted to tell you that I asked Jesus into my life last night. I prayed that prayer you told me, and I asked Him into my life. I know you've been praying for me for years, Princess, and I couldn't wait until 11 a.m. to tell you. I wanted you to know now."

<h1 style="text-align:center">chapter
46</h1>

"It just isn't normal," Steve said. He was sitting cross-legged on the king-sized bed in their room, watching Sam paint.

"Normal?" Sam mused, adding a little blue to the canvas. She was painting a landscape from a photo a client had given her of a seaside garden. "*What* isn't normal?"

"It's just not right," he said. "I mean, they won't go anywhere without each other. Not even to the post office. Frank tried to go the other day, and Francie was right there with him, handing him the keys and pulling her boots on. She quit working just to go. They haven't been apart since the accident."

"Can you blame them?" She picked up a finer brush and started adding sea grass.

"No." Steve said. He watched his wife make delicate strokes of wheat-colored stalks on the paper, blending them into the sand and sea with slight smudges of her brush. "I get it. But maybe they need counseling. It has been nearly six months."

Sam paused and turned to face Steve. She smiled. "We could probably all use some counseling," she said. "Let them heal in their own way."

"I don't need counseling," Steve said. "I'm perfectly okay."

Sam laughed. Steve grinned back. "What?"

"Nothing, dear." She went back to painting.

"I don't know why they don't just kiss and get it over with. Or better yet, jump in the sack together."

Sam didn't respond. Instead, she added some green to her grass.

"They're in love," Steve said. "Everyone can see it."

Sam considered that. "I don't think *they* can," she said, finally. "I really don't think they realize it yet."

"But you agree with me?"

"I think they've been in love since the day they laid eyes on each other," Sam said. "Just give it time."

"Hmmmmpf," Steve said. He laced his fingers behind his head and lay back on the bed to think. But as usual, his mind wandered, and he was asleep in under a minute.

In a month, the business was ready to begin. The machines were up and running, the offices complete, the water, electricity, and plumbing all working.

Now they needed staff.

"I really want a woman to run the business," said Francie, shuffling through resumes at her grandpa's desk. They were back at the farm. "The world needs more women CEOs."

Jack was sitting across from her desk. He looked up from his notebook and frowned. "No you don't," he said.

Jack annoyed her. He had a bad habit of saying exactly what was on his mind. She frowned.

"How do you know what I want?" she quipped.

"Because you like being the only woman," he said.

Francie took a deep breath to tell her part, but Frank broke in from his seat on the couch.

"I have to agree with him," he said.

Francie shot him a look. "*Et tu, Brute?*"

"You have a way about you that works well with men," Frank said. "Don't bring another woman into the mix."

"Are you saying I flirt?"

"No," both men said at once.

"It's more the princess thing," Jack said.

"You know, I hate that word. I hate that title. I should fire you on the spot." She got up from her desk. "You guys figure it out."

"Sit down," Frank said in his usual calm voice. "Jack, quit harassing her. I swear you two fight like siblings. I thought you narrowed it down to three yesterday."

"We did," Francie said, sitting back down while giving Jack a dark look. "And one was a woman."

"I like the one guy," said Jack. "Donald."

"Actually," said Frank, looking over his copy of the resume, "Donald seems to be the most qualified. And he's a Christian. I see he included that here."

"So's the woman," said Francie.

Steve stuck his head in the door. "I still say it's wrong to hire based on religious affiliation." He gave her a cocky smile. "Just sayin'," and he disappeared down the hall.

"It's my company!" Francie shouted after him. "I'll hire who I want!" Why had she surrounded herself with all these *men?*

"We have our third guy," said Jack. "An Asian gentleman. Donald is black. And you have a woman." He glanced at Francie, giving her a look.

"Those three were the most qualified. I'm not trying to run a minority-based business."

"Our office manager is Italian," Jack said. "She has an accent."

"I hired her because she said she'd make cannolis and bring them in," Francie said. "And it *is* New York. It's the melting pot." Rosa was a warm, sharp, organized woman with a large family and a wonderful laugh. Francie had loved her the moment they met. At 52, Rosa reminded her of a younger version of her grandma, which, she admitted to herself, might have had something to do with why she'd chosen her. "My grandma was Italian. I love cannolis!" She laughed. "Okay, so let's bring all three in. We'll start with Donald. His resume is the strongest."

The following week, they hired Donald on the spot.

"He was obviously the best," Francie said. Plus he was a warm, family man, and Francie was trying to build a family-oriented company. And, for her CEO, she had included a question about religious affiliation on the application, even asking what their relationship was with God. She felt a bit of a kindredness to other Christians and wanted one at the wheel of her ship. Rosa was a strong Catholic. As for the rest of the gang, she didn't ask.

Their creative director was a young woman, barely out of college, named Cassie. She was in charge of creating ads. She didn't have much experience, but her enthusiasm had won her the job.

Danny, their fashion designer, was also young, but brilliant, with some awards already under his belt. He preferred runways but was excited about blue jeans and figured he could transform America by clothing them all in Dalton denim. Danny was also flamboyantly gay, and while Francie felt like it was a cliché to hire a gay designer, she loved him right away and wanted him on her team.

"Good job," Francie said to Jack. "We have a company."

"And they all seem *happy*," Jack said. "One big happy family." He grinned at her.

"That's what I want," Francie said. "Why do I always feel like you're mocking me?"

"I'm sorry."

She stacked the papers together, handing them to Jack. "You've got some work to do. I'll see you tomorrow morning."

Francie had a decent routine down. She got up early and handled the horses, did some training out at the track, then returned in time to meet with Jack at 11 a.m. They worked until about one, after which she had lunch. Then she was back outside for a few hours with the horses. By that time the girls were home from school, they ate dinner together, and she did what she called "mom things" until about 7 p.m. After that, she did paperwork for both the farm and the business until about 9 p.m. when Frank came in for their usual evening meeting, which they had started up again.

Francie ate lunch and went down to the barn for a few hours. When she returned, she sat down to take her boots off and glanced over on the peg where Ken had hung his duster. It had become a habit of hers, looking at it every time she left or came in, pretending he was still here.

Today it was gone. So were his boots.

She panicked. She set her own boots aside and ran into the kitchen. Becky was sitting at the table having an after-school snack.

"Where's Ken's coat?" she said.

"I put it away," Becky said. "It was—"

"You put it *away?*" Francie said, her voice shrill. "Where? What did you do with it? Becky, it was mine to put away when I was ready! And I *am not ready!*"

Becky stood up. "You know what? *I was.* You never think about *me*—it's always about *you*. With Ken, I finally, for once in my life, had a *family*, a real family, that did family things and went on vacations together and had *fun!* Maybe that's why you miss Ken so much—because you're no good at being a parent by yourself. It's always about work with you, Mom! Not me!"

"What? Young lady, you wouldn't have half of what you have if I hadn't worked all those hours!"

"You've never thought about me, Mom, ever! Just like you're not thinking of me now. Ken didn't just die on *you*. He died and left me too. I took that coat down because every time I saw it, it reminded me of Ken and of what I no longer have. Mom, I miss him too, and it was killing me to see it every day!" Becky was crying now, her voice shaking.

"*Where* is the coat?" Francie asked through gritted teeth, anger making the blood in her ears pound.

"I hate you!" Becky said. "I hate you for all the years you ignored what I needed, just like you're doing now. You suck as a parent." Becky got up, grabbing her plate and tossing it in the sink, her sandwich uneaten. Francie grabbed her shoulder.

"*Where* is the coat?"

"It's in your closet!" Becky shrugged out of her grasp and went outside, slamming the door shut behind her.

Francie ran upstairs, tripping on the top step. She burst into her room and threw open the closet door. There, neatly folded on top of her stool, was Ken's coat, and his boots were carefully set beside it. Francie dropped to her knees, grasping the coat in her hands, drawing it to her face and inhaling, hoping to catch his scent somewhere. There was nothing. She buried her face into it and cried for a very long time.

chapter 47

STEVE WAS IN HIS GARAGE WORKING on his Vette when he heard a loud roar coming up the driveway. He walked out, wiping his hands on a rag, and saw Jack ride up, straddling a Harley.

Steve whistled. "Wow. Where'd you get that?"

"I bought it," Jack said. "With my new job and all, I figured I'd spend some money on something fun. I've always wanted a bike." He revved the engines again, then sat there, letting it idle.

Steve walked around it, admiring the new shine. "Wow. Top notch, dude. But if I were you, I'd return it."

Jack turned the motor off. "What? Why?"

"Francie hates motorcycles."

"Seriously?"

"Seriously. Dude, get rid of it."

"Why?"

"It scares the horses. But more than that, her first boyfriend was killed on a bike."

Jack took that in. "Well, that was... what? How many years ago? I'm sure she's over it."

"I'm pretty sure she's not."

They heard the screen door open, and Francie came out, carrying a manila folder.

"I'm outta here," Steve said. "Good luck."

He hurried back toward the garage.

Jack sat there, dumbfounded. Before he could think of what to say, Francie was upon him.

"Here." She handed him the manila folder. "The papers you needed me to sign for work."

"Thanks." He took the envelope and swallowed.

"I hope you didn't buy that thing."

"What?"

Her eyes narrowed.

"Oh. The bike. Well, yeah, actually, I did. You want a ride?"

"No. Motorcycles are noisy, and they scare the horses."

"I told him you hated motorcycles!" Steve shouted from the garage.

"Well, I won't ride it around the horses," Jack said.

"I didn't save your life to have you go and wrap your bike around a tree and get yourself killed."

"You don't like it?"

"No."

"So no girls, no cigarettes, and now no bike?" Jack gave her his sideways smile.

"It's your life," she said coldly. "It's not like you're still in prison. If you want to screw around and get lung cancer and get your head smashed in on that bike, it's your choice." She turned and walked back into the house, slamming the door.

Jack took the bike back.

"You need to talk to your daughter," Frank said. Francie was sitting at her desk, pounding at her keyboard, a frown on her face.

She looked up at him and sighed. "I suck at that. I'm a terrible parent, you know that. She hates me."

"She doesn't hate you, but she's hurting. Go. Talk to her. I don't know exactly what went down with you two the other day, but she *is* your daughter. You need to fix it." Then, in his quiet way, he left the room, leaving her to do what she knew she needed to.

She saved her file and got up. She found Becky in the kitchen, stacking cans of cat food in the pantry.

"Mittens was almost out," Becky said. "Sam picked some up for me today."

Francie sat down on the floor next to her and pulled the cans out of the bag, handing them to her.

"I guess that should have been my job as your mom, to make sure your cat wasn't out of food," she said.

"Yeah, well you've never been very good at the mom thing," Becky said.

That hurt, even though Francie knew it was true. There was a silence as the words hung in the air. Finally, Francie said, "I know. I've come to apologize for that."

Becky paused briefly, a can in her hand, but didn't look up. She continued stacking.

Francie cleared her throat. "I, um. You know I love you. And I know I've screwed up. A lot. Not just with Ken's jacket the other day but with everything. I should have been home more. I should have worked less. I just... " She wanted to use an excuse. She wanted to say that she wasn't parented well and had no idea what a good mother should do. But that wasn't exactly true, because her grandma had shown her love. "I don't know."

"Frank says you're driven," Becky said.

"Maybe I'm just scared," Francie said quietly. Becky had finished with the cans and finally looked at her. She searched her mom's eyes for a moment.

"I really miss Ken," Becky said, and her eyes teared up.

"Me too, honey," said Francie, and then Becky leaned forward and let Francie hug her.

"I love you, Mom," Becky said, and Francie buried her face in her daughter's hair.

"I love you too, honey."

chapter 48

RANCIE WAS SCRUBBING OUT BUCKETS in the barn. It had been over six months since the accident, and her hand had healed but not her heart. It was nearly feeding time in the evening. She had had a productive day handling the business end of Dalton Jeans up at the house, then had worked on a new colt she was training to ride. Now she was scrubbing buckets.

She hired people to do these things, but she still enjoyed some of the heavier work of the farm. She often grabbed a pitchfork and cleaned stalls or hauled hay.

She stood up and was rinsing her bucket over the drain when she saw Frank walking down the barn aisle.

"Hey," he said, stopping near her.

"Hi." She pushed a lock of hair behind her ear with a wet hand.

"What happened?" Frank lightly touched her wrist and turned her hand over.

"Oh," she laughed at the scraped knuckle. "I scrubbed too hard, and my knuckle took over from the brush."

He smiled.

"I've got a few errands to run," he said. "We need stamps for tomorrow, and I want to get to the bank before it closes. I'll be home by dinner time."

Francie just stared at him for a moment, trying to figure out why her heart had suddenly started racing. "Do you want me to go with you?" she asked.

"No," he said. "You're busy." He turned to go.

"Frank."

He looked at her.

"What?"

She turned off the hose and dried her hands. "It's just... I don't think... " She stopped, unsure what she was trying to say. "I want to go with you," she finally said.

Frank looked at her. She was wearing torn jeans, and her blue t-shirt was wet and covered in dirt. It would take her time to change, and the bank would be closing soon.

"I'll just stay in the car," she said, knowing what he was thinking.

He looked at her awhile longer, unsure of what to say. Finally, he said, "We haven't been apart since the accident."

"That's not what I'm thinking."

He raised an eyebrow. She sighed. "Fine," she said. "That *is* what I'm thinking."

"I realize we've gotten into this habit of going every place together. But sweetheart, it has been six months. You being in that car with Ken didn't stop it from crashing. I'll be fine. I'll be back."

"You don't know that." Now her palms were sweating.

Near the end of the aisle, a horse nickered and banged his stall door.

Frank smiled. "Navi wants his bucket back."

Francie glanced back at the horse, then finished rinsing the bucket. "Go," she said. "I'll see you at dinner."

Frank stood there, thinking, watching her fill the bucket. When she turned to carry it down to the horse, he turned and left, walking back to the house and his truck.

Francie opened Navigator's door and put the bucket on its hook. "Hi, Navi," she said, petting the horse on the neck as he plunged his muzzle into the cool, fresh water. She noticed that her hands were shaking. Her heart was still pounding. She felt like she couldn't swallow.

"Frank will be fine," she said, more to herself than to the horse. She gave him a final pat and closed the stall door.

But what if he wasn't? What if she never saw Frank again? What if that had been their last conversation ever?

"Hey, Ms. Dalton," said Frenchie. He had arrived to help with the evening feeding.

"Hi, Frenchie," Francie said. He disappeared into the grain room with a wheelbarrow.

Francie thought she heard an engine start, and she jumped.

To heck with this, she thought and took off running. What if he had already left?

Her heart pounding, the blood in her ears, she ran toward the house for all she was worth. She saw Frank's truck starting to pull out.

"Frank!" she screamed. He didn't seem to hear her, and she tried to run faster, feeling like she was about to vomit, the fear was so great in her.

"Frank!" She knew her voice sounded primal as she screamed, but all she could think of was that she had to stop him. He must have heard her, because he stopped the truck. She knew she was a sight, running across the yard like that. She realized tears were streaming down her cheeks.

He got out of the truck and shut the door. "What's wrong?" he shouted. "What happened?"

He ran toward her, and when he reached her, she stopped short. She was out of breath.

"What?" He looked afraid.

"You... you can't leave me," she said. "I can't let you go."

The two of them stood there, Frank slowly letting the tension slide out of his muscles while Francie caught her breath. He pulled a handkerchief out of his pocket and wiped her face.

Then he opened his arms.

"Come here," he said.

She stumbled forward into his embrace, and felt his arms wrap around her and draw her in. She buried her face in his chest and waited until she pulled herself together before she stepped back and looked up at him.

"I suppose you're going to miss the bank," she said.

"It's okay," he said.

"I just... " She stopped, unsure how to continue. "I just... Frank, I can't live without you. I can't even be away from you. I've never been able to live without you."

She looked up into his kind, brown eyes, and years of memories swirled through her mind. He reached toward her and tucked the stray, stubborn curl behind her ear. The intimate gesture felt so natural. His hands felt so familiar.

"Why?" he asked gently.

"*Why?*" she repeated, baffled. "*Why? Why* can't I live without you?"

He nodded. "Why?"

She took his hands in her own. They were warm and strong hands, and she realized that her own had stopped trembling. She squeezed his hands and closed her eyes.

"Because," she said.

He remained quiet, standing there, his hands in hers. He was so close that she could smell his aftershave. She opened her eyes and looked up into his. She felt tears in her eyes again.

"Because," she said quietly, almost whispering. "Because I love you."

He smiled then, still looking into her eyes, calming the pounding of her heart. She loved the deep warmth his eyes had. She felt safe when she looked into them. She held his gaze, afraid of what she had just said, afraid of the words, and yet knowing that no matter how this ended she would still be safe.

"Francie," he said. "I love you too."

"You do?" she asked.

He nodded and moved closer to her. She turned her head up to his and received his kiss. At first it was soft and gentle, a short kiss, but then his lips met hers hungrily, and she took his shoulders and pulled him against her.

She knew then that this is where she belonged. All the years of Frank beside her, helping her, encouraging her, protecting her, all of those times had always in some way been pushing her toward this moment. *This*, this is where she was meant to be. Frank was *home* to her.

They kissed long and hard, and when they finished, they were in each other's arms.

She smiled and buried her head in his familiar chest. "I love you, Frank Weaver," she said. "I don't want to ever let you go."

"You don't have to ever let me go, Francie," he said. "I promised I'd never leave you, and I never will."

She was quiet for a moment. "What will the others think?"

"Who cares?"

Suddenly they heard Steve's voice booming from the front porch.

"It's about time!" he said.

They pulled apart quickly and turned to look at him. Sam was beside him with a dishtowel, drying her hands. She had a huge smile on her face.

"Don't try to act all innocent," Steve said. "We all saw that kiss. It's about time. That should have happened about fifteen years ago. You have our blessing." He saluted them, and he and Sam turned and walked back into the house.

"You can kiss some more," Sam shouted over her shoulder just before she shut the door

"Not if the entire world is going to watch!" Frank said. Then he and Francie laughed.

"Well, I guess we know what they think!" he said.

Neither of them was sure where to go from there.

"I, um, I guess we could still get to the post office," Francie said.

"No, I'm done working for the night," Frank said. "Let's go out to dinner. Just the two of us."

"Like, on a date?"

"Yes. Francie Dalton, I am asking you out on a date."

"Frank, you're my sister's... you *were* my sister's husband. This doesn't seem normal."

"Francie, there's nothing about our lives that is normal. Nothing."

She smiled at that. "You're right." She snuggled back into his arms. "Kiss me again."

In just a month, Dalton Jeans had its first business meeting. Frank, Francie, and Jack flew into New York together for the first time on their private jet.

"If we're going to do all this traveling, we might as well have our own plane," Francie had said, and nobody argued with her.

This was the official kick-off meeting.

Francie was dressed for business with her hair pulled up on top her head. She wore a dove gray skirt and jacket with a light blue blouse.

"Wow," Frank whistled when he saw her and drew her in for a hug and kiss. They couldn't seem to stop kissing nowadays.

They got off the plane and took a taxi to their building, up the twenty floors in the elevator (by now they were used to it) and onto their floor. Rosa greeted them.

"Good morning Ms. Dalton, Mr. Banner, Mr. Weaver."

"Please, Rosa, for the umpteenth time, call me Francie," Francie said, smiling. She loved Rosa, and, as usual for her visits, her office manager had ordered donuts, so she picked up her favorite, the cherry-filled sugar-coated Bismarck.

"You can call *me* 'sir'," Jack said, grabbing a chocolate-coated donut.

"Whatever," Rosa said, slapping his hand. "Those are for the meeting."

"She got to take one."

"She's the owner."

"I'm the VP. That has to mean something. No, wait. I'm the *executive* VP." He grabbed a second donut.

Frank smiled and sat down in the chair next to Rosa's desk as Francie went into her office.

"I'm just going to hang out here," Frank said. "I have my own work to do." He popped open his briefcase.

The meeting room filled up while Francie waited in her office. A soft knock came on the door, and Jack walked in.

"Are you ready?" he asked.

"I'm waiting."

"You're going to be late."

"I'm going to make an *entrance*," she said. "When you bring a horse out for a race, it's always better to wait until people are finished looking at all the other horses and are ready to look at *your* horse. I can't imagine leading a company is that different."

Jack laughed.

"Let's go," she said.

They walked into the full meeting room, and of course, all eyes turned toward them. Francie set her folders down at her place at the head of the table, next to her CEO, and smiled.

"Hi, everybody," she said as Jack sat down to her right. "We all know each other pretty well by now, but this is our first official meeting to get things started. As you know, I own a multi-million-dollar business, but it's a Thoroughbred racehorse farm. I'd like to make this a multi-million-dollar business as well, but I'm a horse trainer, not a businesswoman, so that's why I've hired all of you." She looked around the table at each of them, meeting their eyes. "You guys know your stuff, so together, we're going to make this work and have a lot of fun in the process."

She met Jack's eyes, and he smiled. She had managed to take over the whole room, and yet she could tell people felt at ease.

"I'll just say a few things, then I'm going to let Donald take over. He knows way more about this than I do," she continued.

"Danny, you've come up with some great pieces for our product line. *Great* pieces, awesome designs. I don't know how you did it so fast—blue jeans have never looked better. Let's get some into production quickly so we can wear them and see what we think.

"Cassie, you're our creative bones. We need to get some ads going to start selling what Danny is making. I'm counting on you to make Dalton Jeans ads stand out from the rest. As we talked about, our target market is family oriented. These are jeans for everybody: Mom, Dad, the kids, the cowboys, as well as the supermodel next door." She smiled. "If my sister were still alive, we'd use her in some of our ads. She'd love it." Her voice quavered, so she soldiered on.

"Bart, you are our financial guru. Keep us in line. Let us know *before* we spend too much that we are about to spend too much. At home, I keep buying horses, and Frank has to give me a budget. Do the same for Danny and Cassie."

She turned to Jet, their newest hire, an award-winning photographer in his late twenties.

"Jet, make us look pretty." He laughed.

She glanced at Rosa who was taking notes.

"Rosa, you are my lifeline. Keep me out of trouble."

Then she turned to Jack.

"And Jack, my *executive* vice president." They all laughed, as his title had been emphasized a lot in a teasing way. "Jack," her eyes softened. "Without you I wouldn't be here."

Their eyes met, and in the gulf between them, a million thoughts were shared.

She then smiled at everyone in the room. "Welcome to the family, everybody. Dig into the donuts. Don, head of the ship, I bow to you." She gave her head a little incline and sat down in her seat.

Donald cleared his throat and began to run her company.

Francie was in good spirits the next evening when they left for home. They ordered Chinese take-out to eat on the plane, and she got extra fortune cookies for her two pilots.

They were good men. Geoff and George. She thought it was fun that their names were so close in spelling, like brothers, but the two men weren't related. They had flown together before she met them.

"We come as a pair," Geoff had said, laughing when she interviewed them.

They arrived home late, a little past 10 p.m. They dropped Jack off at his house, and then Frank drove Francie up to her house. He got out and kissed her good night.

"Come in?" she said.

"Not tonight. I'm tired. I'll see you in the morning."

"You don't know what you're missing," she teased.

"Tempt me not, Vixen."

He waited until she was in the door, and then drove back to the barn, to his empty apartment. They hadn't really gotten beyond kissing. It was all still sort of new, and Francie was still processing things.

It seemed everyone had gone to bed already. She tiptoed up to her room and undressed, putting on one of Ken's t-shirts to sleep in. She had kept several of his t-shirts just for this reason. It made her feel close to him.

Then, as she did every night, she went into her closet and sat down on the floor next to his coat and boots. She ran her hand over the duster, and then traced her fingers along its hem. She really wished she had his hat. She had loved that hat, and his tipping it at her was what had first grabbed her heart. She shuddered. She couldn't think about the hat now, though, because when she did, she remembered he'd been wearing it in the accident.

A sob escaped her, but she stifled it. She ran her finger down his boots, tracing the patterns in the engraved leather. What had happened to his hat? Nobody had really told her. What if it had blown away on the freeway, and it was still out there somewhere? She had always assumed it was buried with him. Or what was left of it. Was it crushed? She supposed it was.

Like his head.

She suddenly felt sick and gripped the jacket to her chest. The sobs came hard and fast as they did most nights. She cried until she was spent, and her body was shaking and exhausted.

She kept a box of tissue in the closet and used one now, then sat there until she felt able to speak.

She was in the habit of talking to Ken every night, telling him about her day. She knew that seemed crazy, but she couldn't stop. She knew he couldn't hear her, that he wasn't here, but it felt good to talk anyway. It was a form of therapy for her. She didn't worry about anyone hearing her, because Steve had soundproofed the rooms.

She told Ken about the business meeting yesterday, and how much she liked the staff she had hired. She told him about Jack's confidence and charisma and how everyone liked him and that he would be a good leader. He also worked well with her CEO, which was important.

She told him that Frank had gone with them again, because she still couldn't separate herself from him through travel. She was so afraid that something would happen.

But then she stopped. She hadn't told Ken about *them* yet. She wondered what he'd think.

"Darlin', if you're going to have another man, Frank's the one to have," she imagined him saying.

But what if he said, 'So soon?' instead? It had only been seven months since his death. What was she doing, kissing his best friend and her sister's husband? Why did it seem both weird and not weird all at the same time?

She supposed in some way or another, she had always loved Frank. He was her rock. She told him things that she had kept from her sisters and even from Ken. She went to him for advice. She trusted him.

"I trusted you too," she said out loud to Ken.

"I'm gone now, darlin'," she thought he would say. "Time to move on. Waiting around isn't going to bring me back."

"Why did you have to leave?" Francie asked. Nobody answered. She sat in the closet, her words hanging in the silence that was so quiet it hurt her ears. "I loved you so much." She raised her voice and said again louder, "Ken, I loved you so much!"

When nobody answered, she folded up his jacket and put it back on the chair with his boots tucked underneath.

Then she went to bed. Just as she was settling in, the phone rang.

"Hello?"

"Hey." It was Jack. "It looked like you were still up. I can see a light on in your window."

"Yes, I'm up."

"You sound... stuffy and hoarse. Like you've been crying or something," Jack said. "Are you okay?"

"I'm fine," she said.

"Well, I just... I just called to thank you for dragging me into this business of yours. Dalton Jeans. I know sometimes I'm a pain in the you-know-what, but I really enjoyed our trip, and I'm excited about this company. So... thank you."

Francie smiled. "You're welcome, Jack."

There was a long silence on the phone.

"Well, goodnight." Jack said.

"Jack?"

"Yes?"

"Were you ever in love? Before the war."

Again, there was a long silence.

Then, "Yes."

"Who was she?"

"A girl. Goodnight, Francie."

"Why won't you tell me anything about your past? I understand you not wanting to talk about the bad stuff. But what about the good memories?"

"Good memories go bad. I don't want to talk about her."

There was a short silence. She twirled the phone cord in her hand. "Do you think it's wrong that I'm in love with Frank?" She didn't expect herself to ask this question, especially to Jack, who was as closed to her as any door. Yet here she was.

"Not at all," he said gently. "You're not being unloyal, if that's what you think."

"But it's so soon."

"Or so late. You two have always loved each other."

She didn't want to think about that, or what it meant, or didn't mean, in relation to her marriage to Ken.

"Did you meet her in high school?"

"Yes. Goodnight, Francie," Jack said.

She knew better than to keep pushing. "Goodnight, Jack."

She turned off her light and laid on the bed for a while, trying not to think. After about a half hour, she turned her light back on and went down the hallway to her office. She'd work on some paperwork until her mind settled down.

She was an hour into planning out the next year's foaling season when the phone rang again, still her personal line. She picked it up in her office.

"Hello?"

"Mandy," Jack said. "Her name was Mandy. I was crazy in love with her, and she with me. We wrote to each other while I was in Nam, and Jim said she hung in there while I was in the POW camp. Gave up two years of her life waiting for me, not knowing if I was dead or alive. But then... well, nobody wants to be with a man convicted of treason. She didn't even visit me once. It was over. End of story."

Francie weighed her words carefully. She wanted to say "I'm sorry" or "Ohhh... ", but she held her tongue. Instead, she said softly, "Thank you."

"Goodnight, Princess. Get some sleep."

"Goodnight, Jack."

After she hung up, she realized how exhausted she was. She put her work away and walked back down to her bedroom. She crawled into bed, sliding between the soft covers, and turned out the light. She was asleep in minutes.

chapter 49

THE GROUND SWEPT BENEATH HER FEET in a blur, and she felt his enormous strides eating up the distance between her and the gate. Frank's words rang through her head, "Don't jump that gate," as did her grandfather's of long ago. But she didn't listen to anybody when it came to horses. She followed her heart, and King was tugging at the bit, asking for his head.

"Go ahead, boy," she said and turned him toward the gate. It was a cloudy day, and the wind was whipping in from the sea, blowing her hair back and making her eyes water. Out here, her agenda was gone, and the only thing she felt was the freedom of being on her horse. They knew each other well, and right now, she knew he wanted to jump that gate as badly as she did. He wasn't as tall as Star, and his legs weren't as long, but he could get the height to do it.

She felt him gather his muscles under him and lift, lift her up into the air in a beautiful arc. For a moment, they were flying, the air whooshing past them, the ground silent beneath them. Then he landed and continued on, asking for more rein. She gave it to him, and they galloped toward the beach until his feet started sinking into the damp sand. She slowed him a bit, turned him, and cantered along the beach, the waves crashing up against her legs and his stomach. He was tossing his head, and she was laughing.

They cantered the length of the beach, then she turned and cantered back, stopping at her little cave just a short distance before Frank's house. She loosened the reins and gave her horse his head, and they walked slowly along the surf until he was cool.

The house stood empty. As far as she knew, Frank had never been back in it since the night she had found him there. She wondered vaguely what they would do with it. As beautiful as it was, neither of them wanted to live in it. She turned and rode King back toward her cave. Then she dismounted and took the bridle off of the horse so he could graze.

"Don't wander off and leave me," she said, patting his neck. "I have apples."

She went inside her little cave in the craggy rocks above the beach. She had a plastic tub with a sealed bag inside of it and opened it up. The blanket she kept in there was dry, and she brought it outside and spread it under a tree. It was a hot day, but it was always a little cool at the beach. She pulled a few apples out of the sack she had with her and bit into one. Soon she felt a soft velvety whuffling behind her neck. She reached back and patted King's muzzle.

"You want one too?" she said and bit off a piece for him. She turned and fed it to him, and he chewed thoughtfully, looking out to sea. Then he nudged her.

"Another?" she said, laughing. "Here, have the whole thing." She handed him the second apple, which he bit into with gusto. They finished their apples together, or rather, he finished his first and watched her expectantly as she finished hers.

"I need a snack too," she said, then gave him the core.

King turned his head, his ears pricked in the direction of the farm.

"What?" she said. "What do you hear?"

He listened for a long while, but when nobody showed up, he came back to look for more apples.

"We ate them all, buddy," she said, rubbing his nose. They stayed there for a while, Francie watching the waves and King grazing on nearby sea grass. Finally, Francie got up.

"I guess we should head back. I have a company to run." She slipped the bridle on her horse and mounted. They took their time, walking for a while. Then Francie gathered up her reins. "Let's go," she said and asked him to canter. She cantered him up the grassy slopes away from the water, through the slight woods, and came out into the field heading into her pastures, where she fully intended on jumping the gate again. Instead, she saw Frank's truck parked there, and the gate completely taken apart.

She cantered up to him and pulled King up to a stop. The back of Frank's pick-up was loaded with wood, and he was hammering away. The wood looked new. Some of it still had price tags on it.

"Hey, sweetheart." Frank glanced up from his work, wiping the sweat from his forehead.

"Where did you get the wood?" she asked.

"Up at the lumber yard."

"You *left?* You went out without me?" Her voice had an edge of panic to it. Then she got mad. "You can't just leave! I had no idea where you were. If I had come back—" She stopped, flustered. She wasn't even sure what she was mad about. "What are you doing?" She frowned down at her gate. Her beloved gate.

"I'm trying to save your life," Frank said. He stood and put his hands on his hips, looking at her. She noticed how his biceps bulged under his t-shirt when he did that.

"You're rebuilding the gate," she realized.

"I'm making it a proper jump," he said. "You see"—he picked up a pole—"these will go across the top, and if you hit them, they fall off, so hopefully you and King won't fall and break your necks. For anyone else coming through"—he picked up a large hinge—"the entire gate will swing open and shut. So everyone is happy."

She sat there on King, silently, taking it all in.

"I should have done this a long time ago," he said.

She realized then how much he loved her, really *loved* her. Instead of being angry at her for risking her life (she was still inclined to believe she was perfectly capable of jumping the gate), he had changed the picture. She still had her gate to jump, and he didn't have to worry.

"You're my very best friend," she said, smiling down at him.

"I know." He grinned up at her and then got back to work on his gate. "You can get by. There are no nails on the ground."

She let King pick his way through, then took him back up to the barn where she hosed him off and turned him out into the pasture. He gave a happy little toss of his head and trotted off to the others to graze with them.

"Have fun," she said to him. "Just hang out with your buddies. I have to get back to work, so I can support your eating habits."

But instead, she got two cans of cold Coke and walked back out to the field to where Frank was. She handed him one.

"Thanks," he said, cracking it open and taking a swig. Then he started sawing one of the poles.

She liked to watch Frank work. It made her feel secure somehow, like he was taking care of things.

They shared silence for a while, and her mind wandered as she sipped her Coke. It was hot out here since the sun had come out, but she had a hat on, and the cool drink was helping. She thought about the pile of papers on her desk that Jack had asked her to sign. She needed to do that before 5 p.m., so he could fax them in. Then she thought about the phone call last night.

"Frank, why do you suppose Jack is so closed off to me?" she asked.

"How so?" Frank measured his wood.

"I mean, he won't tell me anything about his past. Like last night I asked him if he had ever been in love back in high school."

"That's kind of a personal question."

"He and I have kind of a personal relationship. Or not. That's why I'm so frustrated. He has lived here with us for about a billion years, and I don't know anything about him. Nothing. He never talks about his past, and he gets angry when I ask."

"So you shouldn't ask," Frank said.

Francie was silent for a while. Then she said, "He's very guarded around me. He won't let me close. I feel like there's this wall between us, which is difficult since we spend so much time working together."

Frank drew a line in pencil where he measured and cut along the line. He held the piece of wood up and started attaching it to the fence post that he had already sunk. There were grooved notches up the side of it where the poles would sit across the gate when he got the other side built.

"Francie," he said as he worked. "I imagine Jack's past is pretty painful, and he's trying his best to forget it. Even the good parts. We know, from what Jim said, that he had a good childhood and wonderful parents. He probably misses them, and I'm sure he wonders about his mom daily. As for a past love... it's not like he can look her up now and take her out to lunch. He needs to live in *this* life, not the life he had."

"I know. I just... it's hard to explain, but when I'm in the same room with him, I feel alone. And at the same time, I feel this... *need*... coming from him. He needs a friend."

"He has me," Frank said. "We golf."

She laughed. "True enough." She took another sip of her Coke. "Maybe he needs to date. But I guess he can't really be himself with anyone else. She wouldn't know his past."

"Neither do you. Jack is the person he is now. He's living in the present. He can be as much as he wants to be."

"I guess."

"My second point. You're a very attractive woman." He looked up and smiled at her, then went back to his work. "You saved his life. You are, in some respects, his very best friend. He's probably just trying to keep some sort of boundary between the two of you."

Francie took the last sip of her Coke. "I guess I never thought of it that way."

"Well, you should. You have a presence. And, in essence, you hold his very life in your hands."

She thought about that for a while, then she left Frank to his work and walked back up to the house to finish hers.

A few days later, Francie was standing in her bedroom, blowing plaster dust away from her face. Steve had really got into his work and was thrilled to be using a sledgehammer. Plaster was flying everywhere. He was taking out more of the wall and knocking into the next bedroom above the living room to expand Francie's room.

"Tell me again why you need more space?" Sam asked, her eyebrow arched. She was leaning against the door frame, watching.

"Who cares?" Steve said. "This is the most fun I've had in decades."

428

"You haven't even been *around* decades," Francie said, wiping dust from her sleeve onto her face as she scratched her nose and smearing it across her goggles.

Francie had thought about hiring the job out, but Steve was so thrilled to take a swing at things that she gave him the chance. Once they were down to the bare bones, she would bring in professionals, but she found this somehow therapeutic. She was keeping the bathroom and walk-in closet that she and Ken had designed, but the wall next to that was going in order to make more space for an office.

"You already have an office," Sam said. She was pushing Francie, but Francie wasn't answering.

"Sam, don't you have a painting to finish?" Francie asked. "Or would you like to break things?" She raised her arms and took another swing, knocking a bigger hole in the plaster wall. She gripped it and hit it harder, then again. Dust flew everywhere, and Sam slipped out of the room, coughing.

"Ready? Again!" Steve yelled, and the two of them hit it, finishing off the largest part.

"This is awesome," Francie said, and they high fived.

Exactly six weeks after they first kissed, Frank was sitting in Francie's bedroom, on her bed, and they were looking at the newly furnished room.

"Interesting," Frank said, looking around. It was essentially the same room, except for a large added space at the back, which went out over the living room downstairs. It made a wonderful sitting space, or office, as Sam had mentioned.

"Interesting?" Francie said. "That's your word for it?"

He smiled. Then he weighed his words carefully. "This extra space—people keep calling it an office. I can see it. A desk under that window would be wonderful. There's plenty of room for bookcases and a few file cabinets, some shelves. Maybe a reading lamp and a couple of comfy chairs there."

"A *couple* of comfy chairs?" she said.

He glanced at her.

She turned red. Why, after all these years, was it suddenly awkward to have Frank Weaver in her room, sitting on her bed?

"I was going to do this more formally at dinner next week," Frank said.

"What? Discuss office design?"

Frank turned to her. "You know perfectly well what." He took her hand. "Marry me, Francie Dalton."

Her eyes lit up. "Yes," she said and threw her arms around him. "I know that wasn't exactly phrased as a question, but the answer is yes." She was laughing into his neck.

He held her to him, feeling her heart beat against his chest. "Oh, Francie," he whispered into her neck. "I will love you forever." He pulled back, taking her face in his hands. "I have always loved you in some form. I don't know how or when it turned to more than friendship, but I know that I can't live without you. You are my life, Francie. My *life*."

"We were meant to be together," Francie said. "I've known that since I was fourteen, and you saved me in that airport."

They looked into each other's eyes. There was so much that didn't need to be said, because they knew each other so well.

"I have a ring," Frank said.

"Really?"

"Yeah. I was serious when I said I was going to ask you at dinner this week. I just knew I needed to be with you forever."

"Me too," she said.

He motioned to the new space in the bedroom.

"And this?"

"Well, you'll need an office... " she said, and they laughed, and he threw her down on the bed and encircled her in his strong arms, kissing her.

"You always have a plan," he said.

"I do," she said. "And that ring? You can still take me to dinner. Surprise me. I'd like that."

Frank and Francie married quietly in the flower garden two weeks after their engagement, with their church's pastor presiding. Becky was maid of honor, and Mickey was the best man. Jessica, Jack, Sam, Steve, and Lexie stood by and heard their brief vows, and then they all went out to dinner. It was a quiet evening, and afterwards, the two newlyweds took a room at a nearby hotel that overlooked the ocean. To the backdrop of waves crashing against the beach below, they made love, and their bodies joined just as their souls had always been.

Walking somewhere in between grief and love, Francie and Frank made their way through the year. The farm was doing well, the horses were winning, and Dalton Jeans was thriving. They learned they could travel without each other, and Francie started going to New York once a week with Jack.

She loved the change of pace and the business attire that replaced her typical barn clothes. She also found that she had a knack for running a company. Her employees liked her and trusted her, and she treated them well. Soon she had a gym and a day care in her business and offered comp time and flexible work hours. True to her intuition, Jack was remarkable at his job, and his natural charm and her confident personality married well in business discussions and won them many new clients.

Jack was polite and easy to work with, and she quit badgering him about his past. They spent a lot of time together, meeting every day in her office, traveling on her personal plane, and eating out together in New York. He began to laugh more and to loosen up, as it appeared that his cover was going to hold. After all, it had been nearly three years, and nobody had come looking for him.

Francie treated everyone well, including her pilots. After a long day or two in New York, she'd get aboard her jet and hand them coffees or pastries or some little thing she had picked up that reminded her of them.

One time she even managed to get an autograph from a Yankees baseball player who happened to be dining in the same restaurant, and she knew that George, her pilot, was a huge Yankees fan. He was thrilled.

"Good morning, Francie," George nodded as they boarded at 7 a.m. one rainy Wednesday morning late in November. "Jack," he nodded again.

Francie handed George and Geoff each a small, wrapped package. "It's from Sam," she said. "An early Christmas gift. Open it."

"It's only November," George said, laughing, but carefully unwrapped the gift. It was a 5 by 7 painting of his three-year old son, George II. "Oh my... " he said, tearing up. "She painted this?"

"From a photo. Remember, I asked you both for photos?"

"Oh, now I'm excited," said Geoff. He unwrapped his gift with a bit more zest. It was a painting of the same size, only of his six-month-old grandson. "This is amazing," he said.

"It's from all of us, really," Francie said. "I bought the frames."

They all laughed, and she and Jack went and took their seats.

"Buckle up," George yelled from the hull. "It's going to be a bit bumpy over Virginia."

The small jet seated eight passengers, with two sets of double seats. Francie sat on the left side, Jack across the aisle from her on the right. They both dumped their stuff in the seat next to them and opened their laptops.

After a while in the air, Francie dug out a bagel and passed the bag across to Jack.

"Mmmmmm," he said, rifling through. "Thanks." He bit into the crusty bagel, dropping a few crumbs on his keyboard.

"Pass the bag back," Francie said.

He held it up. "What? This bag? You gave it to me."

Francie frowned and went back to her keyboard.

Suddenly, his keypad dinged. *You've got mail.*

He opened it. It was from Francie.

Don't eat the blueberry one. It's mine.

"There's a blueberry one in here?" He peeked inside the bag again.

Ding. *I'm warning you.*

He replied. *But I have the bag in hand. You willing to come get it?*

Ding. *Do you really want to mess with me?*

Ding. *I'll take you on. You're just a girl.*

He glanced across the aisle to see her reaction. She shot him a death stare.

You touch that bagel, and you'll find out what this girl can do.

Ohhhhh, I'm shaking.

Come on over here, big guy, and I'll give you something to make you shake.

Jack laughed out loud. *That sounded a bit... inappropriate.*

Francie cracked a smile. *Only a bit?*

I could sue you for sexual harassment. You are, after all, my boss.

Francie laughed out loud then and glanced over at Jack. "Speaking of which, we should get back to work."

He stuffed the last of the bagel into his mouth and reopened his spreadsheet.

"Back to our marketing campaign. Cassie has some really awesome ideas for ads. I'll e-mail you what she sent me last night," he said.

Just then, there was what sounded like an explosion on the right side of the plane. The entire aircraft lurched to the side, knocking most of the stuff off the seat next to Francie onto the floor, and Jack's stuff onto his lap. The plane righted then, but they heard a shuddering sound.

They glanced across the aisle at each other. Then the intercom clicked on.

"This is your captain. Get into crash position. We're going down, but I think I can belly land this baby. It's gonna be rough."

Jack snapped his laptop shut and stuffed it in the back of the seat in front of him. Then he unbuckled and came over to Francie's side, brushing the rest of her stuff onto the floor.

He closed her laptop and took it off her lap, adding it to the stuff on the floor.

"Get down," he said, putting his hand gently on the back of her neck. "Now."

She put her head down on her knees and folded her hands over the back of her head, like she had been taught to do in grade school during tornado drills.

"What happened?" she said to Jack, who was next to her in the same position.

"I think we blew our right engine," he said. "I moved over here to put most of the weight on this side of the plane."

"Shit."

"I would think you would want to pray instead of swear at a time like this," he said.

Her neck was starting to hurt. She could feel the plane vibrating violently beneath her, and their fast descent was making her dizzy.

"Jack... "

She was scared. She was very scared.

"Were you *flirting* with me a few minutes ago?" he asked, trying to keep his voice light. She knew he was trying to distract her.

"I always flirt with you," she said.

"I know. You flirt with everybody. That's how we get so many clients."

"What? I do not."

"You do. You have a presence about you. You don't *overtly* flirt. You just look at them a certain way."

"That's not flirting. I'm just so gorgeous that men desire to please me."

He smiled, despite the fact that he was probably about to die.

"You're not a bit cocky about it either, are you? *Princess.*"

"*Cocky?* Is that seriously the term you want to use in this particular conversation?"

The plane lurched again, and they heard a ripping sound. Suddenly, it was descending faster.

"Prepare for landing!" George's voice shouted through the intercom.

"We're going to die," Francie said. Her heart was pounding. "Frank can't handle it if I die." She started praying fervently.

"We're not going to die," Jack said. "God has let us live through too much for it to end this way."

They hit then, and the plane hit the ground with an earth-shattering thud that knocked their teeth together. It felt like they had slammed into the ground, and Francie was glad her neck was down, or it certainly would have snapped. But the ride wasn't over. They began sliding at what felt like a great velocity across the ground, and Francie could feel it under her feet. The metal belly of the plane started coming apart.

"Hang on!" shouted George. "The landing gear snapped off."

Suddenly, they were in trees, and branches were snapping in through the windows, bursting the glass. Shards fell on Francie's back, and she felt them cutting her skin like a thousand little mosquito bites. She concentrated on breathing and tried not to brace herself for the end. She remembered from her years of horseback riding that if your body is loose when you fall, you hurt fewer muscles. Stay in crash position, but don't sit too tight.

The sound of the branches sliding across the plane's metal hull was deafening. She heard another tear, and suddenly cold air burst across her feet.

Then they heard screams from the cabin, and a loud sound that slammed them both against the seat in front of them, and then ripped their seats right out of the floor. They tumbled forward. For a moment, the world spun around her, and then as suddenly as it had all started, everything went quiet.

Francie opened her eyes.

She was still strapped in her seat, lying on her side toward what appeared to be the front of the plane, up against the wall separating the plane from the cockpit. As she had guessed, the door had been ripped off the side of the plane, and a light snow was falling through on her.

"Jack?"

"I'm okay," he groaned from somewhere behind her. She heard him unclick his seatbelt, and she did the same and rolled out of her seat. She lay for a minute, assessing herself, and realized that she wasn't badly hurt.

Jack crawled over to her and helped pull her into a sitting position.

"I'm okay," she said.

"Me too," he said. He had small cuts on his face and arms but appeared to be otherwise unharmed.

"Did you hit your head?" he asked.

"No. I just sort of tumbled, I think. Rolled maybe."

"Me too."

Jack stood up and carefully brushed the glass from his clothes. "I'm going to go up front and check on George and Geoff."

While Jack was gone Francie stood up and brushed the glass off of herself. She was surprised at how unharmed she actually was.

"They must have brought us in well," she said, proud of her pilots.

Up front, a grisly sight greeted Jack. A pine tree filled almost the entire cabin, and the smell of pine and sap was strong. A large branch had burst through the front of the plane and penetrated George's chest, killing him and pinning him to his seat. Geoff had met a similar fate. There was blood everywhere. Jack had seen a lot of bad stuff during the war, but it didn't make it easier.

"Are they okay?" Francie's voice rang out from the cabin.

Jack quickly stepped back and closed the door.

"No," he said.

"I want to see them."

He looked her in the eye and swallowed.

"They're dead, Francie. The cockpit is pretty smashed up. They hit a tree."

"No," she said, her hand going to her mouth. "I want to see them," she said.

"Don't go in there. We need to concentrate on survival."

Jack looked at Francie. She was wearing a business skirt and blouse. The cabin was freezing, and snow was filtering slowly in through the holes.

"Do you have any other clothes with you?" he said.

"Um," she was fighting back tears. "Jeans. I have some jeans and a sweatshirt."

"Put them on. Leave your panty hose on. Layer. Put on everything you have and move quickly."

"I have my wool coat, too," she said, rummaging around for her bag of clothes. The only clothes Jack had were the trousers he was wearing, his sweater, and a coat. He put the coat on.

"We need blankets," he said.

"They were in the overhead compartment," Francie said, but everything was spilled everywhere now.

"There." She grabbed some blankets. There were only two, and they were thin.

"I think we're in the mountains," Jack said. "I'm going to have a look around. You find food and water and see if there are any matches, or anything we can burn to stay warm. Move quickly."

He hesitated. "Do you have a tracking system or anything on this plane?"

"No," Francie said. "It's just a plane."

"The radio is broken. We'll have to wait until somebody sees our crash. I'm going to go see where we are. Stay here, do what I ask, and do *not* go into the cabin."

"Okay," she said.

Jack climbed out of the plane, his dress shoes slipping and sliding over the wreckage. His feet sunk into the snow and cold spilled into his shoes, soaking his socks.

"Great," he mumbled. But he soon realized that wasn't the worst of their problems. They were in a wilderness, buried inside a patch of trees. With the silver plane on the white snow, there was no way anyone would see them. There was an open patch of snow not far from him, and he looked for some branches to drag there. He could maybe use them to form a message in the snow. He briefly considered pulling one of the pilots out and using their blood for paint. While the idea might save their lives, it was too grisly for him to carry through.

After about a half hour of struggling with branches, his feet were soaked and his hands scratched up, but he had a decent SOS on the ground. Probably too small for anybody to see, but it would have to do.

"Jack?" Francie called from the plane.

"I'm coming," he said, making his way back to the plane and climbing in. Francie had found four bottles of water and set them on the floor in the back of the plane where there weren't any holes. She had circled the seats around it, making them a little hideaway, somewhat protected from the wind. Next to the water sat their bag with the blueberry bagel in it.

"There's nothing to start a fire with," she said. "No matches. No lighter. Did you look up front?"

"Briefly," Jack said. He went back up to the cockpit and rifled through the pilot's coats, which had been thrown on the floor behind them. One was caught under a heavy branch, but he managed to pull the other one loose. Nothing in the pockets, but he brought it back with him and shut the door behind him, swallowing down the bile in his throat.

"Let's sit and wait," he said, making his way over to their spot. "There's nothing out there for us to walk to."

He leaned against the back of the plane and took a sip of water. He had given himself a pretty physical workout.

"Your feet are soaked," Francie said.

"I'm okay."

She pulled off her thick socks and handed them to him. Then she put some mittens on her feet. "I have an extra pair of gloves," she said and smiled.

He pulled off his own socks and pulled on hers. They were a bit small—*quite* a bit small —but stretchy, and he managed to get them to fit.

"At least they're not pink," he said.

She smiled.

"I'm sure Geoff radioed that they were in trouble and gave our location, so help should be on the way," Jack said. "Soon."

"Good." She pulled her coat around her tighter and sat down across from him. "Frank will find us."

"That's what I'm counting on." He handed her Geoff's coat. "Wrap this around you."

They sat quietly for a while.

"I made an SOS out of branches," Jack said. "There was a little clearing not far from here. We have several hours of daylight so the plane should be able to see it."

"Wow. Smart thinking." Francie said. "I tried to send e-mails, but we don't have any signal."

"I hadn't thought of that," Jack said.

"Tell me about Cassie's ideas," Francie said. "We have nothing else to do to pass the time."

They talked about work for a while. They didn't use the laptops, because they wanted to keep the batteries charged for light if they were still here by nightfall. After about an hour of talking, he noticed Francie was shivering.

"Let's move around some more," Jack said. "It will help keep us warm."

They both got up and did some walking and jumping around the cabin.

"Cardio time," Jack said, making his voice sound more confident than he felt.

chapter 50

As soon as Frank heard the plane had gone down, he jumped on the phone and called a fellow horse owner who owned a helicopter and did some work for the National Park Service. That man put him in touch with a private company, and Frank called them. Soon, his house was crawling with people, and he was communicating across the states with others. The kitchen table was covered with maps, and he had drawn in red the plane's flight course.

The authorities were working on it, but that wasn't good enough. He needed to do something.

"She's alive, I can feel it," he said to Sam, who was sitting at the table watching him pace. The kids were all at school and didn't know about the accident. Steve was in California, riding horses.

"Of course," she said, wiping the tears from her eyes. Frank hadn't shed a single tear— he was all business. Sam was totally debilitated by the news. She couldn't fathom losing another sibling. Especially Francie.

"Jack's with her," Frank said. "He has some survival training from the Army. And those are the best pilots she could find. They're good at what they do."

"Okay," said the sturdy young man whose helicopter was parked outside their home in the front yard. "This is where we think they are." He circled a spot on the map. "They went down about three hours ago. Let's fly and see if we can see anything."

Frank had told them under no uncertain terms that he was coming with them. The helicopter was a Priority 1 high-speed search and rescue. Still, it would take a while to get there. On the flight, he planned to go over everything again, so he rolled up his maps and stuffed them under his arm.

"Here," Sam said, handing him a bag. She had packed him some water bottles and an apple, as well as a few energy bars.

"Thanks." He grabbed the bag and started to leave, then turned to look at Sam. "I'll bring her home," he said and gave her a hug.

"I'll pray," Sam said and watched them leave. Then she stood in the empty kitchen and wept.

"I'm exhausted," Francie said. They had been stranded for six hours. "I can't feel my hands or my feet."

Jack had sat back down and was leaning against the wall of the plane again. They had already eaten the bagel and had each drank a bottle of water.

Francie was shivering. Her teeth were chattering.

"Come here," Jack said.

She raised an eyebrow.

He opened his arms. "We're going to snuggle. For body heat. I should have thought of this earlier."

"Snuggle?" Francie said. "Now *you're* flirting." She was teasing, but there wasn't much strength in her voice.

"Believe me, my parts are too cold for any flirting," he said.

She sat down in front of him, and he pulled her back between his legs, back against his chest. He opened up his coat and pulled her inside it, trying to close it around both of them.

He took the blanket he had around his back and put it across her, and pulled the other one over her too, forming a little tent over them both. Then he wrapped his arms around her.

Neither of them said anything for a while. The only sound was their breath, which was forming clouds in the air, and Francie's teeth chattering. Slowly, she started to warm up a little bit.

"I'm so tired," she said.

"That's the hypothermia," Jack said. "It's important that you stay awake."

It felt good to have her close. It had been a long time since he had touched anyone, and he realized how much he missed touch. As if reading his mind, Francie said, "I didn't think you liked to touch."

"I told you, I make allowances for certain situations. This would be one of them." He felt her smile again but only briefly. "One-night stands are the other." She laughed a little, which is what he was looking for. He wanted to somehow keep her awake.

"Are we going to die?" Her voice was small. "I can't die and leave Frank."

"We aren't going to die," Jack said.

"How do you know that?"

"Because Frank won't sleep until he finds you. He's probably not even waiting for search and rescue to find you. He'll mortgage the farm if he has to and buy his own search and rescue firm to come get you."

"He'd better not mortgage my farm," Francie said.

Jack smiled. He was feeling pretty sleepy himself, and he could feel the cold seeping through his back. He rested his chin on her shoulder. Her hair smelled good, and he closed his eyes for a minute.

"I haven't heard any planes," she said, and her voice shook him awake. "I don't think we're in a flight zone."

"No."

She went back to silence. After a moment, her head fell against his cheek.

"Francie, wake up." He shook her a little.

"Sorry. I drifted a bit. Talk to me."

"We could talk about horses."

"My favorite topic."

But then there was silence again. Under the covers, she gripped his gloved hands with hers and tried to rub them a bit, but her hands weren't working.

"I can't move my fingers," she said.

There are worse ways to die, Jack thought. *Much worse.* He gave her a slight hug and tried to pull her a bit closer. She leaned her head back against his chest, but there was no more warmth between the two of them.

"I might as well tell you about my past," Jack said. "That should keep you awake."

"Thrilling tales of old," she said. Then, more seriously, she said, "Only tell me what you're comfortable with. I don't need to know more."

He was glad to hear that she was awake and alert. That gave him some hope.

He took a deep breath, thinking about where to start. He had never shared these stories with anyone. Not even therapists.

"When I was captured in the war, they took me to a camp back in the jungle, away from the POW camps, so there was no Red Cross and no code for them to follow. They could do whatever they wanted to do to me." He swallowed. "For two years, I was tortured." He closed his eyes for a moment, then shook himself out of the past and went on with his story. "I was pretty much alone. The two men they captured with me—you know that they shot them. They kept me alive at first to try to get information out of me, but then I was just their... toy, I guess. Their entertainment. Sometimes, other prisoners were brought in, but they didn't last. They either moved them somewhere else or killed them."

He was silent for a while, and she thought he was done. "I'm sorry," she said. "Jim worried about you. I know he did."

Jack continued. "The scars around my wrists are from where they used to bind me... so they could... do things to me, and I couldn't fight back. But I did. I fought enough once so the ropes cut through to the bone."

He felt her shudder.

"That's why the scars are so bad. They never really gave them time to heal. Sometimes, they got infected, but unfortunately it was never bad enough to kill me."

Under the covers, he felt her lightly grip his hands in hers.

"One of the things they did to me was tie me to a whipping post and beat me. That's why you never see me without a shirt on. It's why I never join the rest of you at the pool or take my shirt off even when its 99 degrees on a typical hot Florida day. The scars are very deep."

"Jack... "

"I guess the plastic surgeon who worked on me was paid to only fix my face, not the rest of me."

His chin was still on her shoulder, and he was speaking softly by her ear. She felt so cold.

"How often did they beat you?"

"A lot. They knew exactly how many lashings it took to nearly kill me, but just enough so I didn't die or black out. They wanted the pain to be the most it could be, so I'd learn my lesson."

"What lesson was that?"

"Whichever one they wanted to think up that day. If I fought back, it was always worse."

He noticed a tear working its way down her cheek. It didn't seem fair that they had come this far only to die now. He sent out a silent prayer to God, a pleading for one more chance for them both. Frank... she couldn't leave Frank.

"We'll get out of this," she said.

Jack laid his cheek against hers. "Yes," he said, closing his eyes again. Then he whispered into her ear. "Thank you."

"For what?"

"For giving me a place to finally feel safe."

He felt her smile.

It was ironic. He felt so safe here at the moment, when in fact, he was not safe at all. He was about to die of hypothermia. Funny how one's perspective of safety altered with one's circumstances, and he had been in much worse circumstances. *Much* worse. *This isn't a bad way to die,* he mused again. But he couldn't let Francie die.

"Francie?" he said. She didn't answer. He tried to shake her, to revive her, but he couldn't get his body to move. *Francie,* he said again, but realized that no sound came from his voice. He couldn't open his eyes, so he kept them closed and dreamed that Frank came in the form of an angel and carried them away.

"There!"

Frank shouted and pointed below. Someone had spelled out SOS in what looked like branches. There was also a path of broken trees where something had crashed and slid into the forest. The plane.

"Oh, God, don't let them be dead," Frank prayed as the pilot lowered the helicopter.

The following evening, after a short stay in the hospital, Francie was back in her own bed, with Frank beside her. They had both turned in early, tired after the adventures of the past day and a half. Jack was settled in his own home, recovered. They hadn't had a chance to talk much.

Frank reached over and put his arm around her. "You have to stop almost dying," he said. "A man's heart can't take much more."

"I'm so sorry," she said.

He buried his face against her chest, and she felt his warm tears on her. "I can't lose you, Francie. I can't."

"Oh, honey," she said, taking his head between her palms. "Look at me." He looked up, his eyes moist. "I'm not going anywhere. Jack told me we weren't going to die, because God had put us through too much to take us home to Heaven now. I believe that. I believe I'm here for a good long while."

"I hope so," Frank said, laying his head down on her chest.

"He saved your life," he said after a while.

"Jack?"

"Yes."

"And Sam said you saved ours," Francie said. "It was your search and rescue that found us. How much did that cost us, anyway?"

"Doesn't matter."

She laughed. "I guess if I wasn't around, it really wouldn't. Thank you. I knew you'd come after us."

"How could I not?" Frank said. "How could I not."

The next day, Francie was recovered enough to walk over to Jack's house. She hadn't seen him since they had been released from the hospital. He was in worse shape than she was but had come home when Frank promised the medical staff he'd check in on him.

She knocked lightly on the door.

"It's open," he called.

She went in. He was sitting on the couch watching football on television, his feet propped up on the coffee table.

"I hear you still have all your toes," she said.

He smiled and grabbed the remote control, turning the television off. "I do. And all ten fingers. I hear the same of you."

"Yep. I'm all here." She sat down on the coffee table across from him, so she could look at him.

"I came to thank you for saving my life," she said. "Apparently, sharing body heat kept us both alive."

He shrugged. "I was just trying to stay warm too."

"They also told me you took the blanket off of yourself and wrapped it around me. Somehow, I missed that, because I never would have let you do it."

"You were pretty far gone."

"I was."

He met her eyes. "Do you remember what we talked about?"

"Yes," she said. "Every word."

He smiled. "Good."

She looked at his wrists and the deep scars that ran around them. Then she looked down at her own hands. "Thank you for trusting me."

"You've never given me a reason not to."

"I won't share what you told me with anybody. Not even Frank. It's your story—you can tell it to who you want to."

"It's fine," he said, shrugging it off. "Really."

She pushed a lock of hair behind her ear. "The funerals are tomorrow. Do you want to ride with us?"

"Sure," he said, fiddling with the remote. Then he sighed. "Another funeral. Two funerals. I just... they saved our lives you know. That was some fancy landing from what I heard. A belly slide in the mountains, and we both survived."

Francie swallowed. "Yeah, I... " she couldn't finish. She thought of the pictures of those babies Sam had painted for them for Christmas. "I know."

They sat there in awkward silence for a few moments, then Francie stood up to leave.

"Take care, and call us if you need anything tonight."

"I'm fine, Princess," he said. "I haven't felt finer in a long time." After she left, he turned the football game back on and opened a bag of chips.

Jack went out later that week to pick up groceries. He was standing in the produce section, trying to figure out if the melon he was holding was ripe or not.

"Knock on it."

He looked up. The voice belonged to a woman across from him, on the other side of the produce stand by the tomatoes.

"Knock on it. If it sounds hollow, it's ripe." Her voice was melodic, soft, with an English accent. She was possibly the most beautiful woman he had ever seen.

Jack knocked. It sounded hollow. "It's ripe," he said.

She smiled, her warm, green eyes sparkling. She had shoulder length chestnut hair that seemed to be both red and brown. She was small, probably about 5' 4", and slender, wearing a fitted t-shirt and jeans that rounded out her hips.

"What else do I need to know about melons?" Jack asked, realizing too late how that sounded. She laughed. He felt his face turn red.

"That depends on what you plan to do with them."

"What would *you* do?" He wanted to keep her talking, just to hear her voice.

"Um, well, most people enjoy them plain," she said.

"Would you like to go out to dinner with me?" Jack asked, surprising himself.

"Yes," she said, smiling. "I'd like that very much." She reached her arm over the produce. "I'm Annie."

"Jack," he said, shaking her hand. She knocked a few tomatoes on the ground.

"Oops!" she said, bending down to pick them up. "Um, I don't usually agree to dates this easily, especially with men I've never met."

"I don't usually date."

They both laughed.

"7:00?" Jack asked.

"Perfect," she said. "Here, let me give you my address." She opened her purse and pulled out a small piece of paper and wrote some information on it. "My number is on there too."

Jack smiled and pocketed the paper. "I'll see you tonight."

"How'd it go?" Frank eyed the flag across the golf course. He measured the distance in his head and swung. The ball went wide and landed to the right, near the sand trap.

"Better than your golf swing," Jack said, placing his ball on the tee. "I took her to that little Italian restaurant in town. She's awesome. We talked for hours."

"And?"

Jack swung his club and didn't do much better than Frank. "We should really give up on this game," he said. "No matter how we try, we don't come close to what Ken used to do."

"At least he's not here to shame us any longer," Frank said.

Jack laughed. "But there was no 'and' last night. After dinner, we walked around town for a little bit and window shopped, and then I dropped her off at her condo."

"That's a change."

"I'm a changed man."

They put their clubs away and climbed on the golf cart. "She's perfect, Frank. Perfect. I can't wait for you to meet her."

Frank looked over at him. "Well, bring her home to dinner."

For their second date, they had an evening picnic on the beach. They bought sandwiches at a little coastal café, and then Jack took her down to the pier, and they ate at a picnic table and watched some swimmers and hopeful surfers playing in the water. Then they walked and talked until long after the sun had gone down.

"I guess we should call it a night," Jack said. "You have work tomorrow."

"So do you," Annie said.

He leaned toward her for a kiss. Their first kiss was light and chaste. Then he kissed her again and felt the urgency in her. Pulling her into a full embrace, he deepened the kiss and tasted the salt on her lips from the sea air. Her hands traveled down his back, and he wanted to ask her back to his place. He wanted more, so much more. But instead, he stepped back a little and took her hands in his.

I can't believe I'm doing this, he thought.

"Annie, I want so badly to ask you back to my place for the night," he said. "There was a time when I did that quite a bit, I'm ashamed to say. But you're special. This is special, and I want to take it slow. I'd like to savor this a bit. I don't want you to be like the others."

Idiot, he told himself. His physical body was very urgently telling him to continue. He took a deep breath.

Annie looked up into his eyes, and he could tell she was pleased with what he had said. "You're amazing," she said, giving his hands a little squeeze. The night breeze lifted her hair up around her face, and the moonlight and nearby streetlamp gave her hair a golden cast. She reached her hand up and touched his cheek, caressing it.

He closed his eyes. The contact felt so good. He wanted more. Just her hand against his cheek stirred so many things inside of him, and he almost changed his mind and took her home. It awakened something in him that he had shut down long ago and hadn't even realized. Touch, he thought, was one of the most powerful senses. It could be brutal, but it could also be sweet. Annie's touch was tender, her caress like a balm to his soul.

When her hand left his face, he opened his eyes.

"I've had a really good time tonight," she said. "Can we go out again when you get back from New York?"

"I'd like that," he said. "I'll be home on Thursday, pretty late. Let's go out Friday."

They made plans, and he dropped her off at her place. As he drove home alone, he reached up and touched his cheek where her hand had been.

chapter
51

F RANCIE AND JACK GRITTED THEIR TEETH and, together, took their first post-crash flight. They were both nervous wrecks, but they made it and treated themselves to a big lunch with chocolate cake and ice cream for dessert at a very expensive restaurant.

"It's a wonder you don't weigh a thousand pounds," Jack said, watching Francie put away the last bite of her cake.

"It's the worry," she said. "I burn calories just *thinking* about flying."

Jack laughed. "I understand."

"Actually... " Francie grinned. "I'm eating for two."

Jack put his fork down and smiled. "Congratulations!" he said. "Life is amazing, isn't it?"

"It is indeed," Francie said happily.

A few months after Frank and Francie's one-year wedding anniversary, Francie gave birth to Andrew Franklin Weaver. She pulled him close to her, breathing in his soft baby scent, and smiled up at Frank.

"Life is good," she said and meant it. He placed his hand on his son's soft head. "It is," Frank said and kissed Francie.

chapter 52

JACK AND ANNIE HAD BEEN DATING REGULARLY for a year, and he brought her home often for dinners with the entire family. Everyone loved Annie, so Francie was actually looking forward to the day out that Annie suggested.

The two women had a great morning. They went to a movie, something smart and sassy and romantic, then they went out to lunch. Francie wore a sundress. She decided it was fun to be a bit girly and had even clipped her hair back with a gold barrette.

They ordered sandwiches and some iced tea and sat down in the shade at an outdoor café to eat and talk about the movie.

After a lot of discussion about what they would have done better and why they loved the main character so much despite the not-too-happy ending, they were only halfway done with their sandwiches, eating at a leisurely pace.

"This is fun," Francie said. "I'm glad you thought of it."

Jack and Frank went golfing nearly once a week. Why should the guys have all the fun? Francie, at first a bit uncomfortable with the idea of a lunch out that didn't involve working, was now thrilled to be out with a girlfriend.

Annie swallowed a bite of her sandwich.

"Francie, Jack is the most amazing man I've ever met," she said.

Francie smiled. "I'm pretty sure he feels the same way about you, judging by the way he lights up when you're around."

"I never felt the need to get married before, but now I see the appeal. I can't stand to be away from him. I wait for the phone to ring. I'm like a schoolgirl!" She giggled. "It's crazy."

"You're in love," Francie said.

"I am." Annie looked across the table at her. "Why don't you suppose he's ever been married? He's quite a catch."

"He says the right woman never came along."

"That's what he tells me," Annie picked at her salad. "What do you know about his past?"

Uh-oh. Francie knew this was coming. She really loved Annie and didn't want to lie to her. And yet, she couldn't tell her the truth.

"Not much," she said honestly.

"He won't talk about it," Annie said.

"No."

"Probably because of the war?"

"He had some bad experiences," Francie said.

"But that's not his whole past," Annie said. "There's an eighteen-year gap. He says he was in the war and talks about times before that. And then he talks about now. That's it. Then there's the gap."

Annie was sharp.

"Have you asked him?" Francie said.

"Yes. He changes the subject."

"Hmmmm."

"Why did you hire him? What were his credentials? He had a résumé, right?"

Francie toyed with her tea, taking a slow, small sip to buy time and weigh her words. Annie waited.

"Annie... he's really good at what he does, and you know, I hired him first to assist Frank, but I needed him more at Dalton Jeans." She took a bite of her sandwich.

"You didn't answer my questions," Annie said.

Francie sighed and put down her sandwich. She looked across the table at Annie, the only girlfriend she had. "Honestly, I don't know much. He's not big into sharing. I think you should let him tell you. It's not right to talk behind his back."

Annie dropped her eyes. "You're right."

"But I can tell you this. He's a good man, and he loves you very much."

Annie smiled. "Yes, those two things I do know."

They finished up their lunch, talking about what they would do on their next girls' outing. Then, they did some shopping. Francie surprised herself by buying a new purse.

That night Francie told Frank all about their day, and he listened with a smile on his face.

"What?" she said when she was done.

"You're so happy," he said.

"Well, I'm embarrassed to say that I guess I've never really had a girlfriend. Just in high school."

"No, you haven't," Frank said. "Sisters, yes. But no girlfriend, at least not as long as I've known you."

"This is so fun," she said. "We're going to do it again next week."

He laughed. "Catching up with Jack and I and all our golf outings."

"Well, yeah. You make it last nearly an entire day. You go out for lunch afterwards."

"Lunch is good. Especially when the golf is bad."

She laughed. "You know, another thing, Annie is so *normal.*"

"Define normal."

"Not like us."

Now it was Frank's turn to laugh. "You mean there's a lack of drama in her life?"

"Yes! Her parents died a long time ago in a car crash, but she has gotten on with her life. She has a condo, goes to work, goes out, spends the weekends doing laundry or going to see a movie with some friends. Normal."

"No near-death experiences?"

"Not that I can tell. And she doesn't work 24/7. She loves her job. Absolutely loves it. She's an engineer right to the core. But when she clocks out at 5 p.m., she leaves it at work and has an actual life. I work—"

"Constantly."

"Yes. Even when I ride, I'm usually working. Training a horse or something. I love what I do, but I don't usually just do nothing."

"You did with Ken," Frank said quietly.

"Yes," Francie said, reflecting for a moment. "I did. But this is different. This is... she's a girlfriend. We can talk girl stuff. She paints her toenails, and I actually painted mine before we went out today. Look."

Francie held up her bare foot, her toenails covered in bright pink.

"Fun." Frank said, grabbing a toe and kissing it.

"I know," Francie said. She shook him off her foot. "But she did start to ask questions about Jack. It got a little hairy there."

"How did you do?"

"Perfectly. You know I've been practicing what I'd say. I managed to say nothing and not lie to her and not make her suspicious. I think. How is this going to end?"

"It will end well," Frank says. "Love triumphs over all."

"I hope so. She's crazy about him, and she makes him happy. He's been a different man since he met her."

"Love does that to you," Frank said, going back to her toes.

She giggled. "I'm not ready for that," she said.

"No?"

"Frank, it's only 8 p.m. I want some ice cream."

She got up, and the two of them went downstairs. Frank dug a carton of Neapolitan ice cream out of the freezer while Francie got two bowls.

"Hey! Where did it all go?" Frank said. "Somebody took the chocolate and left vanilla, which has been infiltrated by the strawberry."

Becky was sitting at the kitchen table eating that very chocolate.

"Caught red-handed, miss," Frank said.

"Hey, first come, first serve," Becky said.

Francie leaned over Frank and dug out the little remaining chocolate.

"Hey!" he sighed dramatically. "You girls are lucky I like strawberry."

Steve came up the stairs, sweaty and breathing hard from working out. He was wearing sports shorts and a tank top.

"I am so frickin' awesome," he said.

"And not a bit conceited," Francie said. Sam wandered in, got herself a bowl of vanilla ice cream, and sat down at the table.

"Seriously," said Steve. "I was voted in the jockey's room as having buns of steel. And I believe they're right. Feel. Hard as rock." He turned his backside toward Francie.

"I am not feeling your buns," she said. "Especially while I'm eating."

"No, go ahead. Grab 'em. Hard as rock."

Francie glanced at Sam for help, and Sam nodded. "Go ahead. They *are* pretty awesome."

Francie reached out and pinched him.

"Ouch!" he said. "So, what did ya think?"

"Sweaty," she said.

"You're just jealous," he said.

"Francie's buns are pretty steely," Frank said. "Even after having a baby."

It was true. She had regained her figure quickly. "So there," Francie said to Steve and stuck out her tongue. Then she took another bite of ice cream.

"Not if you keep eating that stuff, they won't be," Steve said. Then he looked at Sam. "Oh, not you too. All of you—eating this stuff in front of a man who doesn't do sugar. Harsh."

"Have a bowl," Frank said. "You probably burn off more calories in one race than I do in one day."

"Get thee behind me," Steve said.

"Ooohh, Steve quotes scripture," Francie said.

"I'm off to the showers," Steve said. "Ta-ta."

Jack showed up on Monday at 11:00 for their usual morning meeting. He had spent most of the weekend with Annie, and Francie was hoping for details.

"I'm in love," he said.

"Me too," Francie said, swooning. "Isn't it grand?"

"I want to ask Annie to marry me."

Francie looked across the desk at Jack. He had changed so much since he had met Annie. He had a sense of joy that hadn't been there before.

"That's awesome!" Francie said.

"But she says she needs to know my story."

"I assume you trust her," Francie said. "Otherwise, you wouldn't want to marry her."

"Yes."

"Are you asking my permission?"

"Yes. It's your story too."

"Jack, Frank and I knew this day was coming. We all love Annie. You don't need our permission. But you have our blessing."

Jack's smile spread across his whole face.

"Thank you," he said.

After dinner, Jack drove Annie back to his little house at Sunnyhill. He parked the car in the driveway and asked her if she wanted to take a walk. The stars were out, and the night was a bit cool, so she pulled her sweater on, and they walked out over the front lawn and down the pasture fence line toward the grape arbor. They sat down on the swing together.

"I love the stars," Jack said. "They're so beautiful, all those lights up in the sky. And there are stories behind the constellations, you know. Some of them are love stories." He gave her hand a squeeze. "That's why I thought this would be a great place."

"A great place for what?" Annie asked, but the smile she gave him led him to believe she knew what was up. They had been talking about marriage a lot lately.

Jack turned so he was facing her. It was dark out, with only the light of the stars and the moon. He reached over and lit one of the lanterns, creating a soft glow. He could see her face a little better, but the shadows still gave his own some cover.

"You've asked me about my past so much," he said. He swallowed. "I'd like to tell you now." He felt his heart hammering. He took her hand. "You may not like what you hear, but Annie, I want to go into this saying you're the most incredible woman I've ever met, and I love you. I would never do anything to hurt you. Ever. After I tell you my story, I would like to ask you a question."

Annie nodded silently.

"I need two promises from you first," he said. "What I have to tell you could hurt a lot of people if it ever gets out. So no matter how you feel about me afterwards, I need you to promise to keep this to yourself."

Annie nodded. "Okay," she said quietly. "But now you're scaring me a little bit."

He squeezed her hand. "I'm sorry. I'm scared too," he said and gave a little nervous laugh. He glanced up at the house where there was a lone light on in Francie's bedroom.

"Second promise. I need you to think about everything I've said before you respond. Give it a night. We can talk in the morning."

"Well, I may not need to think about it."

"No, I *need* for you to think about it," he said.

She looked at him for a moment before answering. "Okay."

"Okay," Jack said. He took one last look into her eyes and saw the love pouring out. He only hoped it would still be there in a few minutes. He swallowed again. Then in a strong, steady voice, he began.

"I was a POW in Vietnam, as you know, but I wasn't in one of the camps. I was being held somewhere deeper in the jungle. When the war was over, and they found me, I was quite a wreck, physically and emotionally. Our general was a close friend, and he thought it would be better if I had a familiar face pick me up, so he rode on the rescue flight that came to get me. It was him and the pilot and another guy. Apparently, the other guy wasn't on record as being on the plane, because as soon as they got me, he pulled the general's gun, shot him in the head, and then parachuted from the plane. When we landed, I was pinned with the murder and taken to a prison hospital, then put into federal prison. At my trial, I was convicted of treason and sentenced to die in the electric chair."

Annie's free hand went to her mouth.

"I was devastated at my friend's murder and still shaken up from my stint as a POW," he said, "so it was a lot to take in that now I was going to be executed for a crime I didn't commit."

Jack was silent for a moment, to let that sink in for Annie, and to gather his thoughts. He had practiced this so much alone, waiting for this moment, and he wanted to make sure he didn't overload her.

But then how could he not? It was quite a story.

"You must have asked for a retrial. And been acquitted," Annie said.

"Yes, I asked for a retrial. We appealed several times. My dad passed away in the process, and my mom ran out of money.

"Francie's brother, Jim, was my best friend in Nam. We were like brothers, and I was a POW, because when he was captured, I went in to free him. I got him out, but I got caught, so I guess he felt responsible. He came to visit me in prison nearly once a week when he lived in California, and at least once a month after he moved here to the farm."

"You've never talked about him," Annie said.

"He died a few years ago," Jack said.

"I'm sorry. Oh my gosh... you've been through so much."

"After eighteen years behind federal bars, on the night before my execution, I was broken out of prison by a very highly qualified bunch of criminals, given a new identity and a new face, and started over here."

She was silent for a moment, then, "You're... *illegally* here?"

"I'm a fugitive. There was a huge manhunt for me. I'm wanted by the FBI."

Annie swallowed. It took her a minute to find her voice. "Who... who paid for all of that? It must have cost... You didn't steal the money, did you?"

He smiled. "Slow down," he said. "No, I wasn't even aware that I was going to be sprung. I thought I was going to die the next morning."

"So who... ?" Annie looked around. She was sitting in the grape arbor on a 5000-acre farm that bordered the sea, next to a man who was VP for a Fortune 500 company and flew on the owner's private jet. There was untold millions of dollars in horseflesh right down the path from her in the barns.

"Francie," she said.

Jack nodded.

"Why?"

"Because she loved her brother. If this story gets out, we'll both end up on death row."

Annie sat there silently for a few minutes. She was shell-shocked.

"So who are you?"

"Paul Lawson."

Her eyes widened. "I remember the stories. It was all over the news. Oh my gosh." She dropped his hand.

His stomach did a flip-flop. "I was afraid it would be too much."

"No," she said, taking his hands in her own again. "Jack... er... Paul?"

"Jack. It's always Jack. It has to be."

"Jack, I love you. Nothing can change that."

He smiled and brushed a lock of her hair back from her face.

"Francie has gone through great expense and planning to make sure if we get caught it's just her and I going to prison. You can say you never knew about my true identity. That's the story Frank is going to go with. Somehow, she's fixed it so she won't lose the farm either, if she goes down. Which brings me to my question."

Annie looked up at him expectantly and smiled.

"Annie, you've made me feel alive again for the first time in 20 years. You've made my life complete and are such a part of me that I don't feel whole when I'm not with you. I'd like very much to spend the rest of my life with you, and after you think all of this through, I'd very much like it if you'd agree to marry me."

Tears came to Annie's eyes.

"No answer now," Jack said. "Tomorrow."

"Oh, Jack... " she said. "I know I promised. I also know what I'll say. I just... oh, honey." She put her arms around him. "I feel so bad for you." She buried her face in his neck.

"I should have made you promise no sympathy either," he said. "I'm fine now, Annie. I lost a lot of years, but I've made up for them in friends and a wonderful job."

Annie pulled back and looked around.

"So that's why she has all this security."

"Well, not really. That's part of it, but she inherited this farm from her grandparents, and her mom came in here one day and started taking horses. After that, she put the fence up. No one gets in or out without a number of alarms going off."

"Wow," she said slowly, still taking it all in. "Francie's willing to die for you."

"I guess so," he said.

"That's pretty amazing." She opened her mouth to speak, then shut it again. "I'm not sure what to say. You've both put so much trust in me. I feel so honored."

She kissed his hand.

"I see why I need a night to process all of this. I don't guess I'll be sleeping much." She met his eyes again. "But honey, I do promise you this. My lips are sealed. I love you, and she's one of my best friends. If you two are found out, it won't be because of me."

"Thank you," Jack said.

"Jack?"

"Yes?"

"Where did you get those scars around your wrists?"

"That's a story for another night, Annie," he said. "I've given you quite enough to think about."

They embraced, and then he walked her back to his car. He kissed her lightly on the lips and drove her back to her place. They didn't say much in the car. He kissed her again at her door, and she went in.

When Jack got home, it was late. He let himself in the big house with his key and made his way up the stairs to Francie's office. Everyone was asleep, and he found Francie curled up on the window seat, her head on a pillow. She had dozed off. He closed the door silently.

"Hey, Princess," he said quietly.

Her eye fluttered open.

"How'd it go?" she asked.

He sat down in his chair across from her desk. "I think she was shell-shocked," he said, but then he got a grin. "But I think her answer is going to be 'yes'."

Francie smiled and sat up. "That's awesome. I'm so happy for you both! I really do like her."

"Me too," Jack said, still grinning. "I'll go and let you get back to sleep. She's going to call me in the morning. By the time I get to New York, I should have an answer."

"See you in the morning," she said, getting up. "I guess I'll go to bed now. Our flight is at 7:30."

"Goodnight," Jack said and walked out of the room and back to his house. He slept like a baby.

chapter 53

ANNIE WAS UP MOST OF THE NIGHT THINKING, but not about her answer. She knew it was definitely yes. She loved Jack. He was kind and very good to her, and he treated her like she was the most important person or thing in his life, even more so than his job. She had seen so many men choose work over family, which was one reason she had never married.

What she was thinking about was how one man could go through so much and not be bitter. How could he even get through the day? He seemed so well adjusted. He'd told her he had nightmares sometimes—flashbacks, he called them—but that was about it.

It was true that he had a good support group. Francie and Frank were wonderful, and the four of them enjoyed hanging out together. She couldn't imagine a different life.

In the car on the way back to her place, he had told her he needed to live on the farm, and that if she chose to live with him that would have to be their home. He felt safe there, and there were security precautions in case anybody came snooping around. He had places to hide. Plus, Frank and Francie were used to having him there to work on the farm or for the company whenever they needed him.

He worked a lot, and yet he had very flexible hours. If he wanted to take a few hours off for lunch, he did. If he wanted to take an afternoon off to take her to a movie, he did. She liked that.

And she really didn't think she'd mind staying on the farm. It was beautiful, and she loved horses. Maybe she could get her own horse and ride every day. It had been a childhood dream of hers to have her own horse. She had always rented and boarded out the ponies she had shown. Where she had lived in England, there was never a lot of space for land.

She liked the little house, too. It was a bit dark with the natural wood inside, but if they painted the paneling white, that should help out. The backyard was beautiful. She could imagine a garden out there, maybe with a little pond.

She wondered if Jack wanted children. She doubted it and wasn't sure she did either. Maybe, though. She had never given it much thought, since she had been so happy as a single woman. There was just something about Jack when she had first seen him in the grocery store that day. She instantly knew he was someone she wanted to know more. She couldn't explain why.

She was also thankful for his belief in God. Jack had led her into a personal relationship with Jesus. Before, she had always thought of God and religion as something for others. She didn't need it. Her life had been good, and she had been happy without God. But seeing God through Jack's eyes was different. Jack had a peace about him and a freedom because of his relationship with God. He knew he was valued. He found comfort in prayer and had quite a few scripture passages memorized. Because of his beliefs, he treated her with respect, and there was a quiet steadiness about him. He loved her unconditionally, always put her desires first, and he was there to lead her.

Not in a controlling way, but more in a protective way, like the way a man would put a woman on the inside of a street when he walked. She liked that.

Finally, around 3 a.m., she fell asleep. Three hours later, she awoke and picked up the phone by the nightstand. It was morning, and she wanted to give him her answer.

It was a June wedding. Francie held Andy in her arms and let the joy of the day wash over her. The church was decorated with lots of wildflowers, and Jack's pastor was officiating. Frank was the best man, and Annie's girlfriend from work was the maid of honor.

The reception took place in the church basement and was a catered dinner. Jack's "family" from the farm was there. Becky, Jess, and Mickey had come home from college, and they invited Steve's family to fill more space. Becky's boyfriend Rick and his family were also there, as well as a young man Jessica had started dating. Francie noted how her family was growing.

On Annie's side, she had her co-workers and a few neighbors, and two close girlfriends. Her cousins were all in England, and she didn't have any siblings, so no family was there. It was small, but not too small, and they had a DJ with a little dancing.

At 11 p.m., Jack and Annie left for a small house they had rented on the coast about an hour north.

Annie was holding Jack's hand, a huge smile on her face, as she hugged Frank and Francie goodbye. "We'll see you in a week," she said.

"Then you can get all moved in," Francie said.

Jack shook Frank's hand, and then stopped in front of Francie. He met her eyes and smiled. "Thank you," he said.

She nodded. That's all he needed to say. His eyes said the rest.

He tickled Andy under the chin. "I'll see you guys in a week." Then, with his hand in his bride's, he walked out into the night.

Journey's "Why Can't This Night Go On Forever" was playing in the background. Francie turned to Frank, who took Andy from her. "Don't you wish some nights could last forever?" Francie said. "Things are so good now. So happy." She smoothed down Andy's soft brown hair. "So good." Andy took hold of her thumb and smiled at her. She loved spending time with him. Donovan handled most of the racing now, so she could be home more. She didn't want to miss out with Andy, like she had with Becky's earlier years.

Frank put his arm around his wife.

"We've done good, Francie," he said, looking out on the dance floor at Becky and Jess laughing, trying to teach Rick a new dance move. "It all turned out."

"I love that little girl," Francie said.

Then Frank led Francie across the floor.

"Let's go home," he said. "Together. The three of us."

"Our little family," Francie said. She couldn't ever remember feeling so complete.

chapter 54

NEARLY A YEAR LATER, Francie sat at her desk in New York one late May morning, trying to figure out their latest ad campaign. She was very excited about it. They had taken quite a few photos, and she was going over them, trying to figure out which ones she liked the best for their new ads.

She didn't have to do much work though. Cassie was brilliant and had put together some really nice display ads that were going to go in all the major magazines. The theme was family. Dalton Jeans looked good on everyone: dads, moms, kids and yes, even cowboys. Especially cowboys. She smiled at the ad of the cowboy (okay, he was a sexy cowboy, she admitted, even though she was against using sex to sell jeans. He was just... built.) where he held the reins of his horse in one hand and the hand of his child in the other. Behind him, leaning on the fence, was "mom," presumably, her hair hanging down in long waves. Francie had never looked that good just coming from the barn after mothering her own children, but hey, nobody wanted to look at ugly people. That just didn't sell jeans.

She was happy with this particular ad and was wondering where Cassie was. She was expected at this morning's meeting but hadn't been in yet this week, and it was Thursday. It was unlike her not to call in even when she was sick. They only had a vague voicemail from her mother on Monday morning saying that Cassie wasn't feeling well and would be off a couple of days.

Francie was glad for the distraction of this job. Saturday had been Derby Day, and her horse, one of Flame's offspring and the favorite, had finished fourth. She felt that Steve had broken late from the gate, but honestly, he had ridden the rest of the race well, and she was starting to think her colt just didn't have it in him, despite his wins in some major stakes races earlier that year. They were going to try the Preakness in two weeks and see how he fared in that.

Maybe Steve was distracted. He and Sam had put in to adopt Lexie, the little girl Sam had grown fond of while she was teaching art at the orphanage. Francie smiled. She loved the little freckled-face redheaded kid.

Wow, she was distracted today.

She glanced at her clock and noticed that it was time for the meeting. She picked up the four ad layouts Cassie had left her, putting her favorite on top, and went out to the conference room. Jack was already there and so was Rosa. Rosa had ordered a box of donuts, as usual, and set Francie's favorite out on a plate at the head of the conference table. Rosa spoiled her. Everybody knew that the powdered sugar covered raspberry-filled donut was Francie's favorite type so she doubted if anybody would take it, but Rosa always ordered her one and made sure she got it.

"Oh, I'm in heaven," Francie said, sitting down with her coffee and taking a bite of the confection.

"I don't know how you eat so much and stay so thin," said Donald. "I swear I just look at that thing and gain five pounds." Her CEO patted his stomach, which was just a little round.

Jack smiled. "You should see what she orders for *lunch*."

"Why come to New York if you aren't going to eat?" Francie said. "There are some of *the best* restaurants here in Manhattan. I can't help myself."

"Oh, honey, have you tried Tio's?" asked Danny.

Francie looked up with interest. "No. Do tell."

"The best sandwiches in the *world*. And they *deliver*. Try the roast beef with cheese on rye. It's a *melt*."

"Mmmmm," Francie smiled.

"You're distracting her," Jack said.

"Rosa, write that down," Francie pointed to the yellow pad. "Tio's."

"I'll get us menus," Rosa said.

"I already have one," Danny said. "I'll bring it by."

Jack sighed. "Can we move on to ads?"

"Where's Cassie?" Donald said.

"She hasn't called in," Rosa said. "That's not like her. I'll try calling her parents' house again. She's not answering at hers. Or her cell."

They talked about ads, and everyone agreed that the cowboy family was the image they wanted to portray. Jack had a list of magazines they were running the ads in. Danny presented his new line for winter.

Francie listened and slowly ate her donut. She always ate a bit now and saved some for after lunch. Really, it was too much sugar for her, but she loved them, so she always managed to nibble her way through at least one every time she came in.

Later, she ate lunch in the cafeteria with Jack and Danny. Rosa was on the phone and the rest of the gang went out someplace. Danny talked between mouthfuls about his new line. He was quite excited.

After lunch Francie went back to her office to look through more papers. She put in a call to Frank to check on the farm and went to check with Rosa about Cassie.

It was nearly 3 p.m. when Jack came into her office with a pile of folders. She had been sitting at her desk, struggling with the Cassie problem and had decided to ask Jack for his opinion, even though she considered it more of a female issue. She just wasn't sure how to deal with this particular one. And it upset her.

"What's up?" Jack said.

"Close the door," she said.

He did so and came to sit across from her.

"I just found out why Cassie hasn't been in this week. She's not sick. She was raped over the weekend."

Jack's face turned pale. "Raped?"

"Yes. Apparently, she was out with friends, and when she walked back to her car alone, some guy grabbed her. She's scratched and bruised, but mostly it's psychological trauma. She needs some time off, and HR wants me to figure out how much time we should give her."

Jack got up and walked toward the window, his back to Francie.

"How am I supposed to figure that out?" she said. "Surgery, illness, you get weeks. Rape? I can't imagine that's something you ever get over." Francie sighed and put her fingers to her forehead. "She's such a creative, sweet girl... "

"Did they catch the bastard?" His voice was rough.

She looked up. "Yes. He was arrested last night."

"I think they should castrate the sonofabitch. Without anesthetic."

Francie said nothing, a little shocked at his outburst. His back was still to her.

"Wow," she finally said. "Well... we need to figure out how long we can manage without Cassie. I guess we should leave that up to her. Do you think I should call her?"

Jack turned around, and Francie saw how angry he was. His voice was flat when he spoke and cutting. "I don't know what kind of animal he... I'd like to get my hands around his neck. I'd show him some justice and save the courts some money."

Cassie was a favorite of Jack's. Tender, sweet Cassie. But his anger was something stronger than she'd expected.

"Jack?" Francie met his eyes.

"No one should ever have to experience that," he said, his voice catching.

She realized then, what was wrong.

"Oh, Jack."

"No," he said firmly and turned back toward the window. "No, Francie."

His shoulders were tight. He put his hands on the window frame and bowed his head down, taking a few deep breaths.

She felt the blood drain from her face. She wanted to go to him. To help somehow.

"When? In prison?"

"It was a long time ago—things happen in war. It's over. I'm over it, and I'd appreciate it if this was never brought up again."

Her heart went to her throat, as if to still the pounding of her chest. This answered a lot of questions. Why he hated to be touched. Why he pulled away from any intimacy. She didn't know what to say.

"Call her," he said. "Call Cassie and let *her* decide. She needs to feel in control of something, even if it's only the day she returns to work."

He walked toward the door, his back still to Francie.

"Have you ever talked to anybody?" she asked.

"No," he said.

"Does Annie know?"

"I know you want to help, but leave it alone."

And with that, he left.

It was late when they flew home that night. Jack had on his overhead light and was working. The new plane had sets of three seats across from each other. She sat diagonally from him, pretending to work, but really, she kept looking at him. The scars on his wrists were visible even in this dim light, and she wondered what else they had done to him.

Jack looked up, and she dropped her eyes back to her notebook. Finally, she said, "I did what you said. I called Cassie and gave her a choice. She sounded okay. She asked if she could let me know later when she would come back. She misses work. But, like I said, she sounded okay."

Jack nodded. "Sounded okay is different from being okay."

"I know."

They were both quiet, neither looking at each other, each staring at the papers in their lap.

"Well, that's good," Jack finally said. "She'll appreciate that you're being understanding."

Francie nodded. She put her papers together and put them in her folder, then leaned her head back against the seat and closed her eyes. The sound of the plane was comforting, like riding in a car, and quite hypnotic. She concentrated on it, pretending she was driving somewhere on land, but then no, that wasn't a comforting thought either. She decided she didn't really like traveling at all. Cars, airplanes, they all crashed.

Her mind wandered to horses. Now there was a fine ride. She was thinking about King and the gate Frank had replaced. Frank was so kind to her. She was glad Andy had his eyes.

"Annie doesn't know." Jack's voice broke through her reverie. She started, and then opened her eyes slowly. He had turned out his light, and the only lights they had were the dim cabin lights behind them. She could barely see his face in the shadows.

"Okay," she said.

"I haven't told her much," he said quietly. "I'm just not ready."

"Okay," she said again. Then, "I won't mention it to anyone. Not even Frank."

She hadn't told Frank what Jack had said during their ordeal in the plane crash either. It just seemed like Jack needed to trust her.

"It happened when I was a POW," he said.

She hesitated, then asked, "Do you want to talk about it?"

She couldn't see his eyes in the shadows. For a moment she thought he might agree.

"No," he said. "And as I said before, I would like for you to forget about it. You've just been so quiet since then that I knew we had to get this out in the open."

"I'm sorry."

"No. You don't need to apologize. I just don't want you to look at me differently."

"Why would I?"

She saw him smile. "*You* wouldn't, Francie Dalton," he said. "I guess that's why I tell you things."

They were quiet after that, and she leaned her head back against the seat and dozed off, dreaming again of riding King and flying over fences.

The following week, Cassie returned to work. She looked shaky during their morning meeting, but she pulled together

her presentation and shared some of her preliminary ideas for the winter designs Danny was working on. Afterward, Francie called her into her office.

When Cassie arrived, Francie was sitting behind her desk, and Jack was standing by the window.

"Have a seat," Francie said. Jack walked over and closed the door.

"I know your parents have been dropping you off at work this week," Francie said, "but I wanted you to know that I hired security for the parking garage. It's not that I think we need it, but it'll be there if we do."

She knew their garage was safe and that crime wasn't a problem in this area, but it was New York. It was important for her to know her employees felt safe. Everybody should feel safe.

"I also have enough security so you can have an escort to your car every evening after work, or whenever you go out of the building," she said and handed Cassie a slip of paper. "His name is Rip, and he's been with us a long while. I trust him completely. He's the tattooed guy you see in the lobby, and he can kick anybody's butt who gets in your way. I just want you to feel safe. Everyone should feel safe."

Cassie was speechless for a few moments, and then let out a sigh.

"I thought you were calling me in here to ask how I was doing," she said. "That's just not really a question anyone understands the answer to. Unless of course... they've been through what I have."

Francie avoided Jack's eyes.

"Well, I won't ask," Francie said, "but if you ever want to tell me, you can." She glanced at Jack. "The security was Jack's idea. He's in charge of finding areas where we need to beef up security, and he has an eye out to keep everybody here happy and comfortable. We don't want to lose you, Cassie; you're a brilliant graphic artist."

Cassie glanced up at Jack. "Thanks," she said, then looked at Francie again. "Thank you both."

"That's all," Francie said. "You can get back to work. I'm excited to see what you and Danny come up with for the fall line."

After Cassie left, Jack closed the door. "I know this is costing the company quite a bit, but I think it's a good move."

"It is. Our security wasn't optimal. I don't want any creeps sneaking in. And now we have someone to walk us out. It's important to feel safe."

"Yes, it is," Jack said. "Yes, it is."

chapter 55

ANNIE WAS TIRED. It had been another hard night in a year or more of hard nights.

The first nightmare Annie experienced with Jack had been six weeks into their marriage. Everything was going smoothly, and she had moved her stuff in to the little house and seamlessly fit into his life, as he did into hers.

Then one night, around 2 a.m., he woke up screaming, which caused her to wake up screaming. Just as quickly as the screams had started, they stopped, and she found him on the floor, huddled in the corner.

"What?" she said. "What is it?" She was so frightened that she was sobbing.

It took Jack a few minutes to pull himself together. Annie was sitting on the foot of their bed, the comforter wrapped around her, shaking and crying.

"Bad dream," he managed

She crawled down on the floor beside him in the dark and pulled the comforter around him. "It's okay," she said and put her arm around him, meaning to comfort him. He jerked away, as if he had been burned.

"Don't touch me," he said. "Not now."

Annie sat there quietly, calming her own heart and breathing. Finally, she said, "Jack, it's just me. Come on, honey, get up and come back to bed."

"I'm sorry," he said, scrubbing his face with his hands. He crawled back into bed with her. They lay there, side by side, on their backs, both of them looking up at the ceiling.

"Do you want to talk about it?" she asked quietly.

"I don't remember it," he said honestly. "I don't remember what it was about."

Slowly, she reached beside her and took his hand. "I love you," she said.

"I love you too," he said.

Eventually, Annie fell back to sleep, but the first rays of dawn were coming in through the window before Jack finally drifted off.

He had night terrors every few weeks. He was used to them, had grown to live with them, and told her that one bad night wasn't so bad if you had good ones to catch up on sleep.

But for Annie it was difficult. She became nervous and started having trouble sleeping.

"It's hard to wake up to screams," she said to him once. "It scares me to death."

"I'm pretty scared to death at the time too," Jack said.

At first, Annie had tried to comfort him. This proved difficult for two reasons: she was scared herself, having been startled awake so violently, and secondly, he usually didn't want to be touched. Over time, Annie would check on him to make sure he was awake, then go to the couch. But she didn't sleep well there either.

"Jack, I'm exhausted," she said one morning. "I can't keep living this way."

"Annie, it's not like I have a choice. I'd love for them to stop, probably more than you would."

"Oh, I doubt *that*," Annie said. She was tired and had to go off to work. She knew that he would probably get a nap in after his meeting with Francie. He usually did.

"What do you want me to do?"

"Can't you talk to somebody? A counselor?"

"And tell them what? That back before I became a fugitive, I was a POW?"

Annie slammed her coffee cup down on the table. "I don't know. Just do *something*. I'm exhausted."

She had dark circles under her eyes. She had a long day ahead of her and had to lead a team meeting.

"I'm sorry," he said, kissing her as she put her purse over her shoulder and grabbed her keys.

"I know. Me too," she said. She put her arms around his neck and buried her face in his shoulder. "Maybe they'll end."

But they only got worse.

"You look like heck," Francie said to Jack one morning when they met in her office.

"Late night," he said.

She raised her eyebrows.

"Your mind is always in the gutter," he said.

"Not *always*."

"Well, anyway, here are the papers you wanted."

He handed them to her. His hands were trembling, something that hadn't happened since he had married Annie.

She got up and walked around to close the office door, then came back to her desk and sat down.

"Tell me what's bothering you," she said.

He sighed. She could read him like a book. She never pried him about his past or his feelings, but she adjusted her mood or expectations to fit his. She took care of him very subtly, in a way that only he could recognize.

"Annie and I have been fighting a lot," he said.

Francie frowned. This was disturbing news. She loved Annie, and Annie hadn't said anything to her. "Over what?"

"I have bad dreams," he said.

"So? I do too since the car accident."

This stopped Jack. "You have bad dreams?"

"I wake up crying. Frank deals with it."

He studied her for a few minutes. "Why didn't you ever say anything?"

"I didn't think it mattered."

Jack rolled his eyes.

"You never tell *me* about *your* bad dreams," Francie said.

"Anyway, she's a wreck. It's hard to wake up next to someone who wakes up screaming. It's very startling."

"I can imagine."

"She tries to comfort me. I'm not fond of being touched after a nightmare."

Francie was quiet for a minute. "I'm sorry. I should feel for Annie. I've just been through so much I tend to say, 'deal with it,' and move on."

She slipped her hand under her desk and retrieved something. It was a small gold key.

"I want to show you something," she said. "You once told me good memories go bad. That's not always true. I do have a lot of bad memories, and there are not a lot of safe places my mind can go. If I think of my awesome childhood summers, living here and riding Star, I think of *losing* Star. If I remember my happy times with Ken, I remember... losing Ken. But the Bible says to think on good things, so I try to. And the rest of that verse says that the peace that passes understanding will guard my heart. So this is my drawer full of memories, and they make me happy."

She opened her drawer and pulled out the little bottle of sand and told him the story.

"This," she said, pulling out a photo, "is Johnny, my first love. Krista took this picture right before we left on a date."

"You're on a motorcycle," Jack said.

She smiled, remembering the feel of Johnny's leather jacket and his musky smell like it was yesterday. "Yes. And he later crashed it and was killed." Before Jack could say anything, she pulled out the angel figurine Krista had given her.

"My guardian angel," she said. "Krista gave it to me on my birthday one year, the spring before she left for college. I was having a bad day that day."

She set the angel down and pulled on some soft cotton work gloves.

"These were Ken's," she said. "Sometimes I pretend he's holding my hand. If I close my eyes, I can almost feel him." She looked up at Jack and smiled. "It's corny, I know, but it works. If I spend a little time rifling through my drawer here, I feel better." She pulled the gloves off and closed the drawer. "You need to find a happy memory," she said.

He looked across her desk at her, and she could tell that he was uncertain of what to say. "Maybe from your childhood. Your favorite recipe that your mom cooked?" she suggested.

Jack smiled. "Chocolate-frosted brownies," he said. "She had this wonderful recipe she made from scratch. I got to lick out the frosting bowl every time."

She watched his eyes grow distant for a moment. "See?" she said. "They're in there. Your mom would want you to remember."

"Yes, she would," he said. "Yes, she would."

chapter
56

DALTON JEANS WAS THRIVING, the horses were thriving, and for the most part, everybody was happy. Andy was two years old and a thrill to have around. He was an easygoing kid, like his dad, and had Frank's kind brown eyes and shock of sandy colored hair.

Frank was holding him, and everyone had come down to the track to watch White December's maiden run in public. It was about 9 a.m., and Francie had waited until the others were done training before she brought the colt out.

Annie had the day off work and was standing at the rail, holding hands with Jack. They had celebrated their two-year anniversary yesterday and were planning on going to a movie this afternoon.

Sam was there, biting her fingernails. She had already dropped Lexie off at school and had come to watch her husband hop on the gangly two-year old.

A few other trainers and riders had gathered at the rail.

"I hope you have a lot of insurance out on Steve," Red, an old trainer, yelled at Francie as she checked the girth.

"Don't need it, Red. Steve will be fine," she said as she finished tightening the girth. "This horse is running on love."

There was a chuckle along the rail.

"I shouldn't have come," Sam said in a low voice.

"He'll be fine," Frank said. "Francie wouldn't put him in danger. Besides, Steve has been on him back at the farm."

"I know," she sighed.

Jack looked over at her. "What's up, Sam? You're usually pretty calm about his riding."

"I know... " she said. "But he's a dad now. Ever since Lexie came to live with us, I get nervous when I watch."

Annie smiled and put her arm around Sam. "Watch," she said. "It'll be fun."

White December had fallen three months ago during his early training as a two year old. When the bell went off, the gate had only partially opened, and he got caught in it as he bolted out, tearing a gash in his neck and tangling his leg in the door. After surgery to bring him back, he was terrified to go near the gate or to run, and his owner and trainer couldn't handle him. Every jockey that had climbed on him got dumped, and the horse ended up shaking uncontrollably until someone came and took him back to his stall.

His owner had approached Francie six weeks ago and asked if she wanted to buy him. He had good bloodlines but was unmanageable.

"I've heard you have a touch," he had said to her. "He was a good horse. I'd like you to take him."

She paid a price that most thought high, since it was doubted that the colt would be able to prove himself on the track, but she saw more than the others did.

Now Francie held onto her colt and talked to Steve in a low voice so the others couldn't hear.

"He's ready," she said, watching the horse's ears swivel around and take in the sights and sounds. "We're going to break him out of the gate really slow—no bells, no sound—and just canter him up the track to the quarter mile pole and turn him and bring him back. If he's relaxed, you can let him out a bit and take him the whole trip around."

Steve nodded.

"You trust him?" she said.

He rubbed the colt's gray neck.

"Yep. Me and this guy get along really well."

He put his foot in the stirrup and hoisted himself up. Francie waited until he had gathered the reins, and then she let go. She glanced over at Frank, who gave her a thumb's up.

Steve walked him around behind the starting gate, while Francie went up front. He walked December in and stood the colt there, leaving both doors open. December trembled a little bit, and Francie pulled out a carrot and gave him a bite. He chewed it thoughtfully, turning his head to look around the enclosed space, then nudged her for another. She gave it to him. Soon he had orange slobber dripping down from around the bit in his mouth.

"Don't wipe that on me," she said, laughing and pushing his nose away from her. "There's another piece in my pocket. If you take Steve for a nice ride, I'll give it to you after."

She closed the door to the starting gate and stepped back. December snorted and pawed the ground, but Steve stroked his neck, talking to him in a soft voice.

"Amazing," said one of the trainers on the rail.

Francie looked at Steve, who nodded, and she pushed a button, which released the door. December bolted out, nearly out from under Steve, and went sideways across the track.

Steve gathered his reins up tighter and used his outside leg to nudge December back toward the inside rail. He half-trotted, half-bucked across to the rail then stopped, standing splay-legged and panting. He was trembling and sweating.

Francie walked up to him and rubbed his neck again. "I guess you get this now," she said, pulling the carrot out of her pocket. He nudged her a couple of times, as if asking to go back home. But then he took the carrot.

"Let's try it again," Steve said.

They went through the whole thing again. And then again. December kept bolting to the side.

"Let's try these." Francie put some blinders on the colt, blocking his peripheral vision. "Now he has to pay more attention to you."

Steve climbed back on. When Francie opened the door a third time, December cantered out smoothly. Steve stood in his irons and took him around the track toward the quarter pole.

Francie was smiling.

"He's fine now," Frank said. "Look at his ears. He's listening to Steve."

They reached the quarter pole, and Steve let him out a bit. They began a slow gallop around the track. There was a smattering of applause from the folks along the rail, and Francie walked back, all smiles.

"I don't know how you do it," Red said. "That colt was a mess just six weeks ago."

"A little compassion goes a long way," Frank said. "She let him heal at his own pace. She's done nothing but play with that horse. He forgot all about training until she put Steve up on him last week at the farm."

Red nodded, chewing on his gum.

"Wow," Annie said. She had seen White December when they first brought him home and how he climbed, shaking, out of the horse trailer, sedated. The first thing Francie had taught him was to load in the trailer again. She had parked the horse trailer in his pasture, then spent hours just sitting in the horse trailer holding carrots and apple slices, dropping them first at the edge and then further in.

Eventually, curious and a bit hungry, he had taken a bite, and soon he had both front legs in. As Francie earned his trust through brushing and playing, the trailer game because easier, and one day, he just walked right in with her.

Steve finished his mile lap and brought December down to a jog. When he stopped in front of Francie, the horse was out of breath.

"Looks like now we have to get him in shape," Francie said, patting him on the neck. "That winded you a little, huh, buddy?"

Steve hopped down and handed her the reins.

"Good job. Great horse," he said. "Derby material."

Red snorted. "How can you know that with one ride?"

"It's his heart," Steve said, meeting Francie's eyes. "This horse runs because he wants to please us. And he's having fun. He'll run his legs off for her."

"They all do," Red said, giving Francie a thumbs up before he wandered back down toward his own stalls.

Francie took her horse. "Show's over," she said to Jack and Annie. "Thanks for coming."

"Wouldn't have missed it," Annie said.

"Call me when you're ready," Francie said.

"I should be home by two at the latest," Annie said.

She and Annie had planned to go riding in the afternoon, after Annie and Jack got back from their matinee. Jack and Frank were going golfing. Then the couples had planned a late dinner together while Sam watched Andy.

Around 2 p.m., Francie was sitting at her desk working when Annie called. She went down to the barn and saddled up King. Annie came a few minutes later and saddled up Mia Kia, a beautiful bay Arabian mare Francie had given her as a wedding gift. Mai Kai was sweet and gentle but spirited enough to give Annie a good ride. She was also as smooth as a rocking chair.

The two women started off across the field. Francie slowed King down and let Annie open the gate. Mai Kai wasn't a jumper, and Francie respected that and didn't want to show off her own horse. They cantered down the sandy path toward the beach, then rode along the surf, laughing.

"This is awesome!" Annie shouted over the waves. "This is what I always dreamed of doing as a girl!"

They came down and rode on the beach whenever they could, and today was Annie's turn to pack a snack.

They dismounted, soaking wet and tired, and plopped down in the shade under the tree near the cave.

Annie pulled a soft cooler she had tied to her saddle and opened it up.

"What do you have in there?" Francie asked, realizing how hungry she was.

"Some iced tea"—Annie handed Francie a bottle—"and, prepare yourself, chocolate cupcakes, homemade from Doogie's Bakery in town!" With a flourish, she pulled them from her bag.

Francie's eyes widened. "I love you, Annie!" she said, taking her cupcake.

"But first," Annie said, pulling more from her cooler. "Some bread and cheese. Otherwise, we'll be on a sugar buzz."

They laughed and shared their meal in the shade of the old oak.

"That was pretty impressive what you did with December this morning," Annie said. "You should have seen the look on the other trainers' faces. You're kind of like a legend."

Francie laughed. "Oh, I doubt *legend* is the word most of them would use for me," she said. "But he did so well, didn't he? He's come a long way in six weeks."

"Have you missed it?"

Francie had given Donovan all of the horse training for the past three years, during her pregnancy and Andy's toddler years. But when December's owner had offered to sell her the horse on the condition she was the one to handle him, she was thrilled to take him on. Just one horse wasn't too much, and it allowed her to keep her trainer's license current. She had to saddle a certain number of horses in races each year to do that.

"It's good to be back," Francie said. "I figure I'll take it slow this year, and then hopefully next year pick up a few more horses. It all depends. I want to be around for Andy. He's pretty portable right now, but as he gets into school, I don't want to be gone that much, and I'm already in New York a lot."

"Jack told me you asked him to pick out an apartment."

"Yes, I'm tired of hotels. I built a small apartment in the basement of the company for when Donald works late and can't make it home. It should have been the penthouse, but the design just isn't there, and I'm not ready to do more remodeling. Donald loves it. So I asked Jack to find us a place since he's there more than me."

She had only been going every other week, to be home more with her family.

"It'll be easier if we spend the night," Francie said.

"He told me some of the prices for a two-bedroom in Manhattan," Annie whistled.

"Yes," Francie said. "I know. Thank goodness we have a little cushion."

They had dinner at the little Italian restaurant in town where Jack had taken Annie on their first date. Frank paid in celebration of their anniversary.

"Here's to two years," Francie said, picking up her glass of water.

They all toasted.

"Cheers."

"So what was that you put on December's bridle today?" Jack asked. "Blinders, I think you called them?"

Francie nodded and finished chewing her bite of food. "Yes. Blinders. He's spooked easily and was always shying away from things in his peripheral vision, so Steve and I tried them the other day, and I just decided he needed them at the track this morning as well. They only allow him to look straight ahead."

"Isn't that cruel?"

Francie raised an eyebrow. "Me? *Cruel?*"

Jack laughed. "I mean, what if something scary is coming up beside him?"

"He has to trust Steve," Francie said. "Steve had already built up trust with him, and so now December knows that he can count on Steve to keep him safe. December's job is to run straight ahead toward the finish line. He is trusting Steve to protect him from all the things he can't see."

"He only needs to see the finish line," Frank said.

"So he's racing blind," Jack said.

Francie took a sip of her water. "Kind of. He knows where he's headed, but he doesn't know what's going to come at him along the way. And it doesn't matter, because his jockey has his hands on the reins. December trusts that."

"Racing blind," Annie said. "Sounds a lot like life."

It was late when they got home, and Sam had put Andy to bed. Frank and Francie peeked at him in his room.

"Precious," Francie whispered, and lightly kissed his little cheek. "Life is good."

She didn't think she'd ever be able to say that again after her accident, but she could finally say it. The emotional pain wasn't anywhere near gone, but she had gotten to the point where she could push it to the back of her mind. They had taken down any photos of Krista or Ken or the baby and put them carefully into photo albums. They didn't look at them much, and never together. Francie didn't know if Frank looked at them at all anymore, and she had quit going through them so much. It just seemed to open the memories afresh.

That night, they lay in bed together. "God has plans for us," Frank quoted from the Bible. "Plans to prosper us and not to harm us. Plans to give us hope and a future."

"He certainly has," Francie said. She snuggled up into Frank's arms, feeling safe and warm and happy. Sam and Jack and all her other loved ones were safe as well. She went to sleep with the good memories of her time tonight with her friends floating through her thoughts.

chapter 57

IT WAS A COLD, RAINY NOVEMBER MORNING when Annie awoke to her alarm. She shut it off and listened to the rain beating against the window and felt the aching in her limbs. She was so tired that she just wanted to go back to sleep.

Jack had had another night terror last night, and they had both been up for a few hours. She had sent him to the couch, then felt guilty for sending him to the couch, and had gone to sit with him. They'd watched a movie together to take their mind off things. She had gotten into bed about 4:30, and now it was 6:30.

Jack got up and used the bathroom, then went to make her breakfast while she took her shower. This was their routine. He packed her lunches, too, something he had started when they first got married. He spoiled her.

She ate her eggs in silence, then kissed him goodbye.

"I have a meeting this morning," she said. "Do you have a busy day?"

"I have quite a bit of paperwork to do for our new fall line," he said.

"I'll see you tonight."

They kissed, and he handed her a travel mug full of coffee. "It's strong," he said, winking. "I'm sorry about last night."

"It's okay," she said and left for work.

The rain had stopped, and the sun had come out by the time Jack walked back from meeting with Francie. He was happy with the new designs Danny had out, and stores were snapping them up. He whistled as he walked, noticing that Annie's car was parked in the driveway. Sometimes she came home for lunch, and he wondered if she had picked up anything good for him.

"Hi, hon!" he said as he stepped into the house, setting his paperwork on the kitchen table. She was in the bedroom. He went in and saw her packing.

"Annie?"

She looked up at him. She was crying.

"I can't live like this anymore," she said. "Jack, I fell asleep at my desk this morning and my boss walked in and said something to me and startled me so badly that I sat straight up and spilled my coffee. My third cup of coffee that morning."

She sighed.

"I'm not even a coffee drinker," she said. "I prefer tea, but I can't find anything strong enough."

She zipped up her weekend bag.

"I'm going to stay with my friend Diana for a while. Jack... "

She turned to look at him. She started sobbing all over again.

"Jack, I love you so much. You are so amazing and so kind to me, but I just can't live this way anymore. I can't sleep, and when I can, you wake me up with one of your dreams. You're so cuddly and caring half the time, and then the other half, you don't want me to touch you, and

I can't always figure out which is which and when is the right time to put an arm around you... "

She stopped to catch her breath. He stood there, silent and stunned. He had no idea things had gotten this bad.

"Jack, it's killing me to love you. I have to get out of here."

She walked up to him and gave him a kiss on the cheek. "I love you," she said and brushed by.

"Annie," he said, grabbing her wrist. "Wait. Let's talk. Please don't go."

"I'm done talking," she said. "Jack, you won't get help. There has to be someone who can help you without needing to know your past. I've read everything I can on post-traumatic stress disorder and left books lying around the house which you never even open."

"I can get this under control," he said. "I just need to... "

"What?" Annie said.

"I'm trying to put it all behind me," he said. "And it's been easier since you came into my life."

"No, you're not trying to put it behind you; you're trying to *forget* about it. You're pushing it down, which is why it's coming back." She grabbed a book off the coffee table. "Read this. That's what it says in here."

He grabbed the book and threw it down. "I don't need to read this. Annie, some things are better off forgotten!"

"Yeah, that's how everyone around here seems to function. You need to face it, Jack. Until then, it's not going away. I don't even have any idea what happened to you. If you won't talk to me, talk to a counselor."

"Annie, it's not that easy."

"Yes, it is."

"You have no idea."

"Jack, I do. I lost my parents. I'm not immune to tragedy."

"Annie, this is worse than that... this is—"

"Worse than losing my parents?" She laughed, sarcastic. "Wow."

He sighed and ran his hands through his hair. "I didn't mean that. I lost my father. I know what that's like. But sometimes there are just things that are too terrible to get over."

"What about God, Jack? There's the scripture you quote all the time: 'Perfect love casts out fear.' If God is in your life, why do you still have so much fear? Give it to God, Jack."

"Annie, it's not that easy."

"I'm done," she said, grabbing her keys. "I need a break. I can't do this anymore. I love you, but you're killing me."

She went through the door. He heard her drive off.

He stood there a few moments, uncertain of what to do. He hadn't seen that coming at all. He knew she was tired, but he had no idea she had reached her limit.

Her words rang through his head; she had said she still loved him. He glanced at the book on the table. He had looked through it a few times but didn't want to read it. He supposed he should, so he made himself a sandwich and sat down and opened the book.

He got a few pages into it and decided he didn't need the book, he needed Annie. He'd go to her and bring her home, and they could talk. He'd tell her everything he could remember, and he'd open up to her, and maybe she would be able to understand more.

Francie had told him that's it was easier to put up with people's issues if you understand why they have them.

He saw Annie's cell phone on the table. She had forgotten it. He left his uneaten sandwich, grabbed his keys, and drove off to find his wife.

He was on a deserted stretch of road not far from the farm when he heard a loud pop. His car swerved violently to the right. A tire had blown, he thought, pulling over and coasting to a stop. A silver car pulled up behind him, and a man got out.

"Trouble?" he asked.

"I'm not sure," Jack said, getting out of his car. "I think the tire blew."

He went back to take a look at it. There was a perfectly round hole through it. About the size of a bullet hole. His blood went cold.

He turned around, and the man was pointing a pistol at him.

"Get in my car," he said.

Jack was trying to figure out how to kick the gun out of the man's hand without getting shot. He knew he wasn't that fast.

"Let me get my wallet," he said, buying time.

"You don't need your wallet where we're going," the man said.

So it wasn't a robbery. Jack was trying to think.

"Don't you think the cops are going to get suspicious when they find my car?" Jack said.

"I'm not worried about that either," the man said, a wicked grin on his face. "Where we're going, nobody will find us."

Quick as lightning, he reached out with his other hand and tasered Jack. Jack fell to the ground with a thud, and then the man kicked him in the head, knocking him out.

When Jack came to, his wrists were bound and stretched over his head, hooked on a meat hook hanging from some bars in the ceiling. They seemed to be in an old barn, reworked into some type of workshop. He could see a field and a lot of trees out the window.

"I'm glad you're awake," the man said. He looked strong, well-built, and had a nasty scar across his cheek. "As you can see, we're out in the middle of nowhere. No one can find us, and even *more* fun, no one can hear you scream."

Jack looked around the room and saw an assortment of tools he knew were about to be used for torture.

"Oh crap," he said.

The man laughed.

"My name is Reginald Stanton," he said. "Ah, yes, I see you recognize the last name. It was my father you killed on that plane back from Vietnam, where he went to rescue you. That destroyed my mother, you know. *Destroyed* her. You took my entire family from me in that one heinous move."

"I didn't kill your father," Jack said. The ropes were cutting into his wrists, and he winced from the pain. "I have no idea what you're talking about."

Stanton picked up a knife and sharpened it.

"Oh, yes, you do, Paul Lawson. I know who you are. It took me years, but I found you, and now you're gonna tell me who paid to get you out of federal prison. I had taken the day off of work to attend your execution. I asked if they'd let me pull the switch, but apparently that's reserved for the professionals. They have to make sure you fry just right."

He walked up to Jack, so close that Jack could smell his breath. "Are you going to tell me who bought you your freedom, or do I get to play?"

Jack swung his legs up and grabbed Stanton around the middle. He squeezed and tried to take him down, but Stanton thrust the blade into Jack's side, and he jerked away from the pain, which caused him to free the man.

Stanton laughed. "Oh, looks like I get to play," he said. "Well, I have ways to get you to talk."

He leaned forward and sliced through Jack's shirt. It fell from his body. Blood spilled from the knife wound. Then Stanton took a garden hose and turned the nozzle on, spraying Jack down.

"Is that how you plan to torture me, Stanton?" Jack yelled, sputtering. "You're going to *hose* me to death?"

"Oh, no, I'm just preparing you," Stanton said. After he soaked him with the cold water, he turned the hose down to a trickle and swung it up over the pole, so it ran down across Jack's back. Jack looked down and noticed that he was hanging over a drain.

Stanton pulled on some rubber boots and picked up a wand.

"I hear you're a praying man, Jack," he said, turning a knob on the wand. "You'd better start praying." He hit Jack with the wand, and an electric shock went through Jack, causing his body to arch. He yelled.

It only got worse after that.

"Jack was supposed to meet me this afternoon to set up some appointments with potential clients," Francie said to Frank. "I can't find him anywhere."

Frank was stacking hay in the broodmare barn. It was hot, and he had hay sticking to his face and arms.

"I assume you tried his cell."

"I did. He's not answering, and his car is gone. Annie isn't answering, and *her* car is gone, but I assume she's at work. Probably in a meeting. So I let myself into their house, and there's an uneaten sandwich on the kitchen table, like somebody left in a hurry. "

Frank stopped working and put his hands on his hips.

"You're asking for my help?"

He was out of breath and quite dirty.

"Well, Jack's two hours late. I was thinking of taking a drive up the road to look for him, and I sort of don't want to go alone. I just have a feeling."

Frank looked at his hay, then back at his wife.

"Alright," he said. "Let me get washed up."

A half hour later, they were in Francie's SUV, heading down the dusty road that led from their farm. They weren't on the road more than five minutes when they saw Jack's car off to the side.

Frank pulled over, and they got out.

"His cell phone is here," Francie said. "The car is unlocked."

Frank inspected the tire.

"This is weird," he said. "There's a hole in the rubber here that caused the tire to burst. It looks like... like a bullet hole."

"There's blood here," Francie said, looking on the ground. "Dried."

"Let's call the police," Frank said.

"We can't," Francie said, her voice a little shaky. "He's not exactly legal."

She pulled her phone out and fumbled with the numbers. "I guess I'm going to call Mark. I don't know what else to do, and we need help. He's my brother. He'll help us, right?"

Mark had a team out there looking at the car within the half hour. He himself was on his way down from another case and would be there in another hour. Francie was sitting in her car, watching the men work over Jack's vehicle. She was on the phone with Mark.

"What exactly do you know about this guy?" he asked her. "Why would anyone want to kidnap your vice president?"

"How do you know he was kidnapped?" Francie said. "Maybe they killed him."

"No, my men don't think so. There's not enough blood, and if all they wanted was him dead, they would have shot him and left him."

"Oh." Her voice was small.

"We'll find him," Mark said. "He's only been gone a few hours. The trail is still fresh, and they couldn't have gotten far. What can you tell me about him?"

"Just that he's a good man, and you need to find him. His wife went out with a friend, according to her co-workers. She's not answering her phone, but apparently, she was seen about an hour ago leaving work, so she's not with them. She's safe."

Mark couldn't get much more out of Francie, so he promised to find Jack and said goodbye.

"Can you keep what you find out to yourself?" Francie asked him before he hung up.

"Francie... " Mark sighed. "I'll see you soon."

Francie watched his men dust for fingerprints and take impressions of what they felt were the kidnapper's tire prints.

"I can't go to jail now," she said quietly to Frank, who was sitting in the SUV next to her. "and leave Andy."

She turned to meet his eyes. "What if he's dead? Oh, Frank... " Her heart lurched inside of her. She wracked her brain to figure out who might have him.

"I could contact the men who broke him out of jail. They could help me. That's who I should have gone to first."

"Could you even find them?"

"I don't know... "

"We have to act quickly," Frank said. "I'm pretty sure he's in danger."

Francie started up the car.

"Are we going somewhere?" Frank asked.

"We're going to drive around and look for him," she said. "And if we can't find him, maybe we can find Annie. She might know something."

Jack woke gasping on water. He had blacked out somewhere in the middle of the electric shock torture. Stanton was waiting, sitting in a chair watching him.

"I see you're awake," he said. "Shall we begin again?"

He turned on the little tape recorder he had sitting on the chair next to him.

"Now, for the audience, give me the name of the person who bought you your freedom."

Jack spit out some water in Stanton's direction. "Go to hell," he said.

Stanton got up from his chair and punched Jack in the gut. "That's where you are right now," he said, picking up a metal bar. "I'll count to ten, and if I have to ask you for a name again, we're going to play a new game."

"Bring it on," Jack said, his voice weak. He was hoping to get Stanton closer to him again, so he could get in a new kick at the man. But Stanton knew his game.

"I'm a special ops warrior myself," he said, noticing Jack sizing him up. "Don't think you can win this one. I've also read up on some of the things they might have done to you in that private little POW camp they were hiding you in. Horrible things." He shook his head. "If we have to, I'll go there."

Jack had no idea what he was talking about, but he saw a wooden box off in the corner, as well as some ropes stretched across a board. He didn't really want to find out what they were for.

He closed his eyes and prayed for God to release him, to protect him from this man.

I will lift my eyes unto the hills, from whence cometh my help, he said to himself. *My help cometh from the Lord.*

But he was brought out of his prayer by a new pain, this one shooting across his knuckles as Stanton swung the metal bar up and struck them again and again. He heard a few snaps as bones broke.

Oh God, he thought. *Let it be over soon.*

It was dark when Francie stopped the SUV at a gas station. Frank got out and filled it up.

"Mark won't tell me where he is," she said when Frank got back in the truck, "but he thinks they've found a lead. He's chasing it down."

Frank pulled his seatbelt around him. "Good," he said. "I'll try Annie again."

Jack woke up to find himself in a wooden box, cramped into a fetal position. His whole body hurt, and he could hardly breathe. Stanton had beaten him pretty badly.

"Are you awake in there?" he heard Stanton's sickly-sweet voice. "I've got a few more surprises for you."

He heard the click of the tape recorder again. Claustrophobia set in, and Jack started breathing hard, kicking at the crate with his feet, but he couldn't get enough force behind them to do any good.

"If you're afraid now, you haven't seen anything yet," Stanton said. "I saved the best for now."

Jack heard a loud burst and lots of shuffling and yelling. "Get down!" Someone shouted, and there were some shots fired. He tried to peek out of the crate, but pain shot across his back. He couldn't pull in a good breath. He heard what sounded like fighting, and adrenaline surged through him. He started kicking hard at the box, trying to break it apart. But the pain in his side was so bad that he blacked out again.

He woke up with fresh air on his face. Hands were grabbing him, pulling him from the box.

"It's okay, we got ya," one said.

Jack went into full fight mode, kicking and punching with everything he had. More hands grabbed him, and he took a swipe at one man, kicking the guy's legs out from under him. Pain burst through his ribs so badly from the movement that the world swayed. He yelled, ignoring the pain, and went after the man again, but this time, something hard hit him in the skull. He saw lights shoot across his vision and fought more. If he was going to die, he planned to take as many of them with him as he could.

chapter 58

FRANCIE GOT THE CALL when they were on their way back home. It was about 9 p.m. and she was planning to go through Jack's house to look for clues.

"We've got him," Mark said. "Meet us at County General."

Francie turned the SUV around and gunned it.

There was a lot of noise and confusion at the ER. Police and FBI agents were everywhere. Mark was filling out papers, and two men approached her with a warrant.

"Not now," Mark said to them. "Leave her alone."

Francie glanced at Frank, then grabbed Mark's arm.

"I have to see him," she said.

"He's unconscious," Mark said. "We got him here a half hour ago."

"A half hour ago? Why didn't you call me sooner?"

Mark lowered his voice. "We know who he is. Keep a low profile and play dumb."

Francie nodded. Mark took her arm. "You can wait up on the fifth floor. The doctor will be out to talk to you. I have you down as his next of kin."

"Okay."

"They're stitching him up. Looks like his hands are broken too. Francie, it's bad. The man who took him, tortured him. Just prepare yourself."

She nodded again and took Frank's arm. Together, they walked up to the fifth floor.

There were two policemen standing in front of Jack's closed hospital door. They had moved him from emergency into a place where they could keep him safe. Or keep others safe *from* him, Francie wasn't sure which.

Eventually, a doctor walked out of Jack's room. As the door swung open and then shut, Francie saw a few people gathered around a bed, working on him.

She started to go in, and the doctor gently took her arm, stopping her. "He's unconscious right now," he said. "Let my people finish up their work. I want to talk to you, and then I'll let you both in. You're—" He glanced at his chart.

"Francie Dalton and Frank Weaver."

"Okay. Next of kin. Let's go talk. My name is Dr. Tremper."

He steered them into a small, quiet room and closed the door. He motioned for them to take a seat.

"He's going to live," the doctor said right away, and Francie exhaled. She had been so tense that she had nearly melted in the chair.

"Thank God," Frank said.

Dr. Tremper was older, fully gray and had soft hands. He spoke quietly and moved slowly, not in a hurry. He seemed to have all the time in the world for them.

"It's bad," the doctor said. "*Very* bad, and I want to prepare you for what you'll see when you go in there." He cleared his throat, then looked down at his chart. Shaking his head, he put the chart away and looked across at the couple.

"Physically he's going to be in a lot of pain for a good, long while. Right now, he's pretty heavily medicated. I'd say he'll be pretty comfortable when he wakes up, and we do expect him to wake up, because he had a few lucid moments here and there while we were working on him.

"He was beaten badly. He has multiple fractures on his fingers where he was apparently hit with a metal bar. The bruising and swelling are so bad right now that we can't determine what is broken, and we're not going to cast anything until the swelling goes down, so there's no need to put him through x-rays tonight.

"He also has several fractured ribs, and a very big bruise on his side that is clearly in the shape of a boot print, so we know he was kicked, probably multiple times." He paused. Francie nodded to show him she was still with him.

"He was stabbed in the side with a knife, but we stitched it up and stopped the bleeding. It wasn't deep."

Dr. Tremper sighed and rubbed his forehead, as if gathering himself. Then he took a deep breath and continued.

"You'll see burns all across his chest, back, and stomach. We believe he was hosed down and electrocuted. Repeatedly. Electric shock torture is one of the worst and usually a good way to get people to talk. Judging from the number of burns on him, he didn't talk early on.

"He also has a fractured skull. He was beaten repeatedly over the head with a club. We believe this happened *after* he was taken out of the hands of his abductor, and it appears to be police brutality. I was told he fought the police and that they subdued him. He didn't stop fighting until the blows caused a seizure, and he was unable to fight any longer. Then he blacked out, and that's when *we* got him. He was unconscious when he came in. There are also many bruises and scratches on him, especially his arms and face, and his right eye is swollen shut. "He paused. "Your friend was very badly beaten," he said again, quietly. Then he continued.

"Because of the nature of his injuries, you'll be assigned a social worker. He's going to need psychotherapy to recover from the emotional trauma of what he has been through. The physical problems will heal within a couple of months. The emotional trauma will take longer. Ms. Ruth Isadora will be working with you. She's good. You'll like her."

Francie and Frank were holding hands. Frank had unshed tears in his eyes.

"The couple of times he regained consciousness, he fought us and tried to pull his IVs out. He's very pumped up on fear, but I think we have enough sedative in him to relax him for the rest of the night. I didn't put him completely under—it's risky with his head trauma. So I imagine if you call his name, he might rouse again."

They hadn't said a word.

"Do you have any questions?"

Francie shook her head. Frank squeezed her hand.

"I can take you in now. You can stay as long as you want. He's going to need support when he wakes up, and a familiar face will go a long way toward helping him relax."

He led them to the room and opened the door. The room was empty, except for one nurse who was adjusting Jack's IV. Francie drew in her breath when she saw him and covered her mouth with her hands.

"Frank... "

"I know," he said, taking her hand again. He led her over to the bed, and they stood there, staring down at their friend. Frank pulled up a chair for Francie to sit in.

"Why are his wrists wrapped up?" Francie asked.

The doctor glanced at his patient to see if he was still asleep. "His captor hung him by his wrists from the ceiling," he said. "They're pretty torn up."

Frank put his hand to his head and walked away. He stood facing the wall, collecting himself.

"How do you know him?" the doctor asked.

"He's my best friend," Frank said. "We work together, we golf together. We live next door to each other. And Francie, well, he was friends with her brother. She's like a sister to him."

The doctor nodded. "He's in good hands and lucky to have such caring friends," he said. "I need to do rounds. Are you two going to be okay?"

"Yes," Francie said.

He turned to the nurse.

"Abby, I know it's not your job, but can you get them some water?" he asked the nurse.

She nodded and followed the doctor out. She returned a moment later with two Styrofoam cups of water and set them on the table.

"I'll be around if you need me," Abby said. "He might sleep a couple more hours, so try to get some rest while you wait for him to wake up. He's going to need you then."

Francie nodded and thanked Abby. The nurse closed the door quietly behind her.

"Dear God," Frank said. He pulled up another chair and sat by his wife. They just looked at Jack for a few minutes, and then Francie spoke his name.

"Jack?" she said quietly. "Jack, it's Francie."

Nothing.

"Jack?" she said a bit louder.

He didn't move. There was just the steady sound of his breathing.

"Let's let him sleep," Francie said. "I need some time to wrap my mind around what's happening."

Frank stepped out of the room to make some phone calls. When he came back in, nothing had changed. "Sam put Andy to bed. Nobody has heard from Annie."

"What time is it?"

Frank looked at his phone. "Midnight."

"You need to go find her."

"I will." He sat back down and watched his friend sleep. The machine above Jack registered his pulse rate and his oxygen, and every few minutes, the blood pressure cuff would inflate.

"So you know a little about his past?"

"A little," Francie said, glancing at Frank. "He told me a few things when we thought we were dying together in the plane. I was drifting, and he was trying to keep my mind occupied, I think. It worked. I just didn't feel comfortable sharing it with anyone, not even you. I told him he could tell you in his own time."

Frank nodded. They sat there quietly for another hour, listening to the hum of the machines, and the distant voices in the hall. Finally, Frank got up. "I'm going to go find Annie," he said. "Will you be okay?"

"Yes. I'll be sitting here when you get back." She reached up and gave Frank a kiss. "Be careful."

"I talked to Mark in the hall earlier. He said an officer will go with me when I'm ready. He also said to tell you he bought Jack some time."

"They're *not* putting him back in prison?" she whispered.

He squeezed her shoulder. "We'll talk about it later, sweetheart."

He ran his hand through his hair and then left to go find Annie.

It was nearly 3 a.m. when Francie woke up. She had dozed off in the chair. She sat up and rubbed her back, and noticed Jack was stirring in his sleep.

"Jack?" she said.

His good eye fluttered a little, then opened. "Hey, Princess," he said weakly.

She smiled. "Hey."

"You need to hide," he said. "Go. They know who I am."

It took a lot of effort for him to talk.

"We're okay," she said. "My brother is pretty high up in the FBI. He's working on clearing our names." It was a blatant lie; she had no idea if Mark was trying to clear them or if he was preparing their jail cell, but she didn't want to give him something else to be afraid of.

"Hmmmm," he said, closing his eyes again. "I need to get out of here. I can't fight."

"You don't need to fight," she said. "You're safe. There are two armed police officers outside your hospital door. And I'm inside your room. Nobody is going to get past us both."

He lay there quietly for a while, then asked, "Where's Frank?"

"He went to find Annie."

Jack opened his eye again and looked at her. "I don't want to see Annie. I don't want her to see me like this."

"Jack, she's your wife."

"No," he said. "Please, Francie," he struggled to sit up.

"Stop moving," Francie said, watching his oxygen level drop on the monitor. "I'll keep her out."

"Promise."

She was flustered. "Okay, I promise."

"Thank... you." He drifted off again and was quiet for a while. Then he opened his eye, startled, gasping.

"Jack, you're okay," she said. She lowered her voice to a whisper. "You're okay." She softly brushed a lock of his hair back from his good eye.

He met her eyes again. "Don't leave me," he said. "Please."

"I won't," she promised. "I'll stay here with you."

He slipped back into sleep. She sat there with him until 4 a.m., when Frank poked his head in the door. "I found Annie."

Francie got up and walked out of the room, closing the door behind her. Annie was standing next to Frank, who was telling the police officers who she was.

"She's okay," Frank said. "She's his wife."

Francie stayed in the doorframe, the door still shut behind her.

"He's not ready to see you," she said.

Annie stopped short and looked at her. "What do you mean?"

"He asked not to see you tonight."

"That's ridiculous. I'm his wife." She stepped closer to Francie.

Francie put her hand on the doorknob.

"You mean to tell me that you're standing between me and my husband?" Annie asked, a look of hurt and anger in her eyes.

Francie knew her answer was about to change their friendship. "Yes," she said firmly.

Annie laughed and teetered a little bit.

"You're drunk," Francie said.

Annie put her hand to her head. "Maybe a little."

Frank said, "I found her at Diana's. They had just gotten home from the bar."

"You were out *drinking?*" Francie asked. "Do you have any idea what your husband has been through?"

"Frank filled me in. Now move." Annie got right in Francie's face, then staggered and almost tipped over. "I thought you were my friend," she said, slurring her words.

Francie held her ground. "I am."

"We're all tired," Frank said. "If Jack doesn't want to see Annie, I'm going to take her home. Annie, you need to sleep this off."

"I want to go back to Diana's," Annie said. "I left home. I left Jack." She started to cry then.

Frank put his arm around her and led her down the hallway. He called back over his shoulder, "I'll come back in a few hours to get you."

"Okay," Francie said, watching Frank lead her best and only girlfriend out of the hospital.

It had been nice while it lasted.

chapter 59

FRANK RETURNED AT 7 A.M. with a change of clothes for Francie. She washed up as best she could in the bathroom and dressed in new underclothes, fresh jeans, and a t-shirt.

Frank was sitting by Jack's bed when she returned.

"How's he doing?" she asked.

"He hasn't woken up."

"They gave him more pain medication about an hour ago. He'll probably rest for a while."

Frank handed Francie a bagel and a banana.

"Thanks." She peeled the banana and ate it quickly. She was starving.

As she was munching on the bagel, there was a soft knock on the door. A woman stuck her head in.

"Can I come in?" she asked.

"Yes," said Frank, standing.

She offered her hand. "I'm Ruth Isadora, the case worker who was assigned to Jack."

She was older, probably in her late fifties or early sixties, with gray hair and a soft roundness that made her feel grandmotherly. She shook both their hands.

"I'm here to help Jack and to help *you* help Jack," she said. "Together, we're all going to make it through this."

She reached out and squeezed Francie's hands. "I've talked to the authorities and the doctors and an FBI agent who claims to be your brother, so I know some of the story. I was told you are *the woman* to talk to." She looked into Francie's eyes. "It's going to be okay."

She was confident and soft-spoken, leaving Francie with the impression she would be able to make all the bad things go away, at least while she was in the room. "I'm familiar with trauma and have worked with a lot of vets with post-traumatic stress disorder," Ruth continued. "So if we have that, I can help him work with it. He's going to need someone to talk to just to come to grips with the limits his body is going to have for a while. That would be the case with injuries this bad, even if he hadn't been tortured."

Frank pulled up a chair for her.

"I'd rather we talk first in another room," she said. "I try not to keep things from my patients, but I want to start with you two. Is there somewhere we can go?"

"I can't leave him," Francie said.

Dr. Isadora studied Jack for a moment. "Okay," she said. "We can talk later." She took a seat. "Has he been awake?"

"Yes. He's calmer when I'm here."

"Good. I read in his records he was agitated when he awoke. That's good if he trusts you. He needs someone to trust. Where is his wife?"

"She's at home," Frank said. "He doesn't want to see her now."

"He said that?"

"Yes. When he was awake last night."

Dr. Isadora nodded.

"The most important thing you need to know right now is that he's safe. Your brother has been able to arrange it so he can come home to heal. I'm willing to sign any papers I need to in order to make that happen." She looked at both of them. "I'm on your side. No matter who gets involved in this, the courts, the physicians, the family, I am his advocate. It doesn't factor into my job what he has or hasn't done, whether or not he's a criminal. I'm here to help *him*."

Francie nodded, fighting back tears. This woman's kindness and her own lack of sleep were catching up to her. "Dr. Isadora... "

"Ruth. Please call me Ruth."

"Ruth. He's... he's innocent. I need you to know that."

Ruth smiled. "That helps."

Jack was stirring.

"I think we're talking too loudly," Francie whispered.

"No, it's okay. Let's see how he's doing," Ruth said.

Jack's eye fluttered open, and he immediately tried to sit up again, gasping.

Francie stood up so he could see her face. "It's okay. I'm still here. You're in the hospital, and you're safe."

He met her eyes, and he settled back down into the bed, breathing hard, willing his heartrate back to normal. Francie watched the monitor, and slowly, it came back to a normal pulse.

"Francie," he said. "Who is this?" His eye darted to Ruth.

"This is Ruth," Francie said. "She's our friend, your psychologist, and she's on our side."

"I don't need... her," he said, struggling to talk.

"You do," Francie said. "I do too."

"Mr. Banner, is it okay if I call you Jack?" Ruth asked. Jack didn't respond. "I've read your file and know who you really are. The rest of your medical staff does not. You don't have to tell me your deepest secrets—that's not how this works. I'm just here to support you as you need it. But Francie's right— you *do* need me. I'm going to do my best to get you out of the hospital and to keep you out of prison, and it's my word they're going to go on. So you have to work with me."

Jack glanced up at Frank.

"She's good, Jack," he said.

Jack nodded almost imperceptibly.

"Francie... " his voice was hoarse, nearly a whisper.

She pulled her chair closer and sat beside him. "Yes?"

"These drugs... I need less. I can't... fight."

"You don't need to fight," she said. "They said you'd be in a lot of pain without them."

"It's okay," Ruth said. "Let's see what we can do to bring you around more, Jack. What is it about the medication you don't like? You feel too drowsy?"

He nodded.

"We'll let them wear off a little bit, and meanwhile, I'll talk to your doctor. There are other painkillers that won't make you so drowsy. It's all going to depend on how much pain you can tolerate."

"I can tolerate a lot," he said. He tried to rise again.

"Please don't do that," Francie said.

He fell back into the pillows. "Get me out of here, Francie."

"I will. I promise."

Jack drifted off again.

Frank went home, and later on, Steve came in.

"I'm here to relieve you," he said to Francie. He looked at Jack and turned white. "I didn't know it was so bad. Frank tried to warn me but... "

"Steve, I was counting on some levity from you," said Francie.

"Francie, I can't just turn it on," he said. "I'm a jockey, not a comedian."

She smiled, despite it all. "Thanks, but I can't leave. I was just about to lie down here on this chair-bed thing they wheeled in."

"I was given orders from your husband to not take 'no' for an answer," Steve said. "Go. *Get*. Andy needs you."

Ruth was sitting in the room with them. "Francie, go home. You need sleep. I don't have to be anywhere for a few hours, so I'll sit with Steve for a while and fill him in. This is going to be a long road, and you need to be rested and strong for Jack. If you don't take care of yourself, that isn't going to be the case. Go home, be with your little boy, and go to sleep. You can come back tonight. Let's see... it's 10 a.m. I don't want to see you back here until after dinner tonight. Got it?"

Francie hesitated.

"You need to listen to me. I know what I'm doing."

Francie sighed and then got up. "Okay," she said. "But call me if he needs me."

She gave Jack one last look, then turned to Steve. "How am I getting home? Can I borrow your Vette?"

Steve snorted. "That'll be the day. A police officer is waiting in the lobby to give you a ride. You're in protective custody until they make sure there are no more bad guys out there."

"Humph," Francie said, not sure if the protective custody was for her safety or to insure that she didn't leave the country.

Back home, Francie played with Andy and then fixed him lunch. Afterwards, she took a long nap and surprised herself by sleeping until 5 p.m.

"Wow," Frank said when she came downstairs. "You finally got up?"

She smiled and wrapped her arms around him. "Mmmmm."

"You want some dinner?"

"Give me an hour. I'm going for a ride. I need to clear my head. Where's Annie?"

"Staying with a friend. I'll fill you in later."

She called Steve to check in, then, when she was sure everything was okay, she went to the barn.

After a short ride on King and a quick shower, Francie ate dinner with her family. Sam had fixed a roast.

"I've got to get back to the hospital," she said when she finished.

"I'll drive you." Frank grabbed his keys. "Sam's going to put Andy to bed."

Francie hugged her little boy and smelled his sweet hair. *Three year olds are so wonderful,* she thought. It was hard for her to let him go.

"Annie's going to meet us at the hospital," Frank said.

"He doesn't want to see Annie."

"I'm not sure he has a choice. She's his wife."

They met her in the lobby. The two women greeted each other coolly, and when they got to the room, Francie said, "Let me go in first."

Annie stopped and stood with Frank while Francie went in.

Jack was awake and propped up in bed. Some of his bandages had been removed, and the steroids had taken down a lot of the swelling in his face, especially around his eye.

"Hey," Francie said.

"Thank God," Steve said. "There's only so much Pac Man I can play before my mind explodes. Jack has been a gracious host, though. He offered me soap operas."

Steve gestured toward a television, which was turned off.

"You ordered him TV?" Francie said.

"Yes, and got him some food, although he wouldn't eat it. I tasted it. Can't blame him. Stuff's horrid. I told him you'd round him up a Big Mac and chocolate shake before it gets too late."

Francie smiled. "Thanks Steve. Sorry it took me so long to get back."

"See you tomorrow, dude," he said to Jack.

After he left, Francie pulled the metal chair closer to the bed and sat down. "I'm sorry to subject you to Steve for so long. He's enough to drive a person crazy."

Jack smiled.

"You look better," Francie said.

"I feel a bit more human," he said. It was a struggle for him to talk.

"Annie's here," Francie said. His eyes widened, and he started to speak. "She's out in the hall," Francie interrupted. "I know you said you didn't want to see her, but she loves you, and I think you *should* see her. She deserves that much. I don't know what happened between you two, but give her a chance, okay?"

He was quiet for a bit. Then, "I guess."

She watched him for a moment, playing with the corner of his blanket, an odd gesture for such a strong man. He suddenly seemed frail to her.

She reluctantly got up and opened the door. Annie and Frank came in, followed by Ruth.

Annie gasped, then covered her mouth as if to stop the sound from coming out, only she was too late.

"Oh, Jack." Tears sprang to her eyes.

She walked over to his bedside and slowly bent down and gave him a tender kiss on the cheek. "I love you."

He reached up and touched her face with his bandaged hand. "I love you too."

Ruth was standing in the corner, out of the way, looking over his chart.

"They tell me you're coming home soon," Annie said. "I cleaned up the house and put fresh sheets on the bed and put a bouquet on the kitchen table. I'll make you something to eat too... soup? Or... hamburgers?"

Annie sat down in the chair next to his bed and started fumbling with the snap on her purse. "I'm so sorry, Jack. This is all my fault. If you hadn't come looking for me... if I hadn't left... "

"Annie, it's okay," he said.

She looked at him again, then gently reached for his hand. He pulled away. He didn't mean to; it just happened.

"Jack... " She had tears in her eyes. "I've been staying with a girlfriend. You know, Diana from work. She's the one whose house I was going to when... " Her voice trailed off.

"Why don't we leave so they can have some privacy to talk?" Frank said.

Ruth closed the file and went to check Jack's IV. Francie stood up from her chair, uncertain what to do.

"I just need some time," Annie said. "I don't think... "Annie couldn't seem to finish a sentence. She kept fiddling with the clasp on her purse.

Francie felt Frank put a hand on the small of her back to guide her out. She stood her ground, her eyes searching Jack's.

"You need some time," Jack repeated Annie's words, his voice flat. His eyes met Francie's.

Annie turned to Frank and Francie. "Can we be alone?"

Frank whispered, "Let's go," to Francie but she put her hand firmly on the back of her chair.

"Why did that man torture you?" Annie asked.

"I don't want to talk about that now," Jack said.

"Somebody needs to tell me what's going on," Annie said. "How can I help if I don't know the story?"

"Jack?" Ruth said. "Excuse me, Annie. Jack, when's the last time you had some pain medication?"

"They told me the nightmares are worse," Annie said. "I need some sleep. I'm so tired." She had black circles under her eyes and sat, slumped over, barely audible.

"I'm fine," Jack said. He looked tired. Everybody's words were spinning around him. He was breathing heavier. His hands started to tremble. His eyes were darting around the room.

Frank pulled at Francie's arm again, but she pushed his hand away.

"I'll stay part of the night with you," Annie said, reaching for his hand again.

"Don't touch me," Jack said, jerking away from her and ripping his IV out. Medicine started draining out of it, and blood oozed from his arm. "Jack!" Annie said, reaching for the IV and dropping her purse on the floor. Its contents spilled out, and she started to scoop them up.

Frank pulled at Francie again. She noticed that Jack was starting to sweat. He tried to sit up but was unable to push himself up with his hands. He collapsed back onto his pillows, breathing hard.

He gritted his teeth and took a deep breath. "Everybody out!" Jack shouted. "Francie, stay. EVERYBODY ELSE OUT!"

He shouted the words so violently that they echoed around the room. Ruth took Annie by the elbow and ushered her and Frank out, firmly shutting the door behind them. Jack turned so his back was to Francie, and he laid down, trying to calm his breathing and reduce the pain in his rib cage.

He couldn't get comfortable. Francie pulled her chair back up to the bed and sat down.

"I'm sorry," he said, breathing hard. "Annie's going to hate you now."

"That's okay," Francie said. "She'll get over it."

Someone tapped quietly on the door, and Dr. Tremper came in. He sat down on the other side of the bed, looking at Jack. His hands were folded in his lap, and when he spoke, his voice was soft.

"I won't bother you long," he said, "but as your doctor, I'm required to help you." He briefly smiled his grandfatherly smile. Then he grew serious. "Jack, what's your pain level now? On a scale of one to ten, with ten being the worst, where is it?"

"I'm fine," Jack said through gritted teeth.

"Do you want me to leave?" Francie asked.

Jack shook his head no.

"I need a number for your charts," Dr. Tremper said softly. "I don't think you're fine."

Jack was quiet for a few moments. Finally, he said, "Eight."

The doctor glanced at Francie.

"What hurts the most? Is it your head?" he asked.

Jack shook his head again. He was still breathing hard. "The burns," he said quietly.

Dr. Tremper nodded. He filled a syringe and walked over to his patient. "This won't make you too drowsy or do anything else odd to you, but it should help the pain." He pulled up Jack's sleeve and shot the syringe into his bicep.

Then he carefully wiped the blood from Jack's arm where the IV had been pulled out. "If you promise to eat and drink, I can leave this out," he said. His voice was quiet, his hands soft. Jack nodded, never lifting his head from his pillow.

The doctor sat back down and watched his patient for a few minutes. The room was so quiet that Francie could hear the ticking of the minute hand on the wall clock. Slowly, Jack's breathing returned to normal, and he started to relax.

"How's the pain now?" Dr. Tremper asked.

"Three," Jack said.

Dr. Tremper nodded. "Don't let it get that bad again," he said. He glanced at Francie. "Jack, tell Francie when you need more, okay?"

Jack nodded yes. He closed his eyes.

"Can you stay with him a while?" Dr. Tremper asked Francie.

"Yes."

"I'll tell your family to give you some time. I think your husband is going to drive Mrs. Banner home. Ruth said she'd be back later tonight to talk with you."

"Okay," Francie said. "We'll be okay."

Dr. Tremper smiled. "You're in good hands, Jack."

That evening, Ruth came back into the room with Frank. He brought Francie some dinner and set it on the desk.

"How are things?" Ruth asked quietly and sat down in the chair next to Francie. Frank stood behind Francie and rubbed her shoulders.

"Good," Francie said. She had been reading a magazine while Jack slept. The shoulder rub felt good.

Jack opened his eyes and saw Frank.

"Where's Annie?"

"Sorry to wake you," Frank said. "I took Annie back to Diana's."

"I wasn't sleeping. Just resting."

"I've done a lot of marriage counseling, and I know Annie loves you, Jack," Ruth said. "PTSD is tough on spouses too. I think she's just tired and needs some rest. Let's give her a few days."

Jack didn't answer.

"Tomorrow's our golf day," Frank said. "I suppose I should cancel our t-time?"

Jack gave a little smile. "You need... the practice."

Frank smiled. "I don't need practice. I can win without that."

"Not hardly."

Frank gave Francie's shoulder a squeeze. "I'm going to leave my wife here with you tonight and head home. I'll see you both in the morning."

Francie got up and hugged him hard. "Thanks," she said into his ear.

"For what?"

"For being you."

Everybody left, and the room was finally quiet. Ruth had made the recliner chair into a bed for Francie, and she fluffed up her pillow and put on some sheets.

It was only 9 p.m., but Francie was tired. Before she turned in, she peeked out into the hall. The police officers were still standing there, along with Gunny, the new bodyguard she had hired. Gunny was an ex-Marine and had come highly recommended by her security staff.

"Just making sure you're still here," she said.

Gunny smiled. "I am. But they have the man in custody. I think you're both safe."

"Thanks."

She crawled into her makeshift bed and was soon asleep.

She awoke much later to Jack calling her name. She sat up, adrenaline pumping.

"I'm here."

The room was dark, except for the faint light of the machine monitoring his vitals. He was breathing heavily.

"Sorry, Princess. Just a bad dream."

"I suspect you're going to have a lot of those this week." She reached her hand toward his, but he pulled away.

"Don't," he said.

"Do you want to talk about it?"

"I don't remember it," he said.

His breathing returned to normal, and Francie laid back down on her bed. The room was quiet for a while.

"Actually, that's not quite true," he said, his voice low. "I remember it vividly."

"Oh?"

There was a long silence.

"Remember when Cassie was... ?" he began, then took a few deep breaths. "While I was a POW... " He was struggling to get the words out. "There were several men. A gang. I was tied up and couldn't fight but I tried, and that's why my wrists... "

He was quiet for a while. She could hear him breathing hard.

"It happened a lot. It was... brutal."

Francie wanted to reach out to him, but she knew the last thing he needed was sympathy. He was staring at the ceiling, his eyes full of pain.

She sat up and put her hand on the bed rail. "Can I have your hand?" she asked. It felt strange to ask the question. When he didn't answer, she slowly put her hand inside of his, the best she could with the bandages. A tear escaped the corner of his eye and rolled down his cheek. He wouldn't meet her eyes.

"Don't tell anyone else."

She shook her head. "I won't."

"I should have been able to stop it. I tried... it went on for two years, Francie. Two years."

His hands began to shake. Another tear.

"Are you okay?" she asked softly.

He continued to stare at the ceiling. "No," he said. "I'm not. I think I could use some more pain medication."

She called in the nurse, and the woman gave him another shot.

He squeezed Francie's hand with his good fingers. "Don't leave."

"I won't. I promise."

He was soon asleep.

The next morning, they got him up and walked him around. Francie was asked to step outside while the physical therapist assessed him, and he was okay with that. She noticed all the people working with him were women, and she smiled. Good ol' Ruth.

Ruth pulled Frank and Francie into a back room.

"If today goes well, I'm going to release him tomorrow," Ruth said. "It's early, and normally, they wouldn't release him yet, but Dr. Tremper agrees with me that he might be able to rest better at home. He's going to need a lot of care, so you'll probably need an in-home nurse for a few days. He'll need somebody to fix his meals and to be with him at night, I think, until we see how these nightmares go."

"I can do that," Francie said, glancing at Frank.

Ruth looked at Frank too.

Frank shrugged. "He does live right next door," he said. "I can take care of our three year old if he gets up at night."

"I think you need help for a few days," Ruth said.

"We'll be fine," Francie insisted.

Ruth studied Francie for a moment. "You're a very determined woman. You don't trust easily."

"We'll be fine alone," Francie repeated.

"Okay," Ruth said. "In that case, this meeting just got longer. Do you know how to give shots?"

"I give them to horses all the time," Francie said.

Ruth laughed, a rich, deep sound. "Okay." She pulled out a syringe. "But you still have to practice on oranges. You'll have to administer pain medication if needed."

Francie obediently practiced on an orange.

"You pass," said Ruth.

"Ruth?" Francie said. "Jack talked to me last night and told me some of what happened to him in his past." She looked at Frank. "He asked me not to share it with anybody else."

"He trusts you," Ruth said. Her face turned serious. "Francie, it's very important he has someone he can trust. It's amazing what all he has been through, and then to go through this recent attack... quite honestly, I'll be surprised if he completely pulls out of this. He's going to need support, and it looks like he has chosen you. I can't get a word out of him. Also, if he has suppressed memories, as you said, it looks like they're starting to surface. It's not going to be an easy road."

"I'll be fine," Francie said. "And he'll completely pull out of this. You'll see. Are we done?"

Ruth smiled. "You can go."

Francie left, and Frank stayed behind and closed the door.

"Speaking of trust, you're right. Francie doesn't trust easily, and she has decided to trust you. Thank you for that," Frank said.

"You're an amazing couple," Ruth said. "Jack has very good friends. He may be just fine."

Later that day, Francie was home for a few hours, catching up on some work in her office, when her security guard called her.

"Your brother is here to see you. He's alone."

"If he's unarmed, he can come in. Check him good. He carries a second gun in his boot and who knows what else."

There was a moment of silence. Then, "He says it's against policy for him to remove his weapons. He says he's here to offer you a deal, and you'll like it."

Francie sighed dramatically and ran her hands through her hair. "Fine. Send him in."

She called Frank into her office, and they were both there when Gunny let Mark into the room. He left, closing the door behind him.

Francie stood up with a wand.

"Really?" Mark said, holding his arms out away from his sides. "Sweeping me for wires?"

"You can't be too careful," Francie said.

"Of what?"

She frowned, but said nothing and, satisfied that he was clean, sat down behind her desk. Frank was behind her, sitting on the window seat.

Mark sat down in one of the chairs across from her desk.

"Paul Lawson, aka Jack Banner, is on the FBI's most wanted list. That's quite a fugitive you've been harboring."

She was silent.

"Evidence strongly suggests that he did the crime he was in for, which was killing an general of the US Army. But you knew that."

When neither of them spoke, he went on.

"I've talked to some folks, and due to the respectful and productive life he has lived here, it's not likely that he's any longer a threat to the US Government. But more importantly, given the amount of police brutality he faced a few days ago, and given some of the records I pulled up of mistreatment in federal prison by some of the guards there, I believe he has a case against the local police force and the US Government. I'm trying to work out a deal to keep him out of prison. If he promises not to sue for damages to his body, I can maybe get him released of his charges and exonerated. He won't go back to prison. But it's going to take me a while."

Francie was speechless. When she could speak, all she could say was, "Really?"

"Yes, really," Mark said. "Or how about, brother, I was so wrong about my employee, and you were so right?"

Francie ignored that. "So he might be free? Forever?"

"I'm trying," Mark said. "For you."

Francie couldn't stop a smile from spreading across her face. Wait until she told Jack!

"Then there's the matter of who paid for his escape," he said. "Apparently, a high-level team went in and pulled him out, disarming most of the security and managing to get out of there without killing a soul. It seems his benefactor had a conscience."

Mark watched her carefully. She didn't react.

"It was a pretty costly endeavor, I'd assume. Funny how you liquidated your assets around that same time."

"I bought a blue jeans company," she said.

"In New York. Yes, I remember that. A pretty run-down building for all that cash you paid. And you sold Frank your farm? Wow—you were going through a mid-life something or other."

"Just get on with your story," Francie said. Mark smiled. She was flustered and could tell that he knew.

"There is absolutely no trace of who was involved. The people who did it were good, and the trail is cold after all these years. My main suspect is Jim, but he's dead now, so we can't prosecute him. He's probably the reason Jack wound up here at your farm. I'm just glad you were okay, working side by side with a fugitive all these years and not even knowing it." His voice had a trace of mockery to it.

"So that's it?" Frank said. "The story comes to an end?"

"Looks like," Mark said. He looked at Francie. "Your man may be free. And you—you're off the hook. But let's keep his identity under wraps for now."

She didn't know what to say. She wanted to throw her arms around him and thank him for pulling strings, but she didn't want to admit to anything. She didn't quite trust him. She never had.

"Thank you," she finally managed.

"One more thing," Mark said. He pulled a cassette tape out and laid it on her desk. "Stanton tortured Jack to try to get the name of his benefactor, of the person who paid for his escape, and was recording it for proof when he talked," he said. "I've been in this business for quite a number of years, and I've never heard anyone hold up so well under torture. He was prepared to die for the person who helped him and very nearly did. He never gave a name or even a hint of who was involved."

He tapped the tape with his finger.

"It's hard to listen to," he said, his voice softening. His eyes met Francie's. "If you ever question his loyalty, give it a listen. You pick your employees well."

Mark got up. "I've got to get back to work. We have a case back in LA that I have to work for a while. Good luck, and I wish Jack the best with his healing."

After he left, Frank and Francie sat there numbly, looking at the tape for a few minutes. Finally, Francie took it and put it away in her locked file drawer.

"Wow," she said.

Frank came and put his arms around her. "It's over," he said. "Neither of you has to hide anymore."

chapter
60

FRANK PULLED UP IN THE SUV the next morning to take Jack home. Francie wheeled him out in a wheelchair as per hospital policy. There were no cops present, no doctors, not even family. Just the three of them.

When she had told Jack the evening before what Mark had said, he hadn't reacted as strongly as she'd hoped. He just smiled a little and said, "I'm glad you're safe, Princess."

She opened the passenger side door for Jack and, with great difficulty, they managed to get him from the chair to the car. It was hard because his ribs hurt, and he tried to push himself up with his hands, but they were broken, so it was all legs. By the time he moved that short distance, he had broken out into a sweat.

They drove home in silence and got him into his house, where he sat on the couch, resting.

Francie put away the flowers and cards and got him a glass of water.

"Are we all set?" Frank asked.

"Yes, thanks, hon. I'll be home in a bit."

Frank left, and Francie handed Jack the glass of water. He took it awkwardly, holding it with bandaged fingers, and drank.

Then he leaned forward to set it on the coffee table, but the pain stopped him.

Francie took it from him, and sat down on the coffee table, holding it in her hand. "Here's the plan," she said. "I'm going to make sure you have everything you need, then I'm going to go back to my office and work. In the mornings, I'll train White December. He's the only horse I'm working with now, remember? Then I'll come and fix you some breakfast. After that, you can shower or whatever, and I'll come back around 11 a.m. to discuss work with you. If you're up to it. Then we'll have lunch, and I'll go back home until dinner, bring you some dinner, and then come back later. I plan to spend the nights here for a while. Sound good?"

Jack looked at her with tired eyes.

"I don't need your help."

"Yes, you do."

She held up a plastic bag. "I also have a whole bag of syringes here, and when your pain gets too bad, I can give you a shot."

He raised an eyebrow. "You give shots?"

"I sure do. Well, to horses anyway, but Ruth seems to think I'm competent enough to give them to people as well." She smiled.

"I don't need them."

"You can't very well run from me," Francie said.

Jack looked around the room, and his eyes rested on a pair of Annie's shoes by the door. They were her barn shoes, which she probably didn't need where she was. The house seemed so empty without Annie, but Francie didn't comment on that.

"There are canned soups in the cabinet, and I brought the electric can opener over from our house, so if you get hungry before I get back, you can cook," she said. "There's fresh fruit and milk for cereal. I think that's about it."

She looked at his hands and realized that he probably couldn't handle pouring milk just yet. "But I plan to do the meals."

He was looking down at his hands too. He was quiet.

"Hey," she said.

He looked up.

"You with me on this?"

He nodded. "I'm tired now. Can I rest?"

"Yes," Francie said. But she still sat there.

"Out with it, Princess."

She hesitated. "If I leave, are you going to be okay? I mean"—she sighed—"*are* you?"

"You mean, am I going to try to kill myself?"

She swallowed. "You promised me once that you wouldn't."

They looked at each other for a few moments. Then Jack said, "I fought pretty hard to make sure that bastard didn't kill me. I have several people counting on me, so I'm here to stay for as long as the good Lord allows. Okay?"

Francie nodded. "Okay."

She set his glass down on a coaster beside her.

"Jack? Mark told me why Stanton tortured you. Stanton taped it, hoping you would talk. I didn't listen to the tape. But I know." Her voice was nearly a whisper. "Thank you."

Jack absorbed this information for a moment before he spoke. "Well, we have to look out for each other. Isn't that what you said the first day we met? That was all I was doing. Looking out for you."

She smiled and swallowed, fighting back emotion. Then she handed him his cell phone.

"Keep this in your pocket. You have Frank's number and mine on speed dial. Call us if you need us. I'll be back in two hours to help with lunch."

"Okay. Now go. I need some rest."

He laid down on the couch, his head on the pillow, and closed his eyes. "The pain is tolerable now. I'll let you know if it gets worse."

"Okay."

She left.

Surprisingly, they had a good first night at home. The oral painkillers were working well, and Francie didn't need to give any shots. Jack slept soundly, and despite his protests, Francie took the couch and slept well herself. She was shocked when she didn't wake up until 8 a.m. and realized she was very late to the barn.

chapter
61

"HOLY MOTHER OF—" STEVE SAID as Francie walked into the barn. "I thought you were going to sleep until next year."

"Sorry," she said, holding her coffee between her hands. "Do you have time to work December?"

He laughed. "I came down to saddle him. Frank told me to let you sleep, so I figured I could breeze him myself, but since you're here, you can be an actual trainer."

She laughed and led her horse out to the track. She felt good after such a long night's sleep. She had awakened once to help Jack take more pain medication, but other than that, the two of them had slept through the night.

Steve climbed aboard his horse and took him out to the dirt track behind Francie's barn. They had decided not to race him as a two year old, giving him time to relax and fully recover from his wounds. But she was pleased with how he was handling training.

"We might have a Derby contender on our hands," she said when Steve finished and brought the horse back to her.

"That's what I'm thinking," he said, patting his mount on the neck.

Francie cooled the horse off herself, then went up to the house to work in her office for a little bit before returning to Jack.

When she walked into his house, he was fumbling with the can opener. She startled him, and his hands slipped. The soup, half-opened, spilled on the floor. He swore and kicked the can across the room.

"I knocked," she said.

"I know."

He leaned against the counter, out of breath. He was sweating from exertion.

"Go sit down. This is what I'm here for," she said. He said nothing and went back to the couch. She cleaned up the soup and opened another can, warming it on the stove. She poured it into two mugs and took one over to Jack.

"Here."

"I'm not hungry anymore," he said.

She assessed him. His breathing was normal. "How's your pain?"

"Good. Three."

"Well, I'm going to eat." She sat his mug down and sat on the coffee table with her soup.

"We have chairs," he said.

"I prefer this," she answered.

There was a knock at the door.

"Send whoever it is away," Jack said.

She went to the door and saw it was his visiting nurse. She was a petite blond woman in her forties. "I've come to change your bandages," she said in a sweet, cheerful voice. Francie let her in.

"I'm fine," Jack said.

But the woman came over to him anyway with her case of supplies. "Let's get you to your bedroom. I need to take your shirt off to do this."

Francie sat at the table while Jack obediently followed the nurse into the bedroom. She stirred her soup; it was too hot to eat. She decided to look for some crackers.

The nurse had closed the door, but she heard Jack moan loudly from the bedroom, as if in pain. He moaned a few more times. Francie held her box of crackers, unmoving, wondering if she should interfere. She decided not to and sat back down at the table to finish her soup.

The nurse came out about a half hour later, closing the door behind her. "I gave him a shot for pain," she said. "I told him to rest. Those burns are painful, and I can guarantee that changing the bandages hurts."

"Is he okay?"

"He's fine, just hurting. But the shot will kick in soon. I'll be back tomorrow. In the meantime, if you notice any signs of infection—more pain, redness, swelling—you need to call his doctor."

"Okay," Francie said, knowing she would have no idea if infection did set in. Jack would never tell her.

As she was letting the nurse out, Ruth arrived.

"How's he doing?" Ruth asked, looking around the room.

"He's resting."

She and Ruth talked for about a half hour, about bandages and pain medication, and Ruth gave Francie a twenty-four-hour number to call her if she needed her. "For anything," Ruth said.

Then she knocked quietly on Jack's door and heard a muffled, "Come in."

"It's Ruth. Can I talk to you for a few minutes?"

She went in and closed the door, leaving Francie with her empty mug. She came out about ten minutes later.

"He won't talk to me," she said quietly. "He needs to talk to somebody about this. I'm hoping he'll be willing to talk to you."

"Things have been good so far," Francie said.

"It's encouraging that he had a good night. He may be just fine," Ruth said.

But he wasn't.

That night, Francie dreamed about Star. She was sixteen again, riding the mare across the field, grass blowing sideways in the wind. The sun was shining down hot, and Star's hooves thundered across the ground in a rhythmic speed. The gate was ahead of them, and the mare tugged at the reins, asking for Francie to let her jump.

Francie nudged her on, giving her permission. She felt Star gather her muscles and felt the powerful thrust as the horse left the ground, sailing up toward the gate.

Crash!

Something was wrong, and Francie felt herself falling. She heard screams and woke up, grasping the side of the couch and hugging her pillow. She sat up, fully awake, but the screaming continued.

Jack!

Stumbling in the dark, she stubbed her toe on the coffee table and half-hobbled, half-ran toward his bedroom. She heard another crash and flipped on the bedroom light, blinding herself. Quickly, she flipped it off again, now blinded by light spots in her eyes.

"No!" he was yelling, but his voice wasn't coming from the bed.

Her eyes refocused in the dim light cast from the nightlight in the kitchen. He was on the floor against the far wall, his hands over his head, rocking back and forth. Her head spun from getting up so quickly. She bent down, putting her head low to force some blood into it before she passed out.

"Stop!" he screamed, shying away from some unseen terror. "Stop!"

"Jack!" Francie said, getting down and crawling toward him. She quieted her voice. "Jack."

She arrived where he was and kneeled in front of him, unsure of what to do next. She knew better than to touch him.

"Jack," she said, firmly, now in control of herself. "Jack, it's Francie. I need you to look at me."

He held his head in his shaking hands and continued to rock and whimper, some type of noise that sounded half-animal, half-human. One of the splints on his right index finger was torn and dangling. She saw something dark on his white t-shirt and guessed it was blood; he had probably reopened his burn wounds.

He wrapped one arm around himself in a half-hug, keeping the other one on his head, then moaned again as he hit his burns and broken ribs.

"Jack," she said, afraid he'd hurt himself worse. "Jack!" She spoke louder, more firmly.

She had to see his face, to make him look at her. She had to know if he was awake.

She gently took hold of his wrist, to pull his hand away from his face.

He flinched like she had hit him, slamming himself back against the wall. "Don't touch me!" he said. She took her hand away, sorry for what she'd had to do, but it had worked. It had broken whatever dream state he was in. His eyes traveled around the room, then met hers in the near darkness.

"Francie... make it stop. Please." His voice was raspy, his eyes full of fear.

"You're okay," she said, keeping her voice firm and matter of fact. "You had a bad dream. You're safe."

He continued to rock, and the shaking in his hands traveled up his arms and took over his whole body. He sat there, against the wall, shivering and bleeding.

"Make it stop."

She reached over and pulled a blanket off the bed, lightly draping it over him. He tried to grasp it, and his dangling splint caught on the edge, tearing it off. He gasped and put his head back in his hands; the rocking becoming more intense.

"Make it stop. Help me." His voice was a rough whisper.

"Make *what* stop?" she said, feeling a little frightened.

"The war. It won't go away. The men. I need to get out of here."

"Jack, you're home," she said.

He continued to rock, his arms wrapped around himself. The blanket fell off, and she tried to put it back on, but he flinched away from her touch.

"Please don't touch me," he said.

"Jack, I need for you to look at me. I need to know you're here with me."

"I've got to get out of here," he said and tried to get up. The pain in his ribs stopped him, and he moaned, sitting back down and gasping for breath. He was sweating and breathing hard.

"Francie... help me. Make it stop."

She didn't know if he meant the physical pain or the mental pain.

"Do you need pain killers?"

He moaned again, and she saw the bleeding was getting worse. She got up get a syringe full of pain medicine, then saw her phone on the coffee table. She grabbed it and dialed Ruth's number.

"Hello?" came a voice on the other end almost immediately.

"Ruth, this is Francie. I need you to come. Jack's had a dream, and I'm not sure if he's awake."

"I'll be there in fifteen minutes," she said. "Stay with him and keep talking."

Francie went back to the room and sat next to Jack, who was quietly shaking on the floor. She called her security up front and told them to let Ruth in, not to search her, and to please make it quick.

She hung up and waited. It was the longest fifteen minutes of her life. She heard a knock on the door and ran to answer it.

"He won't wake up. I don't know if he's here or still in the dream, and he's bleeding."

"Okay," said Ruth in her calm voice. "Let's see."

Ruth got down on the floor next to him. "Jack? This is Ruth. Francie needs to see your eyes."

"Please, make it stop," he said, his voice so low and full of pain it was almost unrecognizable.

"We need you to sit up first. I need to be sure you're awake."

Slowly, Jack lifted his shaking hand away from his face and looked up at Francie.

"Francie," he said. "Help me."

Ruth pulled out a vial and filled a syringe. "I'm going to give you a shot. I need to touch you to do this." She put a firm hand on Jack's arm, and he flinched but didn't pull away. Quickly and expertly, she pushed the medicine into his bicep, then sat back. "You're going to sleep for a while with no dreams. You'll be okay."

Jack started to relax, and within a minute or two, his head dropped. Ruth caught him in her arms and gently laid him the rest of the way on the ground. Francie got a pillow and put it under his head.

"That's Symatrex," Ruth said. "It'll put him out for about six hours. It's a strong sedative, and it's also a bit of an amnesiac, so he probably won't remember the last twenty or thirty minutes."

"Just as well," Francie said. She slumped against the wall. She hadn't noticed how tense her muscles were until she now tried to relax them. "Wow."

Ruth sat back on her bottom and looked at Francie. "Are you okay?"

Francie nodded. "Yes. Thank you so much for coming."

"I'm going to leave you this vial. Store it in the fridge. Only give the Symatrex to him once a day, or night is more likely when you'll have to use it. It has to go into a large muscle—his arm or his thigh if you can't get to the arm. Only use it when he's like this, and be careful to measure accurately. Like I said, it's a strong sedative."

Ruth tended to his bleeding the best she could; most of it had stopped. She said the nurse could rebandage it in the morning, along with the finger.

The two women stretched him out on the floor and covered him with a blanket. He was too heavy to lift into the bed, and they were afraid of hurting his sides. After Ruth left, Francie changed the sweat-soaked sheets on the bed and remade it. Then she lay down on the comforter, her head on one of his pillows, so she could be in the same room with him. The events of the night had left her exhausted, and she was soon fast asleep.

Francie was sitting at Jack's kitchen table the next morning, going over some breeding contracts. Flame was still making them the most money by far, with his stud fee at one million.

The house was quiet. Sunlight drifted through the front windows and filtered across the floor. Jack was still sleeping in the next room. He hadn't moved all night.

She slept until 9 a.m. and had only gotten up about a half hour ago. She had washed up at the kitchen sink, brushed her teeth, and was now munching on a bagel as she worked.

She heard Jack get up and go into the master bathroom. The pipes creaked as hot water pumped up from the tank and ran through them. The house was still cool from the night with the air conditioning on.

After a few minutes, Jack came out, clean-shaven and dressed in loose shorts and a fresh t-shirt. She wondered how it was he managed to shave so well.

"Good morning," she said, keeping her voice cheerful, as if nothing had happened.

He sat down across from her. She tapped the bag in front of her with her pencil. "Bagels," she said. "That's what they had this morning at the Big House. Sam brought the leftovers to us." She bent her head back to her paperwork. It was amazing how many people wanted to breed their mares to Flame. Lucky guy. She had to be careful, or she wouldn't have any reserved for herself. A stallion could only service so many mares.

Jack sat across from her, looking down at his broken hands. He traced a fingertip down the side of the finger that used to have a splint on it. He tried to rub off some of the adhesive left over from the bandages, but it was too sore. The finger was bruised and still a little swollen.

He started to speak, then stopped. Instead, he reached over and took a bagel out of the bag. He set it on a napkin and stared at it.

"What happened last night?" he finally asked.

Francie kept writing. "You had a bad dream that wouldn't go away. I called Ruth, and she gave you a sedative. We were afraid to lift you up to the bed because of your ribs, so that's why you woke up on the floor."

Jack was quiet, pondering the information she had just given him. He tried to pry his bagel apart to put some cream cheese on it, but he couldn't get his fingers to work, so he gave up and took a bite of it plain.

"Was it bad?"

"Yes." Francie looked up. "How much of last night do you remember?"

"Enough," he said. "I don't remember Ruth being here though."

"The sedative is a bit of an amnesiac. She said you'd lose about twenty minutes."

She went back to her papers, sorting them by months. Most mares were bred early in the year. A horse was pregnant for eleven months, and owners targeted an early spring baby, even as early as February if they lived in a warmer climate. That's because the Thoroughbred registry considered horses' birthdays on January first of their birth year. Racing horses would start in the Kentucky Derby, for example, all as three-year-olds. But, if your horse was born in February, and the other horses were born in April, you would have a two-month age advantage on them. Plus, bigger horses sold better at the yearling auctions.

She glanced up at Jack. His hands were trembling, and he was having trouble with his bagel.

"Where were you last night?" she asked. "During the dream?"

He got up and went over to the sink. Carefully, he took down a glass and filled it with water and took a long drink. He brought it back to the table and sat down. He worked on his bagel some more, and she figured he wasn't going to answer, so she went back to her work.

When he spoke, his voice was so soft she could barely hear him. "A wooden box," he said. "They used to put me in a box. There were men coming to get me. I could hear them. I'm not sure what was worse. Being in the box or going through whatever it was they did to me when they got me out."

She put her pencil down. He was looking down at his hands again. They were shaking more. He swallowed the lump in his throat and closed his eyes.

"I got you out this time," she said. He raised his eyes to hers. "Whenever you come out of one of those dreams, the box or whatever, I'll be here."

He looked at her for a moment, saying nothing. Then he nodded at the bag of bagels.

"There's a blueberry bagel in there," he said. "Do you want to split it with me?"

She smiled. "Remember where we were the last time we split a blueberry bagel?"

"Yes, I do," he said.

"We made it through that together," she said. "We'll make it through this."

She took it out of the bag and cut it in half. "I cut, you choose."

He picked the larger half and almost smiled.

Instead of going to the barn that morning, Francie went home to work out. She wanted to stay while the nurse and Ruth visited, but Jack insisted he would only let her help him if she kept some semblance of a normal life. She wondered what "normal" was.

She was angry. When she found Steve in the basement lifting weights, she asked him to spar with her. He obliged, and the two of them went at it for a while.

"Wow, got a little anger this morning, sis?" he said, ducking a blow she directed toward him. He returned with a round kick, aimed for her midsection, and she grabbed his foot, twisted, and threw him to the ground.

He lay there, laughing. "Apparently so," he answered his own question.

"It's not directed at you," Francie said, wiping sweat from her forehead with the back of her arm and helping him up. "I'm just mad."

"Because of what happened to Jack?"

She swung at him, and he ducked again. She was good—he had trained her well—but he was better. Their usual sparring match was about her holding nothing back, and him defending. Every now and then, he'd throw something at her to see if she was paying attention.

"Because of what happened to Jack, yes. Because of that, because of the whole stupid criminal system, because Annie left him... left us *all* really, and because life just sucks. I mean, how much more do we have to go through?" She got in a nice round kick that hit him on the thigh.

"Ow," he said, hopping back. He jumped at her, grabbed her wrist, and threw her (somewhat gently) to the ground, pinning her down.

"As I recall, you knew this, or worse, might happen when you sprung him."

"I thought I would go to jail. I didn't think he would get tortured."

"Mark was going to shoot him a few years ago."

"Mark wouldn't have shot him," Francie said.

"He'll be okay."

"Let me up."

"You have to figure out how to get up."

Francie thought for a moment. "Unless you want a knee to the groin, then let me up. That's all I can think of."

"Good," he said, "but there's one other way. You could headbutt me. The way I'm leaning in, you'd have me. By the way, how's my breath? I brushed this morning."

She grinned, and he let her up.

"Want to go again?" he asked.

"Yes."

They sparred for a while more. He let her get a few good kicks in.

"Don't let it get to you, Francie."

When they quit, she went upstairs and showered. She no longer had her daily 11 a.m. meeting with Jack to prepare for. The morning visits of his care team kept him busy, and he wasn't yet up to meeting for work.

She wrapped a towel around her hair and returned a call from Rosa in New York.

"Good morning," Rosa said. "How are you? We miss you here."

It was Thursday morning, the time when she and Jack would usually fly in for their staff meeting. She and Rosa talked about the ad campaign and how well it was going and how well their fall line was selling. Their winter ideas were hitting the racks now in some parts of the country.

After a while on the phone, Rosa asked, "What kind of accident was Jack in? You were very sketchy on the phone. Is he doing okay now that he's out of the hospital?"

Francie was quiet, thinking of how to answer. Finally, she sighed and said, "Rosa, I'm not going to lie to you. Just know that he was hurt pretty bad, and it's going to take him a while to heal. He has some bad burns. I don't want to discuss it now, but eventually I'll tell you the story. It's just... complicated."

Rosa, in her usual manner that made Francie thankful every day for hiring her, said, "Sure thing. Just know we're all here for you both."

Francie hung up and sat on her bed. Her Bible lay on her nightstand, untouched since the day Jack had been abducted. Although she hadn't read her Bible lately, she had prayed, nearly constantly, *Please God, help Jack to be okay. Please God, help Annie to be okay. Please God, please God, please God*, but it was more pleading than prayer. She realized that she was angrier with God, really, then she was at anyone else. It was God who had let her down.

She was staring at her Bible and frowning when Frank walked in. He sat down on the bed and wrapped his arms around her. He smelled fresh, like morning air and new hay.

"I love you," he said.

"I love you too," she said.

"I missed you at the barn this morning. Is Jack okay?"

"Yes. I just needed to hit something, and Steve was willing to spar with me."

She felt Frank smile against her cheek. "Good old Steve."

She turned to face Frank. "Actually, Jack's okay now, but we had a really hard night." She told him what had happened and why she had called Ruth in.

"And I'm angry," she said. "Which is why I had to hit something."

"Angry at who?"

"I'm angry at God," she said. "Why did He let this happen? Don't you think Jack has been through enough? And on top of it all, his wife left him. It's just not fair. Isn't God supposed to protect us?"

"He tells us not to be afraid," Frank said. "Which implies there's something to fear."

Francie crossed her arms. "When Ken died, I kept reading Psalm 91 and kept asking God to help me, to protect me. I was in pain, I was sad, and most importantly, I figured if He could take my brother, sister, husband, and niece, what *else* could He do? It became not so much what could God do *for* me, but what God could let happen *to* me."

She wrapped her arms more tightly around herself. "I don't trust God."

Frank reached over, took her Bible, and opened it to Psalm 91. He read it aloud to her.

"Whoever dwells in the shelter of the Most High will rest in the shadow of the Almighty. I will say of the Lord, 'He is my refuge and my fortress, my God, in whom I trust.'"

His voice was steady and strong. Francie had to admit there was something comforting about hearing scripture read aloud.

"For he will command his angels concerning you, to guard you in all your ways."

When he got to that verse, she raised an eyebrow. He paused, smiled, then kept reading.

Francie listened quietly. He finished with, "Because he loves me," says the Lord, "I will rescue him; I will protect him, for he acknowledges my name. He will call on me, and I will answer him; I will be with him in trouble, I will deliver him and honor him—"

"See?" Francie interrupted. "God promises to keep us safe. That's what that Psalm clearly says. To send angels to watch over us and to protect us. Ha! I'm not feeling safe at the moment."

"The Bible never promises us that bad things won't happen," said Frank. "God just promises to be with us when they do. And if we are His children, nothing can happen without His permission, so we have to figure that God allowed this to happen to Jack. I don't think God is happy about it, but we have free will, and man does some terrible things. But God can bring *good* from *all* terrible things. We can always find something good."

"What good came out of Ken and Krista and your sweet little baby dying?" she challenged him. "What good came of *that?*"

Frank brushed her hair back behind her ear and ran his hand down the side of her cheek, gently touching her. He looked into her eyes with his soft, kind eyes that she had always loved.

"Andy," he said.

That silenced some of the anger in her. *Andy.* How she loved that cherubic little three year old.

But she wasn't ready to let Frank—or God—off the hook.

"So it's good that you lost so much to gain Andy? Is that how it has to work?"

"It's not how it has to work. It's just how it does. I happen to believe God wept with us when we lost our loved ones. Then He blessed us with Andy. He gave us back some joy. We're blessed with Andy and with each other."

She lowered her gaze, taking his hand and turning it over in her palm. She traced the lines on it, the fingers. Then she brought it to her lips and kissed it before she spoke.

"I don't mean to belittle what we have... "

"I know. And I don't mean to suggest that I'm glad Krista's gone so I can have you. Never."

"Oh, honey, I know. But you're right. There have been so many blessings, and we've been given so much."

"The kids are in college and doing well. Sam and Steve are adopting little Lexie. She's so wonderful," said Frank.

"The farm is doing good. Dalton Jeans is doing excellent."

"And Jack was saved. Francie, their death, and our resulting faith through it, is what brought Jack to Christ. Don't ever, for a minute, forget that. Jack saw how we continued to love God despite what we had been through, and he saw how God was with us the whole way. God *was.* Then Jack shared his faith with Annie, and now she's a believer too. There's just so much. We can't see as much as God sees. We only see part. We don't know how far back or forward any of this goes."

Francie took his hand and held it against her cheek again. "Thank you," she said softly, her anger gone.

He pulled her to him and hugged her. "I love you, sweetheart."

Francie went back to Jack's house with her arms full of groceries. She let herself in and pushed the door closed with her foot. He was standing in the kitchen by the sink.

"So I figured if cans are too hard to open, I'll get microwavable meals. Just take them out, set them in the microwave, hit buttons. I'll tear the boxes open first."

When he didn't say anything, she looked over at him.

Jack was leaning against the sink, his head down, clenching the sides of the countertop with his hands. He was sweating.

She set the grocery bags on the counter.

"Are you okay?"

He closed his eyes. His breathing was heavy.

"Jack? What's your pain level?"

He spoke through clenched teeth. "I'm afraid to say, Francie, it's hitting about a nine."

"What have you had?"

"The max dose of ibuprofen."

"I'm going to give you a shot." She opened the refrigerator and pulled out the painkiller. She filled a syringe and walked over to him. He had such a death grip on the counter that his bicep was bulging and tight.

"Breathe out so you can relax, or your muscle will be sore," she said.

"Just do it," he said, struggling to speak.

Here it goes, she thought and did what she had been taught by Ruth. When the needle went in, he didn't flinch, and she wasn't sure if that was because he was tough or because she was good. She preferred to think she had done well.

He stood there for a few minutes, eyes closed, while she put the groceries away. After about five minutes, he relaxed and sat down on the couch.

"Better?" she asked.

He nodded.

She opened two microwavable meals and started heating them up.

"Why did you let the pain get so bad?"

"I didn't want to bother you."

"Jack. You are *supposed* to call me. Where's your cell phone?"

"In my pocket."

She sighed and finished cooking their lunch. She took his over to the table.

"Come and sit down and eat."

"I'm fine."

She looked at him for a few minutes. "I'm tired of this 'I'm fine' business. You are *not* fine. I cooked this meal, and I would appreciate if you would eat it."

There was a long silence. Slowly he got up and walked over to the table. He looked so tired. The pain had worn him out.

"What caused the pain to flare?"

"The nurses' visit was a bit rough. She had a mess to clean up from last night. I thought I was okay, so I told her I didn't need a shot. I guess I was wrong."

"What's your pain level now?"

"Francie, eat your meal."

"Not until you answer my question."

"Five."

She frowned. "Next time, don't wait. The doctor said it's harder to get it under control once it gets going."

"I know."

She said a prayer, and they ate in silence. In the middle of his meal, Jack asked if she had heard from Annie yet.

"Sort of," she said. "Frank called her this morning, but she had to get to a meeting, so really all they said was 'hi'." Francie didn't mention that Annie hadn't asked about Jack at all.

"I miss her."

"Me too," Francie said.

"What about Mark?"

"He's still working on your case. It'll be fine." She didn't mention the guards stationed at the gatehouse twenty-four hours a day to make sure he didn't escape. "The man who abducted you—Stanton—is in prison. We're safe."

"There will be a court trial."

"Maybe. Mark has a lot of clout."

"I'm not going back to prison."

"Nope. I won't let you."

He looked at her. "Don't do anything stupid."

"Never." She smiled.

They finished their meal in silence, and Francie started cleaning up. Jack said he needed some rest, went into the bedroom, and closed the door. After she cleaned up, she went back to the house to play with Andy and join her little boy in an afternoon nap.

chapter 62

ANNIE WAS SITTING AT HER DESK, chewing on the end of her pencil, a new habit she had picked up this past week. She missed Jack. She had stopped by the hospital last night to see him, and they told her he had been discharged.

"So soon?" she had said.

"Yes," she was told. It had been against his doctor's wishes, but he and his psychiatric caseworker thought he could rest better at home. They didn't tell her much more, even though she was his wife.

She had driven back to her girlfriend's condo and spent a restless night dreaming about him. She held him in her arms, and then somebody came and snatched him away, and she awoke, startled.

She hadn't wanted to leave him. The idea had crept into her mind slowly, that maybe if she could just get away for a while and catch up on sleep, she'd be okay. Then, that Monday morning she had drifted off in a staff meeting of all places, and her boss had startled her when he called on her with a question. She had felt like a grade-schooler caught misbehaving. Afterwards, he had called her into his office and asked if she was okay. Her work had been suffering, he said, and he was worried that she had fallen asleep at work. Did she need some time off? She had been a star employee all these years, so they weren't going to fire her or anything, but they were concerned. It had been over the past year that things hadn't seemed right with her.

Embarrassed and upset, she had driven home on her lunch break and packed her bags. It wasn't just the dreams, she told herself. They only happened a few times a month, and yes, now she slept lighter and was a bit jumpy because of them. But also, she had to be careful how she touched him. She could never walk up behind him and touch him unexpectedly.

He had been standing at the kitchen sink one day, washing dishes, and she had walked up and put her arms around him, and he had jumped *so* hard and spun around, knocking her backwards and dropping the glass he was washing. Another time she had bent over to kiss him on the cheek. She supposed he was engrossed in what he was reading, but when she reached over the couch from behind, he'd jerked up, and his head had knocked into her mouth and given her a bloody lip.

There were other times too. None of them were his fault, and he was always more than sorry. He tried to make it up to her by bringing her flowers or giving her a back rub in the evenings. She never doubted how much he loved her. And he was great about touching when he expected to be touched.

He loved to hold her hand when they were walking or just sitting on the couch. He put his hand against the small of her back when he ushered her through a door or pulled her protectively close to him on the street. And the sex— the sex was great. He sure knew how to please a woman.

But there was also the thing about his past. He either didn't remember it or wouldn't talk about it. She had no idea what had happened to him those twenty years he had been in prison. *No idea.* And the whole living-with-a-fugitive thing had been harder than she thought.

She caught herself glancing at the newspaper and catching the news here and there, wondering if they were still looking for him. Sometimes, she dreamed they had found him and dragged him away while she stood there, screaming his name. Once she had even dreamed that he was in the electric chair, and someone scary looked at her and said, "You blew it." And then they pulled the lever.

She had never told Jack about these dreams. She didn't want to upset him more or make him worry about her. Looking back, she supposed it would have been good to share them with Francie. Francie was someone she could talk to about these things. Or someone she *could* have talked to. Now she wasn't so sure.

Francie upset her too. She had always known that Francie and Jack had a special connection because of their circumstances, but she wasn't sure what that meant until now. *Now,* it appeared, Francie would do whatever it took to continue to protect him, even if that meant keeping Annie out of her own husband's hospital room.

She was upset with them all, so when Frank had called this morning to check on her, she was short with him. She hadn't even asked about Jack.

She also hadn't told him about the man who'd visited her at work Tuesday morning, the day after Jack's abduction. A man in a dark suit had come and talked to her boss and had her pulled off of a project so they could talk privately outside. He said he was from the FBI. He asked her what she knew about Jack. Was he involved in anything illegal? Did she know why anyone would want to hurt him? His questions were vague, and she answered that she didn't know anything, and he thanked her and left. But that had scared her. What had she gotten mixed up in?

The phone rang and startled her out of her thoughts. It was her project manager, wanting her to rewrite some code for him.

She hung up and put the chewed pencil back in its holder. If she didn't want her entire life to fall apart, she had better get to work.

The nights got worse after that. Nearly every night, Francie had to give Jack a shot to calm him down. She had gone through a vial of Symatrex and had to ask Ruth to bring more. Ruth continued to meet with Jack every morning before his nurse came, but he wouldn't tell her anything. He was pleasant but protective.

"He trusts you," Ruth said. "And right now, *only* you. I don't think it's that he doesn't trust *me*, it's more that he can't handle more than one of us knowing about him."

She was sitting at his kitchen table with Francie. Jack was in the shower. The nurse had given him a shot before she dressed his wounds, saying he could take a real shower today instead of a sponge bath.

Francie nodded. "I'm here for him. He hasn't told me much though. We've been through nearly a week of nightmares, and I've given him shots every time to calm him down. The next morning, he won't face me. He won't talk about it, and he avoids me until the afternoon, when I come in to fix lunch, and then we talk a bit about my morning. Never his nights."

Ruth nodded. "It may just take time. It hasn't even been two weeks since his abduction. He shouldn't even have come home as soon as he did."

Ruth left, and eventually, the nurse came out of Jack's room, and she too went home.

Jack came out and saw Francie sitting at the table.

"You're still here?"

"I'm *back* here," she said. "I left, but your entourage was here longer than usual. It's lunch time."

He sat down across from her, looking tired. He had fresh bandages on his hands.

Instead of getting up to get their food, she sat and looked at him. He stared back at her, and it felt like more than they had communicated in a while.

"I don't want the Symatrex anymore," he finally said. "I want to try to get through the night without it."

She agreed but didn't say so out loud. She remained silent, hoping he would talk some more.

"It clouds my mind," he continued. "It steals my memory, and I can't remember a thing about the nightmare the following morning. Plus, I wake up feeling hungover. I guess if I'm going to work through this mess, I need to be able to think."

She nodded.

"It's going to mean more work for you," Jack said. "You have to deal with me. Are you up for it?"

"Of course," she said.

"What if I'm knocked out with that stuff, and I have a nightmare and can't wake up? And I have no control when I'm on it. I can't protect myself. I can't run. I can't fight. That leaves *you* to protect me."

He tried to put his head in his hands, but that didn't work well with the bandages. He looked like he wanted to hit something. Instead, he kicked the table leg.

Francie raised an eyebrow. "What do you need to fight? Or to run from?"

He pushed the chair back and got up pretty quickly for someone who had broken ribs. "I thought you were going to fix us some lunch," he said curtly. "Call me when it's ready."

He stomped into the bedroom and shut the door.

She sat there, stunned at the sudden anger. After a moment, he opened it and stuck his head out.

"I'm sorry," he said. "I'm really sorry."

"It's okay," she said. "Some days, I feel like kicking something too. Or someone. I'll fix lunch and call you when it's done."

After they had eaten, she pulled out some paperwork. "I'm going to sit here for a while and work. Then I'm off to spend the afternoon with Andy. And nap." She smiled. She started sorting through her pile of papers. "First, though, I need to ask you something." She wasn't sure if it was a good time to bring this up, but now seemed as good a time as any. "Ruth told me something this morning when we talked. She said your doctor called you to schedule a CT scan. Why didn't you?"

"I'm not having a CT scan," said Jack. "I'm fine."

"You may not be fine. You had some bleeding in your head, and they want to make sure you're healed."

"I'm not going. I don't want anyone messing with me. The bandage changes are bad enough. What else do you guys want to put me through?"

"Us guys?" Francie said. "Since when am I grouped in with the rest?"

"I'm sorry," he said.

"Seems you're apologizing a lot to me today. Is something on your mind?"

He looked like he wanted to say something, then changed his mind. "I'm really tired," he said. "I think I'll take a nap." He went and took some ibuprofen, then went into the bedroom, shutting the door.

Jack relented and agreed to go back down to the hospital for his CT scan. The whole trip was a nightmare. Frank drove, and the bumps of the ride hurt Jack's ribs. Jack didn't say anything, but he was gritting his teeth, hoping nobody would notice. At the hospital, he suffered the humility of riding in a wheelchair up to the x-ray room.

He fidgeted in the waiting room while Francie filled out paperwork. Frank leafed through a magazine.

The fluorescent lights, the smells, and the crowd were overwhelming. He tried to leaf through this month's *Sports Illustrated*, but the articles all ran together, and he couldn't make any sense of them. He felt light-headed and closed his eyes. When he opened them again, the lights just seemed even harsher, giving him a headache.

His hands started to tremble.

Francie handed in the paperwork and sat beside him. She leaned toward him. "Are you okay?" she whispered.

"I've got to get out of here," he said. He started to get up.

"Sit," she said.

He remained in his seat. Frank glanced across at them. He raised an eyebrow.

"Mr. Banner?" someone called from the door.

"They're ready for you," Francie said, standing. "Come on. I'll stay with you."

Jack got up, but he didn't walk where he was supposed to . Instead, he walked toward the door and out into the hall. He was walking pretty quickly for someone in his condition, ignoring the pain in his torso.

"Bring the wheelchair," he heard Francie said to Frank and followed him. When she reached him, he was pushing the elevator button.

"I'm not getting a CT scan," he said. "If I die, I die."

The door opened. He went in and hit the close button. Francie stopped it with her hand. "Come on, Frank, we're leaving," she said. Frank got the wheelchair in and the door closed. Nobody said anything on the way down.

"Why don't you at least sit," Francie said.

"I don't need the wheelchair," Jack said.

He walked on his own, back across the parking lot. By the time they reached the car, he was sweating bullets. He leaned against the door to catch his breath, but the hot metal hit one of his burns.

He cursed and kicked the side of the car several times. He couldn't even hit anything because of his hands. Everything he touched hurt some part of his body. Angrily, he tore the splits off of his fingers and flexed them, willing them to bend. It was painful, but not too bad.

"Jack, get in the car," Frank said firmly. Jack climbed in the passenger seat, leaving Francie to sit in back, and slammed the door, hurting his hand in the process. But he said nothing.

Nobody talked in the car on the way home.

At his house, he got out and said, "I need to be alone. I appreciate your help, but I really need to be alone now."

Francie and Frank glanced at each other. Frank nodded.

"I'll be home in a few minutes, hon," Francie said to Frank.

"Francie—" Jack started to protest, but Frank drove off and left her.

"Let's go inside," she said, walking past him and using her own key to get in. He followed her after a few seconds.

She sat at the kitchen table and waited. He walked over to the sink to get a glass of water. His hand was shaking so badly he had trouble holding it. He was sweating and couldn't think, because the pain was roaring through his body. It was blocking everything else out. He felt it wash through him, engulfing him in hot, red flames, reigniting the burns on his torso and crippling the fingers that were trying to hold the glass. Even his eyes hurt from the light, and he started to feel nauseated.

He felt Francie standing next to him.

"Roll up your sleeve," she said. He tried but couldn't, so she did it for him. She pressed the needle into his skin and gave him the shot for pain. He closed his eyes and waited for the relief to come. When it finally did, it was like sweet surrender. It felt so good that he wanted to weep.

"What was that?" he asked, opening his eyes.

"I gave you a little more. Ruth said I could if I had to."

Jack nodded. "Thank you, Princess." He turned and walked toward the bedroom. His head still hurt, and his stomach didn't feel so well. "I'm going to get some rest now. I'll see you at dinner time." He closed the bedroom door.

That night, the dreams seemed worse than before. Maybe because of the outing to the hospital. Maybe because his pain was worse.

"Jack?" Francie always called his name so he would know it was her.

She put a blanket around him.

"I'm going to make some tea with a little sugar in it."

She went into the kitchen and turned on the light above the stove and put on a kettle. It boiled quickly, and she brought a cup back to him. He couldn't hold it.

"I'm trying," he said.

"I know. Here. I can hold it for you."

"No. I'm trying to get over these dreams. I want them to end."

"You might have to talk to Ruth for that to happen."

"No."

Eventually, he took the tea from her and sipped it, but he couldn't relax.

"Let's give you some Symatrex," Francie said.

"What if I dream?"

"You won't." She rolled up his sleeve and gave him the shot.

Ruth was insistent that Jack get a CT scan. She ordered it at 4 a.m., when nobody would be there, and she went with Frank and Francie and had the hospital lower the medical personnel lights. There was no waiting, and Francie stood in the room with Jack, shielded from the x-ray, but able to talk to him the whole time. It was quick, and they all survived. The results came back the next day and his head wounds were healing nicely.

They rebandaged his fingers.

chapter

63

THE DREAMS WERE COMING NIGHTLY, but most of the time, they were able to work their way out of them without using the Symatrex. When Francie woke to the usual screams that night, she got up off the couch and went to him, to see if he was awake.

She had a routine. She wasn't sure "routine" was the word to use, but she knew what to do now. Low lighting, warm blankets, and finally, make him a warm cup of tea. Chamomile, with a little milk and sugar to bring his blood sugar back up. He was burning a lot of adrenaline and calories when he had an attack.

Francie glanced at the clock on his nightstand. It was 3 a.m.. Tonight Jack was sitting on the floor, his back against the wall. She knelt beside him. He was moaning, "No," over and over. His hands were over his head, as if warding off blows.

"Jack," she spoke his name firmly. "It's Francie. Wake up."

It took a few minutes calling his name, but eventually his eyes met hers. "Francie," he said.

"It's just a dream," she said. He was soaked in sweat. He had started to chill.

She stood up. "Let's go to the couch."

He got up slowly and followed her out to the living room, where he sat down on the couch. She draped a blanket over his shoulders. "I'm going to make you some tea," she said. She went and put a kettle on, leaving the lights off. There was a small night light by the stove that cast enough light for her to work by. Jack's nerves were so raw that any bright light, loud sound, or human touch was too much. He couldn't relax unless his surroundings were low in stimuli.

She heard him leave and turned. He had gone to the master bathroom, and she heard him vomiting. He often did that; he was frightened so much by what he saw in his sleep that it emptied him of everything.

By the time he came back, the tea was ready. He sat back down on the couch in the dark, and she handed it to him. She could smell mouthwash on his breath.

"Be careful, it's hot," she said. He was shaking so badly that he couldn't take the mug, so she set it on the coffee table.

"I'm going to get you a clean shirt," she said. "That one is soaked. Can you take it off?"

She went to his drawer and pulled out a clean t-shirt. When she came back, he had his shirt off. She moved his tea over and sat down on the coffee table across from him, their knees almost touching. She looked at him.

"You okay?" she asked, making sure to make eye contact with him.

"Yes," he said so quietly she almost didn't hear him.

"Are you still with me?"

He nodded and reached for the shirt. She handed it to him, but instead of taking it, he slowly took her hands in his broken ones and bent his head down onto them and the soft shirt she was holding.

"I can't do this anymore," he said, and a sob escaped him. He hadn't broken down once in tears, not once the entire time. He had been angry, upset, frightened—but had never broken down.

Another sob came from deep within him. And then he bent forward, his forehead on her knees, and wept. Great sobs came from him, and his entire frame shook with them. The white bandages on his back were all she could see, and they stood out, moving like bones in the darkness of the room.

"Oh, Jack," she said and felt her own tears trickling down her face. She gently pulled her hands out of his and put them on his shoulders, then she touched the back of his head, smoothing his hair. "We're going to make it through this."

His face was on her knees, and she realized the new t-shirt was getting soaked with his tears. She let him cry, and it seemed to go on for many minutes. She tried to keep herself composed, but silent tears were running down her face.

Please God, she prayed. *Please ease his suffering.*

Eventually, he sat up. She handed him the shirt, and he put it on, and she realized that most of the tears had fallen onto her knees and soaked into her pajama pants.

She draped the blanket over his shoulders, and he tried to pull it closed in front of him, but his hands wouldn't work.

She did it for him.

"It's never going to end," he said. "I can't keep doing this."

"Tell me what you saw," she said gently. "Tell me about the dream."

He shook his head. "I can't."

"Yes, you can. You're the strongest person I've ever met."

She moved to sit beside him on the couch, so he wouldn't have to look at her while he talked. The room was quiet, except for the chattering of his teeth, and eventually, even that stopped as he warmed up.

He took a deep breath. Then he began to talk.

"When I didn't... *cooperate*... they put me inside of a box and kept me there for days. It was small, hot... " His voice was shaky but strong. He swallowed and continued. "There was a slit near the floor, and I would lie down and try to get air. Sometimes they'd take me out and tie my wrists together, and then they'd take turns beating me. They got bored, I guess, and I was their entertainment. It would go on for hours. Then they'd throw me back into the box."

He took another deep breath. His body shuddered. Francie moved her hand over by him, palm up, and he slowly took it, gently lacing his bandaged fingers between hers. He swallowed hard and continued.

"This particular dream... they... " He paused.

She could see the side of his face in the dim light. A new tear trickled down his cheek.

He bowed his head, fighting back the emotion. "I can't talk anymore," he said, his voice hoarse. "The memories... that's enough." His hands started shaking again. She held onto the one she had.

"You're safe now," she said. "They're just memories."

"I want some Symatrex," he said. "I don't want to remember."

"You need to remember," she said.

He put his head in his hands and leaned forward, his elbows on his knees. "Oh, God... "

She put a hand on his back. He flinched, but she kept it there. She rubbed his back gently, up by his shoulders, where there were no burns or broken ribs. He started weeping again. "Oh, God... Francie, make it stop. Please."

She wanted to. She wanted to give him the Symatrex and make it all go away for him. Go away for *her*, too, so she could crawl back on the couch and fall back into her own dreams of horses and Andy. Sweet little Andy.

"Jack," she said. "Look at me."

"I can't... "

"Look at me." She moved across to the coffee table again. Sitting directly across from him, she reached out and gently took his hands, pulling them away from his face. He looked across at her, and she knew he saw her own tears reflected in the dim light. She kept her voice strong.

"We're going to get through this together, okay? I'm here, and I'm not going anywhere." She sat there, holding his hands in hers until his breathing began to calm again. "They're just dreams," she said again. "Just bad memories." She let go of his hands and handed him his tea.

He managed to take the mug and get a few sips down. He leaned back against the couch, and she got her own mug and sat beside him again. They sat in silence, sipping their tea.

"Let's go to bed," she said after a while. They had been up a long time. He nodded.

Jack went into the bedroom and climbed into bed, curled up on his side, and pulled the comforter around him. He lay there, his eyes wide in the darkness, still trembling a little. Then he felt Francie climb onto the bed behind him.

"What?"

"Shhhh," she said, laying down next to him. "It's okay. You're under the covers, I'm on top of them. We're fine. I'm not going to leave you alone tonight." She lay down next to him and put her arm around him, over top of the comforter.

He felt her warm presence and closed his eyes, new tears coming. Her touch was so comforting, so needed, and he felt the tension and cares of the past few weeks melt away. Soon, he was carried into a deep, dreamless sleep.

The next morning Francie was sitting at the table, munching on a piece of toast, when Jack came into the kitchen. He sat down across from her, beard stubble on his face.

"It's 10:00," he said.

"I know. I didn't wake up until 9:30," she said. "I guess I missed horse exercise time."

She motioned to a plate covered with a pot lid. "Breakfast should still be warm."

He lifted the lid and pulled the plate over to him. Scrambled eggs and toast.

"Thanks." He bowed his head and said a silent prayer and picked up his toast. After a few moments, he said.

"About last night... "

She looked up at him when he didn't continue and raised her eyebrows. "Yes?"

"I... " he searched for words, watching his fork move the eggs around in his plate. "I don't expect you to keep doing this. You should start spending nights at home, before it becomes too much, before it... before you... " his voice trailed off.

"Before I leave you?"

He met her eyes.

"Jack, I'm not going to leave you. I'm not going anywhere."

Neither of them said anything for a while. The sun slanted across the kitchen counter from the window above the sink, lighting up dancing dust particles. The clock quietly kept up its tick-tock beat, a noise only noticeable when the room was absolutely silent.

"Thank you," he said quietly.

She smiled. "And if we ever sleep together again, I expect *you* to fix *me* breakfast."

He looked up at her and laughed. It was the first time she had heard him laugh since the abduction.

They both laughed until they had tears in their eyes, and Jack was holding his ribs, grimacing at the same time. Finally, they wiped their eyes with their napkins, both of them spent from the emotions of the past twelve hours.

"We do lead an interesting life," he said, still chuckling.

Frank was standing outside of Annie's workplace when she got off that evening. "We need to talk," he said. "Let's go for a ride."

No "hi" or "hello" or "how are you", Annie thought, and his serious face and tone scared her. She had her gym bag in the car and had planned to head over there for a workout before she went home. It helped her nerves. She almost protested, but she was afraid of the news he bore. Was Jack worse? Was Jack *dead?*

Swallowing, she nodded and followed him back to his SUV. She got in and buckled up, and he started driving, heading out toward the coast.

"Is Jack okay?" she asked, her voice trembling.

Frank glanced over at her. "He's not dead, if that's what you're asking."

She turned to look out the window and let her stomach settle. He drove them to a place above the water where they parked on a paved area above the beach under a tree. They could see the ocean waves crashing below. A couple of surfers were trying to ride the waves. He kept the car running and the air on.

Frank felt like using Francie's wand on Annie, to make sure she didn't have any listening devices on her. He had actually brought it along, but he didn't want to treat her like a common criminal, and besides, she hadn't known he was coming. He didn't quite trust her. He didn't quite trust anyone at the moment, and it upset him that he had taken such a dim view of the human race lately.

"I've called you at least five times a day every day," he said. "You've never returned one of my calls."

"I was waiting for Jack to call me," she said.

"Jack probably can't even dial the numbers," Frank said. "Both of his hands are broken. But you would know that if you ever came to see him."

He saw the anger boil up inside of her.

"He didn't want me. And I *did* come back. I went back to the hospital a few days later and was surprised to find that he had been discharged so soon."

Frank thought about this for a moment. "Then why didn't you call home?"

"I don't know," she said. "How is he?"

"He's horrible," Frank said. "His body is broken, and the torture caused all of his buried memories to resurface, so he has PTSD from something that happened to him over twenty years ago, plus he's trying to deal with the trauma of what happened to him a few weeks ago. All of that on top of the fact that *his wife left him.*"

He hadn't meant to be so harsh with her, but he was feeling pretty angry himself now.

"This is all my fault," she said and started to cry. "If he hadn't come looking for me in the first place, none of this would have happened. That's when that man grabbed him."

"No, Annie," he said, his voice softer. "You can blame yourself for other things, but don't blame yourself for that. Stanton had been planning this for a while and would have gotten Jack sooner or later."

Annie blew her nose.

"Why did they discharge Jack so soon?"

"His case worker, Ruth, thought he could rest better at home. He has a nurse come in once a day to change his bandages, and Ruth stops by daily also."

"But he's alone the rest of the time?"

"No, Francie is staying with him, especially at night."

Annie couldn't stop the flow of tears. Nor could she stop the anger that welled up in her at the mention of Francie's name. She still pictured her standing in the doorway at the hospital, as if daring Annie to walk past her.

"I hate her," she said.

Frank looked over at her. "Why?"

"She's with him, and I'm not."

"That was your own choice," Frank said.

"No. He told me to leave. He told us all to get out of the room except for *her*."

So that's what this is about, Frank thought.

"Oh, geez," he said. He rubbed his forehead with his hands. "It's not like that, Annie. I live with her. I'm over there enough that I live with them both. It's not like that at all."

She wiped her eyes and fished in her purse for another tissue.

Frank sighed. "Francie misses you. She said the other day that its times like these when she could use a best girlfriend. She actually said, 'I miss Annie.'"

Annie found her tissue and wiped her eyes, fighting back more tears that were threatening to come. She stared out across the ocean, wishing she was a girl back home in England and that none of this was happening.

Frank looked out over the same ocean and felt the anger draining out of him. When he spoke, his voice was quiet and gentle.

"When Francie pulled Jack out of prison, she created a bond between them that the rest of us will never understand. I don't think she meant to. When she first started, this was supposed to be Jim's thing, and she was only funding it. But the people they hired wanted to deal directly with Francie, so she got pulled in. She and Jack's lives have been intertwined ever since, because if either of them were found out, they'd both go to prison. For life. Or get executed. She was willing to die for him right from the start, and he has proven that he's just as willing to die for her. It's hard to come in between a bond like that. That's something you and I just have to accept."

Annie was silent. The sky was turning a soft gray color. It looked like rain was moving in.

"Also, they're the only survivors of a plane crash. That alone is enough to bring them together."

"I guess I wasn't prepared for all of this," Annie said. "I didn't expect all of this when I married him."

"You had a choice," Frank said.

"No," Annie turned to him. "No, I *didn't* have a choice. That's what none of you understand. I was already in love with him when I found out who he was, and about all of this... this... espionage or whatever you want to call it. It wasn't fair. He never should have even pursued me. What was he thinking? He should never even have had plans to marry."

"He didn't," Frank said. "He had given up women and was ready to lead a bachelor's life. But then he saw you. Annie, he *loves* you. You changed his life. You made him a better man. He was happy with you."

Annie's tears started again.

"I know you love him too," Frank said. "Come home."

"It's too late," she said. "I've messed up too badly."

"It's never too late. If anyone understands that, it's Jack."

Annie looked at her watch. "I really need to get going," she said. "Can you take me back to my car?"

Frank looked at her, waiting, willing her to say that she was coming back.

"Please, Annie. He needs you."

"Frank... I have to get myself together first. I can't deal with this. I don't know how you guys do it. It's too much for me. I've led a simple life all these years—even when my parents died, that was *horrible*—but I was on my own here and only saw them once a year when I went back to England. It just seemed like they were away. It hurt, and for a few years it was really hard, but I had a good job here... *have* a good job... and good friends, and I got along okay. I didn't have a lot of tragedy."

Frank nodded his head and slowly put the car in reverse. He turned around and pulled onto the road, taking her back.

"Just think about it," he said. "At least call him. Tell him you still love him."

Annie didn't answer, and they were both silent the rest of the way back. It was raining when she got out. "Thanks," was all she said. She covered her head with her purse and ran to her car. Frank watched her through the raindrops until she disappeared behind the rain-soaked windows of her automobile.

Francie stopped by to check on Jack before dinner. He was sitting on the couch.

"I brought you something," she said. She was carrying a small gray and white kitten she had brought up from a litter in the barn. He was finally old enough to wean. She held him up. "You need a kitten."

He looked at the kitten.

"I don't want a kitten."

"But this kitten needs *you*. He's way too cuddly to be a barn cat, and I need to get rid of them all. I can't bring him in *my* house, because Mittens likes being the only cat. He needs a good home."

"This isn't a good home. I don't even like animals."

"You keep saying that, but you've lived here for years. You need to get over that not liking animals thing."

She dumped the kitten onto his lap. The kitten started to purr, as she knew it would, and rub against his hands. He reluctantly petted it on the head. It purred louder and arched its back against his hand in pleasure, then settled down on his chest and started to fall asleep.

"I can't keep this cat," he said. "I don't even have a litter box."

"Yes, you do," Francie said. She went outside and came back in with a litter box, a bag of litter, and kitten food. She unpacked it all, along with two bowls and a few cat toys.

"You're unbelievable, Princess," he said. He started to protest, but as he looked down at the kitten, he realized it was sound asleep.

"Where do you want the litter box? I think the bathroom is the best place."

Without waiting for his answer, she disappeared into the bathroom to set it up.

When she came back that evening with a hot plate of dinner for Jack, the kitten was curled up on his lap, and he was dozing on the couch. She quietly set the plate on the table and got out some silverware. The noise woke him.

"Dinner?" he said.

"Yes. I see you two have made friends."

"Spike says I'm warmer to sleep on than the bed you made him in that old box."

"Spike?"

"Do you have a problem with his name?"

"Well... he's just so cuddly and cute. Not really spiky."

"We are manly men who live in this house, and we have manly names. Nothing cute and powder-puff about us."

Francie laughed. "Unless you count the time you had a tea party with Lexie and... "

"All right," he said, laughing. "Enough." He got off the couch slowly, carefully lifting Spike with his bandaged hands and placing him on the cushion. The kitten stirred, then went back to sleep.

One sunny day in November, Alexis's adoption became final. Steve, a very proud papa, declared November 21, "We Love Lexie Day," and Sam made a big chocolate cake with pink frosting and chicken pot pie for dinner, because those were Lexie's favorites.

The house looked more like a carnival than a home. Pink balloons and crepe paper were strung haphazardly everywhere (Lexie and Andy had insisted on helping with the decorating), and there was confetti sprinkled on the table.

Everybody was there, and Francie had talked Jack into joining them. As soon as he walked into the house, Andy hugged him "very gently" as his mother had told him, and Lexie ran up and said, "Oh, hi Uncle Jack. I haven't seen you in a while. Have you been on vacation?"

Jack laughed. "Vacation? Yeah, something like that."

They gathered around the big dining room table to eat.

"Honey," Steve said to Lexie, "when that Christmas toy catalog comes in the mail, you circle everything you want, and I'll try to get it *all* for you."

"Oh my gosh," Francie said, rolling her eyes and spearing a potato from her pot pie.

Lexie giggled, which sent little Andy into spasms of laughter.

"Uncle Steve! She won't have room to sleep if you buy her *everything*," Andy said.

Six weeks had passed since the attack on Jack, and this was the first "normal" evening Francie had enjoyed. It felt good to be sitting at the table with everyone. Well, everyone except for Annie.

But nobody mentioned her.

It was all about Lexie. She had settled into their lives long ago, but it was good for it all to finally be official. Sam was beaming, and they talked about 4-H, ponies, and swim lessons.

"I don't need swim lessons," Lexie said. "I'm a horse rider. I'll just stay on land."

She viewed swim lessons as a waste of her time, time she could otherwise be spending on top of her pony, Pippin.

"You live on a peninsula, so you need swim lessons," Steve said for the hundredth time. "What happens if you fall off the edge of Florida some place?"

Lexie giggled again. "Uncle Jack," she piped up, "Can you please pass the pot pie?"

"*More* pot pie?" Sam said. "Wow. You were hungry. Hand him your plate."

Jack reached over and dished out some pot pie for her.

Physically, Jack was doing better. The last of his bandages had been removed that day. The burns had healed nicely, for which Francie was sure he was thankful. She had never seen the burns, or any part of his body in the light without a shirt for that matter—the nurse had handled it all. His fingers had mostly healed too, and his last splint had been removed. He had refused to go to the doctor's office for any of it, and instead, paid out-of-pocket for the expense to have his doctor come to his house. His ribs were even doing better, and he could finally take deep breaths without pain.

Dr. Tremper had decided he could forego any more x-rays and just "go on instinct." Francie appreciated his willingness to treat Jack according to Jack's needs instead of according to "policy." She had told him so when he left that day.

After cake and ice cream, Jack pulled out a small package. "Here, Lexie," he said. He had asked Francie to pick up a gift for him. "After you open this, I'm going home. I'm tired."

"From that long vacation you were on," Lexie said, taking the package. She opened it, and there was a tiny pendant of a pony on a gold chain.

"Ohhhhhhhhhh!" Lexie's eyes went wide, and she gasped in wonder. "Oh, Uncle Jack, it's the most beautiful thing I've ever seen. Thank you!" She set it down, ran around the table, and threw her arms around him. Francie cringed, but Jack hugged her back. "You're welcome," he said. "I'm glad you like it."

"Uncle Jack, catch ya next time," Andy said, holding out his fist for a fist bump, like Jack had done with him so many times. Unlike Lexie, Andy had seen Jack several times over the past weeks, but he was elated when he noticed the bandages were off his hands. Jack fist-bumped him. "Your boo-boos are all better?" Andy asked.

"Yep, buddy, they're all better." He rubbed Andy's soft head of hair. "Goodnight."

He left, and Lexie finished opening up her gifts.

"Is it Lexie's birthday?" Andy asked again. He had asked that question several times; he just couldn't figure out what they were celebrating.

"Sort of," Francie said.

He took his mommy's hand and climbed up in her lap. He watched as Steve put Lexie's pony pendant around her neck.

"I love Uncle Jack," he said, laying his sleepy little head back on Francie's chest.

"I do too," she said quietly, smoothing his hair. Then she watched her new, "official" niece open gifts and waited her turn for a hug.

chapter 64

ANNIE HAD BEEN HAVING HEART PALPITATIONS. They'd gotten bad enough that she'd gone to see her doctor. Her doctor checked her thyroid, gave her an EKG, and did all the standard tests. Everything came back normal, as she suspected they would.

"Stress," her doctor told her.

She made a decision to take some time off of work. She'd go back to England. She hadn't been there in many years and wanted to see her grandmother again. She'd visit old friends, poke around places where she had grown up, and see if she could find herself.

Maybe she could finally relax.

She knew she was a coward, and she hated herself for it. While she made plans to leave, she tried to figure out how to tell Jack. She thought of just showing up at his door, but she knew if she saw him, she'd have to stay, and the only way to save herself was to run. She'd picked up the phone at least a dozen times that week to call him and always put it down.

In the end, she ended up writing him from the airport, moments before she boarded her plane.

Francie was making a strong pot of coffee. It was 1 p.m., and she had stopped in at Jack's to drop off some paperwork and the mail. He had started working again, and she needed him to look at some sales figures. It had been a hard night, an early morning, and they were both exhausted.

She was looking for cups when her eye caught the writing on one of the envelopes. Her heart jumped when she picked it up.

She handed it to him. "It's from Annie," she said.

He glanced at her, and she went back to the cupboard, making herself busy getting mugs out. Jack opened the envelope and read the short letter, then threw it down on the counter. She resisted the urge to ask what it was about, but it didn't seem positive.

He roughly pushed his chair back and stood up. He walked to the bedroom.

"You might as well read it," he said over his shoulder. He slammed the door shut behind him.

Francie picked up the note.

Jack,

I am going home to England. I want to visit my grandma for a few weeks. I haven't been feeling well. It's anxiety, I guess. I hope to pull myself together and will come see you when I get back. I love you.

– Annie

Several unpleasant names for Annie went through Francie's mind. Who would send a *letter?* Not a visit, not even a phone call, but a *letter?* For over six weeks, Jack had never heard from Annie once and now this.

She decided then and there that they needed to write Annie off. Annie was going home to England. *Home?* And would come see Jack when she got back? *Really?* What a... Francie stopped herself from swearing.

She looked at the bedroom door and wondered if Jack was okay. Who would be okay after *that?* She thought of knocking, then thought better of it. Instead, she gulped her coffee down, left the papers on the table, and headed to the barn to work off her anger.

Later that afternoon, Jack walked slowly over to the Big House. Frank was upstairs, working in Francie's office, and Jack sat down in his usual chair across from the desk.

"Hi," Frank said.

"Hi." It felt good and familiar to sit in his chair. Almost normal. Jack really missed his job and wanted to get back to it, more than just the paperwork he had been doing from home. He missed the people, and he missed New York. He definitely needed something.

"What's up?" Frank said, setting his work aside. Frank was like that—always ready to listen, no matter who bothered him or when. People came first with Frank, and Jack appreciated that in his friend.

"Nothing much," Jack said. "I just came to try out my chair and see if I still fit in it."

Frank smiled. "How's the kitten?"

"Spike's fine. Actually, what I came to do was to thank you for all you've done these past weeks, but especially for letting me borrow your wife."

Frank smiled. "Oh, it's not like I *let* you borrow her. Francie does what Francie wants to do."

Jack laughed. "Don't I know that."

"Anyway," Jack continued, "I think I'm doing better now and can stay by myself at night. I need to start doing that at some point and now seems just as good a time as any."

"Francie and I have talked about that," Frank said. "We think you should come and stay here at night. We have the room down at the end of the hall. You'd have your own bathroom, and nobody else uses that bedroom. It has always been the guest room. She even mentioned putting a litter box in there so Spike can come."

"Stay here? And wake everybody with my nightmares?"

"You've forgotten that the walls are soundproof."

"Oh, yeah."

Jack was quite for a while, thinking. "No," he said. "I need to do this. I need to get back to normal. I need to learn to live alone."

Frank looked at him. Jack knew he looked healthy. He hadn't lost too much muscle tone thanks to physical therapy, and his body had healed up nicely. There were no scars on his head anymore, and with the bandages off, he looked good as new. He knew better though; the walk over here had taken its toll. He tried not to show it.

"Francie told me about the letter from Annie this morning," Frank said.

Jack nodded. There was nothing much to say. Frank changed the subject.

"So what does Francie think about you staying alone?"

"I haven't told her. I figured I'd go at it through the side door and tell *you*, because I know what she's going to think about it."

"What does Ruth say?"

"Haven't mentioned it to her either. It's just something I have to do, Frank. I need to try to get back to being independent. I'll be fine. I can always call you if I need somebody."

"Okay," Frank said. "I'll tell Francie. She usually listens to me. *Usually*."

Jack smiled. "Thanks, pal. That's what I was counting on."

He got up and started the slow, tiring walk back home.

chapter
65

THEY STARTED WALKING FOR EXERCISE. Francie figured they could talk about work while they walked out to the beach and back, or at least part way there and back. Jack needed to get back in shape and rebuild his stamina. He also started coming over to the house to lift weights in the basement again. It was slow work, because he was tight and sore, but he was getting there. At first, he worked with a physical therapist, but that only lasted two times, then he continued on his own. He preferred it that way—to work alone.

By early December, he had stayed nearly two weeks by himself. The nights were bad, and he missed Francie. Sometimes he was up all night after a bad dream. He started watching late night TV, Spike curled up with him. Other nights, he managed to get back to sleep. Overall, he was getting there. It was just slow.

Frank was glad to have his wife back in bed. They started going to bed early, both of them exhausted from the past two months. They'd read a little while, maybe give each other back rubs, then turn in.

They decorated for Christmas that year. It was the first year since they had lost Krista that they dug out her angel collection and put it up around the house.

"We could use some angels watching over us," Francie said. She shed some tears as she remembered her sister, but she also had fun telling Andy about all the angels and about his Aunt Krista.

"She was beautiful, like an angel herself," Francie said to him.

Steve got really into the lights and covered the house in them for Lexie's sake. He managed to do it all without falling off the roof, but Francie told Lexie the story of him swinging from his ankle one year anyway.

"And your Aunt Francie *left* me there!" he said.

"And I would do it again," Francie said.

They baked cookies and took the kids to see Santa. They made lists, wrapped presents, and decided to go out and cut down a tree instead of putting up their usual artificial one.

Only once did Jack call Francie to come over after a dream. She and Frank brought him and Spike to the Big House that night, and he and the cat slept well.

"I have an early Christmas gift for you," Mark said though the intercom from the front gate. "Why do you always have your people interrogate me before you let me in?"

Francie pushed the intercom button from her desk. "Go ahead," she said to Matt, who was on watch. "Let him in."

"I'd like Jack to be there too," she heard Mark's voice. She glanced across her desk at Jack, who had been working with her on some spreadsheets. She agreed reluctantly and hung up.

"Let's see what he says," she said to Jack, then picked up her phone to call Frank. She asked him to let Mark in the house and come up to her office with him.

"I have a gun hidden in this room," she said to Jack. "If he gets out of hand, I'll threaten to shoot him again."

Francie laughed, hoping to ease some of the tension. The morning had been going so well. Jack just sighed and put his paperwork down. He stood up, walked over to the window, and looked out across the field at the horses.

Soon Frank knocked and entered with Mark.

"Hey Francie!" Mark said. He walked across the room and gave her a hug. He sat down on her couch. "Everybody have a seat," he said. "I come in peace. You'll like this visit, I promise."

Jack remained standing by the window but turned around to face Mark. He put his hands in his pockets and leaned back against the window seat. Francie swiveled in her chair. "Make it fast," she said. "I have a conference call."

"Ouch," Mark said. "No brotherly love. Well, I've managed to pull some strings, and Jack won't be going back to prison." He waited for some cheers or something, but they all kept staring at him silently. "Really," he said.

"What about all the 'evidence' you keep telling me you have about him being guilty and all?" Francie said.

"Like I told you before, dear sister, due to the mistreatment here and in the federal prison system, he has quite a lawsuit. Jack, if you sign away your rights to sue for damages to your body, they will drop all charges. It's going to take a while for this to become official. To save face, you're being asked to keep quiet about who you are. If it leaks out, you're back in the slammer. Give us six months to a year, maybe longer, then you can "come out" if you want, but do it quietly and not publicly. I expect you'll want to contact your mom then. She's alive and doing well, but you can't contact her until this is officially over."

Francie glanced at Jack when they mentioned his mom. He gave her a quick smile.

"As for me, I still don't trust you," Mark said, looking at Jack. "I think you're guilty of that murder and who knows what else. But you seem hell bent to save and protect my sister at all costs, and that goes a long way with me. So you've bought your life back."

Mark stood up and looked at Francie. "I suppose I'm not invited to Christmas this year?"

He waited, and she sat there, unsure. "Will you even be in the country?" she asked.

"Maybe. I'd love to mingle. Get to know your family better." He glanced at Jack again.

"Call me the week before. We'll see how it goes," Francie said. "Mark, I don't want it to be this way. I don't. You know I love you. But I don't trust you."

Mark laughed. "I'm not the only one in this family who plays dirty, Francie. Your hands aren't so clean either, are they?"

She didn't reply.

"Good day, my friends." He turned to Jack. "Congratulations."

He patted Frank on the shoulder and turned to leave.

"Mark," Jack finally spoke. Mark turned to look at him. "Thanks."

"You're one tough dude," Mark said. He shook his head. "You surprised me, and that doesn't happen often. If you *are* innocent, the US can be proud to have a man like you on our side."

With that, he turned and left.

Francie broke out into a big smile. "Well, Jack Banner, you're officially a free man!"

Frank got up and pounded him on the shoulder. "Let's go golfing tomorrow to celebrate."

Christmas Eve was a crowded affair. Becky came home with her boyfriend, Rick the Rock Star, as Ken had always called him. They were engaged. Jessica was dating a very handsome Latino man whose parents owned an Andalusian horse farm in Texas. She brought him home. Mickey was engaged to a sweet girl named Vicky (everybody loved the rhyming of their names) and she came as well. Steve's parents and his brother stopped by, and the house was filled with people. They had a huge Christmas Eve dinner, mostly catered (Francie refused to cook), and Sam baked cookies with the kids. They ate those for dessert. They went to the 7 p.m. family service at church, then came home and opened gifts. The house and tree were beautiful, and Christmas lights and candles gave a soft glow to the room that evening as they all sat around and talked.

The little kids were sent to bed to wait for Santa to come, and the older kids broke off into couples or groups to chat or play computer games.

Francie was sitting at the dining room table, squinting at Christmas cards in the "mood" lighting that Steve had created for the kids. She and Frank had been cracking nuts and eating them, but then Frank went into the kitchen to wash dishes, bless his heart.

Jack had been quiet most of the evening. Now he was sitting by himself in a corner, a goblet of water in his hands. He was twirling the glass around by the stem, watching the water flop around. Francie knew he missed Annie. With all the couples and children in the room tonight, Francie could tell he felt very alone. She wondered, briefly, what Annie was doing to celebrate Christmas in England.

"Merry Christmas," Francie said, going over and sitting down beside him. He glanced up at her. "It's a few minutes after midnight. Merry Christmas."

He smiled. "Merry Christmas, Princess," he said. She reached out and gave his hand a little squeeze.

"I need to go help Frank with the dishes," she said. "Then off to bed."

Jack sighed and stood up. "I'll dry," he said.

The three of them worked together in companionable silence until the task was done. It was a good evening.

Jack knew that Francie was glad Christmas was over and that she could get back to some routine. In early January, Francie was nominated for several Eclipse awards for Thoroughbred racing, so she went to New York for the banquet. She and Donovan received a few awards and so did their horses. Steve was recognized for his riding. It was fun, and Francie bought tickets for Jack and Frank. Sam stayed home with the kids.

It was nice to have the apartment to stay in, although Steve flew home the next day. On Monday, she and Jack went to the office for the first time in three months.

Everybody was happy to see them, and Rosa embraced them both and had their favorite donuts and a hot pot of coffee waiting for them.

"I love this woman," Jack said, biting into his cinnamon crusted bagel. Nobody asked any questions, and Jack didn't offer any answers as to where they had been or what had happened.

Jack went into his office and closed the door. He sat in his chair and swiveled around a few times. Then he looked through his desk drawers and straightened a few things around on his desk. It felt so good to be back. This was as close to normal as he had felt in a long time. Here, he didn't miss Annie so much, because she had never come to New York with him. Here, he wasn't Jack who had been abducted; he was Jack, *executive* vice president and a man very capable of leading them. He led staff meetings and sealed deals. He was solid, strong, and in control.

At their staff meeting that morning, Danny introduced the new spring line: products Francie and Jack had seen samples of online but not in person. Cassie followed up with their marketing plan. Bart then gave them a financial update. They had had an overwhelmingly good sales period over Christmas. Francie's little business, staffed mostly with amateurs, was possibly going to hit the Fortune 500 this year.

Francie smiled. "You guys are amazing," she said. "Jack and I haven't been very involved these past few months, and you have not only held the company together but raised it a few notches. I love you all!"

Cassie smiled. "We missed you guys," she said.

Morale was high at Dalton Jeans. Francie walked through the entire building after the meeting and talked with other employees. She saw that the daycare was running well, and several people had their children at their desks with them, coloring or cutting with scissors. One mother, Karen, was nursing her baby discreetly in her office when Francie walked in.

"When he's done, you can see him," Karen said. "I'm so happy, and thank you so much for your relaxed policies. I need to work, but I would never have been able to leave him. I had no idea I'd feel this way after he was born. This is perfect. After he's done eating, I just take him back to daycare for his nap, and I can go check on him during the day. Thank you." She was beaming with happiness.

When Francie got back to her office, Frank was waiting for her.

"Rosa says you only order lunch from Tio's," he said. "I'm hungry. Let's order."

"Oh!" Francie clapped her hands together. "Yes! Feed me now! Tio's! Oh, Frank, it's to *die* for." She pulled out a menu. "Here."

Then she dialed Jack.

"Rosa's ordering lunch from Tio's," she said. "Put in your order."

She hung up. "It's soooo good. And did you see that Rosa had my favorite donut waiting for me? I just love this place."

Francie twirled around her desk. She grabbed the latest jeans, which were hanging on a clothes rack nearby. "And these. Wow—did you see what Danny did with the pockets?" She noticed Frank was laughing at her. "What?"

"You're having fun," he said. "It's just fun to see you... having fun."

"It is a bit like playing," she said. "I get to run this place. It's sort of like playing employer and dress-up all at the same time. Oh, and I didn't tell you. We're flying Rick the Rockstar in for a photo shoot. Danny says if we can get his butt into a pair of these, they will sell like hotcakes."

"I thought you weren't using sex to sell," Frank said.

"Rick isn't sexy—he's my soon-to-be son-in-law," Francie said. "So ewww. No, we're using his rising popularity. Celebrity, Cassie calls it."

"I see."

She threw her hands up into the air. "I *love* this place!"

chapter
66

FEBRUARY WAS NOT FRANCIE'S FAVORITE MONTH for many reasons, but mostly because it marked the anniversary of the car crash.

She went into February this year like she always did, full steam. After two months off of work with racing, she started the horses back in training and helped Donovan ship them off to the tracks he was running them at. She pulled December out of his rest and started prepping him for racing with her eye on the Kentucky Derby.

"This horse can do it," Steve said, and she agreed. He wasn't one of *their* horses—he wasn't from one of Flame's bloodlines—but he was her rescue, and it made it all the more special because he wouldn't run for anybody else. Not even Donovan.

One hot morning, they went to the barn to feed. It was a Monday, so most of the staff was off since Francie preferred them to work the weekend.

"I noticed a tree fell and broke part of the south side pasture fence," Frank said. "I'm going to call Jack and see if he can help me fix it,"

At 10 a.m., under blistering heat a bit uncommon for Florida that time of year, Frank, Francie, and Jack were out in the pasture, ripping apart a section of the fence to replace it. A few curious horses stood nearby, watching.

"You start digging that one out," Frank told Jack, pointing to a fence post. "I'll start on this one."

Francie was kneeling between them with the parrot jaws, trying to cut apart the branches of the tree that had smashed the fence down when it fell on top of it. She was sweating buckets.

She glanced at Frank, then Jack. They were both covered in dirt. A bee buzzed at her, and she shooshed it away, but it came back, so she took her hat off and swatted at it. It left and that's when she saw Jack out of the corner of her eye. He jumped up and staggered back from the fence post like he had been bitten, and for a moment, she thought he had found the bee's nest. He backed up a few more steps and dropped the shovel, clutching his head with both dirt-encrusted gloved hands. Francie was about to shout "bees!" when she realized that nothing was buzzing around him.

She glanced at Frank, who was still digging away at his post, trying to chop the splintered part out of the ground.

"Jack?" she said, standing up and wiping her hands on her jeans.

He didn't answer, so she took a few steps toward him.

Just then, Frank's post snapped, making a loud crack, which spooked the horses that had been watching. They snorted, turned tail, and ran. Jack, startled by the noise, dropped his hands and said, "I've gotta get out of here," then took off at a brisk pace back toward the barn. His hands were shaking, and his eyes had that terrified look in them that Francie had seen so often at night.

"What on earth?" Frank said.

"I think he just had a flashback," Francie said. "I'll see if he's okay."

Frank looked at the dropped shovel, the half-finished fence post, and the nearby horses who were now cantering around the pasture, bucking in pretend terror. They snorted at him as they brushed by.

"But we have a downed fence and horses... "

Francie sighed, exasperated. "I knew we should have locked them up."

"But you said they like to help," Frank said lightly.

She looked at him.

"Go," he said. "See if he's okay. I can handle a few loose horses."

"Thanks."

Francie took off running toward the barn. By the time she got there, Jack was at the water pump, splashing water on his face.

She caught up to him, out of breath.

"Jack?"

He turned the water off and wiped his face on his shirt. "Tell Frank I'm sorry. I can't do this right now."

He was short of breath and trembling.

"Jack... "

"Francie, not now. I need to be alone."

He left the barn and went off toward his house.

Francie stood there a moment, undecided, then turned to go back to help Frank.

"I don't know," she said to his questioning look. "He wants to be alone. I'm pretty sure it was a flashback."

It took them two more hours, but they managed to finish up the section of the fence by themselves. The horses came back to watch. By the time they were done, Francie was soaked with sweat.

At home, she took a long, cool shower, ate a bite of lunch with Frank, then went up to her office to get ready for her 1:00 meeting with Jack. Dalton Jeans was on her agenda for the next two hours.

She wasn't sure if he would actually show up, and decided that if he didn't, she was definitely going to go check on him. But he came, on time, and sat down in his chair, handing her a folder of papers to sign.

She didn't open the folders but instead, just looked at him.

"Flashback?" she said.

He nodded.

"You okay?"

He held up his shaking hands.

"Do you want to talk about it?"

"No." The word came so abruptly it cut off the end of her sentence.

She took a deep breath, and then opened the first folder. "We got the fence fixed," she said conversationally. "The horses were transfixed by the whole thing." She glanced across at him. He was looking down at his hands, fiddling with his pen. "So tell me what I'm signing here."

"Umm... those on top are for the ads we placed... in New Vogue and Country, er, Country something or other." He stood up. "I can't do this. Francie, I need the rest of the day off."

He started to pace.

"Tell me," she said.

"No. The point is to *quit* thinking about it. "

"And how's that working for you so far?"

"You know, you're not a therapist," he said, turning on her in anger. His hands went to his head, and he rubbed his temples. He was breathing hard, hyperventilating. "You don't always need to try and fix me. Sometimes, you just need to let things go. I need some air."

He walked out, slamming the door behind him.

She sat there, staring blankly at the papers for a few moments. Then she picked up her phone and left him a simple message. "If you want to talk, you know I'm here."

She didn't expect a reply and didn't get one.

That night, she insisted that Jack sleep in his room at her house. He had been edgy all evening and didn't eat much dinner, distracted. He had thought the kids would bring him out of the past, but he couldn't seem to get over the anxiety that had started that morning.

He gathered his things from his house, left Spike with an extra helping of dry food, grabbed his laptop, and settled in early in the guest room to get some work done before bedtime. But he couldn't think. He was exhausted from his day. He saw that the clock said 10 p.m., so he closed his laptop and lay down, turning off the light. He was asleep almost instantly.

It was 2 am. when her cell phone woke her up. Francie grabbed it. It was Jack.

"Francie... " She could tell by his voice what he needed.

"I'll be right there," she said. She pulled on some sweatpants and made her way down the dark hallway to his room. He was sitting on his bed, his head clutched in his hands, rocking back and forth.

"I had a nightmare. I can't make it stop," he said, his voice panicked.

She sat down beside him on the bed. "How long have you been up?"

"About two hours." His voice was raw, raspy. "I can't make it stop."

"Tell me about the dream."

"I can't."

His shirt was soaked, and he was cold now, shaking. Francie went over to his drawer and pulled out a fresh t-shirt. He kept some clothes here since he stayed over so often.

"Here," she said, gently handing it to him.

In the darkness, he pulled off his other shirt and put the dry one on. She pulled a quilt off the nearby chair and put it over his shoulders. "Please make it stop." He was rubbing his temples, his voice barely a whisper. "It won't stop. I can't keep going on, Francie. It's too awful. Please."

There was a light knock on the door. Frank. Jack got up and went to the bathroom, while Francie quietly asked Frank for some tea. "And bring the Symatrex, just in case," she said.

Frank left to go make tea, thankful he had the easier of the two jobs.

Jack was running water for a long time in the sink. The door was open. "What are you doing?" Francie asked.

When he didn't answer, she went to the doorway. Jack was scrubbing his hands with a nail brush.

"I can't get the smell of dirt off of them," he said.

"Dirt?"

He swore and turned the water off, wiping his hands on the towel. He paced back to the bedroom and sat on the bed, his trembling causing the bed frame to shake. He put his hands back to his head. "God!" he shouted. "I need it to stop!"

Francie sat down beside him. "Jack," she said. "It's okay."

"Francie, I need you to help me. I need some Symatrex. *Please.*"

"I asked Frank to bring it up with the tea," she said. She wanted to rub his back or do something to comfort him. "Can I touch you?"

"No."

Frank knocked again and entered. His eyes weren't adjusted to the darkness, so he held out the tea, and Francie took it. She put both cups on the nightstand and took the Symatrex from him.

She gave Frank a kiss on the cheek. "We'll be okay now," she said. "Get some sleep. I'll be there eventually."

He left, and she made her way back over to the bed and handed Jack his tea. His hands were shaking so badly he couldn't take the cup.

"Tell me about it," she said. "We can work through this."

There was a long silence. Finally, he took a deep breath and let it out slowly. "They... " he began. "When I was a POW, they... "

He stopped. "I can't."

He put his head in his hands.

"Francie," he lowered his hand and held it to her. She took it. He hung on, as if for dear life. She felt him trembling beside her.

"I need the Symatrex," he said, squeezing her hand. "Please." His voice had taken on a begging quality, and she felt guilty for waiting so long.

"Okay," she said. "I need some light." She let go of his hand and leaned over to turn on the nightstand light. She got a syringe out and filled it from the little vial.

"Why don't you lie down," she said. He slid over and laid down on the bed, his back to her. She rolled up his sleeve. "Okay," she said. "Here goes."

"Wait."

She paused.

"What if I dream?"

"You won't."

"Okay. I'm ready."

She pushed the needle into his skin and plunged the medicine into his arm. He flinched a little, then raised his arm up and took her hand.

"I'm afraid," he said as the medicine started taking hold.

"I'm here."

"Don't leave me."

"I won't," she promised. As he fell asleep, she pulled the quilt up over him. She was exhausted, both from her morning working on the fence and from her worry over Jack this afternoon. She thought of Frank in their warm bed down the hall, then looked down at her friend, who was finally resting, unconscious on the bed beside her. As she reached over to put the needle away, exhaustion overtook her. She lay down beside him, on top of the quilt, holding his hand in hers, and started drifting off.

Frank peeked his head in.

"Francie?" he whispered. "I came to put the Symatrex back in the fridge."

She weakly pointed to it, her eyes closed.

Frank stood over her, looking down at his wife, laying on the bed, her hand holding his best friend's.

"Francie," he said in a whisper. "You do realize you're in bed with another man?"

"Mmmmmm," she said, nearly asleep.

"It doesn't seem right."

"I'm on top of the covers. He's underneath," Francie mumbled. "He's unconscious. Nothing to worry about."

Frank looked down at them for a few minutes, watching Francie, who was now fast asleep. He thought he should care, but he realized that he didn't. After all he had been through in his life—heck, just in the past few months—this seemed inconsequential. He leaned down and kissed Francie on the cheek. He pulled a blanket over her.

"Goodnight, sweetheart."

"Mmmmmmm," she said.

Then he turned out the lamp on the nightstand and left, quietly closing the door behind him.

Francie slept late the next morning. She was surprised when she woke up, and Jack was gone. It was 10 a.m.

"I've got to get out of this habit," she said to herself, rubbing her eyes. For years she had been an early riser, at the track before the sun was even up.

She sat on the edge of the bed for a few minutes, then heard some pattering down the hallway. Andy burst into the room.

"Momma!" he said. "I love you!"

She gave him a hug, smelling his little boy smell.

"I love you too!" she said.

"Andy, don't wake Momma!" Frank whispered and looked in the room. "Well good morning, sleepyhead," he said, holding a spatula. "Pancakes, downstairs."

"Good morning," she said, getting up and wrapping her arms around him. "Or good afternoon."

"It's not that bad—yet," he said. "At least it's still morning. We all slept in. Andy didn't get up until 9:00."

"Wow," Francie said. "I guess it's a good thing I have staff to feed the horses today."

"Jack went home. He says he'll see you at one." Frank hurried back down the stairs to flip his pancakes, and Francie went to wash up. After breakfast, the three of them went down to the barn. She found Steve, and they exercised December.

"A Derby hopeful should be on a schedule," Steve said.

"I know," Francie said. "But I thought about it—this is good for him. He's flexible. He's getting used to running in the afternoon heat. He should be fine on the racing circuit due to his flexible nature."

"You just keep telling yourself that."

December worked beautifully and happily, and Francie headed to the house feeling pretty good. She'd had a great seven hours of solid sleep last night, and a few hours earlier before her sleep had been broken by Jack's phone call. She stretched as she walked back toward the house, rubbing her arm. She was a bit sore from digging out that fence post yesterday.

Andy stayed at the barn with Frank, so Francie could work in her office for a few hours.

She took a break around noon and went down to fix herself a cup of soup. She sipped it in her office, moving from horse papers to Dalton papers. At exactly 1 p.m., Jack walked in.

"Good afternoon, boss," he said. He sounded tense.

"Hey," she said. She glanced at him but didn't say anything about last night. She had learned not to talk about it the next day.

He sat down in his chair and showed her a graph he had been working on. It traced the growth of different articles of clothing they had made, along with purses and accessories, and how much they sold during which seasons.

She noticed his hands weren't shaking.

"This is awesome," she said. "Thanks. If you could present that at Thursday's meeting, that would be great. And get a copy to each member of the team."

"Of course," he snapped. "I didn't make it just for us to look at."

She sat back and folded her arms across her chest.

"Don't start giving me attitude," she said. "You asked for the Symatrex, so I gave it to you."

"It has nothing to do with that."

"Let's not pretend this is about work." Every time she gave him the drug, he was mad at her the next day. And grateful. It was a strange mixture of emotions. Ruth said he was probably embarrassed of being so needy and wasn't sure where he stood with her because the drug blocked out part of his memories. How much of a coward had he made of himself? How much had he asked for or fought off the drug she'd eventually given him?

She tried to cut him some slack. She knew it wasn't personal.

"I hate that drug," he said.

"And yet you needed it. End of conversation."

"You slept with me in your husband's house," he said.

"You were upset." Francie said. "You asked me not to leave."

Jack lowered his eyes. "And Frank?"

"Don't worry about Frank. He came in and kissed me goodnight."

Jack shook his head. "You have to quit doing this for me."

"I'm here as long as you need me. You know that."

They were quiet for a while, then he said, "I'd be glad to show the graph at the meeting on Thursday. I made up a Power Point. Why don't you take a look at it?"

He opened his laptop and slid it across the desk to her. As she was looking at the presentation, he got up and closed the office door and sat back down. When she looked up at him again, he was pale.

"This is very good," she said, then glanced at the closed door. "But I'm guessing we're not going to talk about this now."

He fidgeted with his pencil for a moment, then looked up at her. "I thought a lot this morning about what happened yesterday, and if you want to hear it, I'll tell you about it."

She closed the laptop, then sat back in her chair, her hands on her lap. "Of course," she said.

He swallowed. "When I was digging... you were right. I had a flashback. The dirt triggered it," he said. "It was bad. I was right back there in the camp. The smell of the dirt, the feel of the dirt. I was *there*, no longer standing in the horse pasture. Then I couldn't get that memory to go away. Sometimes I can push them back and go on. But not yesterday. I thought by nighttime that I was okay, but it came back in the dream. I remember asking you for the Symatrex. No, actually, I think I was *begging* you, and you didn't want to give it to me. I'm sorry I put you though that."

"No, it's okay. I should have given it to you sooner."

"I don't remember much... but I remember asking for the shot."

He paused for a moment, looking down at his hands. They were steady, but his breathing had increased. He looked back up at her.

"They had a certain punishment for me," he said. "When I fought too much during the... " He swallowed and looked back down at his hands. "I was punished. They thought this would make me quit fighting, because it was quite a terrifying punishment."

Now his hands started to shake. He sat forward, rubbing his face. He took another deep breath. When he continued, his voice was strong.

"They used to tie me to a board," he said. "Flat to it, on my back. Then they'd throw me face up in a grave and start shoveling dirt on me. They told me they were going to bury me alive, and I'd die slowly, suffocating under all that dirt. They'd shovel and get me pretty covered up, laughing the whole time and taunting me, and then they'd pull me out. They had figured out just when to get me before I passed out from not being able to breathe." He had watched Francie as he talked, and saw the blood drain out of her face. "That was my punishment when they felt I had misbehaved, and they promised me that one day, their leader would no longer find interest in me and that is how they would kill me. They would bury me alive."

Francie was speechless.

"That's where I was yesterday, instead of standing in that horse pasture," he said. "I was back in that grave. And I was back there last night in my dream."

When she could finally speak, Francie said, "I didn't think it could get any worse. I don't even know what to say to you. 'Are you all right?' sounds... stupid."

He was trembling. "I need some fresh air," he said and stood up.

She started to say something else to him but was so upset by what she had just heard that she couldn't say anything.

"Are you okay?" he asked.

She nodded. He turned and left.

After a minute of stunned silence, Francie got up and closed her office door. Then she put her face in her hands and wept.

She could no longer work, so she went to the barn. She avoided Jack for the rest of the afternoon, and he didn't show up for dinner. Frank kept asking her what was wrong, but she wouldn't talk.

"Later," was all she said to him. "I can't right now."

They ate dinner in silence, except for the happy bubbling chatter of Andy. Sam and Steve had taken Lexie out for dinner.

"I need to do something," Francie said to Frank that evening after they cleaned up the kitchen. "I have an idea. Can you watch Andy for a few hours? I'm going to the barn."

"Sure," he said. "Are you okay?"

"I think so. I think I've figured it out."

When Jack opened his door, Francie was standing there with his laptop. She handed it to him.

"I need you to come with me," she said. "I have something for you."

He pulled on his boots and followed her to the barn. It was quiet, and the horses were munching the last of their hay. The staff had gone home for the day. A few horses stuck their heads over their stall doors and quietly whickered a greeting. She went down the aisle, rubbing King on the nose as she passed, and stopped in front of a stall door. She took the halter off its hook and haltered the filly inside.

"This is Terra," she said. "Her full name is Sunnyhill Terra Cotta, because of her color, but I call her Terra for short. I know you've probably seen her over in the other barn. I just brought her to the main barn last night. She's my favorite, aside from King."

She led Terra out and put her in the cross ties. She picked up a brush. "When I get upset, you know I come out here to the barn. I brush my horses or go for a ride, and it clears my head. After you and I talked today, I needed something to clear my head, so I came out here. It's like therapy."

She picked up another brush and handed it to Jack.

"I was planning to make Terra my other riding horse. She's two and nearly old enough, which is why I moved her to the main barn. But what do I need with another riding horse? So I'm giving her to you."

"Me?" he said.

Jack stood there, holding the brush, watching Francie brush down the long, smooth neck of the Arabian filly. The horse was beautiful. She was a light bay in color, with a shiny black mane and tail. She had three white feet that came up just past the cornet band and a small star on her forehead.

"Come here," Francie said gently, and Jack walked toward her. She took his hand that was holding the brush and ran it down Terra's shoulder. "Go with the grain of the hair."

"Francie... I'm not really a horse person."

"I need to help you, Jack. You told me not to try to fix you, just to listen. I can't. I need to fix. And this is what helps *me*. I want to give you a horse. You'll bond with her, and she'll be the greatest therapy you can imagine. I know she will. She's got a gentle spirit and really wants to please."

He looked at the filly, who turned her head back and nuzzled him for more brushing.

"You brush this side, and I'll get her other side," Francie said.

The two of them worked on the mare in silence. Francie finished and took a different brush and handed it to Jack. "For her mane," she said. She got herself a similar brush and started working on the tail.

Jack found the strokes to be therapeutic. As he worked, his mind calmed with the rhythmic motion of his hands and the stillness of the barn. The warm body beneath his hands responded in subtle ways to his touch, and he marveled at how her skin could detect even the lightest pressure.

He thought about arguing with Francie, but she had been right about the kitten. He found Spike's presence very comforting and loved the way the little guy followed him around and slept on him while he watched television or read.

After Francie finished with the tail, she picked up a hoof pick.

"To clean out her feet, you stand like this," she said, demonstrating with her back to the horse's head and her shoulder up against the horse's shoulder. "I pat her shoulder, then run my hand down her leg, and she picks up her foot."

The horse did as she described.

"This is called the frog." She pointed to a triangular section inside the bottom of the foot. "It's like her shock absorber. It's a tender area, so you pick around that area and clean the hoof out, like this. Once you start riding her, you'll want to make sure there are no stones in there before you take her out."

She did the front and back of Terra's right side, then handed the hoof pick to Jack.

He only hesitated a little, and then followed what she had shown him. He cleaned out the other two hooves.

"So that's about it," said Francie. "She's a clean horse now."

He put the hoof pick back and turned to pet the mare on her face. She lowered her head and nuzzled him. He blew softly on her nose, the way he had seen Francie do with so many other horses, and Terra blew softly back, communicating with him. Then she nuzzled him again, asking for more petting.

"Okay," he said.

"Okay, what?"

"Okay. I'll let you give me a horse."

"Really?" A big grin spread across Francie's face.

Jack smiled and patted Terra on the neck. He had his own horse.

After that, Jack started talking to Ruth. Although she had been coming regularly for the past four months, he hadn't said much to her during their hour-long sessions.

The next one went differently.

He figured he had shared some of his most horrific memories with Francie and survived, so maybe it was time to start talking to the expert. He wanted to get better. He *needed* to get better, so Francie could get back to her own life. He owed her—and Frank—that much.

So when Ruth showed up, she expected their typical friendly chat time, and his shrugs and vague responses to her questions. Instead, he was the one who started the conversation.

"I know you've put up with a lot of my BS these past few months," he said. "I appreciate that, and the fact that you've been patient with me, understanding that I wasn't ready. Now I'm ready to start talking. Where do you want me to start?"

"Why not at the beginning," Ruth suggested.

So he did.

chapter 67

Early in March, Jack was in his kitchen, cooking dinner for himself. He was making a beef stir fry, and had several things going in the pan, and the rice bubbling nearby in a pot. He loved to cook and had lately returned to that passion.

The television was on. He had rented a sci-fi movie that he was looking forward to watching with dinner, but now the sports network was playing in the background.

Spike was rubbing against his leg, hoping for a dropped morsel.

Jack had returned from the barn about a half hour before. He went several times a day now and had started taking Terra treats. Now she greeted him with a loud whinny every time he stepped in the barn. He had surprised himself by falling madly in love with the horse very quickly. She loved him right back. He was bordering on what he might call happiness.

His veggies were finished, and he added the cooked meat, stirring in a spicy sauce from a bottle, then dumped the whole skillet full of food over a plate of rice. He poured himself a glass of iced tea and carried the whole thing over to the coffee table. He picked up the remote and had just hit "play" when there was a knock on the front door.

He got up and opened it, expecting to see Francie or Sam or anybody from the Big House. Instead, it was Annie.

"Hi," she said.

He stood there, too stunned to speak, then shot a look up at the front gate.

"They let me in," Annie said. "I still live here."

He put his hand on the doorframe, blocking her way in.

"No, you don't," he said. "Not anymore."

He saw the hurt in her eyes.

"I'm back from England. I want to talk."

"I don't want to listen," Jack said.

"I still have a lot of my things here," Annie said. "Can I at least come in?"

It was true, she did still have a lot of her things here. Jack hadn't touched them. The dresser drawers were still full of her clothes, as was half the walk-in closet he shared with her. Most of her shoes were still here. He often wondered how she survived on the little she had taken with her when she left. She had only planned to be gone a few days—not five months.

Jack stepped aside.

"Get your stuff, and get out," he said.

Annie came in and glanced at his dinner in front of the TV. Spike rubbed against her leg and she looked down, startled. "Oh! You got a cat!"

Jack didn't say anything, and he paused his movie. His food was getting cold.

"Hurry up," he said, his arms crossed.

She looked at him, and her hand went to her heart.

"Jack, I'm so sorry," she said. "I love you. I was just scared. I was overwhelmed and tired and just couldn't function and then my grandma finally gave me a place to rest and talked some sense into me. Please, let's just talk." The words spilled out of Annie so quickly she couldn't stop them.

"I never meant to hurt you. I just needed to get away, just for a few days. I didn't expect Stanton to happen and then you were so hurt and didn't want to see me, and you threw me out of the hospital room and let Francie stay, and I was so hurt and thought you hated me." Her words came out in a rush, tumbling over each other. "You never called me. I even came back to the hospital to see you, but you had been discharged already."

She took a deep breath and laughed nervously. "I had planned what to say to you today; in my head, it was going to be a lot more organized and calmer."

Jack stood there, glowering at her, but there was a slight hesitation in his eyes.

"Get your stuff," he said.

She turned and went into their bedroom. Things looked a little different. The bed had been moved a little father over, and he had a new bedside lamp. It looked like the carpet had been recently shampooed. She opened her drawer and was relieved to see that her clothes were all still there. She pulled out a scarf, then realized she didn't have anything to pack it in and sat down on the bed, holding it.

Jack was standing in the doorway.

She looked at him again, holding the scarf up to her face and smelling the familiar smells of home. She closed her eyes and pretended, just for a moment, that she was back, two years ago, right after their marriage when she was so happy.

None of this had been his fault. He had always been good to her. She had let him down.

She got up from the bed and slowly walked over to him. She stood close enough so he could smell her cream rinse, a favorite of his. Her hair hung loosely on her shoulders, and she had worn a shirt that she knew was a favorite of his. His handsome face was right there, and she longed to touch it. "I missed you," she whispered.

"Annie, don't," he said. His life was finally getting back on track. He didn't want this.

She leaned in and kissed him lightly on the lips. Her smell, her touch, intoxicated him. It had been a long time. A very long time.

She put her hand on the side of his cheek, gently touching him. "I'm so sorry," she said. Tears welled up in her eyes. The shame and guilt she felt was almost too much for her. She knew she'd have to work a million years to make it up to him, and even then, that wouldn't be enough. "Can you give me another chance? I know I don't deserve it. Let's just talk. Let me tell you what my grandma said. I know I've been wrong. I've been selfish. I've been a fool and a coward. Jack, please let me stay. At least for a while."

He didn't answer, and she leaned forward, kissing him again. Her heart ached for him, and her insides quivered. She wanted more. Apparently, so did he.

He tasted her lips and put his hand around her lower back, pulling her into him. They kissed long and hard, and he found out how hungry he was for her. He ran his hands through her hair. She took his hand and pulled him toward the bed. Clothes came off rapidly, and they were kissing more. He gently laid her on the bed and laid down on top of her. He kissed her throat and she cried out, wanting more and pulled him down on her.

Jack's food sat outside on the coffee table, forgotten, except by the cat, who delicately licked around the spicy parts and enjoyed the plate of meat his owner had left there for him.

"Just like that, you just took her back," Frank said. They were golfing the next morning. Annie had left for work.

"Well, not *just* like that. We have a lot to talk about."

"You slept well?"

"We didn't do much sleeping," Jack said, hitting the ball with his nine iron.

Frank whistled. "Nicely played." They watched the ball land on the green, near the tee. "So she seduced you."

"Basically."

Frank sighed and hit his own ball, which fell far short of the green. It wasn't going to be a par for him on this hole.

"Francie's angry."

"I figured as much."

"Francie doesn't trust easily," Frank said, capping his club and climbing in the golf cart. "She trusted Annie, and Annie left her. That's the way she looks at it. She was fuming mad when she woke up this morning and saw her car still there."

"She can't be happy for us?"

"Not yet. Trust must be rebuilt. This is Francie we're talking about."

Jack wasn't sure what he felt. He didn't trust Annie either. And truthfully speaking, it hadn't been trust he was thinking about last night. It was sex.

"I'm a fool," he said.

"No," said Frank. "I don't think so. I think you're wise to try again. She's your wife, and judging by the way she left at the beginning of all of this, she was fleeing for her life. She was really struggling with something, and it sounds like now, maybe, she has worked it all out."

"She's bringing the rest of her stuff back today. She has been living with her girlfriend all these months, except for when she was in England."

"When did she get back?"

"She got back in February. She took a few weeks to think about it all and process what her grandma said about love and marriage and second chances. Maybe this is it."

"I hope so. I believe in second chances."

"Me too."

After dinner alone with Annie, Jack walked over to the Big House.

"Hey, Princess," he said. Francie was sitting at the kitchen table, doing watercolors with Sam and the two kids.

"Hey," she said.

"Can we talk? Privately?"

Francie nodded reluctantly and put her brush in the water. "Andy, finish painting Momma's horse for her, will you?"

"Okay, Momma."

Francie followed Jack upstairs. He closed the office door.

"Don't hate me," he said.

"I don't hate you."

"It just happened. She caught me off guard, and I'm not going to lie—there was sex involved."

"Ewww."

"And Francie, she's my *wife*. She's begging for a second chance. I have to give it to her. She keeps saying she was overwhelmed by all of this and scared. I know what it's like to be afraid. I have to cut her some slack."

Francie sat down heavily in her chair and twirled it back and forth.

"I know. I'm happy for you."

"No, you're not."

"I just don't trust her," Francie said. "Not yet. That's going to take time. Frank is all ready to work on this too. I will do my best—for *you*—but don't expect miracles in only a few days."

"Okay."

"Jack, this is just too fast. Why can't you just ask her to take it slow, and then actually do that? Have a few dinners together before she moves back in."

"It's not like I can *un*-invite her. I already told her she could move back in."

"Was that right after the sex?"

He frowned at her. "None of your business."

"I'm not so sure about that. Who's going to help you pick up the pieces if this falls apart?"

"I get it. You did all the hard work and here she comes after the hard part is over, waltzing in to 'take care of me'."

Francie sighed. "It's not that. I don't know. It just doesn't feel right."

He sat there for a while, contemplating. He had gotten himself into this. He could get himself out of it. But he wasn't sure he wanted to. He really loved Annie.

The next morning, Annie left the house early and stopped by the track, where she knew Francie would be. Steve had just finished with December, and he brought him back for a cool down.

"Barracuda, 4:00," he whispered down to Francie. She turned to look and saw Annie walking toward her.

"Hi," Annie said.

"I see you've come back," Francie said.

"Look, you have a right to hate me," Annie said. "But I really want to start over. Francie, I miss you."

Annie was sincere and looked hurt when her old girlfriend didn't embrace her. Instead, Francie got right in her face.

"Jack is just getting his life back on track. If you break him, I'll be on you like a bear on honey, and you won't set foot on my farm again as long as you live, you got it?"

Annie swallowed. "I guess I know where I stand with *you*," she said. "Yes, I got it. I'm not here to hurt him. Or you."

She turned and started walking back to her car. "I really do want to try to be friends again," she said over her shoulder.

Steve walked the horse up and stopped behind Francie.

"Wow," he said. "Maybe I called the wrong woman 'barracuda'."

"Steve, shut up," Francie said.

"Absolutely not," Ruth said when she came for Jack's session the next day. "You can't move in."

"But I *live* here," Annie said.

"You forfeited that privilege when you left," Ruth said, not unkindly. "Jack is in recovery, and we need to take this slowly. I'd prefer you didn't spend the night again, at least for a while."

"How long?" Annie asked.

"Let's give it a week and then see," Ruth said.

Annie decided to spend a few nights at her friend's house and move slowly. She wanted to show everyone she was trustworthy and wasn't going to jeopardize Jack's recovery. So they started dating again.

They met in town for dinner and walked along the beach, with Jack's bodyguard, Gunny, always in the background. Most evenings, she came to the house, and they made dinner together and talked. Finally, after a week, she just stayed late and decided not to go home. Ruth agreed they could give it a try.

Jack slept well most nights. He welcomed Annie's warm body next to his, even if Spike was a bit miffed about losing his spot. But the cat got over it and eventually warmed up to Annie as well.

Annie seemed genuine. She moved slowly, and whenever Jack needed space, she backed off. She only asked him once or twice what had happened to him, and she didn't push him when he didn't answer. He slowly started to trust her.

After about three weeks together, he began to tell her small things about himself. Just *small* things. No details, but it was enough that he was sharing *something* with her. He balanced her need to know with his need to remain a man in her eyes. She needed to know the things that had happened to him, why he was sometimes averse to touch, why he startled so easily, and why he had nightmares. But she didn't need to know details.

She handled the nightmares well when they came. She did what Francie had told her to do. Keep the lights dim, put a warm blanket around him, bring him some tea with a little sugar in it.

They started to work things out.

Francie began to relax. She left Jack on weekends to put December into some pre-Derby stakes races. Her horse won a small starting race, then took the prestigious Santa Anita Derby by three lengths. Suddenly he was the horse to watch.

She came back home after her weekends away, thrilled to be back in racing. Andy and Frank went with her—she wasn't going to leave Andy like she had Becky. She was careful to keep her trips short, and she often took her son to New York as well. Jack came for the Wednesday-Thursday trips, and they stayed in the apartment, usually with Frank.

Jack was doing well.

At the end of that three weeks, when he was home, he had a nightmare that Annie couldn't pull him out of. He was huddled in the corner of their room, on the floor, and kept asking her to make it stop. This went on for a half hour, and he was shaking so badly she was afraid he was sick. Desperate, she realized he was going to need the medication, and she fumbled with the Symatrex, thinking she'd give him a shot like Ruth had taught her to with the orange. It took her three tries to get the syringe filled because her hands were shaking so badly, and when she got to Jack, she froze. She couldn't do it. Needles had always made her queasy, and she was afraid she'd hurt him.

"Just do it," Jack said. She hesitated, and he ran to the bathroom and vomited. As she heard him retching for the second time that night, she picked up the phone and called Francie.

"Francie," she said, "I need your help. I can't give him the shot."

She was horrified to realize she was crying. Within minutes, Frank and Francie were both there. She met Francie at the front door and handed her the needle. Francie went straight to the bedroom with it.

Annie looked at Frank, and tears started falling. "I blew it. He needs me, and I blew it. I'm such a stupid idiot." She began to sob, and Frank pulled her against his chest in a bear hug.

"It's okay, Annie. You've been doing wonderfully. Francie had to call Ruth the first time too."

"It's horrible. He's so sick. So terrified."

"I know." He kept her enfolded in his arms, letting her cry.

Francie found Jack in the bathroom, sitting on the floor, leaning against the wall.

"Hey." She knelt down next to him. He wouldn't meet her eyes.

"I'm so cold."

"Let's get you to the bed."

She reached for his hand.

"Don't," he said, getting to his feet. He almost fell twice but made it to the bed and sat down on the edge. Francie closed the bedroom door and sat beside him.

"Do you want to do this without the Symatrex?"

He just sat there and shook.

"Jack?"

She reached her hand out to him, palm up. He took it and laced his fingers though hers.

"Where's Annie?" he asked.

"She's out in the living room with Frank. Do you want her?"

"No."

He looked at the needle in her other hand. "I hate that stuff," he said.

"I know. You don't need it."

"I do. I want it. I want this to go away."

He pulled his hand away from hers and buried his face in his hands. "Oh, God... "

He rocked back and forth on the bed, as if in physical agony, then ran to the bathroom again.

When he returned, he was spent.

"Lay down," Francie said. "I'll give you the shot." She knew he wasn't going to be able to relax on his own anytime soon. He laid down on his side, facing away from the door, curled into a fetal position. "I need to turn on the light."

She reached for the bedside lamp and clicked it on. She saw a tear escape the corner of his eye.

"What if I dream?"

"You won't."

She rolled up his sleeve.

"Don't leave me."

She didn't answer, unsure of what to do. Instead, she inserted the needle and pressed the plunger. She held his hand as he drifted off toward sleep and peace.

She sat there a moment, waiting to make sure the medicine took effect. Then she reached over to switch off the lamp. It was then that she noticed the bedroom door was open. Annie was standing in the doorway.

"Thank you," Annie said, sniffing.

"He's out. He'll sleep for about six hours," Francie said.

She walked past Annie and out into the living room, putting the medicine away.

"I'm sorry. I failed. I thought I could do it."

Annie was looking for encouragement. When Francie kept working and didn't say anything, Frank gave her a look. She closed the refrigerator door and turned toward Annie. She felt a stirring of pity inside her, but even more, she felt a longing to have her girlfriend back.

"Annie," she said. "It's okay. It's hard on all of us. You did fine. I'm glad you called me. Frank and I are here if you need us."

"He wants you to stay," Annie said. "I heard him say that."

"He won't know if I'm here or not," Francie said.

"He will when he wakes. You can sleep on the couch."

Francie hesitated. Frank took her elbow and steered her toward the door. "We're good," he said.

"Yes," Francie said. "He needs *you*, Annie. Just be here when he wakes up. Make him a nice breakfast. He's usually starving."

Annie nodded. She looked very small and frightened.

Francie went out the front door, and Frank followed her. It took them both a long time to get back to sleep.

chapter 68

"Yes! Yes! Yes!" Steve pumped his hand up and down as he sailed across the finish line in the Bluegrass stakes, two lengths ahead of the favorite. He patted December on the neck and slowed the horse down. "We did it again, boy!"

By now, the horse was national news, as were Francie and Steve. The "wonder team," people called them. Another impossible horse plucked from a life of abuse, running out of love for its trainer. That's what the stories said, anyway.

And Steve was the only jockey who had been able to stay on him.

They accepted their trophy in the winner's circle.

"Where next?" the announcer asked.

Francie looked at Steve and smiled. "I guess we're headed for the Kentucky Derby!"

Applause went up from the crowd, spooking December. Steve laughed and raised his crop in salute. "We're off!"

Annie felt Jack snuggle up next to her in bed and put his arm around her. It was late April, and there was a soft rain on the roof, lulling him to sleep. Annie smiled and grasped his hand, pulling his arm tighter around her.

"Goodnight, love," she said.

It had been a wonderful couple of months but, at the same time, difficult. Jack had only needed the one shot, but she still had to be careful when she touched him. He was as kind to her as ever, though, and trusting. Although she tried not to show it, it upset her when she learned of some of the things he had been through. She wasn't sure how to act around him. Suddenly, not touching him made more sense, so she tried to do that less, and yet he pulled her toward him more, like now.

He seemed to need her now more than ever.

Mark had visited her at work. She told Francie and Jack about it that evening and was sure from Francie's look that Francie had called Mark and gone off on him later that evening. Still, it had scared Annie. Mark was friendly enough but was looking for answers from her. Answers she wasn't sure how to respond to. How long had she known? Was Jack really guilty? She refused to talk, Mark had left angry, and Annie was upset.

That night, though, she was feeling happy, and after several uneventful nights, she had finally relaxed again. She drifted off to sleep to the quiet rain.

Sometime in the darkness, she was ripped out of a dream by Jack yelling. He sat up, swearing, on the edge of the bed.

"Jack?" she said, sitting up behind him.

"I'm fine, Annie. Go back to sleep."

He was shaking, she could see that much. Her heart went out to him, and forgetting, she reached out to put her arms around him.

He responded with a defensive backward swing of his arm, which caused his elbow to land right into her nose. She yelped and fell backward off the bed with a thud. Jack leaped away from her on the other side of the bed, as if struck by lightning.

She heard him hit the wall hard, with his back against it, then suddenly, he must have realized what he had done.

"Oh, Annie! Oh, geez. Are you okay?"

He ran around the side of the bed to her.

"No. I think my nose is broken."

Jack held out a hand and helped her up. She went into the bathroom and switched on the light.

In the bedroom, Jack was still trying to get his bearing. His dream kept coming at him, and he was trying to focus on the present and on Annie. "Annie... " he said. The room began to swim. He put his head in his hands to try to think.

"Jack, help me out here," Annie said, trying to keep her voice light. "I'm bleeding pretty badly. Can you get me some ice?"

Jack stumbled into the kitchen in the dark. He opened the fridge and forgot why he was there. He could feel them behind him. He turned, backing into the fridge and spilling the milk.

"Pull it together, Jack," he said. But he couldn't. He picked up the phone and dialed Francie. "We need you," was all he said before he sank to the floor.

Frank whisked Annie off to the hospital, while Francie stayed behind to clean up the mess. She had moved Jack to the couch, and he was sitting there with a cup of tea and a blanket around him.

"I hurt her," he said when Francie finally came to sit down.

"She'll be okay."

"I'm so sorry. I'm trying not to do this anymore. I'm really working with Ruth. You can ask her."

"I know."

Francie sat down beside him. "What was the dream about?"

"It wasn't that bad. I would have been okay if she hadn't tried to touch me. I just... something in me snapped."

He stood up. "I need some air," he said. "Don't follow me. Please. I'll be back." He went outside and shut the door.

"I dropped Annie off at her girlfriend's house," Frank said early that morning when he got back. It was about 4 a.m. "She needs a break."

Jack was sitting on the couch. Francie was asleep in the armchair.

"Okay," Jack said quietly and went in the bedroom and shut the door.

Annie did come back, but only for a few days. She couldn't get her nerves under control, and the pain and swelling in her face only made it worse.

"I'm leaving," she said to Jack. "Just for a while."

He nodded and quietly watched her pack up her things.

"Maybe," she said at the door, "maybe when I come back, we can paint this room. It's so dark. Then we can build a separate bedroom. I can sleep in there. We'll start off together every night, then move to separate rooms. We'll make it work."

"Okay," was all he said. He was tired. She closed the door behind her.

chapter 69

ONE BRIGHT MONDAY IN MAY, Francie was back in her office reading the new *Sports Illustrated* magazine. She was on the cover. Or rather, her horse and jockey were on the cover.

"A Cinderella Story," the press was calling it. White December had captured the Derby and was on his way to the Preakness and a potential Triple Crown victory.

"He can capture the Belmont," Steve said of the third race. He was sitting across from her. "But I'm not sure about the Preakness. He likes distance."

"I agree," Francie said. "You'll have to watch the other horses closely this week. Let's follow them and figure out our strategy."

They high-fived across her desk, and Steve ran off to catch a flight to ride in some races in New York the following morning.

Two weeks later, Jack was buying stamps in town at the bank. Everybody at the farm was in a celebratory mood, and it was contagious, so he was in a good mood. Francie's horse had only come in second in the Preakness, but the news was still focusing on December more than the winner.

Things were neutral with Annie. She had called him several times, and he had called her, but he hadn't seen her. She needed time to heal, she said.

It was lunchtime, and he was feeling a bit hungry. There was a little sandwich shop next to the post office, and he went inside and ordered something to go. While he was waiting for it, he saw Annie.

She was sitting at a table in the corner with another man, laughing. The man cut off a piece of the pie he had and offered it to her, right from the fork. She refused to let him feed her, and instead, took the fork in her own hand and ate a bite.

She smiled and nodded, as if it tasted good. The man said something, and she laughed again.

Jack got up and walked over to their table, anger boiling inside of him. Annie looked up, startled to see him.

"Oh... Jack," she said. "Hi. This is Dave. Dave, this is my husband, Jack."

"Hi," Dave held out his hand. Instead of taking it, Jack said to Annie, "Can we talk a minute?"

"Um... sure." She wiped her mouth with her napkin and got up. "Excuse us," she said to Dave. "I'll be right back."

They walked to the back of the restaurant before Jack rounded on her. "Who the heck is that?"

"That's my new boss. We work together."

"It looks like you're doing more than that."

"What? Oh, you've got to be kidding."

"From his body language, he wants way more from you than your engineering skills."

"You have got to be kidding!" she said. "You think I'm... oh my gosh, Jack. He's just a friend, and we're having lunch."

"I don't like it."

"I don't care."

"You're still my wife," he said.

Anger flashed in her eyes. "I don't belong to anybody," she said.

"Well, you certainly don't belong to *him*. Stay away from him. We're not divorced. Or even separated. As a matter of fact, what *are* we?"

"We're finished with this conversation," she said and turned to leave. He grabbed her wrist.

"Don't let him touch you," Jack said. "He's after more than your work skills. I can tell."

"Yeah? Well, at least he hasn't given me a broken nose," she said and jerked her wrist away from him.

Jack heard his number called for his sandwich. He stood there, watching Annie grab her sweater and purse and say something to Dave. Dave stood up and threw some money on the table. Annie swept out of the restaurant, and Jack walked up to get his sandwich. Dave stepped in front of him.

"Stay away from her," he said to Jack. "She's trying to heal. She can't do that with you around."

Just as Jack was about to plaster the man's face into the lunch counter, Gunny stepped in between them. "Is this man bothering you?" he asked Jack. Gunny loomed over everybody, and his presence alone was enough to make most men back off.

Dave swallowed. "Call your dog off," he said to Jack. "No wonder she doesn't want to be with you. You travel with a circus."

Gunny delicately grabbed Dave in some subtle spot on his hand and twisted, just enough that Dave's knees started to buckle. "Let's walk outside," the bodyguard said. "Say another word, and I'll break your wrist."

Dave turned three shades paler and nodded. The two men walked out front together, while Jack paid for his sandwich.

When Jack got outside, both Annie and Dave were gone.

"Did you kill him?" Jack asked hopefully.

"No. Just gave him something to think about."

"Thanks."

"Yeah, well, you can't get into any fights. Remember, Mark is itching to find a reason to toss you back into the slammer."

"I know. Thanks again."

"That's what I'm here for."

Jack could have let it go, but Annie called the next day and said, "I'm stopping by tonight. I need to get some things."

She showed up with Dave.

Dave had the sense to wait in the car.

Jack watched her pack. "Are you taking *everything?*" he asked. Spike was rubbing against her legs as she worked. She stopped to pet him. "I don't think this is working," she said to Jack.

"What?"

"This." She spread her hands around, gesturing at everything. "Us. And this place is so dark. You really need to paint it. It might perk you up."

She stuffed a few more things into her bag and zipped it up, brushing past him to the front door.

"So I nearly get killed, my recovery has been hell, and you pick this particular period in my life to leave me?"

She turned. "I know. I just can't deal with it. It's anxiety. My stomach is bothering me, I'm getting headaches. I know the timing is bad. I'm helping to make this the worst six months of your life, and I'm sorry."

"Oh, no," he said, crossing his arms. "The *worst* six months of my life would be the part I keep dreaming about."

She sighed. "See? The dreams. I can't even relate to what you're going through. How am I supposed to be able to help you?"

"You don't have to fix me, Annie. Marriage is about love. For better or worse. Until death do us part, in case you forgot your vows."

"I didn't realize the 'worse' was going to be this bad," she said quietly and took a step backward, as if afraid of him.

He sat down at the kitchen table. "Can't we at least talk about this?"

"Not now," she said. "Dave's waiting. I'll call you."

And she left.

"How the hell did he get past you?" Francie shouted at her security staff. She never yelled at her staff.

Matt spoke up. "We searched him and swept the car. It was clean."

"We searched him good. I personally gave him a thorough pat down," Gunny said. "He didn't enjoy it, I can assure you." He winked at Jack.

"You did say we could let anybody in if they were approved by someone who lives here," Matt said. "Annie lives here."

Francie ran her hands through her hair. "Not really!" she said.

Frank put a hand on her shoulder. "We need to figure out Annie's status."

"I say we ban her completely," Francie said. Frank squeezed her shoulder a little, trying to calm her.

"Stop it," she shook him off. "I'm mad."

"I'm not ready to ban her yet," Jack said. "We're not over. We're just taking a break." Then his voice got firm. "But if that Dave character sets foot on this property again—"

"Okay," Frank interrupted. "Dave is definitely banned. Annie is not—for now. The security staff did what they should have done. Good job, guys. That's it." He put his arm around Francie's shoulder. "Let's go."

She didn't like being "managed", and he knew it, but she also knew that she was about to explode, so she let him lead her away.

"Bitch," she mumbled under her breath when she was out of Jack's earshot.

Frank sighed. "Drama," he said.

chapter
70

66**I**'M GOING TO LEAVE YOU FOR A FEW DAYS when the Belmont rolls around," Francie said. "Sam is coming with us, so you're going to be in charge of the farm. The barn staff will be here, and Gunny, of course, and the other security staff. Ruth has promised me she'll be on call 24/7, as usual—"

Jack interrupted her. "I'll be fine. *Fine*, Francie." He smiled for added emphasis. After the last incident with Annie, she knew he had been trying to move forward, for Francie's sake, if for nothing else. She was happy with how he was doing. This last race of the Triple Crown meant a lot to her, and she and Steve were having a lot of fun with all the national media attention, not to mention how good it was for business.

"If I have any problems, I'll call Ruth. And you'll have your cell phone on you. The only thing that could go wrong is a bad dream, and I've pulled out of them without you before."

She frowned.

"I *have*. I'll be fine."

As he talked, he unloaded a few gallons of paint from his car, along with brushes and rollers.

"What are you doing, anyway?" she asked, curious.

"I guess I should have asked you first, since technically, it's your house," Jack said. "But I was planning to paint. I'm tearing the paneling out and sanding down the drywall, then I'm painting the whole thing white. That's how Annie has always wanted it, and I always said no. Is that okay?"

Francie waved a hand dismissively. "Do whatever you want," she said. "It's yours. But what if you need Symatrex?"

He turned to look at her. "I'll be *fine*," he said, dragging the word out for emphasis.

"Okay." After a moment, she asked, "Why do you care all of a sudden how Annie wanted the house?"

He hesitated. "I won't lie to you, but I didn't want you to worry, so don't. She told me she was stopping by this weekend. Probably on Sunday. She said she was coming home and wanted to talk."

"No," Francie said. "Not while I'm gone."

"Francie, I'm a big boy."

Francie looked at him. Every ounce of her being was shouting *No! No! No!* but she remembered Ruth's words when this whole thing began: *Try to take care of Jack without assaulting his manhood. You have to leave him with some dignity. He needs to make his own choices. He needs to feel in control of his life.*

She took a deep breath. "Okay," she said. "You're right. You'll be fine." She forced a little smile that she hoped looked reassuring and picked up a paint can to help him carry stuff into the house.

He chuckled. "How painful was that for you to say?"

Jack stepped back from the wall he was painting, humming to Bruce Springsteen's "Glory Days" that was pumping out of the radio.

Not too shabby, he thought as he looked up and down the room. The white really did perk up the place. Now with the new sofa and love seat he had purchased, the place would be all white.

Of course, he'd have to get pillows of some sort. He remembered Annie saying florals in brilliant colors contrasted well with the white. That might work.

A drop of paint fell off his brush and landed on Spike, who had the misfortune of having decided to rub against Jack's legs. His fur stood up on his back, and he streaked into the bedroom to take cover under the furniture and lick the offending mess off himself.

"Spike, you crazy cat, that'll kill you," said Jack, laughing as he balanced the brush on the paint can, and went to find his feline friend. After wiping his hands off on a wet rag, he reached under the bed to grab Spike.

He was greeted with a meow that definitely sounded like complaining.

"If you'd come here, I'd get it off of you," he said, reaching farther under the bed. "It's not like I did it on purpose. Although, I always did want a spotted cat."

Then he heard a noise that made him freeze. It sounded like Annie's red Cougar pulling up into the driveway. He knew the sound of that car well, because he had listened for it to pull in the drive thousands of times before as he cooked dinner for her while she drove home from work.

His heart skipped a beat, and he pulled himself out from under the bed, brushing himself off. Then he walked into the living room and turned off the radio.

He heard a car door shut. It was Annie. He knew it was. He hadn't expected her visit until tomorrow. "I'm coming home," were the words she had used on the phone. "Let's talk."

He started toward the door, but her entrance cut him short.

"Annie," he said.

He knew he must be a sight in his jeans with the knees torn out and his untucked blue t-shirt splattered with paint.

"Jack," was all she said, still standing motionless inside the door.

It was a perfect moment as he gazed across the room at her. The light silhouetted her slim figure and highlighted her auburn hair in red. She looked good. She hadn't really changed in the three weeks she had been gone. He had so many questions. Where had she been? What had she been doing? Did she miss him even half as much as he missed her?

He already felt warmer, thinking of her curled up next to him tonight. As he looked at her, the anger, the mistrust, the hurt he had been feeling for weeks was gone in an instant. He knew he was hard to live with, that he didn't deserve her, and yet here she was, back, willing to work things out.

Her intense green eyes met his only briefly, and then looked around the room, taking in the changes.

"This looks good," was all she said. Then her eyes fell on her hands.

"I've come to get the rest of my things," she said, walking toward him. "You can read this while I'm packing."

"What?" He was confused. She handed him a manila envelope.

"I want a divorce, Jack."

He went numb as she placed the envelope in his hands. No, this wasn't right. Something wasn't right. His knees felt weak, and he pulled the chair out from the table and sat down. She was gone already, in the bedroom—*their* bedroom—and he could hear her pulling open drawers.

"Oh, hi, Spike. How ya doin' sweetie?" Annie's soft voice carried out of the bedroom.

With trembling fingers, Jack tore open the envelope and looked at the papers. Annie had already signed them. He was confused. She had told him she was coming home.

"It's simple, really," Annie was saying to him from the bedroom. "You can have everything. I took $10,000 out of savings, and that's all I want. None of this is your fault, so I don't plan on leaving this marriage with more than I came into it with."

He was shaking. He laid the papers down on the table and crossed his arms to try to get some control of his hands.

"Annie," he was finally able to say. "I... I love you." The words sounded pathetic, helpless, to his ears. He only hoped she felt the emotion they carried.

She carried two suitcases out and set them by the front door. He noticed she was taking the floral ones he had given her. The ones she was supposed to be taking on their anniversary trip later this year.

She turned to face him. Her eyes were dry, making him ashamed of the tears that were welling up in his own. He got up and walked over to her, putting his hands on her shoulders.

"Annie, I'm begging you, give us a chance. I love you. We can make this work."

"Jack, I have been giving this a chance. I've given this marriage a chance for four entire years, and it's killing me. It's not that I don't love you. That has never been the issue."

"Then Annie, *stay*. Love is all we need." He was pleading with her now.

Annie took hold of his wrists and firmly removed his hands from her shoulders.

"I can't live this way anymore," she said. "This is killing me. You've been through so much, and I didn't know any of those things when I first fell in love with you. And I thought I could deal with it, I really did. I thought love was enough. But it's not. The nightmares, the anxiety that you constantly feel... I don't understand that, and I don't know how to deal with that."

She was starting to cry. Jack started to put his arms around her again, and she backed away. He noticed he was trembling worse now and cursed inwardly. That was just the thing she hated. He was what she hated.

"I want to have children, and we can't. We can't raise children under these conditions, with their father waking up in the middle of the night screaming from nightmares. I thought I could deal with that and just be a good wife and that love would be enough."

"You *are* enough," he said. "You're enough for me. Annie, I'm trying to change. Look at what I've done here." He swept one trembling hand to take in the room. "I've lightened it up, and you're right, it really does look better. And you should see what I've done to the garden. I've put in the wrought iron gate you always wanted. Come and look." He reached for his wife's hand, and she jumped back, like he had shocked her.

"No," she said. "Jack... love is *not* enough. I can't love you, not in the way a wife should. You won't let me touch you half the time. And when you do," she swallowed. "The... things... that they did to you... it's always there, in the back of my mind. They... raped you, and I don't know how to deal with that. I don't know how to make love to you or even how to love you. Sometimes just my hand on your shoulder is enough to upset you. You... you *broke my nose...* when I touched you...."

Jack sat back down in the chair. He couldn't seem to stand up anymore. The room was swaying back and forth. Annie was starting to blur. He thought it must be tears in his eyes, but when he wiped them, the room rocked more wildly.

"You can have your lawyer look those over," she said, motioning to the papers on the table. "But I don't want anything."

"Annie, please, can't we just talk about this? You said you were coming home."

"No," she said. "Dave is waiting for me. At the front gate," she added bitterly.

"Dave?"

"Goodbye," Annie said through her tears. "I really do wish you the best."

She picked up her two suitcases and turned, and he watched her walk out of his life. He heard the trunk slam shut, and then the car door. And then it drove off down the driveway. From his chair, he could see the gate, and he watched as she said something to Gunny. She slid over, and Dave climbed in the driver's seat. Then they drove out and disappeared from view.

If only his hands would quit shaking, he could think better. He needed to get his car keys and follow her. That's what any worthwhile husband would do—chase after her and show her how much he loved her. And maybe beat the hell out of Dave.

He tried to get up from the table, and a wave of dizziness hit him. He grabbed the table, and adrenaline pumped through his body as he tried to steady himself. That made the shaking worse.

There was Annie's Xanax in the cabinet above the microwave. He managed to reach it, hanging onto the counter to steady himself. He shook two pills out of the bottle and downed them without water.

On his way into the bedroom, he was blinded by black spots floating before his eyes, and then the dizziness hit again. He made it to the bathroom before he vomited up the Xanax.

Sweating, he splashed his face in the sink. *This is why she can't stand to be around me*, he thought, but then another wave of nausea forced him to concentrate on survival.

He needed to call somebody. Staggering out of the bathroom, he grabbed the comforter off of the bed. He was so cold. If only he could stop the shaking.

He rummaged through the dresser drawer, looking for Ruth's number. He couldn't find his cell phone, but he found his wallet and stuffed it into his pocket. If Ruth's number wasn't in his office, he would call somebody else. He needed help.

The office was across the kitchen, and he was halfway there when he stumbled and fell over the chair. Cursing and holding his injured knee, he rocked back and forth, blinded by another onslaught of tears.

"Francie," he whispered. But the room was silent. Francie was in New York. He was alone.

There was Symatrex in the refrigerator. He had never given himself a shot before, but he needed to stop the shaking. Then he would be able to think better. His head was throbbing, and his heart was racing—he couldn't quite seem to catch his breath.

He pulled open the refrigerator door from where he sat and reached up for the syringes. His fingers fumbled, dropping the syringe twice before he got the cap off. The dosage said three mililiters. He filled it to the mark, squinting against the light in the kitchen, barely able to read it. Then he injected it in his arm. It hurt like hell.

Unable to stifle a cry, he pushed in the plunger and then jerked out the empty syringe. He sat there, waiting for the drug's almost immediate relief. When none came, he began to wonder if he had gotten the right dosage.

"Three milliliters," he read. *Okay.*

He got another syringe down and after several attempts managed to fill it. Only enough to stop the pain. He couldn't handle any more pain.

He plunged it in his arm and watched as blood dripped from the injection site. He pushed in the plunger, only slightly aware that he had administered four milliliters. Spike came out of the bedroom and brushed against him, and he dropped the medicine. That was the last thing he knew.

chapter 71

GUNNY FIGURED HE SHOULD GO CHECK ON JACK after Annie left, especially since she had been with Dave. He knocked on the door a few times, but nobody answered. He turned the knob. It was unlocked, so he let himself in.

He saw his boss lying on the floor, unconscious. He ran to him and knelt down, checking for a pulse. Then he pulled out his phone and dialed 911.

Jack awoke into a nightmare. Bright lights were shining down on him, and he was stretched out on a table. He tried to sit up and was told gently to lay still, so, of course, he fought harder. More hands pushed down on his chest, and then they clamped down on his wrists. He felt bands tighten down on his arms and his legs, pinning him to the bed. That's when he started screaming.

Gunny couldn't get through to Francie's phone, so he called Rosa. Thank God she was in the office. He figured she might have a better connection since she was in New York.

He knew there was a therapist involved too, but he didn't have her number with him, and he couldn't remember her last name. Everybody called her Dr. Ruth. She must be affiliated with the hospital. He grabbed a nurse and tried to pepper her with questions, but she was in a hurry and pushed him away.

"Hey," said an officer. "We don't allow guns in the hospital." Gunny, protesting strongly, was escorted outside. He'd have to find Ruth another way.

Francie gave White December a pat on the neck and let Steve take him out onto the track. She went up to her box seat and looked through her binoculars at the familiar green and gold silks of Sunnyhill.

"He looks good today," she said to Frank. "December is at the top of his game."

Frank chuckled. "You keep going back and forth on whether or not you think he can last the whole mile and a half. Usually, you're more sure of things."

"I know. This particular horse keeps surprising me. Steve and I aren't sure if he's a distance horse or a miler. Maybe he's both."

Sam was biting her nails. "With Steve on him, he'll win," she said.

Francie looked at her. "Nervous?"

"Yeah. Not sure why. I used to be the one on the horse. Things change when you have kids."

Francie smiled down at Andy. "They sure do."

The band struck up "New York, New York," the theme song for the Belmont, and everybody sang along. It was a beautiful day, warm and sunny, and the track was fast.

The horses were loading into the starting gate when her phone rang.

She looked at Frank then and shrugged with an "I don't know who it could be" look written on her face.

Everyone who had her cell phone number was here, except her secretary Rosa, and she wouldn't be at work today, or bothering Francie during the race.

It rang again. She had about thirty seconds before the race started. She squinted to get a better look at White December as he quietly loaded into the gate. Then she answered her phone.

"Francie Dalton," she said, slightly irritated. It never occurred to her to be worried. Probably some racing fan who had found her number.

"Francie Dalton?" The voice on the other end was unfamiliar.

"Yes? Who is this?"

Next to her, Donovan squeezed her shoulder.

"This one's ours," he said.

Francie saw her face up on the big screen as ABC's cameras panned across the crowd.

"This is Dr. McMurtry at County General in Florida," said the voice on the phone. "There's been an... accident... involving Jack Banner. You should come."

Her world stopped for a moment. Jack. He was home alone. Annie was coming to visit... but that was supposed to be tomorrow.

Just then the bell rang, and thirteen horses burst from the starting gate.

She got there in just over three hours. Gunny was outside the hospital, having been banned for bringing in weapons, and Francie made a mental note to check on hospital policy and bodyguards and who she could sue later. Gunny told her the room number, and she ran up the stairs and burst through the door, out of breath, and probably startling Jack and making the situation worse.

But she had heard his screams from the stairwell.

"I'm here," she said, taking his head in her hands. She waited until he made eye contact.

"I'm here," she said again. "You're safe now."

Jack was sleeping when Ruth got there; he had relaxed enough so whatever was left in his system was taking effect.

Ruth sighed and sat down in a chair next to Francie's. Francie had Jack's hand in hers, and Ruth laid her own over top of theirs on the bed. She gave a gentle squeeze, and Francie felt her eyes sting with tears.

"Not again... " Francie whispered. "He can't take anymore."

"I know, honey," Ruth said in a quiet voice. After a moment, she added, "He came in with a lot of Symatrex in his system, along with some Xanax. He's lucky to be alive."

"We can't keep him here," Francie said. "You have to get him moved before he wakes up."

"I know." Ruth looked around at the tiny, enclosed room with no windows. "I will. Let me go sign some paperwork. Then you and I need to talk."

The day had been hard. It was Sunday afternoon, and after discussions with various doctors, Ruth arguing with everybody, and Dr. Tremper being brought in, it was decided that Jack could go home under Francie's watch. Ruth had the last say, and had consented, although the paperwork hadn't moved as quickly as either of them would have liked.

Francie sat alone with Jack in his room, waiting for another hour until the doctor got there to sign the release. It was nearly dinner time, and her stomach was starting to growl.

Jack was angry. Over the past twenty-four hours, he had gone back and forth from anger to depression to anger again. But it wasn't a productive anger. Francie was used to him being strong, a fighter, and instead, he was turning the anger inward, against himself and against God. He seemed ready to quit.

But at the moment, his anger was fueling him again.

"I don't see why I'm still here," he said. He was dressed and ready to go, sitting on the window ledge, looking out across the parking lot. Francie was in a metal chair by his bed, checking the messages on her phone. Work never waited.

She looked up. "You know why you're still here."

"If they're so worried that I'm going to kill myself—well, I could do it here just as easily as at home. Look. Scissors there—"

Yeah, where were those the other day when I needed them? Francie thought.

He looked around. "There's an IV there. I could stab myself repeatedly with a needle."

She closed her phone. "Don't be morbid."

"Stupid people."

"We both know you're fine. That's all that matters."

"I'm not fine," he said. She looked up at him. "I'm done. I'm tired. I'm finished."

"What does that even mean if you don't plan to off yourself?"

He rubbed his hands across his face, and she was sorry for the words. She was just so antsy herself.

"I'm not going back to church," he said. "Ever."

"Maybe I won't either," she said. She put her phone in her pocket and stood up to stretch. He looked at her.

"It's fine by me," he said finally.

"Jack... " she softened her tone. "Let's not do this..."

"Francie, I don't need sympathy. Go. Leave me alone. I'll take a cab home."

"Don't."

He stood up and kicked the recliner, and it slid across the room, hitting the wall. The fast movement made him dizzy. He put his hand to his head.

"You need to eat," she said.

"Stop mothering me."

They looked at each other across the gulf of the room. "I don't need anybody," he said quietly. "I need to get used to being alone." He sat down on the window ledge, his anger quickly fading. ` Francie thought.

"I'm sorry," he said, leaning his head back against the window and closing his eyes.

"Me too."

Ruth poked her head in. "Ready?"

"Yes," they both said together.

Ruth rolled a wheelchair in. "The chair is hospital policy. Don't cause problems. They've given me heck about letting you go."

Jack sat down in the wheelchair and let Ruth roll him out of the hospital.

Neither he nor Francie spoke on the ride home. Gunny drove. When they got to the house, Francie followed him in. Jack went right into the bedroom and laid down, pulling the covers up to his chin. He felt light-headed, which Ruth had said he probably would for another day. His system was still in shock from the overdose.

He was tired. He closed his eyes.

Francie fed Spike and cleaned out his litter box. She rubbed the cat behind the ears and talked to him for a few minutes, assuring him that everything was okay. Then she went to the bathroom and opened the medicine cabinet.

They told her to take everything out. Pills, razor blades. That would include knives in the kitchen and anything else potentially dangerous. Heck, he could hang himself on a window blind cord if he wanted to. She went back and sat down at the kitchen table, running her hands through her hair. She'd leave everything where it was. Give him his dignity, at least.

She had brought her laptop but didn't feel like working. Instead, she put her head down on the table in her arms. The clock ticked. Spike settled down at the foot of Jack's bed.

Time moved forward slowly, eerily, until it was finally time for Francie to fix a meal. She judged 6 p.m. as mealtime, and she got up and started banging some pots around, hoping to wake Jack up.

She didn't know what to fix him. Soup seemed like an insult. He wasn't sick. She thought of steak, but nothing was thawed, and it seemed like too much work to cook. She opened the freezer and found a few TV dinners in there. She opened them up and started the microwave.

Then she went to Jack's room.

"I'm fixing us some dinner," she said. "It'll be ready in a few minutes."

"I'm not hungry," he said from his bed. She stood in his doorway until the microwave beeped. Then she went and took the meals out and sat them on the table with two glasses of water. She waited. He never came. Finally, after a half hour of staring at her own meal, she tossed both of them into the garbage. It was only 6:30.

She laid down on the couch and went to sleep.

She awoke at 1 a.m. and again at 6 a.m. Both times, she checked on Jack, and he lay in bed in the same position, breathing, but not moving.

At 6 a.m., she went to the barn. She did her chores and then came back to the house.

"Jack, it's eight o'clock. You've been in bed for days. Get up."

"I'm tired," he said. "Just let me sleep."

She sat on the edge of the bed. "Don't let her do this to you," she said. "We've both been through too much to give up now. I need you today for the Dalton fall project. The new clothing line is out."

She went and fixed him a bowl of cereal. She heard him get up and use the bathroom, then shuffle out unshaven. He sat down in front of his bowl of oatmeal.

"I'm sorry it's not more exciting," she said. "You need to go grocery shopping."

He didn't say anything. He stirred the oatmeal around in the bowl.

"I'll leave you here to shower and eat, then I expect you at my place at 1 p.m. Okay? Just come over to the office, or if you're still light-headed call me, and we can meet here. Ruth is coming over later too, but we can meet first. We need to get some work done."

He nodded, stirring his oatmeal but not eating.

"Jack."

No response.

"Look at me," she said, her voice pleading.

He looked up.

"I need for you to be okay," she said. She fought back the lump in her throat.

He nodded. "I'll be at your office at 1 p.m," he said.

He didn't say anything else, and after a while, she went home.

At 1:30, she sat at her desk, tapping her pencil. He was never late. She was half mad at him and half afraid to go over there, wondering if he were dead. Well, only one way to find out.

Frank was running errands, and Andy was at day camp on a field trip. Sam was chaperoning. Francie had originally wanted to chaperone, but the trip was the Monday after the Belmont, and she had planned to be in New York right now, celebrating.

She went over to Jack's house and let herself in. He was still in bed.

"Jack, get up," she said.

"Not today," he said. "Go away. I'm fine."

She sighed dramatically and pulled up his window shade, letting sunlight spill into the room. He moaned and pulled the covers over his head. She raised the second shade.

"Get up and get dressed. I'm fixing you something to eat."

She went into the kitchen and made a can of soup. He still hadn't come to the table. Angry, she went into his room.

"You told me not to pity you, so I'm not going to start giving you pity now," she said, angry. "Get up!" He didn't respond. "I'm not going to let you throw your life away. Now get up, and let's get some work done." She grabbed the covers and jerked them off of him. He was lying on his stomach, wearing nothing but boxers. He grabbed the covers, pulling them back over him, but he wasn't quick enough. She got a good look at his back. The scars were there, but she also noticed the finely sculpted muscles. *Oh,*

Jack, she thought. *If you take your shirt off, it's not the scars people are going to be looking at. It's your physique.*

"Francie, I could have been naked," he said.

"I've seen plenty of naked men," she said. "I wouldn't be impressed. Now get up." She tried to keep the anger in her voice, but the fact was, she wasn't angry anymore. She was about to cry.

"Francie, just leave," he said, his voice sounding as tired as she felt. He turned away from her, facing the wall. "Please leave me alone. You always try to save me. I don't want to be saved. For once, just let me go."

"Jack... "

"Go!" he said, anger in his voice now.

"I need you to choose to live," she said, her voice breaking. "Please."

He didn't respond.

She backed out of his room, tears cascading down her face. She turned and stumbled on the door frame. She let herself out his front door, not looking back. She left the soup sitting on the kitchen table, untouched.

In the yard, she willed herself to not cry. She swallowed and took deep breaths. "Hold it together, Francie," she said. "You've got work to do. Hold it together."

By the time she reached the kitchen, she had herself under control again. She sat down at the kitchen table, swallowing the lump in her throat.

"Mommy!" Andy had just gotten back from his field trip and was sitting at the table with Frank, playing with some trucks. He threw his arms around Francie's neck.

"Hey, sis!" Steve came into the room, fresh from his win in New York. "Awesome horse you have! I wanted to ask you what you thought. Did you see how Jimmy came after us at the half pole?"

"How's Jack?" Frank asked.

Francie felt like she was suffocating as the voices swirled around her. She tried to take a deep breath and couldn't. Tears filled her eyes.

"I can't do this anymore," she said. She unwrapped Andy's arms from around her neck and stood up. "I can't."

"Francie?" Frank said. She held up a hand to stop him. She ran from the kitchen, up to her bedroom, and closed the door. She buried her face in her pillow and wept like she hadn't wept since Ken had died. Eventually, the tears subsided, and she was exhausted.

When Frank came in a little while later, she was lying in bed on her side facing the wall.

"Francie?" he said. "Are you okay?"

"I'm going to bed," she said.

"It's 3:00 in the afternoon."

"I'm tired."

Frank sat on the edge of the bed and laid his hand on her shoulder. "What happened?"

"Jack needs some time," she said.

"Ruth called. I had to let her in his house. She said Jack wouldn't respond to her. He wouldn't even get out of bed."

Francie didn't say anything. Frank squeezed her shoulder. "Get some rest," he said. "Maybe that's what you both need. Just some rest."

It rained all night. When Frank came to bed around 10 p.m., Francie still hadn't moved, and that worried him. He got ready, then turned out the light and crawled in beside her. He put his arm around her. She turned toward him, sniffling a little, and buried her head in his chest. He let her cry, holding her, her soft hair under his chin. "It'll be okay," he said, although he had no idea if that was true or not. She cried herself out, and eventually fell asleep in his arms.

He lay there for a while, trying to figure out what had happened. He knew he should probably have gone to check on Jack after dinner, but he had asked Gunny to do that instead. He was angry at Jack. It was irrational anger, he knew. None of this was Jack's fault, but if it weren't for Jack, his wife wouldn't be in this bout of depression.

He eventually drifted off to sleep.

The alarm woke him the next morning at 7 a.m. He had to get Andy ready for camp. Francie made no move to get up, so he rose quietly and let her sleep.

When he got home, he came in the bedroom and raised the shade. "Francie, get up," he said pleasantly. "You've got about a million emails and several phone calls, and you really should go check on Jack. Ruth wants an update. She called me this morning. Her mother is in the ER, so she won't be over until later today, probably this evening, but she said she's going to get here eventually."

Francie didn't move.

"Get up, hon," he said.

Francie slowly got up and sat on the edge of the bed. "Okay," she said quietly.

"I have a meeting in town this morning. Call me later to let me know how things are. Sam is home for a while if you need her." He hesitated. He hated to leave her, but she seemed to be moving. He leaned across the bed and gave her a kiss.

Then he left, closing the door behind him. Frank didn't usually worry, but this morning, his stomach was tight with uncertainty. He had never seen Francie like this.

Frank left, and Francie wandered into her closet to pick out some clothes. She saw Ken's duster sitting up on her shelf and pulled it down. She wrapped it around herself. It had lost his smell long ago. She closed her eyes for a minute, trying to pretend it was about six years ago and that things were okay.

Instead, she started to cry again. She put the duster back on her shelf and crawled back into bed. She covered up her head.

When Frank returned at 1:00 with Andy in tow, she was still in bed. He tried to call Ruth but got her answering machine. "Has anybody checked on Jack?" he said to Sam. Sam was making sandwiches.

"No," she said. "Lexie had baseball camp this morning. We've been gone all morning."

He sat there for a while. "I guess I'll eat."

"She won't get up?" Sam asked.

He shook his head.

"I can take the kids this afternoon," Sam said. "Steve is gone, and I was going to take Lexie to the pool in town with her friend. They have a kiddie pool. You want me to take Andy after his nap?"

He did. Frank worked for a while, then realized that Francie had been in bed for twenty-four hours. He went into the bedroom.

"Francie," he said. "Get up and get showered."

She didn't answer.

Suddenly, he was angry. He closed her door and marched over to Jack's house, feeling the heat rising in his face. His fists clenched and unclenched at his sides. He let himself in, not even knocking. Spike ran to him, meowing and demanding food.

The house was dark, the shades in the bedroom pulled. Jack was in bed.

Frank went in the bedroom.

"Enough feeling sorry for yourself," he said. He heard the anger in his own voice. "There are more people at stake here than *you*. My wife has been in bed since she left your house yesterday. She won't eat, she won't talk, and she won't get out of bed. She's depressed, Jack. After all she has done for you, you can't do this to her. You get your sorry butt out of this bed and come over there and say something to her to fix this situation, or I'm coming back over here to *get* your sorry butt out of bed. I'm not going to lose my wife because of you."

He stormed back out of the bedroom and slammed the door for emphasis as he left the house. He was sorry he hadn't taken the time to feed the cat.

He went back to work in Francie's office. After about an hour, there was a soft knock on the door. He looked up. It was Jack, clean-shaven.

"Can I go in her bedroom?" he asked quietly.

Frank looked at his friend. If ever a man looked beaten, it was Jack. He had dark bags under his eyes, and his shoulders sagged. He had lost that charming twinkle in his eyes, and his voice was rough, as if he hadn't spoken in days. His wrists were raw from his fight with the restraints at the hospital.

"Yes," Frank said. He wanted to say more, but what was there to say?

Jack went slowly down the hall and knocked on Francie's door. When he didn't get an answer, he let himself in. She was lying on her side, facing away from the door. He went over to the bed and sat on the edge of it.

"It's me," he said. "Jack."

She didn't respond. He could tell by her breathing that she was awake. He cleared his throat. A lump formed in it, and he fought back tears. "I've come to tell you, Francie, that... " He took a deep breath. He didn't need to cry on her. Not now. He looked around the room and wondered at all the heartache she had cried through here. She had been through so much herself. He looked at the small figure lying on the bed, under the covers, not responding to him for the first time since he had known her. He cleared his throat and tried again.

"I'm choosing life." His voice was rough, raw. He fingered the comforter. "I'm choosing to live. But I'm going to need your help." He swallowed again, the weight of his words like a stone around his neck. "Please."

He sat there for a while, waiting for her to respond. She didn't. He placed a hand on her shoulder, which was buried under the comforter. "I love you, Princess. You're the best friend I've ever had."

The room was quiet. He gave her an awkward little pat on the shoulder, then got up to leave. It seemed like a very long walk back home.

Francie laid there for another hour, pondering what Jack had just said. Finally, as she had always done her entire life, she gathered her strength and got up. Jack needed her. She had never let her family down, and she wasn't about to start now.

She showered and dressed and went downstairs. Frank quietly folded her into a hug. "Welcome back," he said. She pressed herself against him for a moment, gathering strength. She was tired, deep down in her soul, but determined.

"There's something I've got to do," she said.

"I know." He let her go.

She walked over to Jack's house and knocked on the door. He opened it.

"Let's take a walk," she said. "Terra is probably missing you right now."

He nodded and pulled his boots on, and the two of them walked slowly, side by side, toward the barn, where Francie knew how to fix things.

<h1 style="text-align:center">chapter 72</h1>

THE WEEKS PASSED, and they got back into their routine. Jack was sleeping in his house, alone most nights. He hadn't called Francie once. He said he was okay and was never taking Symatrex again. He continued to meet with Ruth every other day for a therapy session. He was working really hard, and the nightmares had practically stopped.

He started spending more time around the Big House. When it was Francie's day to cook, he hung around the kitchen, helping out. He was always available to help Frank with farm chores, as well as keep up his role as VP for the company. He took over evening watering duty on Mondays, when the barn staff was off. Work was like a balm to him, as was his horse and his cat.

He and Frank, or sometimes he and Francie, worked at getting his horse trained to ride. He kept busy, dealing with Annie's absence by not dealing with it.

He wouldn't talk about anything personal. He became closed off, like he had been when Francie had first met him. He wasn't rude, and he hung around, but he refused to talk about anything painful, except with Ruth. Francie was quiet—she never pushed—but he knew she missed him. The two of them went through the motions of running the farm and the business, and the tough daily grind of living with their pasts. They laughed and joined in on family conversations, but they both carried a deep sadness inside of them.

One day, Frank showed up in the office for Jack and Francie's 1:00 work meeting, which he never attended. He came in uninvited, closed the door, and walked past Francie's desk to sit on the bay window seat.

They both looked at him expectantly.

"Yes, dear?" Francie finally said. She and Jack were both poised, laptops open, ad designs up on their screens, ready to get to work.

Frank laced his hands together and looked at his wife and best friend. They had both been moping around for weeks. Frank had spent a lot of time thinking and praying and had some things he needed to say. He took a deep breath.

"I've come to talk," he said. "I want to know how you're doing, Jack. And we've all been dancing around the Annie issue for weeks."

Jack closed his laptop with a snap. "Did you know about this?" he asked Francie accusingly. "This meeting feels like a set-up."

She shook her head. "You know I wouldn't do that to you."

"I don't need to *talk*," he said and got up.

"Jack, *sit down*." Frank's voice was quiet but firm. There was a tone in it that neither of them had heard before. Jack looked at his friend's serious face. He sat.

"I'm going to start by saying I've put up with a lot from you two over the past few months. You've spent a lot of time together. A *lot*. You've shared the same bed on at least two occasions that I know of."

Jack dropped his eyes to his hands.

"Amazingly, none of that has bothered me," Frank continued, "but I think after all I've put up with, you both need to listen to what I have to say. And I have a lot to say. I, at least, deserve your time. Agreed?"

They both nodded.

"So let me talk. Just listen for a while. Don't interrupt."

Francie closed her laptop. She leaned back in her chair, unsure of where her husband was going. Jack sat back, humbled, and gave Frank his full attention.

Frank sat there a moment, gathering his thoughts. "I think it's fair to say we've all been through a lot," he began. "I don't think I could have gone through what you went through, Jack, and still be sane. I'm amazed and awed. So is Ruth." He looked over at Francie. "And you know I think *you're* amazing, sweetheart. I always have." She smiled at him.

"Now bear with me, because I'm going to preach a bit," he said and pulled out a little pocket Bible. "I know you all feel like God has deserted us." He flipped through the pages until he came to the scripture he wanted. "But I've been thinking back on it all. God has been in this whole story. I'm sure He wept with us when bad things happened, but He brought something positive out of it all.

"Jack, if you hadn't saved Jim back in the war, he wouldn't have been home to save Francie that evening she walked into a bad part of town. Your actions saved her life. Jim felt responsible for your capture, we all know that, and because of that, you're sitting here now. We wouldn't have Dalton Jeans if we didn't have you, and what a blessing that company has been! Not just because Francie's having fun with it, but because it's financing the farm. That was always a worry; would we make enough this year to run the farm another year? Now, even if the farm goes belly up, we've got a second income."

He paused. "Let me read this. 'I have plans for you, declares the Lord, plans to prosper you and not harm you, plans to give you hope and a future'."

He closed the Bible.

"I know you've been harmed," Frank said. "It seems like God is going back on His promise. But what I really think it means is, in the end, we're still His. There's hope in that." He flipped to another passage. "'Nothing can take you out of the hand of God.'" Frank looked up at Jack. "*Nothing*. You're His, and He loves you."

He closed the Bible again. "God never promised us that life would be easy. As a matter of fact, He more or less says it *won't*. In Psalms He says, 'Yay, though you walk through the valley of the shadow of death, you will fear no evil. For I will be with you'" He doesn't say 'if' we walk through that dark and scary valley. He says you *will*. Jesus says, 'Take up your cross and follow me.' A cross? It's not an easy journey, but God promises to be with us every step of the way."

He flipped to another chapter. "But this is the scripture that really got me thinking. Paul says in 1 Corinthians, 'For now we see through a glass, darkly; but then face to face: now I know in part; but then shall I know even as also I am known.'" He looked up at them. "We can't see the whole picture now. God has plans and can use whatever randomness happens to us in this world, and I know He is using us now. We don't know how far back it goes or how far into the future. If Krista and Ken hadn't died, we wouldn't have Andy. What if it's not about Francie and me at all? What if God's plan is for Andy? Maybe he's going to be a great evangelist or find a cure for cancer! God can take what hurt us and put a blessing in it. And Jack, what if this isn't about you either? What if all of this came about for some future reason that we can't see yet? I think what

God is calling us to do, above all else, is to trust Him. Just *trust* Him."

Frank rubbed his face with his hands.

"That doesn't take away from what has happened to you or make it small in any way. I just want you to see that it's not the end, and that God loves you enough to take this mess and turn it into a blessing. Somehow, somewhere, He will bless you."

He flipped to one more passage. "Joel 2:25 says, 'I will restore to you the years the locusts hath eaten.' You've lost a lot." He looked at Jack. "A *lot*. More than most men could bear. But you aren't most men. You're a man with God on his side, and that means that anything is possible. *Anything*."

He closed the Bible and set it down. "I love you both," he said, "and I know you're weary and hurting and angry. Just don't give up on God. Let Him be your strength."

They all sat there quietly. Finally, Frank said, "I guess I'm done." He glanced over at Francie. Her eyes were moist.

"Your grandpa knew what he was doing when he gave you this farm," Frank said. "You've turned it into a safe haven. Look at how many of us have come here to heal." He reached for her hand and gave it a squeeze. "I'm grateful for that."

Jack leaned forward in his chair and put his face in his hands. He rubbed his eyes. "Me too," he said, sitting back. "I'm grateful for that too."

The rain had stopped, and a small shaft of sunlight was peeking through the clouds. It shone across the desk and touched Jack's hands. He turned them over in the light, looking at his scars, and the lines that had begun to get deeper with age. Then he looked across the desk at his friends and smiled. "Thank you, Frank," he said.

Frank got up and squeezed Jack's shoulder as he passed by. "I'm going to get back to work," he said. "Thanks for letting me interrupt your work time."

Jack walked into the kitchen later that week. Francie was at the counter, chopping vegetables. It was her turn to cook.

"What are you making?"

"Stir fry," she said. "Andy loves it, especially with a sweet and sour sauce. I'll have plenty. You can stay for dinner."

"Sure. Can I help?"

"I'd *love* help. You know how much I love to cook," she said wryly.

He laughed and washed his hands in the sink, then grabbed a cutting board and knife.

Francie handed him a head of cabbage. "You can start with this."

The two of them stood there in comfortable silence, chopping vegetables. Jack's cell phone rang. He pulled it out of his pocket and glanced at it.

"It's Annie," he said.

Francie looked up. "Don't ask me if you should answer it. I'm staying out of this."

It rang a second time and a third. He pushed a button and sent it on to voice mail.

"She called yesterday too," he said. "I ignored it. She left a message. Said she wanted to meet."

Francie raised an eyebrow and then went back to chopping. They hadn't heard from Annie since she'd dropped off the divorce papers. Nothing. Not a word. Not even an inquiry as to why they hadn't been signed yet.

Jack began chopping again. Neither of them spoke. After about five minutes, the phone rang again. He received so many work calls that he had to look at it.

"It's Ruth." He answered it.

"Jack," Ruth said in her usual, cheerful voice. "How are you?"

"I'm fine," he said. "Are you calling just to chat, or did I miss our meeting? I thought it was tomorrow."

He raised an eyebrow at Francie.

"It is tomorrow," Ruth said. "But I had something I wanted to tell you. Annie came in to talk the other day. She has something to say that I think you need to hear. She wants to meet. You need to answer her calls and set up a time. I can be there if you want, but she'd prefer to talk to you in private."

Jack didn't answer. He wasn't sure what to say. After the incident with the divorce papers and the Symatrex, Ruth had strongly and firmly told Jack not to interact with Annie under any circumstances unless they talked about it first. Now here she was, changing her mind.

"I don't want to see her," he said finally. "I'm done with Annie."

"I don't think you are, hon," Ruth said. "Just meet with her, just this once, and hear what she has to say. As your therapist, I'm asking you to do this."

Jack sighed. Francie, who could hear in the silence of the kitchen, had put her knife down and was standing with her hand on the counter, looking at him.

"I trust Ruth," she whispered.

He trusted Ruth too. "Okay," he said to his therapist. "I'll call her."

After he hung up, Francie said, "You can go up to my office if you want privacy." She looked over at him. "Are you okay with this? I'm trying not to interfere, because you know how I feel about Annie. It's Ruth who I trust in this scenario."

He nodded. "I'm okay." He went upstairs and called Annie. Their conversation was brief, and they agreed to meet at the pier in town in an hour.

"What's the hurry?" Francie asked.

"I just want to get this over with," Jack said.

"Take Gunny."

"Of course. Ruth told me not to go alone. As we all know, I've agreed to listen to Ruth."

Gunny drove Jack to the pier.

The day was overcast. Annie was standing on the pier, looking out over the ocean. Jack sat in the car and watched her for a minute. She was wearing a blue, print dress that was blowing in the wind. Her hair was down, and she kept pulling a sweater tighter around her shoulders because of the chill off the ocean.

He glanced at Gunny. "Cover me," he said with a sardonic smile.

Gunny smiled. "Sure thing, boss."

Jack got out and walked toward his wife.

Annie turned and saw him coming. He walked casually across the street toward her, taking his time. She had forgotten how handsome he was, and her stomach did a little flip at the sight of him. She pulled her sweater tighter around her, more from nerves than the chill. Then she said a brief prayer under her breath.

She had no idea how this was going to go.

"Hi," she said awkwardly when he reached her.

Jack nodded. "Hello, Annie."

She was as beautiful as ever, and he felt his heart tug. Not for the Annie she was now, but for the Annie she had been, when they were together and happy. He wanted to close his eyes and go back to those times, but he forced himself to remain here, on the pier, in this moment.

He put his hands in his pockets and stood a few feet from her.

"What do you want?" he said.

"Thank you for coming," she said. "I know I don't deserve your time. I said a lot of things I shouldn't have said and acted horribly—"

"I'm not here for an apology, Annie," Jack said. "Just tell me what you came to tell me."

She swallowed. "Of course. I'm sorry." She pulled her sweater closed with her hands. Tears welled up in her eyes.

"I was reading my Bible the other night, and God spoke to me. He said, 'it's not over, it's only the beginning.' Jack, I live in the present, and it's sometimes hard for me to see the future. I've always had trouble getting past what is happening *now*, for what could be. But now I have a reason to hope in the future. And so do you."

She smiled. "Jack, you're going to be a daddy."

He stood there, shocked. He had been over a million things in his mind that she was going to say, and this hadn't been one of them.

"Are... are you sure?"

"Yes!" Tears were now rolling down her cheeks. "That night I came home the first time—I had stopped taking my birth control pills, and you and I... well," she laughed. "Then I started feeling awful and throwing up, and I just thought it was all stress. It was hormones! So I went to the doctor, and she confirmed it. I'm pregnant!"

Jack felt a smile spread across his face. He had never even considered a child, not with his past and his life. He laughed out loud, then. "Annie, I don't know what to say!"

"Can I have your hand?" she asked. She reached out gently and took his hand and placed it on her belly. He felt a roundness to her that hadn't been there before.

"Oh my gosh," he said, tears springing into his own eyes. "Oh, wow."

He laughed, and so did she, and the two of them stood there, laughing and crying, unsure of what to do next. But it didn't matter, because between them, under Jack's hand, was their future.

chapter
73

JAMIE ANNE BANNER WAS BORN SIX MONTHS LATER. Her daddy was in the room to catch her as she came out, and he cut the umbilical cord. Her mommy hugged her to her chest and cried tears of joy.

The very next day, they took her home together, where they had built a little bedroom for her off of the kitchen and decorated it pink and purple. Her Aunt Francie and Uncle Frank—her godparents—were there to greet them all with a warm meal.

She was too young to know what had transpired over the past few months before her birth, about the talks with Dr. Ruth, and how her mommy had asked both her daddy and Francie for another chance. All she knew, or felt, was that her mommy and daddy sat close together, holding hands, and she was enfolded in a world of happiness.

For the first three months, she would sleep in a bassinet in their bedroom. Her Daddy slept well most nights, and on those he didn't, she never woke. She slept soundly through it all.

Her mommy settled into motherhood well, quitting her job and leaving behind all the people who had been telling her for months to leave her daddy. Annie knew she had a higher calling and could finally give her family the love and help they needed.

"Someday, little Jamie," her daddy said to her that first evening home. "Someday, I'll tell you stories about your namesake, and how I came to be here."

Annie leaned over and let the baby wrap her hand around her finger. "And you can grow up here, honey, at Safe Haven, and learn to ride horses and play in the surf. It'll be a grand life."

Jamie didn't know about these things, but she knew she was hungry. She started sucking on her hands, and Jack handed her over to her mom to breastfeed. He looked at both his ladies and smiled. Life was good.

chapter 74

One Year Later

JACK WALKED INTO FRANCIE'S OFFICE with a smile on his face.

"I got this in the mail a little while ago," he said. He pulled an official looking document out of an envelope and handed it to her. It was his pardon, finally, releasing him of all criminal charges and guaranteeing his freedom.

Francie read it. "Oh, Jack," she said. "Wow."

He sat down in his chair. "The first thing I did was call my mom. I've arranged a flight for her, and she'll be here tomorrow afternoon." He laughed. "I can't wait to see her."

"Neither can I!" Francie said. "She can stay in the guest room as long as she wants."

"I'm not letting her out of my sight," he said. "Gosh, I've missed her."

Then he grew serious. "They sent me something else too," he said. He pulled a ribbon out of the envelope. "It's a soldier's medal. They give it to someone in service who saves a life," he said. "I want to give it to you. You deserve this more than I do."

He handed her the ribbon. She took the silky red, white and blue colors in her hand and opened her mouth to say something, but he stopped her.

"Put it in that drawer of memories you have there," he said, "and every time you look at it, know how grateful I am."

He jumped up from his chair. "Now I'm going to go ride my horse. And I was thinking, in another year or two, we have to get Jamie a pony!"

He turned to go, then stopped at the door. He looked back over his shoulder.

"Thank you, Princess."

He walked out.

She heard the back door close as he left the house. She ran her fingers over the shiny ribbon, then held it to her heart. She closed her eyes for a moment, breathing it all in. Then she unlocked her drawer and set it inside, on top of all her other memories.

She locked it back up and went down the hall to share the good news with Frank.

He was standing at their bedroom window.

"Come here," he said when he saw her. "Quick. Look at this."

She walked over and stood beside him, looking down and across the pasture toward the barns. Jack and Annie were walking hand in hand, and Jack was holding Jamie with his other arm. The evening sun was setting behind them, silhouetting the little family in its golden color.

"You did that," Frank said. "You made that possible."

"*We* made that possible," Francie said. "You and me. It has always been you and I, together."

She turned toward Frank. His kind brown eyes gazed into her blue ones. "And it always will be," he said. Then he smiled. "We're alone for at least another hour before

Sam gets home with the kids. I can think of something else you and I do well together."

She laughed, and he pulled her into his arms and into a long, passionate kiss.

the end

Acknowledgments, Disclaimers and such

Spoilers!
Don't read until you finish the book!

Thank you to the incredible number of people who beta read this book for me over the years. Your support, comments and critiques gave me the resilience to tackle a book of this magnitude. I couldn't have done it without you.

I started writing this book to answer the question, what happens to our faith when really bad things happen? When I began this book I was very young, way too young to be able to answer those questions. I had to live a whole lot more life first. I have worked on this book, making changes, editing, rewriting, for decades. I'm still not sure I have the answers; as a matter of fact I know I don't.

I know some of the plot lines are crazy. My young James Bond mind made up all sorts of scenarios to test my characters' faith. Now that I am older, and hopefully, a more seasoned writer, I can definitely see the challenges and believe-ability of some of my plot lines. But in essence, what I was trying to do is answer questions about faith, which I think still works.

This book has had about a dozen beta readers. One woman came back and told me that there's no way so many bad things would happen to one person. With that, I disagree. I have lived enough life to know that God allows more challenges on some than others. While these specific scenarios may not be the exact challenges a person might go through, their magnitude and number are spot on.

The parts of the book I do feel very confident about are the horse parts. I have been a lifelong equestrian, a fan of horse showing and racing, and I write from deep experience. I hope Francie's love and passion for horses comes through in my writing, as well as the power of animals to heal what troubles our souls.

Francie is not perfect. None of us are. She comes from a traumatic childhood, and is searching for love, sometimes hurting the people who want to love her the most. She wants to be safe, above all else. Don't most of us wish for that as well? But she means well. I tried to make her as real as I could, bad decisions and all.

I hope this book touched you on some level, and mostly, I hope that you walk away from it knowing that we don't see the whole picture. Not yet. God is still at work in us, and around us, and He is taking our circumstances and using them to perfect His will – something more glorious than anything we could ever imagine.

For now we only see in part. But someday... someday we will see the whole picture.

God bless.
Pam

about the author

PAMELA GOSSIAUX is the international bestselling author of the *Horses and Hearts Inspirational Romance* series, the *Russo Romantic Mystery* series, the romantic comedy *Good Enough*, the YA book *Ordinary Girl*, and the inspirational books *Why Is There a Lemon in My Fruit Salad?* and *A Kid at Heart*. She is also a keynote speaker, freelance writer, and teaches writing workshops. She lives and writes at her horse farm in Michigan, where she resides with her family and an assortment of pets. Visit her website at PamelaGossiaux.com. Follow her on Instagram, Facebook, Twitter, and BookBub. To receive updates, news, and special offers, sign up for her newsletter.

www.ingramcontent.com/pod-product-compliance
Lightning Source LLC
Chambersburg PA
CBHW061044210726
48294CB00001B/28